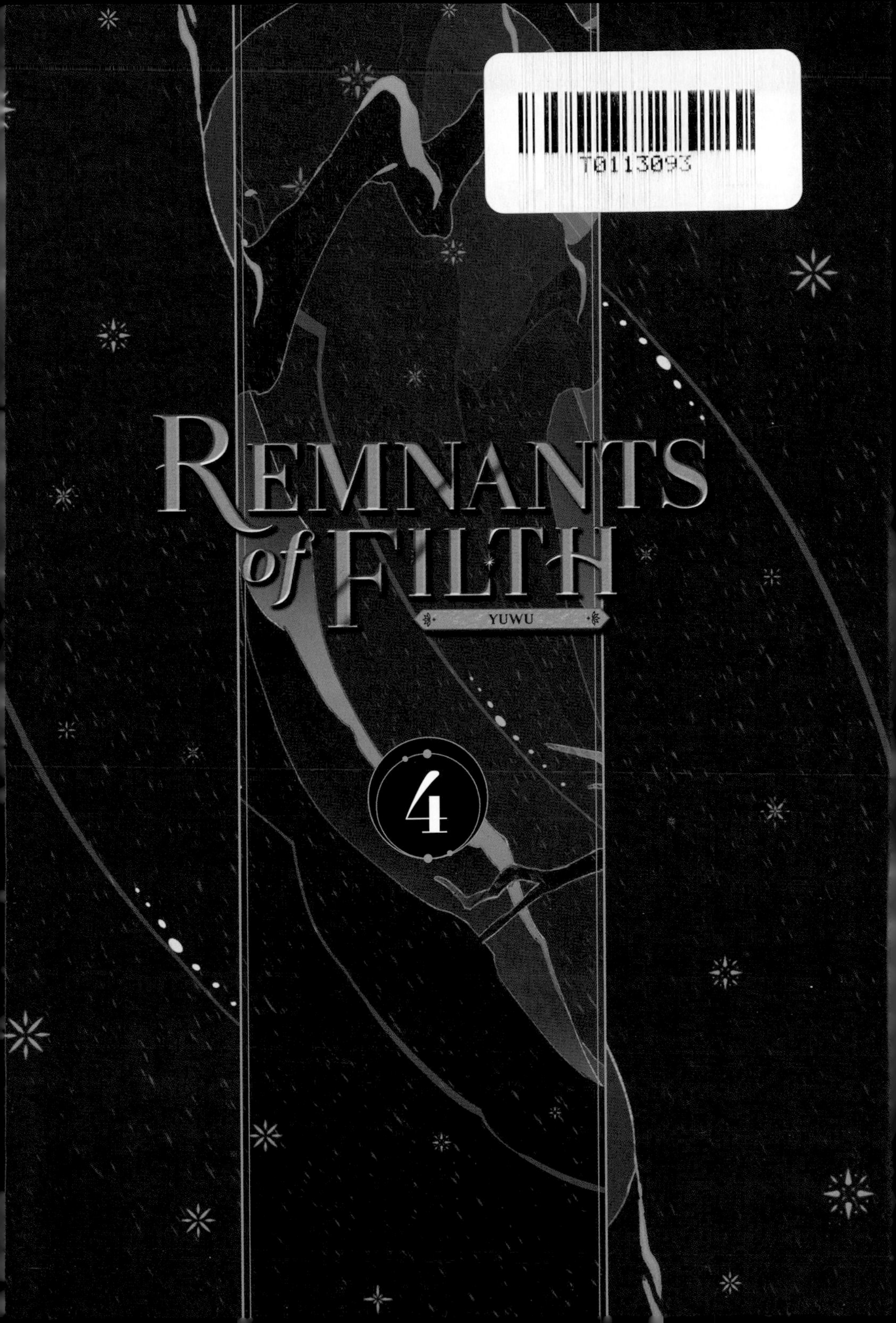
REMNANTS of FILTH
YUWU
4

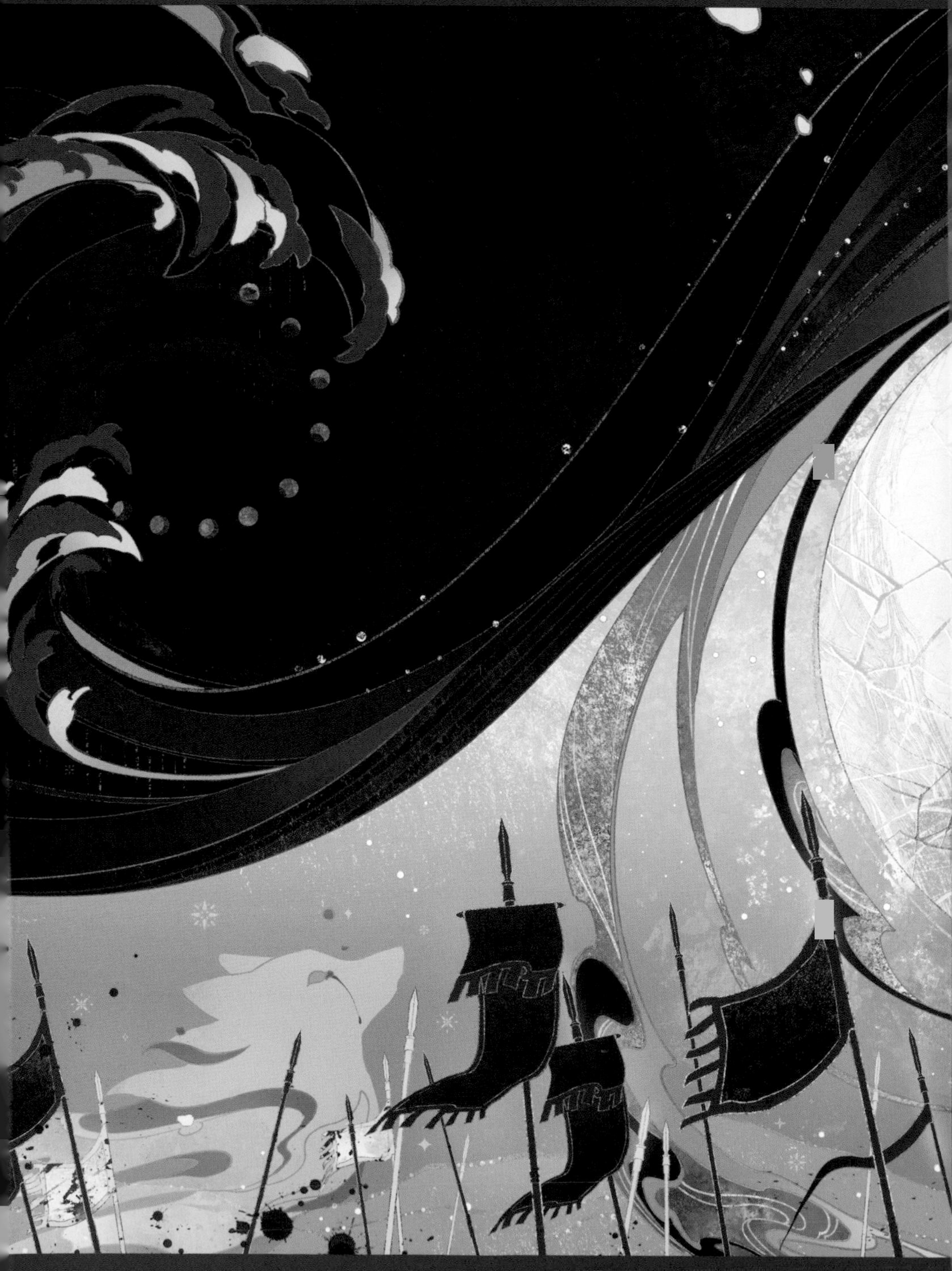

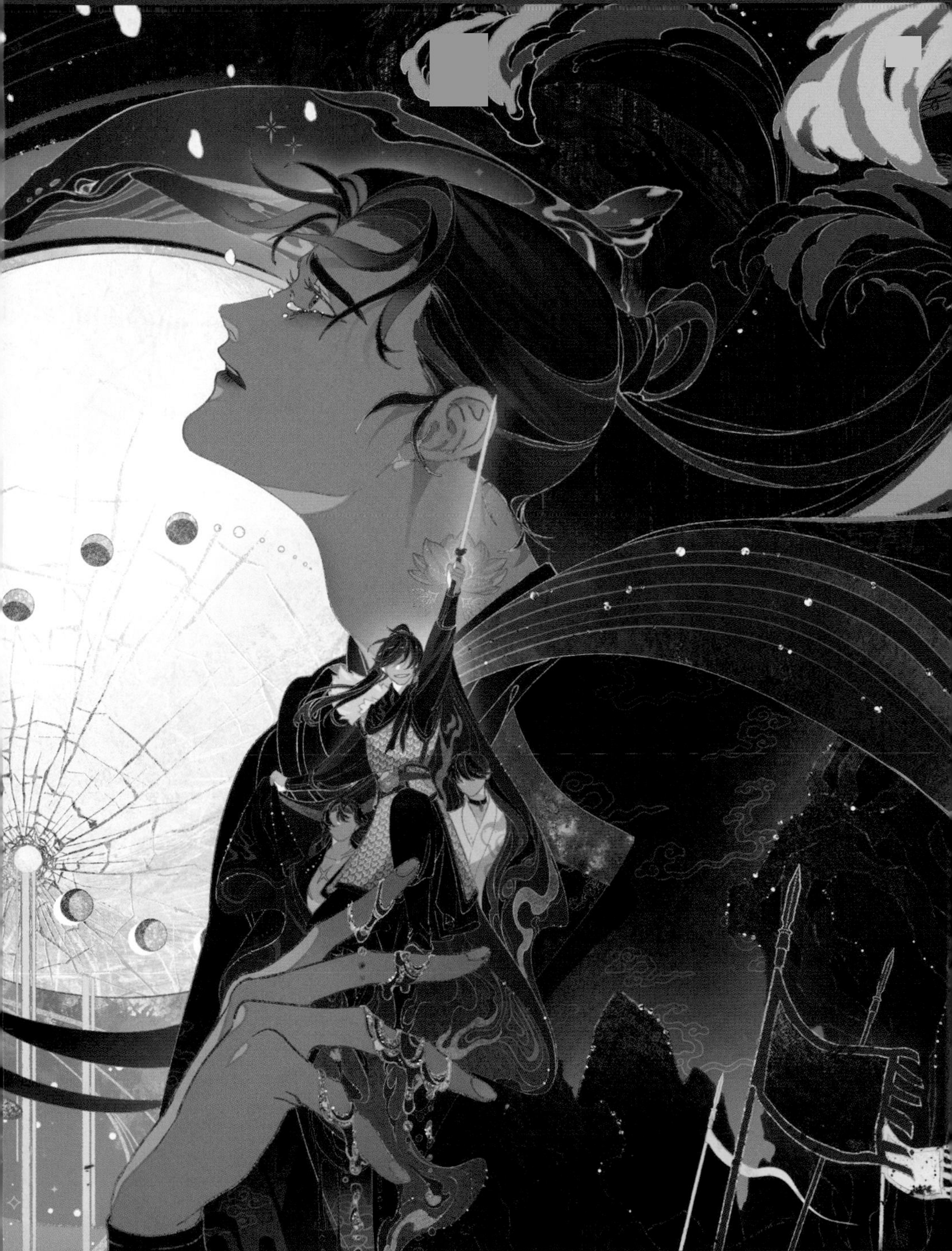

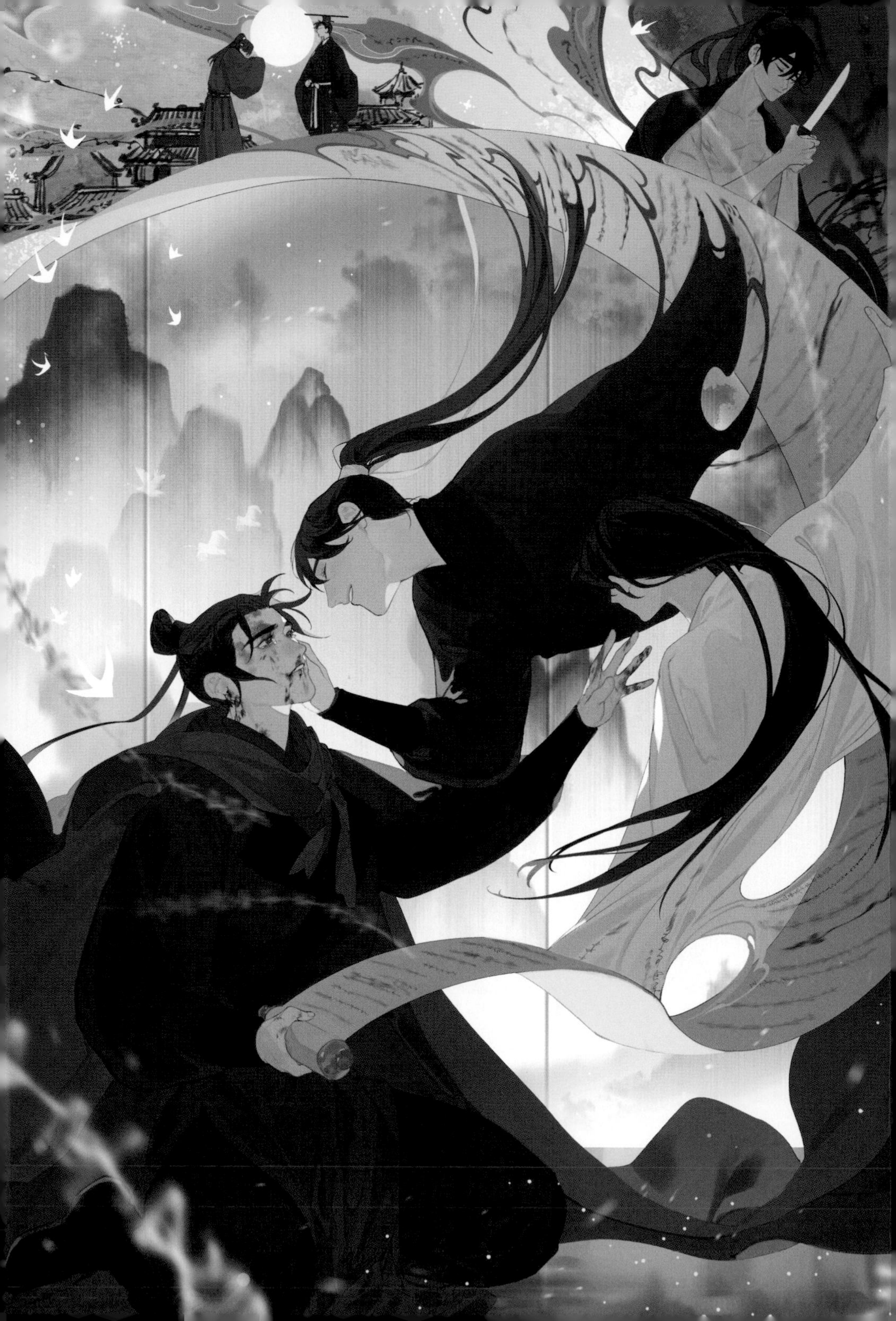

REMNANTS of FILTH

YUWU

4

WRITTEN BY
Rou Bao Bu Chi Rou

ILLUSTRATED BY
St

TRANSLATED BY
Yu & Rui

Seven Seas

Seven Seas Entertainment

REMNANTS OF FILTH:
YUWU VOL. 4

Published originally under the title of 《余污》 (Yu Wu)
Author © 肉包不吃肉 (Rou Bao Bu Chi Rou)
U.S. English edition rights under license granted by 北京晋江原创网络科技有限公司
(Beijing Jinjiang Original Network Technology Co., Ltd.)
U.S. English edition copyright © 2024 Seven Seas Entertainment, Inc.
Arranged through JS Agency Co., Ltd
All rights reserved.

Cover and Interior Illustrations by St

Seven Seas press and purchase enquiries can be sent
to Marketing Manager Lauren Hill at press@gomanga.com.
Information regarding the distribution and purchase of digital editions is available
from Digital Manager CK Russell at digital@gomanga.com.

Seven Seas and the Seven Seas logo are trademarks of
Seven Seas Entertainment. All rights reserved.

Follow Seven Seas Entertainment online at
sevenseasentertainment.com.

TRANSLATION: Yu, Rui
ADAPTATION: Neon Yang
COVER DESIGN: M. A. Lewife
INTERIOR DESIGN: Clay Gardner
INTERIOR LAYOUT: Karis Page
PROOFREADER: Stephanie Cohen, Hnä
COPY EDITOR: Jehanne Bell
EDITOR: Kelly Quinn Chiu
PREPRESS TECHNICIAN: Melanie Ujimori, Jules Valera
MANAGING EDITOR: Alyssa Scavetta
EDITOR-IN-CHIEF: Julie Davis
PUBLISHER: Lianne Sentar
VICE PRESIDENT: Adam Arnold
PRESIDENT: Jason DeAngelis

ISBN: 978-1-68579-761-4
Printed in Canada
First Printing: July 2024
10 9 8 7 6 5 4 3 2 1

TABLE OF
CONTENTS

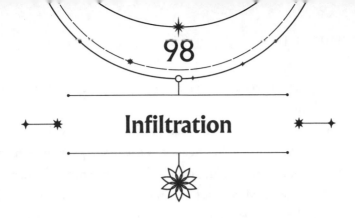

Infiltration

MO XI AND GU MANG looked out over a sunken area surrounded by dense forest. Crosses of petrified wood lined three sides, covered in chains and shackles—execution platforms. An enormous blood pool was carved out of the middle; within it, skeletons tangled like flotsam as centuries' worth of the dead rose and fell on the churn of its bloody waves.

The fire bat tribe had built a pavilion that extended over the pool's surface, lit by temple lamps balanced on delicate stands, each gleaming brightly in the gloom of the night. The pavilion's construction was exquisite, but a closer inspection would make anyone nauseous—the ground that looked to be composed of fine sand and rounded cobblestones was in truth strewn with countless human teeth. As for those temple lamps, their stands were curving human spines and their bases human skulls... This pavilion was built from human bones.

Mo Xi stared in silent distaste.

"Look over there, in the middle!" Gu Mang exclaimed.

Mo Xi glanced over. In the center of this pavilion that was like hell on earth sat a beautiful woman who appeared around forty years old. She wore gauzy robes and splendid jewelry, with a gold and jade circlet resting atop her brow. Her aura was one of overwhelming luxury and poise; the other bat demons were like planets orbiting her star as they moved around her, trembling in fear as they waited on her whim.

"That must be Wuyan," Gu Mang muttered. "How strange. She doesn't look like the peerless beauty in the first legend, nor the old demon hag in the second. She seems like a pretty normal queen."

Mo Xi knew Gu Mang was referring to her looks and nothing else, because at that moment, a bat demon official in military uniform was kneeling at her feet. She was held down by two attendants, and half her face was covered in blood; one pointy bat ear had already been hacked off.

Wuyan twirled that ragged ear in her fingers, fiddling with it absentmindedly. As they watched, she dipped a finger into the oozing blood, painting it over her shining nails as if applying cinnabar stain. "You've searched all day and haven't found a thing," she said leisurely, still playing with the ear. "Instead, you allowed someone to kidnap this venerable one's medicine—Shunfeng-er, why should I let you live?"

The official was shaking. "Your Majesty... Your Majesty, have mercy..."

"This venerable one has shown more than enough *mercy*. You were in charge of guarding the pill room, yet this venerable one's most important source of blood has slipped through your fingers." Wuyan's tone was hard, her red eyes narrowed. "Do you know this is a crime punishable by death?"

The official trembled, unable to form words.

Wuyan raised her hand, fire blazing from her palm. In a blink, the angry flames burned the ear to ash. "Attendants."

"Here!"

Pinky delicately raised, Wuyan assessed her freshly painted nails then pointed a red-tipped finger at the official kneeling on the ground. "Shunfeng-er is incompetent, her mistake unpardonable. Throw her into the cauldron to be...hmm, boiled alive."

The cruelty of the punishment made both Gu Mang and Mo Xi blanch.

"Your Majesty! Your Majesty, spare me!" The official wailed hysterically. "I beg Your Majesty, let me redeem myself! I'll catch A-Rong and those little thieves who trespassed onto the island! Your Majesty—*Your Majesty!*"

Wuyan ignored her completely. The attendants dragged the official away, her desperate screams piercing the dark forest like claws, tearing the night apart.

It was a long time before they stopped.

Wuyan sighed. "Had this venerable one not been so compassionate for so many hundreds of years, we wouldn't be suffering such incompetence." She looked up and addressed another bat demon kneeling by the pillar. "Shunfeng-er's disciple?"

The bat demon squeaked in terror.

"Did you see how your shifu ended up?"

"I s-s-s-saw, saw it!"

Wuyan smiled thinly. "Do you want to end up like her?"

"N-n-no! I don't! Not at all!"

The bat queen's smile froze on her face. "Where's your gratitude, then? Shouldn't you make yourself scarce and start tracking down the trespassers with the other squads?"

"Yes, yes!" The disciple staggered to her feet and fled in abject terror.

Wuyan closed her eyes and leaned back against the soft cushions to rest. "A-Fang, come," she said with a wave of her hand. Her handmaiden A-Fang hurriedly stepped forward and bowed. "How many Xueling Pills are left in our stores?"

"Your Majesty, Miss Rongrong was sick the past few days, so her blood couldn't be used. Only two pills remain."

"Two pills..." Wuyan sighed. "In that case, I won't take one today. The yin energy in this blood pool is strong enough; I can delay it a short while."

"So that's how it is," Gu Mang said quietly.

Mo Xi turned to look at him.

"I was confused why Wuyan didn't personally track us down. Something so serious happened on her island, yet she only dispatched her subordinates with orders to kill us. Now it makes sense," said Gu Mang.

"Hm?"

"She probably damaged her vital energy with her reckless cultivation method. Now she has to take a Xueling Pill every day to relieve the pain. Without Rongrong, her source of medicine's been cut off, so she's conserving her remaining Xueling Pills until she gets Rongrong back. The next best thing is to stay by the blood pool instead of running about; its yin energy will minimize the damage to her body." Gu Mang prodded Mo Xi with his elbow. "Hey."

"What."

"Do you still have that life crystal showing Yue Chenqing's condition?"

"I do," replied Mo Xi. "What of it?"

"If the queen doesn't plan on personally seeking us out, Murong-xiong should have no problem fending off other demons." Gu Mang paused. "We came to rescue Yue Chenqing, not to make trouble; we shouldn't fight if we don't have to. We have two objectives: lift the curse from Yue Chenqing and make it off of this island safely. Well then, why not get closer to the queen and monitor her movements? She's set a barrier over the island to stop us escaping—but every barrier has its weak point. I'm thinking if we study her, we can figure out where the barrier is weakest and escape when the time is right. Just keep an eye on Yue Chenqing's crystal to make sure he's okay."

Mo Xi thought it over and agreed. "But how are you going to get close to her?"

"About that—to be honest, sometimes the Liao Kingdom's spells are much more useful than Chonghua's." With a snap of his fingers, a tiny flame appeared at Gu Mang's fingertips. He tossed this flame toward the sky, where it instantly scattered into countless colorful butterflies that covered them both.

"You're casting a Liao Kingdom black magic spell on me?!" Mo Xi's voice was low but severe.

He was almost inaudible, but Gu Mang wasn't taking any risks. Reaching up, he gently tapped Mo Xi's lips. "Little beauty, why are you fussing? Listen to Gege and hush."

Mo Xi was rendered entirely speechless.

"Things like spells—if they're not hurting anyone, does it matter if they're from the Liao Kingdom or Chonghua? If they work, they work. Where did all these strict rules come from?"

More and more colorful butterflies gleaming with spiritual light amassed until the two of them were enveloped in a dazzling brilliance. Fortunately Gu Mang had set down a concealment spell beforehand, or they would have been instantly discovered by the fire bat patrols. The light glinting from the butterfly wings brightened to a blinding white before gradually winking out. Gu Mang chuckled. "Look at me now."

Standing before Mo Xi was a pointy-eared fire bat handmaiden with a scarlet mark on her brow, her face bright and pretty. Her slender, shining, blue eyes peered at him over a charmingly sloped nose, and her lips seemed to curve mischievously even when she wasn't smiling. This bat demon had her own distinct beauty, but upon closer examination, each of her features were unmistakably Gu Mang's.

Mo Xi was flabbergasted.

"Illusion Butterfly Transformation Technique. My own invention," Gu Mang said, producing a little mirror from his qiankun pouch. "Take a look at yourself."

Mo Xi grabbed his wrist and growled, "You changed *my* face into a servant girl's too?!"

Gu Mang only smiled and held up the bronze mirror. Mo Xi had no desire to see such a terrifying reflection; he shoved the mirror back down. Gu Mang held it up again, and Mo Xi again pushed it away. Finally, Gu Mang relented. "All right, I know your temper, so I transformed you into a guard. There's nothing for you to get mad over."

He held up the mirror once more.

Mo Xi shot a glance at his reflection and saw his features had indeed changed. He had gained a pair of pointy bat ears, and his skin had paled to a bone-white with lips as red as if he'd drunk blood. He glanced downward; his black clothes trimmed in gold had likewise transformed, turning into robes identical to those of the Bat Island guards.

Gu Mang patted his shoulder. "Let's go."

Low-level bat demons surrounded the blood pool pavilion, so the pair hid in the trees to await their opportunity. When a servant girl and a guard at last approached, they sprang out and struck them unconscious. Gu Mang dragged the two bat demons into a secluded corner and collected their waist tokens. "Put this on just to be safe."

Gu Mang and Mo Xi each took a waist token. After concealing their human scents, they slipped into a group of bat demons as they passed by. Yet it wasn't long before a burly female bat demon noticed the newcomers and began to berate them. "Hold it! What's up with the two of you? Don't you have work to do?"

This female bat demon had a deeply wrinkled face and carried a whip. She thrust her chin toward Gu Mang and Mo Xi as she rebuked them with a hand on her hip. "Her Majesty is displeased tonight; don't you think you should wise up? Or do you want to be sucked dry and turned into leather?!"

With a twitch of her hand and a shake of her flabby white arm, her whip cracked toward them like a swift snake. As the long whip was about to strike Gu Mang's face, Mo Xi's hand shot out, catching the lash head-on.

Silence fell over the group. The rough whip had cut Mo Xi's palm open; blood seeped between his fingers.

"What are you doing?!" the bat shouted. "You dare defy me?!"

Mo Xi looked up. "You said it yourself: Her Majesty's mood is foul tonight. If she sees a servant girl with her face ruined for no reason and finds it inauspicious, I'm afraid we'll all be made into leather."

Among demons, the fire bat tribe was not known to be particularly intelligent. Faced with this explanation, the female demon stared blankly and came up with no retort. At last she snorted. "Fine, I'll let you off this time, but see if I don't get you the next..."

Gu Mang answered with a smile. "Jiejie is right. I understand; I'll never do it again."

This bat was quite slow-witted. She smugly snorted again and pulled back the leather whip, fastening it at her waist.

"Jiejie, actually, we're not idle," Gu Mang wheedled. "It's just that our companions were too fast. We were a step behind, and all the work was snatched away. Jiejie, if you're willing, give me something to do. I'd like to take some of your burden."

The bat demon looked him up and down. "Little lass, you have a silver tongue in that pretty mouth." She thought it over and waved her hand. "All right, go make up a plate of sweet melon and fresh fruit. Bring it to the inner courtyard." After giving her orders to Gu Mang, she turned to glare at Mo Xi. "And as for you. It's not your break time. Can't you keep it in your pants for one second? Stop trying to hook up with every female demon you see! Go patrol!"

Mo Xi had experienced his fair share of struggles; this wasn't the first time someone had ordered him around. But no one had ever ordered him around while daring to pelt him with words like "stop trying to hook up" and "keep it in your pants." His face was almost green as he glared back at the bat demon.

"What are you glaring for? You're a puny little guard; you dare defy your superiors?"

"Jiejie, don't blame him," Gu Mang hastily cut in. "He was born with a face that begs to be punched. He looks like he's giving you attitude, but in reality, he thinks Jiejie's words are very wise."

"Is that so?" the bat demon asked skeptically.

Expression chilly, Mo Xi fell silent for a few moments, then stiffly spat, "Yes."

The bat demon was still suspicious. Gu Mang shot Mo Xi a significant look; he obviously wanted him to explain himself more fully. Mo Xi could do nothing but grit his teeth and say: "Madam, your advice is invaluable. In the future, I will certainly...avoid immorality. Thank you for your wisdom."

With the bat demon successfully diverted, Mo Xi and Gu Mang split up to tackle separate tasks. The inner courtyard of the pavilion was the queen's private quarters; male guards were forbidden entry. Mo Xi went to patrol a different area of the blood pool, while Gu Mang descended those steps made of human bone and carried a plate of fruit into the heart of the pavilion alone.

As Gu Mang turned a corner, a line of servant girls emerged. The demon at the front glanced at him. "Delivering fruit?"

"Yes."

"Bring it to the agate pool. Her Majesty is there now."

Of course Gu Mang had no idea where the agate pool was, but the bat demon subconsciously tilted her chin as she spoke. Gu Mang was clever; he snapped up that tiny little detail and smiled. "Right away."

Fruit platter in hand, he sought out Wuyan. He soon found that this so-called agate pool was a heated bath filled with boiling blood. The human blood inside was millennia old, prevented from drying out or rotting by some unknown method unique to the fire bat tribe. Steam slowly unfurled from its surface like a hot spring.

Queen Wuyan sat at the edge of the pool. She had already undressed; a scarlet bathrobe was draped carelessly over her shoulders, revealing snowy white arms and a good half of her ample bosom. Her jade-pale legs were like rippling milk, astonishingly tender as she dipped her toes into that thick blood and splashed up droplets like shining red beans.

Wuyan's personal servant girl, A-Fang, was arranging her mistress's hair in preparation for her bath when she spotted Gu Mang out of the corner of her eye. "Your Majesty, the fruit is here," she said. "Would you like to bathe first, or enjoy some refreshments?"

"So many horrid things have happened today. I've had my fill on anger alone," Wuyan said bitterly. "What's the point in eating?"

A-Fang shot Gu Mang a look, indicating that he should set down the plate of fruit and withdraw.

Gu Mang obeyed, depositing the platter and retreating to the side of the room with eyes lowered. He had no interest in watching women bathe. Besides, although Wuyan maintained herself well, he couldn't miss the fine wrinkles at her waist and neck. Even if she was a demoness, it didn't feel right to see such intimate details. But what choice did he have? Any one of Wuyan's movements might reveal the clues he needed. He watched her carefully, doing his best to avoid lingering on certain areas.

Wuyan shrugged off the red bathrobe that concealed her figure and slipped into the blood pool, completely naked. Closing her eyes, she sighed quietly in relief before stretching her arms and leaning against the side of the pool. She let her attendants scoop up the warm, flowing blood with small bamboo cups and pour it over her back.

What Gu Mang saw next left him astounded.

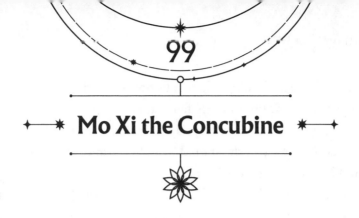
Mo Xi the Concubine

AS THE HOT BLOOD washed over Wuyan's skin, those fine wrinkles slowly vanished. Wuyan's appearance was undergoing minute changes in the steam of the pool. The loose skin of her face became taut and flawless: the faint crease between her brows seemed to smooth, the sagging folds at the corners of her mouth gradually disappeared, and the fine lines on her lips faded to nothing. Her entire figure grew so tender and delicate that she resembled the first flower bud on an early spring branch.

The blood bath transformed the dignified beauty of a lady in her forties into the fresh loveliness of a gorgeous young maiden. She was exceedingly charming, like a white blossom soaking in the red blood pool. As she absorbed the blood of humans who'd perished thousands of years ago into her veins, her skin flushed with color and her features turned dewy and pristine. Wuyan cupped a handful of blood in her palms, sipping delicately through scarlet lips. After a few swallows, her lashes fluttered open—even her eyes had become as clear and pure as those of a girl in her twenties.

Watching this outrageous scene unfold, Gu Mang was struck by a realization: Wuyan *was* the devastating beauty in the Liao Kingdom's legends, as well as the wrinkled and white-haired old hag!

This bat queen couldn't figure out how to cultivate into immortality. And she did not merely fail, but even severely damaged her vital energy, making her age rapidly. A demon's natural lifespan was long; at Wuyan's age, she should be in her prime. How could she possibly be willing to lose her beauty?

The Xueling Pill refined from the blood of the feathered tribe should have the same effect as the agate pool—no, it must be even stronger. Not only could it repair Wuyan's vital energy, it could restore her body's youth. Perhaps the blood pool could return her to her early twenties, and only briefly, but the Xueling Pill... The Xueling Pill probably returned her figure and features to her teenaged appearance and kept them that way for a long time.

Wuyan soaked in the pool, its yin energy revitalizing her fully. She glowed with youth from the inside out; even some of her unhappiness seemed to have dispersed. When she spoke again, her tone was relaxed. "A-Fang, say, who are these people who came to the island?"

"According to the shangao, there are four of them, all men," A-Fang replied. "But the shangao swears a lot and never says anything reasonable, so that's all I could learn."

"Four men." Wuyan sniffed. "This venerable one doesn't go out to kidnap people anymore, yet these ants still come swarming to my island. They deserve to be made into my personal playthings."

A-Fang said nothing.

I was right, Gu Mang thought. *She didn't say "keep" them as playthings—she said "make." This bat queen really is carrying a torch for someone; that's why she used gu worms to change Yue Chenqing's features. Which poor bastard is so charming a bat queen would yearn madly for him all this time?*

"Your Majesty, most humans live but a few decades. The last time, when that cultivator came to the island asking for medicine to save his mother, he only lasted a dozen years before he died. How long do you think you can play with these four?"

Wuyan lifted a finger from the pool; dark red beaded at its tip. "They dared steal this venerable one's feathered tribe medicine. After the way they've angered me, so what if they don't last long? Anyway, they're mere puppets, they're not..." She paused; the innocent expression disappeared from her tender and tranquil face and was replaced with a seething madness even demonic magic couldn't disguise. "They're not the real *him*."

"Your Majesty..."

"Forget it. I won't bring it up again." Wuyan leaned back, head pillowed against the stones at the pool's rim. "He's an immortal," she chuckled, "but this venerable one lost real affection for that craven traitor long ago. After all these centuries, the only thing this venerable one can't forget is his handsome face. Creating an identical copy is nothing difficult."

Gu Mang was shocked—*What?* The man Wuyan had set her eyes on was an immortal? But after the shock passed, things started to fall into place. Of course... Why else would she so insistently defy her nature as a demon to cultivate, attempting to step onto the immortal path rather than the demonic way? It seemed it was because her Prince Charming was an immortal.

Since antiquity, immortals and demons had stood opposed; how infatuated must this bat queen have been to try changing her own nature to be with such a man? And that immortal later became a "traitor"—he must have somehow disappointed her greatly. Not only did she fail to cultivate into an immortal, she ended up with a sickly body that was deteriorating in the prime of her life.

Thus her old infatuation had decayed into twisted obsession. She wasn't willing to meet any men who weren't of her tribe, but if a human man happened to trespass onto Bat Island, she would transform him into that remembered immortal, then toy with him and torture him to death.

Looking at this demon, Gu Mang thought her worthy of both hatred and pity. He couldn't help but sigh.

A-Fang was still massaging Wuyan's shoulders. "Yes, we'll catch those four wretches, as well as the little rascal they wanted to snatch away. We'll feed them gu worms to change their faces, wipe their memories, and keep them on the island to serve Your Majesty obediently. Hmph! That's letting them off lightly!"

Wuyan's mood was brightening. "You always say just what I like to hear," she said, smiling. She turned her head. "Bring the fruit over. This venerable one will partake."

Gu Mang gathered his wayward thoughts and calmly raised the white jade plate in both hands. He crossed over to the agate pool and knelt deferentially. Wuyan picked through the fruit with slender, snow-white fingers. Eventually, she pointed at a small pile of lychees. "These—peel them."

"Yes, Your Majesty," replied Gu Mang.

A servant girl hurried over with a small celadon bowl. Gu Mang nimbly peeled the gleaming, translucent lychees, six in all, and arranged them in the bowl. Wuyan plucked out one and closed her cinnabar-stained lips around it, filling her mouth with its tangy sweetness. She savored it and said, "These lychees are extraordinarily good today."

Gu Mang smiled but made no sound. He had placed a Soul-Recording Spell on the plate of fruit when he brought it over, then layered some other illusion spells he had once thought useless for battle to hide its traces. Under the spellwork, the lychees tasted uncommonly sweet and delicious.

His talent for spellcasting was outstanding, and the fire bats were exceptionally simple-minded; Gu Mang's plan went off without a hitch. When Wuyan ate the lychee, the Soul-Recording Spell would disperse within her, absorbing all the memories Gu Mang needed. Later, he would only need to recite the incantation, and this intangible spell would disengage from Wuyan's mind, return to Gu Mang, and present all the information it had collected.

Wuyan finished the fruit and wiped her fingers with a silken handkerchief offered by a servant girl. Sated, she lazily closed her eyes and reclined against the side of the pool to soak further.

The most important step was completed—Gu Mang sighed in relief. But a moment later, he heard A-Fang ask, "Your Majesty, will you require a guard to service you tonight?"

Gu Mang choked mid-sigh. *S-service?!*

"Xuannü's[1] dual cultivation method boosts longevity. This venerable one can't take a Xueling Pill today, so I must collect yang to mend yin. Of course a guard's services are required."

Gu Mang stared in horrified silence.

"Go make arrangements for this venerable one."

"Yes, Your Majesty," answered A-Fang.

A-Fang left, while Wuyan remained in the blood pool. This beauty seemed like a female ghost that had crawled out of purgatory, indescribably exquisite. She stuck out a pinky, studying the vermillion at her fingertips, then said absently, "This venerable one is in an ill humor today. Prepare some fragrance and liven things up for me."

"At once, Your Majesty!" Two bat demons came forward from either side, each holding a teardrop-shaped crystal bottle filled with petal-pink flower nectar incense. They knelt by the pool, bending their elegant necks to pour the perfume into the crimson blood.

---

1   Xuannü (玄女), also known as the Dark Lady, the goddess of sex, longevity, and war.

Within seconds, the hall filled with fragrance, its heady scent dispersing throughout the entire pavilion and drifting outward. The scent was syrupy-sweet, a kind of fragrance Gu Mang had never smelled before; it seemed to be a blend of all the scents he liked. He smelled grass, the perfume of a lotus pond in summer...and the clear sweetness of honey.

As he marveled that there could be a scent on earth so perfectly suited to his tastes, he saw out of the corner of his eye the expressions of intoxication on the faces of the other bat demons. Now that was a bad sign. This fragrance must be like the ephemera Murong Lian smoked—it had a hypnotic effect.

Gu Mang shook his head vigorously and began circulating spiritual energy to suppress the incense's effects. Refocusing his mind, he looked around again. As expected, all the demons in the pavilion wore expressions of perfect bliss, as if they might ascend to heaven at any moment. Wuyan leaned against the side of the blood pool, her features becoming increasingly alluring under the influence of the incense. She was as languid and soft as rich spring soil, her coquettish eyes like rippling silk, her carmine lips lightly parted.

This gentle illusory fragrance bled outward like ink on paper. A short time later, A-Fang returned. "Your Majesty, the guards."

A row of bat demons filed into the pavilion behind her. All had broad shoulders and narrow waists, their faces compellingly handsome. Gu Mang swept a glance across them, his eye immediately catching on the one with the most gallant features.

As expected, Mo Xi's name had been called. But judging by his expression, he didn't yet know why. He knitted his swordlike brows, eyes skimming the group of demons before him. His gaze paused fleetingly on Gu Mang, then slid away, some faint confusion showing in his eyes.

Oh no, thought Gu Mang. Mo Xi was the type who was beautiful but oblivious. Usually, his glacial expression was sufficient to reject a crowd of wild admirers, dashing their hopes with a single sharp look. Yet as soon as he encountered something he didn't understand, confusion would surface upon his features, thawing that bitter coldness and revealing a face that was young and guileless.

In brief, he was a beauty.

At this point, there was no way to hide Mo Xi's attractiveness; Gu Mang could only hope that Wuyan had peculiar tastes, or that she was blind. He began to pray: *Don't choose Princess, don't choose Princess, Princess has an explosive temper, you can't handle the consequences...*

He was still chanting devoutly when Wuyan lifted a finger and pointed it right at Mo Xi. "It'll be you."

Gu Mang stared in horror.

Mo Xi blinked in confusion.

Wuyan stretched languidly and rose from the blood pool. The fire bat tribe had a unique constitution—instead of staining her body red, the blood rolled off her like normal hot spring water to reveal her naked body, supple as white jade.

This demon's lack of propriety made Gu Mang want to bash his own head in. Wuyan stepped straight out of the bath. Gu Mang only saw her bare back, but where Mo Xi stood... He would be seeing her front...

Gu Mang risked a peek at Mo Xi's face. A series of vivid colors passed over it like a rotating carousel lantern. But the fire bat tribe wasn't sharp and had difficulty reading expressions, and the incense fumes had dulled Wuyan's focus and self-restraint. She saw only Mo Xi's handsomeness and none of his menace. The bat queen spread her arms provocatively, then gathered her hair and clicked her tongue. "What a hopeless little servant you are. I've selected you to attend me—did you freeze up in joy? Come, help this venerable one dress."

After such an invitation, what more did Mo Xi need to hear? His eyes flew wide as he first stared at Wuyan in shock, then swung his gaze over to Gu Mang, who guiltily lowered his head.

Mo Xi seemed to choke on his words. He slowly looked back at Wuyan, his handsome face going a stunning shade of green.

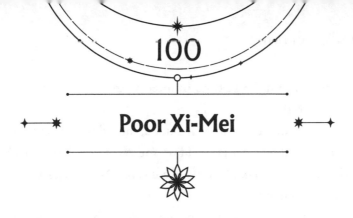

100

Poor Xi-Mei

THE HONEYPOT SCHEME was a time-tested ploy recorded in *The Thirty-Six Stratagems.*[2] A beauty sent into an enemy's sumptuous tent could become the poison that brought them down—but not every beauty was suited for this kind of work. For instance, you might send out the famed seductress Diaochan[3] to co-ordinate a plan of attack from within and without. But if you tried to do the same with a legendary female warrior like Mu Guiying?[4]

Gu Mang was intimately familiar with Mo Xi's temper. Mo Xi could weather injury or insult without batting an eye, but romantic liaisons between men and women were intolerable to him. When Mo Xi was young, he had watched his mother and uncle carry on a sordid affair, and as an adult, he compulsively avoided relationships. He couldn't abide women having improper thoughts about him. In all his thirty years, Gu Mang alone had managed to mess around with him without getting killed.

Upon seeing Mo Xi's hands clench into fists, teeth visibly grinding in his handsome jaw, a thousand ideas flashed through

---

2   A sixth-century treatise outlining a series of stratagems used in war, politics, and civilian life.

3   A beautiful woman from Romance of the Three Kingdoms who seduced the warrior Lü Bu and convinced him to kill the warlord Dong Zhuo.

4   Legendary female warrior from the Generals of the Yang Family saga, and a symbol of courage and loyalty.

Gu Mang's mind. At last, he shouted with a bolt of inspiration, "Why is it you?!"

All the bat demons, Mo Xi included, turned to stare at him.

Wuyan narrowed her eyes. "Hm? You two know each other?"

Gu Mang knelt, faking flustered concern. "Your Majesty, p-please forgive my rudeness."

"This venerable one asked you a question. The two of you know each other?" Wuyan glanced at Gu Mang, then at Mo Xi. "He's... your lover?"

The fire bat tribe were demons that sprang from the union of beasts and depraved members of the feathered tribe. Naturally, they had no taboo against taking others' husbands or wives. If Gu Mang lied and said Mo Xi *was* his lover, this bat queen might find the prospect more thrilling and be less likely to let him go. So he quickly put on a hateful expression as he looked up to answer Wuyan. "How could I be his lover? I'm not even done loathing him. Your Majesty, forgive me, I was overcome with revulsion, which is why I offended Your Majesty."

Wuyan's curiosity was piqued. She blinked her bright brown eyes. "How did he provoke you?"

Gu Mang rose and pointed an accusing finger at Mo Xi. Without blinking or stammering, he announced, "He can't get it up!"

Both Mo Xi and Wuyan were completely taken aback. A hush fell over the pavilion. The female demons all eyed Mo Xi, whispering among themselves. A few of the younger ones couldn't hold themselves back and tittered loudly behind their sleeves. Meanwhile, some of the male demons who had entered with Mo Xi looked at him with undisguised sympathy.

"How do you know?" asked Wuyan.

Gu Mang ignored Mo Xi's stare, which seemed ready to slice him to ribbons, and blurted, "Your Majesty, I dual cultivated with him before, but he was unreliable and damaged my vital energy! How could I let this go?"

The gazes on Mo Xi became judgmental. It was one thing if he simply wasn't up to the task. But how bad did his technique have to be for him to injure the demon dual cultivating with him? Even Wuyan had her doubts now. She had planned to use the blood pool bath and Xuannü's dual cultivation technique to repair her vital energy because she couldn't take a Xueling Pill. If she was led astray by beauty and chose an unreliable guard to serve her, the results would be the opposite of what she wanted.

She turned at once to rage at A-Fang. "This is the man you picked?!"

Terrified, A-Fang blanched and dropped to her knees. She kowtowed in apology, then spoke sternly to Mo Xi. "What are you still standing here for? You want to anger Her Majesty further?! Get the hell out!"

Mo Xi was so furious he was shaking from head to toe, yet he had nowhere to vent his anger. In the end, he shot a last vicious glare at this crowd of lunatics, then glowered at that lying ruffian before turning to leave.

Wuyan announced to the remaining male demons, "This venerable one is weak today. If any of you are unreliable, get lost. If you remain here and this venerable one picks you and you hurt my vital energy, I promise you can't bear the consequences!"

The fire bat tribe was licentious by nature; those male demons were all too eager. Upon seeing their queen's naked, supple body, and breathing in that incense, their faces flushed and their eyes shone. They clamored to offer their services.

"I can do it!"

"Your Majesty, I can!"

"Your Majesty, I'm great in bed!"

Gu Mang looked on incredulously. Thank goodness these demons were slow-witted. If this were the cleverer Qingqiu fox tribe, the mishap would not have been settled so easily.

It seemed Gu Mang had gotten into the queen's head. In the end, she picked a tall, strapping demon with thick hair and retired to her rooms with him. A-Fang closed the door for them and turned to the other demons at the agate pool. "All right, that's it for tonight. You're dismissed. Go cultivate and gather energy for Her Majesty."

"Yes!" the demons chorused.

The crowd hastily dispersed. Gu Mang saw that some of the female demons looked anxious. They rushed over to the male demons the queen hadn't selected, fighting among themselves to speak with them first.

Gu Mang's suspicions were roused. Why were they in such a rush? What did *go cultivate and gather energy for Her Majesty* mean? As he muttered to himself in contemplation, he tidied up the fruit plate in a corner and slipped out of the pavilion before he could be noticed. Unexpectedly, his questions were answered the moment he left the inner courtyard.

Just outside, those female bat demons and male guards had already paired off, embracing passionately. Even the wrinkled and pudgy female demon who had struck him with the whip was looking for a male demon to join her. Those who found partners to consort with disappeared into a number of simple thatched huts on either side of the pavilion. Soft thumps and gasps already rose from several huts with their curtains pulled down.

As Gu Mang watched, wisps of white smoke floated up from the huts where the demons were copulating and wound toward the inner courtyard of the pavilion, finally converging above the queen's abode.

So. Not only could Wuyan restore her energies from cultivating the yin and yang path, she could also harvest the spiritual energy created from dual cultivation between her tribe members.

Even Gu Mang, shameless as he was, had to blush at this. Still, he had to marvel: this fire bat tribe was born of the feathered tribe's beastly dalliances, yet they could use sex to increase and mend their energy. The living things of the Nine Provinces were wondrous indeed.

Without warning, a heavy hand came down on his shoulder. Gu Mang was already on edge in this erotic atmosphere, terrified that some hapless male demon would try their luck with him. At this unexpected touch from behind, he jerked his head around—but before he could get a clear look at the newcomer's face, Gu Mang had already been pinned from behind as his assailant's other hand came up to cover his mouth. The demon said not a word as he dragged Gu Mang toward the nearest thatched hut.

Gu Mang panicked. This bat demon was shockingly strong, but using magic would instantly give Gu Mang away; all he could do was squirm. His strength was no match for his assailant's. Not only was Gu Mang unable to struggle free of his grasp, the demon had covered Gu Mang's mouth so tightly he couldn't make a sound. He shoved Gu Mang into the hut and tossed him roughly into a pile of straw. The bamboo curtain tumbled down, blocking the moonlight and plunging the small hut into darkness.

Sunk in that soft heap of straw, Gu Mang's scalp prickled. The fire bat tribe descended, however crookedly, from the feathered tribe, and the feathered tribe were birds. The most primitive areas of their territory—the places where they mated, for example—followed the instinctive habits of demon birds. Thus this sex hut contained no bed, but a nest-like pile of straw. The pungent scent of it assaulted Gu Mang's nostrils, along with a primitive beastly musk, so intense he almost choked.

To fight or not to fight? Do nothing, and this male bat demon would take him by force in the dark. Fight back, and not only would he fail in his mission to crack the barrier around the island, he might also put Yue Chenqing and the others in danger.

His mind buzzed with worry. As that tall figure stalked toward him, Gu Mang shrieked miserably, "Dage! If you have something to say, let's talk! I-I-I'm just a fledgling! I'm not suited for yin and yang dual cultivation! Consider someone else!"

The demon ignored his rambling. He hauled Gu Mang around and pressed him into the straw pile.

"Mother! Fucker!" Gu Mang shouted. "You still won't stop? You—fucking—get off—to this—huh?!"

"Keep shouting." His assailant spoke at last. His voice, low and electrifying, made Gu Mang shudder against his will. That cornered, furious, strained, frustrated voice spoke right in his ear, rising and falling with its owner's damp, scalding breaths. "And I really will fuck you to death."

Gu Mang blinked.

"I've fucking had enough! Don't think I won't do it!" After what seemed like an age, the large hand around Gu Mang's throat finally let go. As the other demon stood up, a fireball ignited in his palm, illuminating the small straw hut. Mo Xi was biting his lip in the orange firelight, staring daggers at Gu Mang as he lifted that handful of flames. Those pretty phoenix eyes contained fury, yet were also tinged a delicate red. In a departure from his usual fastidious propriety, the collars of his robes were in disarray from Gu Mang's struggles beneath him.

Gu Mang rubbed at the five livid fingermarks on his throat and gasped for air. He rolled his eyes. "Are you crazy? All I said was you couldn't get it up!"

Mo Xi clenched his teeth. "You couldn't keep your mouth shut?!"

"Was I supposed to stay quiet and wait for you to start a fight, then?!" Gu Mang nearly retched, heaving for breath. His blue eyes were misty as he looked up at Mo Xi. "Looks like I should have said *Yeah, this guy is totally hung, seven rounds a night is no problem; he'll satisfy you so completely you'll wish the night were longer* and let the queen yank you like a concubine into her bedroom to disgrace you a hundred times over!"

"You—!"

"*You* what?" Gu Mang plunked himself down on the pile of straw and took a great lungful of air. "You scared the shit out of me just then; I really thought you were some bat demon in heat…" he mumbled. When he finally recovered his composure, he pulled himself upright and looked up at Mo Xi. "Let's talk business. How's Yue Chenqing?"

Mo Xi tamped down on his anger. "No change to the crystal," he replied.

Gu Mang rubbed his neck again and coughed a few more times. "That's good. Oh yeah, put out that flame. This bamboo curtain doesn't block light, and bat demons don't like fire. If they see it, they'll know something's wrong with this hut."

"I set down a light-concealment barrier."

"It's better to be cautious."

After a pause, Mo Xi snapped his fingers. The fire winked out.

Gu Mang sat and breathed steadily. "We're almost finished here. Try to be patient," he said. "As soon as I pull out the Soul-Recording Spell I left on Wuyan, we'll know where we can leave the island."

With that, Gu Mang began to mouth the incantation. Motes of white light streamed slowly from the pavilion, passing through the walls of the hut and converging at Gu Mang's fingertips. Over the space of an incense time, a pearlescent ball of light coalesced in Gu Mang's palm.

"Look, this is Wuyan's mind." Gu Mang sighed in relief. "I recorded the secrets of the barrier, and also asked it to find the reason she wants to make people into puppets. Seeing as Yue Chenqing fell victim to her gu, I thought it best to know."

He filled Mo Xi in on everything he'd heard by the agate pool. Mo Xi frowned. "Wuyan was betrayed by an immortal?"

"Sounds like it," Gu Mang replied. "There's a good chance we'll catch a glimpse of that heartless and disloyal immortal in this portion of her mind. Hold on a moment."

Mo Xi didn't have much interest in any heartless and disloyal immortal. But upon seeing Gu Mang's earnest expression, he opted to stay quiet.

Gu Mang twitched his fingertips, and the glowing ball rose into the air, floating at eye level. "Tell me," said Gu Mang, "why do you infect the men that come to the island with gu?"

The pearly white ball gradually filled with color as a hazy scene took shape on its surface. The indistinct murmurs of someone's innermost thoughts surrounded them—it was Wuyan's voice.

"This happened back when I was young," she said softly.

At these words, the scene in the glowing ball began to change.

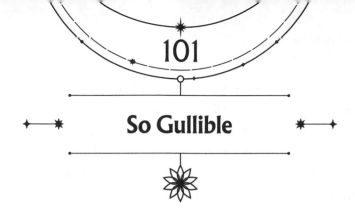

So Gullible

"**M**ANY YEARS AGO, the Dream Butterfly Islands were at war. The demon population on a neighboring island outgrew their lands, and their people had nowhere to go. To expand their territory, they broke our alliance and invaded the islands belonging to the fire bat tribe. After many months of fighting, the invading demons killed the queen—my mother—and massacred the other bat tribes on the island." A crowd of demons slaughtering their fellows appeared in the ball of light. Its pearly gleam darkened, veiled with a bloody haze.

"I was the heir to the bat throne. Those demons saw me as a thorn in their side and sought to kill me. My elder sister used herself as bait to help me escape, but I was severely wounded... My wings were broken, my tendons snapped, yet I drained my spiritual energy to flee. I was too scared to stop...but I didn't know where to go..."

Furious waves crashed within the ball of light, thunder and lightning interweaving. "I flew over the sea in bat form for many, many days, when I met a great storm. My strength was flagging and my wounds were festering. Finally I could fly no more; I tumbled from the sky onto an unfamiliar island. The moment I fell, I knew I hadn't landed in any ordinary place. Its spiritual energy was too strong—this was the home of immortals."

In the vision, the young Wuyan flapped her ragged wings, attempting to take flight again and again to no avail. "I was terrified," she said. "Ever since I was little, I was told immortals loved to kill demons. I lay in the grass, thinking how I'd survived the battle between demon tribes only to die at the hands of an immortal. I wanted to struggle to my feet and fly from the island, but I didn't have the strength. No matter how I tried, my wings could no longer carry me. But my flailing attracted the attention of a passerby. Someone was walking through the flowers, walking toward me..."

The bat with broken wings collapsed into the grass, near death. She was gravely injured; her thin wing membranes were torn, and blood stained the leaves beneath her. Her black eyes were wet and wide, the picture of misery. As she lay helpless, a white-soled silk shoe with blue trim appeared in the glowing ball and stopped next to her. An elegant, fine-boned hand reached down and gathered her up. That person carefully protected her, supporting her in his palm.

Gu Mang was smug. "Look, didn't I say the heartless and disloyal immortal would appear?"

The field of view in the ball of light slowly moved upward, from that white silk shoe to those spotless sleeves...

Once the immortal's face came into view, both Gu Mang and Mo Xi were stunned.

"The Wise Gentleman?!" Gu Mang exclaimed in surprise.

Mo Xi's eyes widened. "Headmaster Chen..."

The "heartless traitor" looking out from the ball of light was none other than Chonghua's sage from centuries ago—Chen Tang, the Wise Gentleman. It beggared belief. As far as they knew, Chen Tang's cultivation was remarkable and his character faultless, but he was still a normal human. He had never ascended to become an immortal.

"How could this be..." Gu Mang mumbled.

Mo Xi stared at that glimmering ball of light with a frown. He shook his head. "Let's keep watching."

In the vision, Chen Tang stroked his porcelain-pale fingers across Wuyan's fuzzy forehead. His soothing touch passed jade-colored spiritual energy to this little demon hanging onto life by a thread. The scene in the glowing ball slowly widened to show an isolated, near-uninhabited isle—but it wasn't Bat Island.

The island in the vision was undeniably strange. Its climate was difficult to discern, for it was filled with flowers and trees laden with ripe fruit. Winter's plum blossoms, summer's lotuses, autumn's osmanthus, and springtime's peaches and plums were all seen. The fertile land was awash in beautiful blossoms, and at the center of the island was an altar constructed from a single massive stone. The altar was empty save for a jade qin table with a five-stringed jiaowei[5] guqin arranged on top.

Gu Mang turned to Mo Xi. "There is much I still can't remember. Is this island part of Chonghua?" he asked.

"No." Mo Xi stared at that flowering isle. "This island doesn't fall within Chonghua's territory."

Gu Mang stroked his chin. "How curious. Chen Tang the Wise Gentleman appearing alone on a deserted island outside Chonghua..."

He had no time for further thought before Wuyan's voice sounded again, this time filled with endless disappointment, frustration, and longing. "Perhaps it wasn't my time to go, or perhaps the tales I was told as a child were false—but after the immortal on this island found me wounded, he never tried to hurt me. He took me back to his living quarters and did all he could to heal me."

---

5   Meaning "scorched wood," first made by a notable scholar of the eastern Han dynasty who created a qin with a beautiful tone from a piece of burned wood of the parasol tree.

In the ball of light, Chen Tang carried the injured bat to a wood cottage near the little island's shore.

"I was badly wounded, and my dear mother and sister had perished in the terrible battle I'd fled," continued Wuyan. "Intent on escape, I'd had no time to grieve, but now that I was safe, I was overcome with heartbreak and cried day and night." In the small room, Wuyan—having recovered her human form—was huddled in a ball, tears streaming down her face. "The immortal kept me company. He wasn't scary like the ones in the demon tribe's tales. He treated me kindly, consoling and comforting me... Under his care, my spirits slowly lifted. I stayed for a long, long time. Later, I discovered the island moved from place to place. It never stayed in the same spot for long..."

Gu Mang and Mo Xi exchanged glances. What kind of island was this, covered in flowers and drifting untethered on the sea? It was like nothing they had heard of before.

"Regardless of season, the island existed in an eternal spring. An immortal lived there, so the spirits of the plants flourished," Wuyan said. "But aside from the flowers and trees, we were the only two on the island. He was kind and good, but far too mysterious. He wouldn't tell me where he came from—he wouldn't even tell me his name. After living with him so long, all I knew was that his surname was Chen."

"So it really was Chen Tang?" Gu Mang murmured.

"But what could I do? I called him Chen-gege." Within the glowing ball, Wuyan had regained some of her spiritual energy and, with it, her human form. She sat by the verdant altar with her delicate legs bandaged, but she didn't seem to be in pain. Her bright eyes never strayed from Chen Tang's figure.

"Chen-gege came to the altar and played the qin every day. The music was beautiful; each time he played, illusory haitang petals fell swirling over the island. I thought this was his immortal magic and begged him to teach me, but he always demurred. He said the haitang flowers didn't fall because of him. When I pressed him, he only smiled. But he was beautiful when he smiled. I saw him every day, and each time I saw him smile I was happy. Our time passed like this. Day after day, he treated my wounds, and I listened to him play the qin. And then one day..." Wuyan paused. "I discovered my view of the world had changed.

"Before that, I had the sky, the flowers, the trees, and Chen-gege in front of me. They were all very pretty, and it made me happy to look at them. But one day, I discovered that although the sky, the flowers, and the trees were still there, they no longer caught my eye. Instead, it was as if they had given all their color to Chen-gege."

Wuyan said: "I finally understood. I had fallen in love with him. He saved my life, treated my wounds, and soothed my grief. He shattered my previous impression of immortals..." Wuyan's inner voice sounded like any young girl's, pleasant and sweet, like crisp fruit on a branch. "Though he was so mysterious and taciturn, though he was an immortal and I a demon, I loved him. And I was going to make him love me back."

A brief silence.

"But he turned me away."

The ball's pearlescent glow dimmed. Within it, Wuyan was standing by the qin altar, face in her hands, tears falling between her fingers with a soft patter. It was clear her attempts to win over Chen Tang had failed. When Wuyan's inner voice spoke again, she sounded tearful. "He was completely shocked when I confessed my feelings," she said. "He said we had only known each other a few months. How could I feel love for him?

"But isn't love just a feeling? It can be slow and steady like a stream, or something you grasp in an instant. No matter how I pleaded with him, he rejected me in no uncertain terms. He said I could stay on the roaming immortal island until my injuries healed; then I must leave. I told him that I really did love him, but he said we didn't share the same path. I told him I would cultivate the immortal path for him, but he said he wasn't an immortal."

Wuyan paused. "*Liar.* If he wasn't an immortal, how could he move the island? If he wasn't an immortal, why would petals fall when he played the qin? I interrogated him, but he refused to answer. In the end, all I asked was whether or not he thought I was pretty. I would spare no effort to become whatever type of woman he liked. But he said his heart was for the Dao and that he desired nothing else."

At this, Gu Mang sighed. The fire bat tribe wasn't sharp to begin with, and on top of that, the emotions of demons were more stubborn and unreasonable than those of humans. Chen Tang obviously had no feelings for her, but she still hounded him for an explanation. She must have worn him down to the point of helplessness. Cultivators would often say their hearts were for the Dao when they needed to reject a particularly persistent admirer. In most cases, as soon as they heard these words, there was nothing the rejected party could say no matter how infatuated they were. At the very least, it was easy to accept since they weren't losing to a rival.

And indeed, Wuyan said as much: "I wasn't satisfied with his reason, but what could I do? I couldn't possibly stop him from cultivating, could I? In the end, I had no choice but to leave the immortal island. But before I left I decided to be stubborn one last time. I told him, since you're a gentleman, you must be a man of your word. You've rejected me today because your heart is for the Dao, with no desire for anything else—so you can't lie to me. He said he wasn't lying. So I asked him to pinky-promise with me. I used a demonic spell from the fire bat tribe to tie an invisible thread on his pinky—if he ever went back on his word and married another woman in the future, I would find out. And then I would...I would..."

Wuyan sounded lost. Even she didn't seem to know what she would do if Chen Tang married in the future. The scene in the glowing ball shifted again, this time showing the familiar coast of Bat Island.

"After I returned to Bat Island, I went through many trials and became the queen of the island. Yet I longed for him. Every night, I summoned the thread on my finger. When I saw it was still there, I would know he had kept his promise to love no one else. I clung to hope deep in my heart. I went against my nature to cultivate the immortal path...all in the hope that there would come a day I'd see him again. I hoped he would see my sincerity and know my feelings were true. I hoped I could change his thinking. So I kept cultivating and waiting, year after year. Until one day..."

The voice paused, and the ball of light darkened. Within, Wuyan was flying into a rage, as if she'd gone mad. "One day, I found that thread...had broken."

Gu Mang turned to Mo Xi in astonishment. "Did Chen Tang marry before he died?" he asked Mo Xi.

Mo Xi frowned, leveling a doubtful gaze at the ball. He shook his head. "No. He had no wife or children."

"Then did he have any similar-looking siblings?"

"No."

"Strange," Gu Mang said. "According to Chonghua's annals, he died killing the demon beast. But that doesn't line up with Wuyan's story at all." Gu Mang's brow furrowed as he continued in a low murmur. "I've always felt Chen Tang seemed familiar somehow. Like I've seen him somewhere before. What's up with this person?"

As he pondered, Wuyan continued to speak. Like muffled thunder from an approaching storm, her voice slowly transformed from sorrowful to ominous. "He married. He changed his mind, but not for me," she seethed. "For some woman I didn't even know! So much for 'heart for the Dao, desiring nothing else'... He *lied* to me! He looked down on me because I was a demon and he was an immortal! As soon as a suitable immortal pursued him, he changed his tune! He never intended to tell me the truth! I wished for nothing more than to rush over and rip that man-stealer to shreds, but I didn't even know what the bitch looked like! I was there *first*!"

Wuyan's fury echoed in their ears, as piercing as bared claws. "I knew him first! He promised me! He was disloyal and heartless! *He broke his promise!*"

Gu Mang sighed to himself. He'd really expected it to be a typical story of a fickle man, but against all odds, it wasn't so. This fire bat demon queen had staked it all on a one-sided infatuation. Chen Tang never loved her in the first place, and rejected her the only way he could. She tried to force him to love her, but feelings could never be forced. Nor did it matter who had come first. It was true that Chen Tang had promised he wouldn't marry, and had broken that promise, but this couldn't truly be deemed a "betrayal."

"I left the island to look for him, but the world is vast, and I had no idea where he and that bitch were hiding. On top of that, I was cultivating the immortal path against my nature; for this, I paid a heavy price. I was still young, yet my hair had turned white, my body shriveled and shrunken. Only the Xueling Pill made with the blood of the feathered tribe could return me my youth and strength. But *why*?!"

In the glowing ball, Wuyan had become a wrinkled old woman raging within the palace. A servant girl trembled as she presented a Xueling Pill to Wuyan on the throne. The instant she swallowed it, it was as though an unseen hand smoothed the wrinkles from her face; her aged skin became delicate and supple once more, and her withered features regained their beauty.

Her youth could be returned with forbidden medicines. Only the innocence in her eyes was forever lost.

"Mother was right. Immortals really do kill demons. Some kill our bodies while others kill our hearts! Liar! Liar... I don't understand these men who aren't of my tribe... I never want to see creatures like that again."

By now, Wuyan had descended into a frenzied madness. On the one hand, she believed Chen Tang could still change his mind; she harbored the deranged hope that her lost love would come see her again. On the other, she developed an extreme hatred for men of any other tribe, demon or human. She issued an order: if foreign men came to the island, they would be fed gu worms to change their appearance into Chen Tang's. She would use them however she pleased, easing her longing for a brief time.

"For a love like this, once is enough. I'll never make such a mistake again..." Her soft voice faded like ripples on a lake's surface, slowly falling quiet.

Once her story ended, Gu Mang stood and extinguished the ball of light. All that remained was a wisp of white that curled up and floated into his head—the result of him sharing minds with Wuyan and mastering the Bat Island barrier.

Silence reigned inside the thatched hut. Gu Mang said nothing after completing the spell, and Mo Xi's head ached from the demon tribe's overzealous emotions. He kneaded the bridge of his nose and his forehead in frustration.

The fire bat tribe was beast-like, and their love and hatred came down to something like this: *If I love you, I'll make any sacrifice for you.*

If you don't love me after that, then you're heartless. The situation was a little more nuanced than that, but Gu Mang still felt rather speechless.

Mo Xi sat on the pile of straw, his head pounding. "What *is* this…"

Watching him, Gu Mang slowly formed a cunning idea. He broke the silence to ask with interest, "What about you? Have you ever had similar thoughts?"

Mo Xi lifted his head, confusion in his black eyes. "What?"

As Gu Mang looked into his limpid, uncomprehending eyes, he felt a twinge of reluctance. But he hardened his resolve, quirking his lips into that infuriatingly roguish smile as he reached out to lift Mo Xi's defined jaw.

Perhaps Wuyan's rambling really had made Mo Xi's head spin, or perhaps Gu Mang's loaded question had stunned him—whatever the reason, Mo Xi didn't resist. He let Gu Mang's finger tilt his face up, staring blankly at the man in front of him.

Gu Mang smiled. "Have you ever resented me like that?"

Mo Xi continued to stare.

"Have you ever thought, no matter how much you sacrificed, or how much you changed…" Gu Mang's finger slid down inch by inch, past that chiseled chin, along the rolling jut of Mo Xi's throat and down to his lapels, slowly coming to a stop on the left side of Mo Xi's chest. "I never actually loved you."

Gu Mang's fingertip tapped against that spot where he had once personally stabbed Mo Xi. A smile like fleeting mist played upon his lips as he pressed down lightly. The wound had long since healed, but the grisly scar remained. Through Mo Xi's clothes, beneath Gu Mang's fingers, it faintly began to throb once more.

Arm propped on his knee, Gu Mang knelt in the straw. He leaned down to stare at Mo Xi, who was sitting in front of him, and his mouth split into a grin as he asked, "General Mo, have you ever felt the kind of resentment she did?"

The confusion on Mo Xi's face disappeared with this. Gu Mang was smiling, but he might as well have slapped Mo Xi across the face. Mo Xi was stung; he hadn't expected this strike, and heartbreak spilled from his expression almost instantly. He turned away, biting his lip. Only after a long moment did he gather up his dignity and turn back to Gu Mang, fixing him with a vicious glare. "Chen Tang never said he loved Wuyan."

"So?"

"But you..." Mo Xi spoke with difficulty. "You did."

"Oh. Did I?" Gu Mang paused. "Then let's say I did. But you should understand, what men say in bed in a moment of pleasure can't be taken seriously." Gu Mang heaved a sigh. "Back when I slept with those girls, I would also tell them *I love you, I care about you, you're the only one for me.* When I was happy, I would say I'd pluck the moon from the sky for them. But look at you—you're a grown man. These words wouldn't fool silly little brothel girls, yet you believed them."

He sighed, reaching out as if to pat Mo Xi on the head. But before he could complete the motion, Mo Xi slapped his hand away.

102

Sharing a Room

THE SMILE on Gu Mang's face froze. Something stirred faintly in the depths of his blue eyes, but only for the instant it took that apathetic smile to return. He looked down at Mo Xi's handsome face, at this man who currently resembled nothing so much as a dog betrayed by its master or a cat whose tail had been trod on; sorrow and wounded pride merged on that bone-white face. Tears gathered in Mo Xi's eyes, but he still stubbornly held on, gritting his white teeth as he stared back at Gu Mang with a fierce arrogance.

"So what if I did. I'm not like you—I can't be so careless toward everything."

Gu Mang paused, then burst into laughter. "Look at you—and to think you looked down on Wuyan. Aren't you the same? She insisted on forcing it, and you insist on believing it."

The tendons on Mo Xi's pale hands were pushing through the skin, but Gu Mang acted like he hadn't noticed. "There's really very little difference between you. Both of you think what you gave wasn't reciprocated, and spent so many years stewing in resentment—"

But he didn't get to finish. "Gu Mang," Mo Xi cut in, pinning him with a stare. "Are you being serious right now?"

"Why wouldn't I be?"

"You think I resented and hated you all these years because what I *gave wasn't reciprocated*?!"

Gu Mang looked into the flickering depths of Mo Xi's eyes and almost felt sorrow. But after a beat, all he said was, "Why else?"

Mo Xi closed his eyes. "If I hated you for that, why would I have bothered begging you to turn back at Dongting Lake... Why would I have bothered keeping your soldiers, or hoped you wouldn't go to the Liao Kingdom—if I were only upset because you never truly loved me, do you think you could still stand before me and say these things now?"

Long-suppressed emotions ripped a hole in Mo Xi's facade of calmness. He finally erupted. "If that were my grievance, I've had plenty of opportunities to vent my discontent. I could have taken you by force, humiliated you, poisoned or drugged you. Yet I've done none of those things; do you think it's because I don't know how?! I saw you as my comrade, my friend, my..."

My beloved. My god.

What I hate is your betrayal, and the way you changed. You didn't just abandon me—you abandoned your brothers, your dream, your fathomless glory.

You abandoned the man you used to be.

Mo Xi's eyes were red-rimmed. "Had you chosen any other path, I wouldn't have blamed you, even if you had nothing more to do with me for the rest of your life. Gu Mang—back then, you nearly ripped out my heart."

Gu Mang's hands shook slightly.

Mo Xi looked up at him, black eyes dull as a starless night. As he gave voice to the emotions trapped in his breast for too long, he rasped, "Couldn't you see?"

For a while, Gu Mang couldn't speak. Those dark eyes hurt too much to look at. Gu Mang remembered the first time he encountered them, back when they looked nothing like this.

The first time he saw Mo Xi, he was standing beneath one of the academy's osmanthus trees, his gold-trimmed black robes embroidered with the soaring snake emblem. His high ponytail was bound with gold ribbon, and a jade bow rested in the crook of his arm as he sighted a distant target. The wind rose and set his sleeves to fluttering. Sensing someone's eyes on him, Mo Xi turned back and glanced at Gu Mang.

Those eyes were like deep, still waters, clear and bright as an ethereal lake. His gaze held little emotion; it casually slid away from Gu Mang.

After that, Gu Mang encountered him again and again at the academy. He saw him sitting alone on the stone steps reading a book, then eating alone leaning against a tree. He saw him leaving the academy's cultivation practice field, walking with his ribbon in his mouth as he gathered his hair into a ponytail, his pale, slender neck emerging from sweat-soaked robes.

He was always alone.

"The young master of the Mo Clan is so arrogant."

"Who cares how powerful his spiritual energy is? He still has no friends."

"You should hear the headmaster go on about him—how he's so *talented* and *hardworking*. I heard, ever since he entered the academy, he practices at the archery range every day until the hour of hai, long after dark. Heh, who does he think he's putting on a show for?"

Gu Mang had heard the same sentiment many times by now. Long before Mo Xi knew Gu Mang, Gu Mang was well aware of the name *Mo Xi*. He was the subject of whispered discussions in the academy and his lord Murong Lian's mockery; without intending to, Gu Mang had inadvertently learned a great deal.

Among noble young masters, bad tempers, arrogant natures, phony reputations, and reckless ambitions were only too common. Gu Mang assumed Mo Xi had no one to blame but himself and didn't think too kindly of him either.

So it went until the day Gu Mang passed by the fields and saw two of the academy slaves kneeling before Mo Xi. The holy weapon Shuairan crackled in his grip. Gu Mang saw a young master using his status to bully slaves and was about to speak up for them when he heard one of the slaves sniveling through tears as he kowtowed. "Mo-gongzi! Mo-gongzi, we're sorry! W-we didn't steal your money pouch on purpose, it's just...it's just..."

The thin, sickly-looking girl beside him cried, "It's just that we're starving. We offended Murong-gongzi a few days back, so the head housekeeper cut our rations... My brother w-was afraid that I might fall ill from hunger, and you're a-always alone...that's why we had the guts t-to try...try and steal your..."

Mo Xi stared at this pair of siblings. Slowly, the red light of the whip Shuairan dimmed to nothing in his hand. Head lowered, he took his money bag from his qiankun pouch and left it on the stone steps. Then he turned to leave.

Watching this play out from a distance, Gu Mang was stunned. Because of what Hua Po'an had done, the disciples of the cultivation academy were forbidden from interacting with any slaves not their own—and they most certainly weren't allowed to help them. That was the greatest taboo at the academy. But Mo Xi had acted instantly and silently, with no expectation of reciprocity. As if what he'd done was natural.

Back then, Gu Mang had felt something he couldn't put into words as he watched the little lord's fluttering silhouette recede. But he still wouldn't have paid any special attention to Mo Xi had things ended there. What truly surprised Gu Mang was the news that spread like wildfire through the academy a few days later: the darling of the heavens Mo Xi had been whipped in punishment for violating academy rules.

"So even he can't escape punishment, huh?"

"He thinks he's better than the rest of us. This whipping will finally knock him down a peg!"

"I heard it's because he gave his money pouch to a pair of slave siblings; everyone knows that's against the rules. Usually he's faking diligence, but I guess now he's faking kindness. What a hypocrite."

Gu Mang felt something entirely different in his heart as he listened to the crowd pass judgment on Mo Xi.

When he returned to his room, he heard Murong Lian's unbridled laughter from the courtyard. "That Mo asshole is such an idiot! They were just faking it to trick him—I really didn't expect him to take the bait so easily, ha ha ha ha!"

"My lord is so clever and wise. Mo Xi doesn't stand a chance!"

"Hmph! No matter how strong his magic is, he won't be nominated for the outstanding student award after breaking the academy's greatest taboo. He thinks he's a match for me?" Murong Lian snickered. "He's ten years too early."

Only then did Gu Mang realize the case of the "starving" slave siblings had been completely orchestrated by Murong Lian to frame his rival. After those siblings took Mo Xi's money pouch and cowrie shells, they turned around and brought them straight to Murong Lian, who filed a complaint with the academy's discipline elder. Mo Xi, he claimed, had openly defied the academy's rules and secretly consorted with slaves.

Mo Xi was the only son of the Mo Clan. He would escape severe punishment, but he had still violated the academy's greatest taboo.

By no coincidence, the discipline elder was a friend of Wangshu-jun's family; of course he favored Murong Lian. Thus, Mo Xi was whipped.

At the time, Gu Mang had belonged to Murong Lian; he and Mo Xi had no connection whatsoever. Yet this young master's actions had left him stunned; slowly, he found himself caring for this Mo-gongzi whom he didn't know. He couldn't say anything to Mo Xi, much less visit him or make his sympathies known. But that incident planted the seed of affection in his heart.

Destiny determined all, and those fated to meet never escaped its pull. A few days later, Gu Mang was walking down one of the academy's tree-lined paths. The jade-green lawn was deserted save for a youth sitting alone against a birch tree.

Mo Xi sat in shady silence, nibbling on a zongzi and absorbed in a bamboo scroll spread over his knees. That pale cheek like fresh snow still bore a whip's scar from his punishment, but he didn't seem to mind. Mo Xi's lowered lashes were still so thick, his gaze still so clear, free of resentment. A ripple spread through Gu Mang's heart—he thought this young master was beautiful beyond compare.

He stood behind a tree for a moment, gazing at that lonely, elegant figure from afar. At last, Mo Xi noticed this overly intent gaze and looked up from his scroll. Their eyes met.

Gu Mang stared in silence.

Mo Xi stared back in confusion.

This was the first time Gu Mang met those ink-dark eyes. His palms were a little sweaty. He'd always been a cheerful person, but for some reason, he felt anxious. Part of him wanted to smile at Mo Xi, but another part didn't know what to do.

At that moment, Lu Zhanxing happened to pass by. Spotting Gu Mang, he waved and shouted, "Mang-er! What are you standing there for?"

Gu Mang turned to answer, breaking away from Mo Xi's gaze and striding off into the distance.

The noble Mo-gongzi surely hadn't recognized this nameless little nobody. He probably didn't remember their first meeting on that tree-lined path. But Gu Mang remembered. Those eyes like black jade… In his mind's eye, they were pristine, containing a purity he wanted to protect with all his heart.

In the present, Gu Mang sighed, looking into those eyes so close to him in the thatched hut. They held hate, resentment, pain, dissatisfaction; stubbornness and ruthlessness flashed in their depths. But Gu Mang remembered: the first time he saw Mo Xi, all they held was a solemn integrity.

In the end, this was what they had become.

Gu Mang turned away. He was afraid if he kept looking he wouldn't be able to stop himself from saying certain things. The heart where his core had shattered was already aching.

In the silence of the hut, Mo Xi murmured, "Gu Mang. Wouldn't it be nice if all I wanted was to have you? Things would be so much simpler if that were the case."

Gu Mang didn't answer him.

"But what I wanted was for you to come back."

There was nothing Gu Mang could say. He sat down on the pile of straw, sinking softly into its depths. With a long sigh, he leaned back, staring blankly at the ceiling.

He knew he needed to maintain boundaries with Mo Xi. Mo Xi was his poison, one that was deadly and without an antidote. He strove to build a wall between himself and Mo Xi, but the moment he saw those frustrated, sorrowful, heartbroken eyes, his hands would shake as he tried to lay down the bricks.

He very, very much wanted to leave this small, thatched hut.

Other than the straw, all he could smell was Mo Xi's faint scent. He wore a cold and hard mask, but he didn't know how long he could keep it on in front of Mo Xi. In the end, Gu Mang sprang to his feet. He dusted the straw from his clothes, walked to the doorway, and peeked out through a crack in the curtain.

The bat demons outside were still looking for partners. It was a chaotic scene, definitely a poor time to leave. He could do nothing but sit back down next to Mo Xi and stare into space with his chin in his hand. He didn't plan to keep hurting Mo Xi; that would only hurt him too. But they couldn't just sit here like this either. Gu Mang changed the subject: "Where's Yue Chenqing's life crystal?"

"In my qiankun pouch."

"Take it out, let's have a look."

After a moment, Mo Xi fished out the stone, inlaid with swirls of agate. It shone brightly, its gleam growing more resplendent as they watched. Gu Mang took it into his own palm and examined it a while, then returned it to Mo Xi. "Looks like everything is going smoothly on Jiang-xiong's side. There's no rush to leave then. Let's wait until those bat demons are in the huts. It's too busy outside."

Mo Xi ignored him. After his outburst, he had sunk into this wordless silence. Gu Mang knew he must have truly hurt him. Of course Gu Mang knew what he'd said was absurd—how could Mo Xi be the same as Wuyan? They really had come together so passionately, so desperately. He had slept with Mo Xi enthusiastically, yet now he was criticizing Mo Xi for making a big deal of it. He had so clearly seen Mo Xi's attempts to protect him, Mo Xi's despair, Mo Xi's willingness to sacrifice his life to make him turn back...

Yet in their current circumstances, what could he do but make Mo Xi hate him, make him leave him? Mo Xi's heart was soft. He was a man of upright character, and while he might have looked ruthless and cold, Gu Mang knew he was kinder than anyone.

This kindness was like the aid he offered those academy slaves—it too easily became a weapon others used against him. Since Gu Mang had already chosen this path, he didn't need Mo Xi's pity, indignance, or dissatisfaction, and he especially didn't need the slightest hint of his love. He only needed Mo Xi to hate him completely.

But when he was so close to him, breathing in his familiar scent, Gu Mang felt the same disquiet he had in the past. He knew distinctly what he had to do, yet he couldn't stop himself from clinging to one pitiful scrap of delusion—that everything could still be changed, that he could still get as close to him as before, like a moth flying into flame. A delusion that he could still hold this man, lose himself in him... That he could use the excuse of momentary passion to say *I love you* one last time without hesitation.

How nice that would be indeed.

They sat on the straw, each lost in their own thoughts as they waited for the bat demons to find their mates and disperse. Suddenly, a pair of embracing bat demons staggered past the hut, breaking the silence. Through the hanging bamboo curtain, Mo Xi and Gu Mang could see them kissing as if they were glued together and hear their flirtatious giggling.

"Stop rushing me, won't you?"

"We're gathering vital energy for Her Majesty, aren't we in a rush?"

The female demon's laughter was muffled by more kisses. "*Mmph*... You're just using Her Majesty as an excuse. Don't you want to..."

The following words were drowned out by heavy panting.

Gu Mang couldn't resist shooting a glance at Mo Xi, who noticed and turned his face aside. Just as Gu Mang thought Mo Xi would continue feigning deafness, Mo Xi asked without preamble, "What does *gathering vital energy for Her Majesty* mean?"

"Oh," Gu Mang replied. "I think Wuyan can absorb the spiritual energy produced by the bat demons when they copulate. It's probably a unique trait of the fire bat tribe."

Mo Xi didn't make a sound, but from what Gu Mang could see of his side profile, it looked like he was mouthing *Ridiculous*.

"Fire bats are promiscuous by nature; it's not so strange," Gu Mang said. "Once they've entered their nests, we'll leave."

That pair of lovebird bats were still kissing hungrily outside the curtain, their passion palpable even from their silhouettes. But when they tried to push the curtain aside to enter, the male bat stopped. "Aiya, this one's taken."

The female bat's voice was soft as flowing silk. "The one next door's empty. Let's go there."

The two bats stumbled into the hut next door. Just as Mo Xi breathed a sigh of relief, they heard a *thump* through the wall beside them. The two bats were pressed against the wall of their hut, just a few feet away—now, the sound of their coupling echoed even louder in Gu Mang and Mo Xi's ears.

"Ah...not so fast... S-slow down..."

Mo Xi's face instantly darkened.

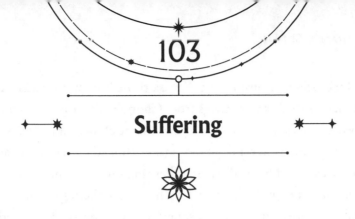

103

Suffering

THE HUTS WERE SMALL, with little distance between each one and its neighboring abode. On top of that, the bat demons were a shameless bunch; soundproofing was the furthest thing from their minds while building these huts. Some probably felt it was more thrilling this way.

But Gu Mang and Mo Xi were mortified.

The two bat demons were in quite a hurry and wasted no time getting down to business. They had to be pressed up right against the wall; Gu Mang and Mo Xi could hear faint wet squelches. Gu Mang peeked over at Mo Xi; he couldn't see Mo Xi's expression in the dark, but the man was radiating an almost physical gloominess.

Gu Mang cleared his throat, turned his clear blue eyes toward the hut's ceiling, and began to hum.

Mo Xi stared at him like he was a madman.

He was looking for a way to distract himself from the uncomfortable noises of the demon beasts next door, which he quickly managed to do. In the past, Gu Mang had played songs for all sorts of occasions on his suona. The melody he hummed now was every bit as brassy as the ones he used to favor, with many twists and turns. While those two bats were immersed in each other on the other side of the wall, Gu Mang was humming a little tune in an impossibly infuriating style.

He'd originally just meant to mask those intrusive sounds—but all these melodies were songs from Chonghua that he'd forgotten when he lost his memories. He'd played some of them at Jiang Yexue's wedding; others he'd played in trenches choked with the smoke of war. Back when he made these notes sing on his suona, there had been many people by his side. Lu Zhanxing hollering; Jiang Yexue smiling. Those army ruffians sprawled out beneath the splendid, spangled sky, raising cups of wine to their lips as they laughed and watched him by the dancing light of the bonfire.

Mo Xi too would be among the crowd, gazing at him with those night-dark eyes that shone so bright.

As Gu Mang hummed, he stopped caring about the noises from next door. He shifted into a more comfortable position, lying back in the pile of straw with his arms pillowed behind his head, bouncing one long leg as he focused on the melody. After a time, he paused. He turned to Mo Xi, who was sitting in the darkness, and asked teasingly, "Do you like it?"

"...You want to bring the neighbors over?" Mo Xi replied darkly.

"I won't." Gu Mang leaned back against the straw, one hand tapping his knee, softly keeping time. "Watch, they can't stop me."

A few minutes later, the sounds on the other side of the wall were replaced by angry pounding.

Mo Xi looked at him reproachfully. His eyes seemed to say, *What are you going to do about this?*

Gu Mang was in no rush. He tied off his tune with a grace note and let the sound fade. "What's wrong, dear neighbors?" he asked lazily.

"What are you doing in there? Are you screwing or not?!" the male bat demon growled from the other side.

Hearing him say *screwing* so obscenely, Mo Xi seemed to choke.

But Gu Mang was a vulgar person, so he laughed. "Oh, we're screwing all right."

Mo Xi stared in silence.

"Then what are you singing for?!"

"That's just how I am. When I'm enjoying myself, I like to hum a tune."

The rage of the bat demon next door could've burned through both walls. "When you get done good you like to hum 'Moon Reflected in the Pool?!'"[6] he snarled.

"Yep; when I come, I even double the tempo."

This response silenced the bat demon along with Mo Xi.

Bouncing a slender leg, Gu Mang toyed with a piece of straw as he continued, unabashed. "It's just a personal quirk. We were here first; if you don't like it, pick a room farther away." He paused, then added roguishly, "The demon I'm with is a great lay. Once I really get into it, who knows, I might find myself singing a jig or two. Brother, are you sure you don't want to move?"

The bat demons next door muttered curses at him. Despite their eagerness, it seemed they couldn't maintain the mood under threat of such a performance. The fire bat tribe was hedonistic and single-minded. In the heat of the moment, the last thing they wanted to deal with was a lunatic who sang double time when he came. After kicking the wall and swearing a few more times, the other couple left to find another hut.

Listening to their shouts of "Lunatic!" and "Freak!" as they hurried away, Gu Mang cackled silently in the pile of straw. As soon as they were gone for good, he couldn't hold back his laughter any longer. His shoulders shook, mirth coursing through him like ripples through water. "Ha ha ha ha—"

---

6   Formal mournful traditional song.

"You..." Mo Xi said.

"Arguing or explaining really won't do you any good sometimes." Gu Mang looked at Mo Xi with gleaming blue eyes, misty with suppressed laughter. He grinned. "You've got to either ignore them or prove you're crazier than they are. Works every time. But Xihe-jun, I'm afraid you couldn't learn this trick. You're far too prim and proper."

Mo Xi said nothing.

Several minutes passed, and Gu Mang felt they'd waited long enough. He pushed himself up from the pile of straw and took a step toward the door. Perhaps he'd gotten up too quickly after being sprawled out on his back for so long—he immediately felt lightheaded.

Even while angry with him, Mo Xi's question was reflexive. "What's wrong?"

"I...don't know, I'm a little dizzy." Gu Mang rubbed his forehead. "I'll be all right in a bit." He crossed to the doorway, twitched the bamboo curtain aside with a pinky, and peered out. There were only a few bat demons in sight; most had already paired off and disappeared into the thatched huts flanking the path. The pavilion made of human bones was deserted but for the faint haze of incense smoke glowing softly in the light of the moon.

Gu Mang waved Mo Xi over. "All right, we can sneak out now."

Mo Xi came to stand beside him. The two watched through the crack as the last pair of bat demons ducked into a hut. Gu Mang reached out to lift the curtain.

The instant he touched it, a red bat insignia glowed to life on the surface, so suddenly it burned Gu Mang's fingers. He snatched his hand back. "What the hell?!" he exclaimed.

Mo Xi reached out as well and received a similar scorching. "There's a barrier on the door..." he murmured.

Barrier techniques had never been Gu Mang's strong suit, but they happened to be Mo Xi's. Slender, pale fingers moved over the barrier sigil inch by inch, reading the spiritual energy flow. His brows drew together in a frown. "It's a one-way barrier. Anyone can enter from outside, but to leave from inside..." Mo Xi hummed quizzically, as though he thought he might have read it wrong. He ran his fingers over the edge of the bat sigil a few more times. Whatever suspicions he held seemed to be confirmed; Mo Xi's expression turned ugly as he lowered his hand in silence.

"What is it?" Gu Mang asked.

Mo Xi said nothing. He walked back to the straw heap, sat down, and closed his eyes. "We'll wait until daybreak to leave."

Gu Mang's eyes flew wide in surprise. "Why?"

"Don't ask questions."

In the glow of the barrier's red light, Gu Mang could see Mo Xi wore an expression of embarrassment. Just as Gu Mang was about to say more, another wave of dizziness washed over him. He had no choice but to stand quietly and wait for it to pass before walking over to Mo Xi and sitting down.

Gu Mang was clever. If Mo Xi wasn't willing to explain, he could guess. "This barrier doesn't stop people from entering, but it stops them from leaving. Then its purpose must be to ensure those who enter complete some task before they leave. All the thatched huts must have the same barrier as this one. We can't get out, but those two bat demons from before could."

Mo Xi didn't reply.

As Gu Mang thought it over, his gaze roving back and forth inside the room, it gradually dawned on him. There was nothing here except a pile of soft, thick straw. The bat demons entered to do one thing: dual cultivate and send the spiritual energy they created into their queen's pavilion.

He glanced at Mo Xi's shuttered expression once more. The answer was plain. "I get it—the barrier will check to see if the people inside have had sex or not. It won't let out the ones that haven't, right?"

Mo Xi neither confirmed nor denied. "As soon as the sun comes up, the barrier will lose its effect. We can go at dawn."

But this dawn wouldn't come so easily. Gu Mang tossed and turned, uncomfortable and unable to find sleep. The dizziness from earlier hadn't receded; if anything, it had intensified. He felt as though a fire had sparked to life in his belly, the dry heat spreading like ink on paper, rendering his breaths harsh and labored.

At first, Gu Mang thought he'd overtaxed his weakened body, so he put his discomfort out of his mind. But as it worsened, that strange heat made him prickle all over. Even his fingertips were trembling...

By now Gu Mang couldn't possibly fail to realize what was going on. He sat bolt upright, panting lowly, and yanked open his lapels. He stared at the moon outside the bamboo curtain, his eyes flashing as he recalled what he'd seen in the pavilion.

"Bad news," he said. "There's a problem with that fragrance from the blood pool." He swiped a hand over his face and patted his cheeks, trying to make himself more alert. "Mo Xi?"

Mo Xi was sitting with his back against the straw heap; he hadn't slept. At the sound of Gu Mang's voice, he turned.

"Do you feel weird at all?" Gu Mang asked.

"No. What's the problem?"

Gu Mang swallowed. Those fire bats hadn't gone running into the huts just because of the queen's command—the fragrance released from the blood pool contained an aphrodisiac. But why wasn't it affecting Mo Xi? Was it because he hadn't gone to the pool, and only breathed in a small amount of the scent in the air?

Noting his silence, Mo Xi asked, "Is something the matter?"

"I..." Gu Mang paused. "No."

He lay back down on the straw, his back to Mo Xi, and began silently reciting sutras, trying to suppress the agitation that was growing stronger and stronger. But whatever fragrance the bat queen had poured into the blood pool was extremely potent, the equivalent of casting a spell on all the inhabitants of the pavilion to send them into heat. Unbeknownst to Gu Mang, this perfume only affected demons. Mo Xi was a human; of course he wouldn't feel anything. But Gu Mang was different; his body had been tempered in the Liao Kingdom, fused with the essence of a snow faewolf's soul. Even if the fragrance didn't have as strong an effect on him as on pure demons, it was still frightfully powerful. After reciting a heart-calming sutra seven times over, he couldn't alleviate the dry heat burning through his body. Gu Mang grimaced and curled in on himself as he faced the wall, his breaths slowly quickening...

What the hell.

Demon beasts were different from humans. Under normal conditions, humans could overcome their lust—it was uncomfortable, certainly, to be left without relief in the thick of desire, but it was no more than discomfort. Beasts and demons were not the same. When animals in heat couldn't find relief, their lustful torment was agonizing; even their bones ached with it.

Gu Mang swallowed thickly and closed his eyes.

He didn't want Mo Xi to discover the state he was in, but he couldn't control the effects of the incense, which seemed to take hold of his body as if in retaliation for his abstention. Because he hadn't obeyed the fragrance's commands, every sense that triggered lust was amplified. He could smell that scent he knew too well on Mo Xi's body: his faint, distinctive fragrance, and the masculine musk beneath.

Gu Mang's hands balled into fists in the straw. He bit his lip and slowed his breaths by sheer will, but he couldn't suppress the pounding of his heart. Right now, he truly hated this body the Liao Kingdom had tempered... This body that ran with beastly blood, that forced him to submit to the aphrodisiac and recall those absurd, passionate scenes of the past. Gu Mang's lashes fluttered, hiding the wetness in his eyes...

I can't think about it. I won't think about it.

Shattered images flashed before him, defying all reason. The lust in him longed for Mo Xi's scent to envelop him, yearned for Mo Xi to embrace him from behind as he had in the past, pressing his searing chest to Gu Mang's spine. It demanded that they make love just as wildly as they had back then, that thick root pushing into yielding spring mud, the air filling with the earthy scent of petrichor. The soil was soft and saturated, and when that great cedar dove in, rivulets of spring water burst from its depths, pooling on the forest floor.

Can't think about it.

Won't think about it.

But somehow what sprang to mind was the scalding heat of Mo Xi's breath when he bit Gu Mang's earlobe, his ragged panting in the heat of desire—

"Gu Mang."

A questioning voice, its timbre low and alluring, broke through those torrid memories. Curled up with his back to Mo Xi, Gu Mang shuddered against his will. Try as he might to hide it, Mo Xi still noticed something amiss.

"What's wrong?"

"I..." The instant Gu Mang opened his mouth, his voice was so hoarse even he was taken aback. He swallowed, forcing his voice to steadiness, hoping he sounded a little more distant and a little less shaky. "I'm thinking about some personal matters; it's none of your business."

These words were frosty, and Mo Xi was prideful. As Gu Mang expected, he dropped the issue after being jabbed like that. Gu Mang breathed a soft sigh of relief as he lay facing the wall of the hut, worrying his lip between his teeth. When he opened his eyes, they glimmered with scattered light; he was in such pain they had already filled with tears.

The desire induced by the fragrance was insidious: the harder he tried to suppress it, the stronger it became. Gu Mang's senses screamed. They couldn't endure any more stimulation—he had merely heard Mo Xi's voice and he could feel his body going weak. In the secret recesses of his heart, he found himself thinking how that voice had once murmured his name against the back of his ear while its owner held him from behind, thrusting into him as the sweat between their bodies threatened to fuse them together...

Gradually, Gu Mang's vision blurred. It was too hot; it was genuinely too hot. His heart was beating so rapidly...

He wished the Time Mirror hadn't given him his memories back. Wouldn't he be better off now if he was still the version of himself who knew nothing of passion? Then he wouldn't remember any of these absurdities from the past, nor the thrill and pleasure of sharing Mo Xi's bed.

Gu Mang squeezed his eyes shut. He was on the verge of falling apart. The snow faewolf blood was welcoming the poison inside his body without hesitation, burning away his human rationality piece by piece.

The man he loved, the man he'd slept with, his only beloved, the one he was doomed to part with, the one he wanted but could never have—that man was right behind him, only a few steps away.

And they were in a nest beasts used for rutting, filled with the heady scent of sex.

The hand Gu Mang clenched beneath the straw was trembling, his tendons protruding. He was afraid that, in the next second, Wuyan's maddening miasma would destroy him, and he would do something reckless—something regrettable.

After a moment of hesitation, his blue eyes snapped open. He reached down as if he'd made up his mind. With his back to Mo Xi, Gu Mang unfastened his belt and took hold of himself with a shaking hand.

He swallowed the groan that threatened to escape.

Gu Mang's clear blue eyes were wide as he panted in silence. It had been a very long time since he'd done anything like this. He had to avoid Mo Xi's notice, so he moved surreptitiously. His hand stroked clumsily up and down, but it was like giving a parched traveler a single sip of water: wetting his lips begat an even greater heat and thirst.

He couldn't speed up or tighten his grip; he couldn't make any conspicuous sounds. It was like drinking poison to slake his thirst. Slowly, the rims of Gu Mang's eyes grew red from discomfort and frustration; the faewolf blood rushing through his veins was about to drive him mad...

But he couldn't even moan aloud.

Even with his last scrap of rationality, he remembered he shouldn't get involved with Mo Xi. On the day he chose to defect, he had pushed Mo Xi to the side, then dug a chasm seething with hatred between them. He shouldn't have gotten close to him again...

"Mngh!"

A strong hand grabbed him from behind; Gu Mang flinched violently. He heard Mo Xi's voice: "Don't move."

His thoughts were in such disarray, the physical stimulation so devastating, that Gu Mang hadn't noticed anything while so focused on chasing his own release. When those warm, firm, familiar arms caught him by surprise and pulled him into an embrace, Gu Mang's eyes flew open. The shock of it—the overwhelming thrill of it— dragged a moan from him. "*Ah...*"

He saw sparks. For an instant, his head spun; everything was blurry, yet he instinctively tried to escape. He felt shame, alarm, contrition...by the time Mo Xi's hand wrapped around him, Gu Mang was nearly in tears. There was pleasure, yes, but also a despairing reluctance.

Mo Xi's low voice sounded in his ear, just like in his memories, except this time it held hesitation and resentment. "*This* is what you meant when you said you were fine?"

104

Inseparable Hearts

M
O XI HAD REALIZED something was wrong with Gu Mang a long time ago. It was just that after each round of questioning, Gu Mang insisted he was fine. Mo Xi truly didn't want anything to happen between them that shouldn't. Although he was fully aware of what was going on, he did nothing.

But the straw hut was too small. He couldn't stop himself from glancing again and again at that man curled up in the corner, as far away from Mo Xi as he could manage. He knew Gu Mang was unwell and trying to hide it. He'd even noticed when Gu Mang's hand started to move.

In Mo Xi's eyes, Gu Mang had really let go of the past, and really wanted nothing more to do with him. So—even this dissolute army ruffian who'd once laughed and said, *It's just sleeping together, it's good as long as both people enjoy it*, would rather suffer in silence and touch himself than reveal his arousal to Mo Xi.

This man could smile at Jiang Yexue and speak nicely with Murong Chuyi. He could even be warm and soft to the little bird he brought back mere hours ago. It was only toward Mo Xi he was cold.

Gu Mang had really let go of him.

Mo Xi wanted to pretend he hadn't seen anything. The pathetic scrap of self-respect and pride he retained urged him to turn aside. But when he heard Gu Mang's suppressed, painful panting...

He couldn't bear it.

In the end, even he didn't know what he was feeling as he rose and approached that curled-up silhouette, bending down and taking him into his arms.

Gu Mang's instant flinch of surprise and muted groan set Mo Xi's heart trembling. Mo Xi steeled himself, then resolutely broke his vow not to touch Gu Mang again; he took that pitiable shaft into his hand. Gu Mang unthinkingly pressed back into Mo Xi's chest, his jaw tilting, his neck arching. "Don't...don't..."

"Close your eyes. Just pretend it isn't me." Mo Xi's voice was low and husky.

Gu Mang's brow furrowed, words stuck in his throat. His body was in such a fragile state, but his soul remained unyielding. He wanted to say, *How could it be anyone but you?*

It's always been you. Mo Xi, only you...

But in the end, this unspeakable love could only ever be just that: something he wanted to say and nothing more. One thought the other had severed all ties, and the other thought his own heart made of iron and steel. Each had their reasons, both unwilling to open their hearts to each other again. It didn't matter—passion and desire were a bottomless abyss, and they had already stepped into that nothingness long ago, tumbling endlessly downward. It was all darkness, and the only thing they could hold onto was each other.

Mo Xi's hand started moving, and the last of Gu Mang's resistance collapsed. The final mote of clarity he had was just enough to keep him from calling Mo Xi's name in the heat of passion. He was like a beast trapped in the sea of desire, struggling desperately to free himself from this cage of bygone love, but there was no escape. Mo Xi knew him too well; he stirred the fire within him too easily, weakening his limbs, drawing moans from his lips. Gu Mang threw his head back, panting in Mo Xi's embrace.

His disappointing flesh, so prone to tears, had already allowed his eyes to redden, their slender corners misty with unshed tears. He trembled all over, slack in Mo Xi's arms. Clinging to that last thread of rationality, he hoarsely cried, "L-let go of me..."

His tone was harsh, but his voice was surpassingly soft, quavering like it might melt. He'd meant it to be a fierce rebuke, yet it left his mouth as an unintelligible moan. "Please, let go..."

In the end, Gu Mang's cries devolved into pathetic begging. Heaven only knew how much agony he was in, forced to take control of his love at the same time as he wrestled with his primal desire. He'd lost his memories, walked down a path of no return, and had two souls carved out of him. He didn't know how long he could keep the awareness the Time Mirror had returned to him; he didn't know if this clarity the heavens had bestowed in pity would be taken from him just as easily. He had lost so much. The man behind him was the last bit of light and warmth he had to hold.

But still he restrained himself. "Let...let me go..." Gu Mang cried brokenly.

Let me go; don't come closer. I've been tempered with bestial blood, but I'm still human. I would still feel unwilling, I would still regret the path I chose. But I can't turn back, so please...stop torturing me... All that lies before me is a frigid night. Your warmth will make me hesitate, will keep me from moving forward.

I'm already a traitor. Mo Xi, I don't want to be a coward too...

As Mo Xi held him, he too was in pain. Between the two of them, who was supposed to let go? Who was supposed to release the other? Since Gu Mang didn't want Mo Xi to touch him, Mo Xi had uttered that pathetic line, *Just pretend it isn't me.* And yet Gu Mang still rejected him. This jolt of pain made Mo Xi loosen his grip.

Like a swallow freed, Gu Mang startled up from the ground and made a valiant attempt to get to his feet so he could put some distance between himself and Mo Xi. But the demon blood was surging inside him, and his desire clouded everything. He felt weak, utterly sapped of strength. After unsteadily lifting his shoulders, he fell right back into the straw.

How many unknown pairs of demons had coupled in this hut? The golden straw was suffused with a sharp musk. A muffled whimper issued from Gu Mang's throat. He turned over, his clear blue eyes wide and vacant.

He watched Mo Xi stand up, and he saw his own reflection in Mo Xi's eyes.

This was honestly pathetic. He knew what a sight he was, while here was Mo Xi, still so properly attired; even his lapels remained neatly folded. The fragrance's effects were roiling stronger and stronger inside Gu Mang. He knitted his brows in pain. Lifting a hand to ward him off, he began, "You..." He wanted to say, *You need to go away, stop looking.* But the dry heat was rushing upward. He bit down on his lip and didn't finish his sentence.

Mo Xi misunderstood; he thought Gu Mang had reached out to pull him closer, and took hold of Gu Mang's hand.

It was like lava bursting through rock at long last. The whisper of skin against skin finally broke Gu Mang's self-imposed shackles; he had been strained to his very limit. With this touch, human reason yielded to demon blood.

He couldn't get up—instead he dragged Mo Xi down. Caught off guard, Mo Xi fell heavily on top of him; their combined weight sank into the soft straw. Gu Mang arched his neck and grimaced, a muted groan issuing from his throat. He was shaking unbearably. As he pressed close to Mo Xi, he could feel that long-lost desire, that terrifying hardness, pressing into his abdomen through both their clothes.

Whatever remaining strength he had fled. His lips quivered, and his blue eyes glimmered with shattered light. He had managed to say *let go of me* earlier, but the intense, bestial lust in him now burned red-hot, dyeing the rims of his eyes scarlet. He could only gaze at Mo Xi's handsome face and bite his lip, unable to say a thing.

Instinct made him sincere, urged him to speak the truth. All these years, after all these years... He had done countless ruthless deeds and walked countless bloody roads. He had abandoned everything, save for Mo Xi. Gu Mang hadn't abandoned Mo Xi; he had cut himself away from him. Holding the knife, inch by inch, he'd carved into his own flesh and dug Mo Xi out of his heart.

Only after he'd come out of the Mirror with those lost memories did he truly reunite with Mo Xi. When he'd seen Mo Xi amid that bloody rain, his heart had raced frantically, but he buried it all beneath callous apathy.

But how could that be the honest truth? He loved him so much, missed him so much. He missed him in the barracks, missed him in battle, missed him in every plaintive melody. In the depths of his shattered memories, he loved him, cherished him, and longed for him.

He tore into his lip viciously, tears shining in his eyes. It was partly because of this tortuous desire, but even more because he really had been destroyed so utterly. He wanted more than anything to be recklessly selfish for once. He wanted to say, *Just fuck me, okay? Fuck me. Please... Save me, I've been soaking in a sea of blood for eight years... Will you hold me again...?*

Oh, I missed you, Mo Xi... After I cut you out of my heart, that scar never healed.

Gu Mang blinked, feeling something wet and hot spill from his eyes and drip into his hair. Mo Xi reached out to touch his face, but he snatched Mo Xi's hand. Mustering all his strength and awareness, he rasped, "Fuck me..."

He saw something flash in Mo Xi's eyes, a light that had nothing to do with lust.

Gu Mang felt as if his heart was being cut out, as if he was being cooked alive. He closed his eyes and swallowed. "I will...pretend..." Those fingers around Mo Xi's wrist were shaking, shaking. "I will... pretend you're...someone else."

He opened his eyes to see that the spark in Mo Xi's gaze had gone out. In its place was a frost that could chill one to the bone. He looked deeply wounded. But just as Gu Mang was accustomed to using laughter to hide his heart, his little shidi Mo Xi had finally learned to use coldness to hide his feelings. His Mo Xi would never again be the youth who rushed to confess his love on a snowy night.

Neither could return to who they used to be.

In those black eyes, pain sank beneath the ice that floated up. "As you wish." Mo Xi ground the words between his teeth.

Gu Mang felt himself flipped over with a terrifying brusqueness. A hand pressed him face down in the straw. This position...and this setting. It was purely a physical release. It had nothing to do with love.

The aphrodisiac had left Gu Mang achingly sensitive; his skin bloomed red in the wake of Mo Xi's touch. He kept his head down amid the golden stalks, his face pillowed on one soft cheek as he struggled for breath. His mind was a morass. He felt Mo Xi un-ceremoniously tear off his clothes; his hands seemed to move with vengeance, or with rage. Before he removed Gu Mang's underclothes,

Mo Xi pressed against him through that final thin layer, hot as a brand, and viciously thrust forward.

"*Ah*...!" Gu Mang gasped aloud at that feeling he'd craved for so long, crying out hoarsely as his fingers clenched around a handful of straw. How useless he was, this man who had been losing and losing since the battle of Phoenix Cry Mountain—to the imperial court, to political machinations—and now he was losing to desire.

Mo Xi unfastened his own black-iron belt buckle with a crisp click. "Imagine whomever you'd like."

Gu Mang buried his face in the pile of straw, unable to say a single word. He hardened against his will at Mo Xi's touch. Mo Xi picked him up and sat him between his legs, facing away, that thin layer of underclothes the last thing separating them. Mo Xi's cock was already fully erect, pressing menacingly between Gu Mang's thighs but not yet forcing its way in. He held Gu Mang in his lap as he caressed his feverish and sensitive body from behind. Rough hands pulled Gu Mang's lapels aside and pinched at his hardened nipples.

"Ah..." Gu Mang panted, caged between Mo Xi's legs. He couldn't help the hoarse moan that spilled from him, but just as he gasped, Mo Xi's fingers pushed into his mouth.

They'd engaged in plenty of outlandish acts in the past. Back then, Gu Mang had coaxed Mo Xi along and taught him, step by step. So many years had passed, but Mo Xi hadn't forgotten these lessons. He was only abstaining from sex; he wasn't all that innocent. It was just that he'd long ago chosen a certain person and had no desire to sleep with anyone else.

Those fingers curled into Gu Mang's mouth and pressed down on his tongue, sliding rhythmically in and out in an unmistakable cadence. That stiffened cock beneath him was also thrusting again and again against his underclothes. At each motion Gu Mang let out a muted groan. The demon blood in his body made him more sensitive; his pants were already growing damp.

He hazily tried to turn, to glimpse the man he loved so deeply. But Mo Xi removed his own pitch-black hair ribbon and bound it over Gu Mang's eyes.

"You..."

"I'm sure you'll feel better if you don't have to see my face."

Long lashes trembled beneath the ribbon. Gu Mang didn't know what kind of expression Mo Xi wore when he said these words; he hadn't time to consider it before he was pushed into the soft straw. He felt coolness on his lower half; Mo Xi had torn away that final layer of clothing.

Gu Mang swallowed thickly. He couldn't think anymore, his mind was blank, but this wasn't a comfort to him—his need was about to be satisfied, but his sanity was on the verge of destruction.

Mo Xi didn't kiss him, nor did he lovingly caress him. In the past, Mo Xi had always approached Gu Mang with adoration; this was the first time he'd ever simply stripped Gu Mang's clothes and taken out his cock to press it between his legs. The wetness at its tip slicked over his entrance, rubbing back and forth...

"Why are you shaking so much?"

Gu Mang couldn't respond. Mo Xi was holding him from behind, but Gu Mang's legs felt completely boneless; he was pushing his body to its limit just to stay upright. He wasn't trembling from pleasure, or out of fear. He and Mo Xi had made love so many times; he could still feel the ghost of it, regardless of how many years had passed.

His mouth wobbled. "It's fine," Gu Mang forced himself to say.

But when Mo Xi touched the ribbon that covered his eyes, he found it soaked with tears. "...Does it bother you so much to be with me?"

Gu Mang's teeth sank into his wet lower lip. He couldn't see, but he could feel Mo Xi take hold of his jaw, forcing him to turn his head. His lips were so close Gu Mang could feel every breath. "Even though the aphrodisiac got you into this state, you still don't want to do this with me. Is that right?"

Only silence answered him.

"Gu Mang," Mo Xi continued. "How you must loathe me."

He picked up Gu Mang and laid him face up, back in the hay. Gu Mang didn't know what was happening; he reached up to pull the ribbon off and felt his wrist yanked back down.

Mo Xi had been driven crazy. He was such an upright person, but his suppressed emotions twisted his voice almost past recognition. He didn't let Gu Mang touch the ribbon. Instead, he lifted Gu Mang's legs and bent to pin him beneath his body.

Gu Mang had nearly bitten through his lip to silence himself, yet the press of that firm and hot chest still wrung a tiny, broken whimper from him. Mo Xi brought the wet tip of his cock to Gu Mang's soft, quivering entrance, nudging against it but not pushing in. Very quickly, Gu Mang could bear no more. "M-Mo Xi..." he gasped impatiently.

"Are you sure you want to call my name?"

Gu Mang swallowed hard. Even his toes were curled tight. "You... *ah*...!"

The tip of that burning shaft breached him, and Gu Mang arched his back and cried out. Demon beasts frequently coupled with no regard for sex, and Gu Mang's tempered body possessed certain of their traits—his hole could secrete the same thick fluid as the demon tribe.

Mo Xi clenched his jaw. "How are you...so wet..."

He *was* wet, he could feel it. Gu Mang panted for breath. His entrance was already ridiculously soft and slick. Mo Xi had only thrust the head halfway in, but his hole was already sucking thirstily at Mo Xi's cock. When Mo Xi moved, soft, wet sounds issued from where they were joined. Gu Mang shivered with the thrill of it.

"I-inside... H-hurry up..." Gu Mang was almost sobbing.

"Who are you thinking of?"

Gu Mang whimpered. "I can't take anymore..."

Even a gentleman could be driven insane. Mo Xi had never considered himself a gentleman, and Gu Mang...well, he had really pushed him too far. After barely entering, Mo Xi pulled out again. Gu Mang's legs wrapped limply around Mo Xi's trim waist, shaking and helpless.

"Is it Lu Zhanxing, or someone you met in the Liao Kingdom, or..." Mo Xi gritted his teeth. "That black-clad man who convinced you to defect inside the Time Mirror?"

"No..." Gu Mang's chest heaved. "No...no..."

"Or is it the man who gave you that brocade pouch—the one I've never even heard of?"

Dazed and near tears, Gu Mang mumbled, "I don't know..." as if he hadn't heard a single word Mo Xi said. "I don't know..."

He'd been pushed to the edge of his endurance, his cock painfully hard. Any more and he wouldn't know if Mo Xi was helping him with the poison or aggravating his torture. "Stop asking me..." Gu Mang hoarsely cried, his hands scrabbling for purchase. Finding Mo Xi's wrist, his fingers closed around it in an iron grip. "Come in... Fuck me... It...it hurts..."

Neither of them made a sound.

Just as Gu Mang became convinced that Mo Xi would abandon him, his legs were viciously yanked upward.

Mo Xi didn't know if he was doing this for his own pride, for Gu Mang's feelings, or so that two people with inseparable hearts whom fate had sundered could finally find a hard-won excuse to lose themselves in each other. The truth was, in the depths of their hearts, they had yearned for such an excuse for a very long time.

"Tonight is only to help you with the poison. Don't..." Mo Xi paused. "Don't think of it as anything more."

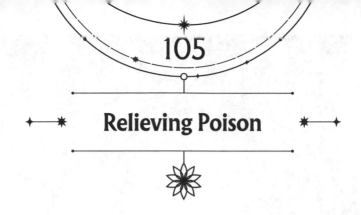
Relieving Poison

GU MANG'S ENTRANCE was so hot and wet, Mo Xi didn't need to open him like in the past. He only pushed two fingers inside, bending and working them, and that slick warmth sucked them in.

Mo Xi inhaled sharply. So the Liao Kingdom's tempering had extended even to this. As he thought of that brocade pouch with its unknown giver, and the black-clad man in the Mirror who'd pushed Gu Mang to defect, he suddenly felt unsure. Was Gu Mang's current state merely a side effect of the demon blood in him, or had someone molded him to this purpose? He'd thought the Liao Kingdom only needed a commander and not a plaything, but Gu Mang's newfound sensitivity set his imagination running wild.

He stared down at the face obscured by his black ribbon and withdrew his sticky fingers. Gu Mang had been panting through parted lips all along, but when Mo Xi's fingers slipped out, his brow furrowed deeply, and he began to shake. Mo Xi knew the poison had nearly broken him; he would collapse if he didn't find release soon. He smeared that wetness over his own straining erection and lined himself up, ghosting against Gu Mang's slick and eager hole.

Gu Mang's fingers were clutching at the straw, his bestial instinct growing stronger and stronger as his human rationality dwindled to nothing. His scalp prickled at the sensation of a blazing-hot cock

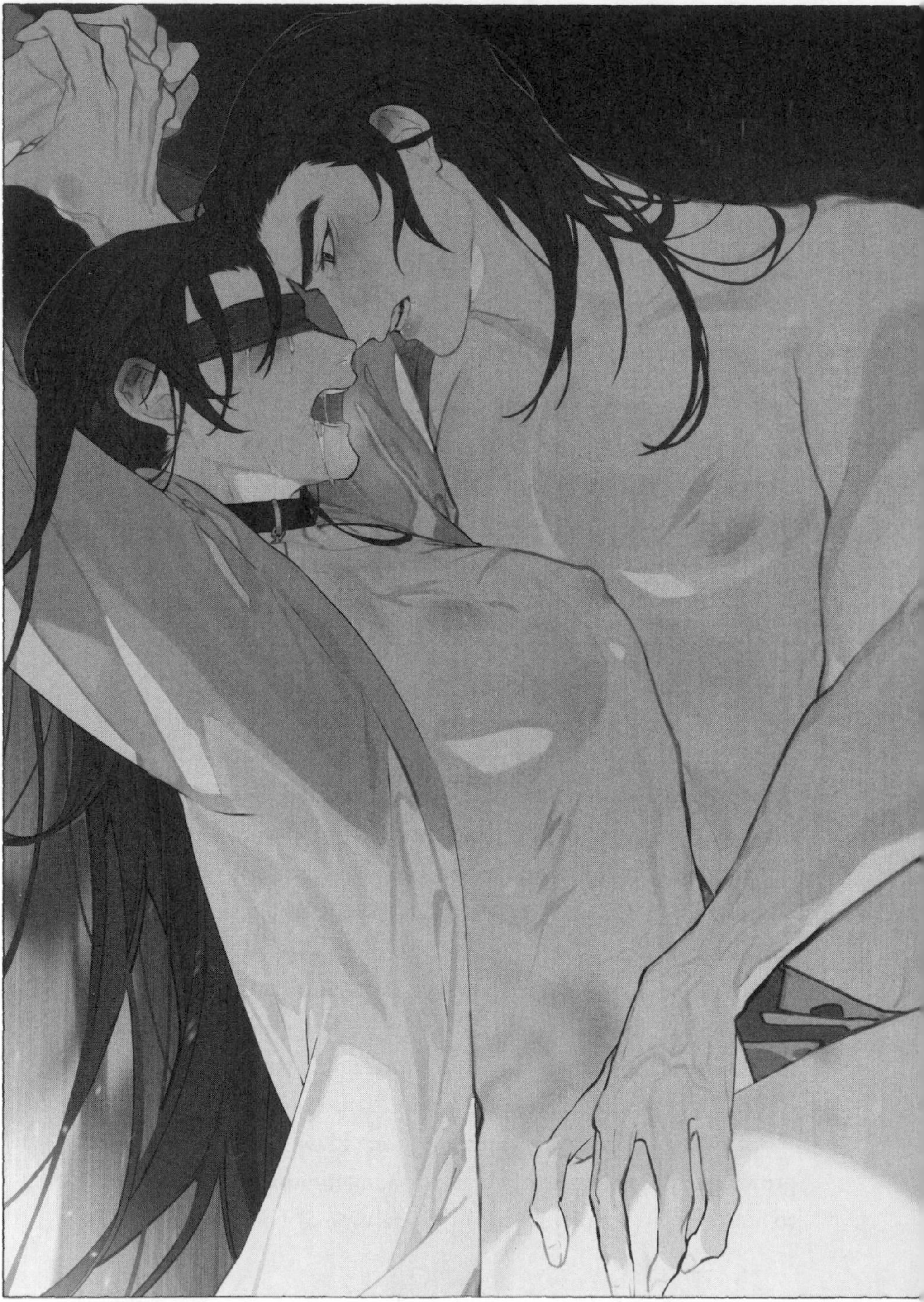

pressed to his rim. His legs unwittingly spread wider, welcoming and begging that man to thrust in.

"Come in... Fuck me... M-Mo Xi..."

The syllables of his name broke like a sob as they escaped Gu Mang's lips, finally setting Mo Xi's desire ablaze. His eyes darkened as he took hold of Gu Mang's hips and slowly pressed his thick shaft inside. Gu Mang's tempered body clenched, tightening thirstily around his length, the warm slickness responding audibly to the intrusion.

"Ah..." Gu Mang knitted his brows, arching his neck as he gasped. "Come in, all the way..."

Gu Mang's body now could be fucked as easily as any demon beast. Mo Xi was terrifyingly large; in the past, Gu Mang would be shaking from pain by the time he was halfway inside. Yet tonight, Gu Mang had taken it so quickly that he still craved the feeling of being stretched.

Mo Xi couldn't say what he felt: impatience, worry, heartbreak... Regardless of all else, the physical pleasure was undeniable. Gu Mang had been gone for eight years, and he had been abstinent for eight years until today, when pretense allowed them to entwine once more.

"Faster... F-fuck me harder... *Ah!*"

As Mo Xi viciously thrust in, Gu Mang's moans rose in pitch. The hut filled with the sound of their rough panting. Gu Mang's legs, already shaking and weak, were locked around Mo Xi's slender waist. Unable to see, he only felt that something impossibly hot, thick, and hard had buried itself to the hilt inside him, as if it wanted to pierce his belly through.

"Ah...*ah*..."

To be taken so forcefully and invaded so thoroughly by pleasure was like drowning. Gu Mang, irreparably broken, mumbled dazedly, "Come in... All the way in... *Ah!*"

Mo Xi leaned forward to grab Gu Mang's hand and forced him to press down on his own abdomen. "Can you feel it? In all these years, who else has fucked you this full? If anyone has...could he satisfy you? Could he fuck you this deep?"

His voice had always been low and sensual; now it was even more alluringly husky. His head was lowered, his lips almost brushing Gu Mang's ear. When the fevered heat of Mo Xi's breath fanned his face, Gu Mang's eyes went glassy and unfocused beneath the blindfold.

Before Gu Mang could return to his senses, Mo Xi began to move, driving hard and fast into his soaked and clenching body.

"Ah...*ngh ahh*..." Scalding heat surged into Gu Mang, each stroke threatening to run his soul through. The love he was denied and the lust he was lost within became a roaring spring that engulfed him totally. There were no sounds in the hut except the clap of flesh against flesh, the soft, slick noises that accompanied each thrust, Gu Mang's half-lucid moans and Mo Xi's ragged breathing.

"*Ah*... Deeper...Mo Xi... Mo Xi...go deeper... *Aaaah*..."

Scorching hardness and clenching walls melted together, loath to part, love and desire becoming water that flowed between them. Gu Mang's every moan earned him a vicious thrust, filling him to the brim each time. Caught in the pleasure of being fucked so hard, past the point of endurance, Gu Mang desperately clung to the man atop him. Their skin beaded with sweat that mingled, seeming to draw them ever closer.

In the throes of this fervid entanglement, Gu Mang all too quickly came apart. He was so close; he lifted his hips to welcome Mo Xi's thrusts. Mo Xi knew precisely where he was most sensitive and made sure to hit it with every stroke, making Gu Mang's skin tingle with pleasure. But his bestial instinct and the aphrodisiac demanded more. He wanted Mo Xi to fuck him deeper, to hammer that spot harder, so he canted his hips to meet Mo Xi's again and again. "R-right there...fuck me...ah," he gasped. "Mo Xi...*ah*..."

Just as Gu Mang was on the cusp of release, Mo Xi suddenly pulled out. A shudder racked Gu Mang, as if his soul would leave his body along with that heavy shaft. Slick dripped out after it, the sensation so unpleasant Gu Mang's toes twitched.

"M-Mo Xi?" Gu Mang said in confusion and torment.

Gu Mang heard a soft sigh right by his ear. "Didn't you say you don't want it to be me?" He found himself hauled upright and flipped over. "On your hands and knees."

Mo Xi's grip tightened on Gu Mang's hips as he lined himself up, took a breath, and thrust all the way in.

"*Aaahhhh*...!" The sensation of being fucked from behind was much more intense. Mo Xi grabbed at the hair ribbon, forcing Gu Mang to arch his back. Gu Mang panted, whimpering brokenly as Mo Xi drove against his prostate at a punishing pace. The two of them were in the most primal position, rutting like beasts, Gu Mang subjugated beneath Mo Xi. He was being fucked to the point of tears, until he was so hard it hurt; he felt as if his stomach would split. "Ah...Mo Xi..."

"Good?" Mo Xi rasped.

"Yes...please, please, faster... I'm going to..." Face down in the straw, Gu Mang started to cry. Mo Xi was fucking him with such force that his voice broke with each thrust. He was being driven insane by the pleasure and pain of a human body enduring the enormity of bestial lust. "I'm going to come...ah..."

Mo Xi reached over and took hold of Gu Mang's weeping cock. Gu Mang's eyes immediately widened as he cried out in shock. The blindfold, loosened in the onslaught, slipped down, exposing teary blue eyes. They were utterly blank, twin pools of desire.

It didn't take long for him to come in Mo Xi's hand, shudder-ing as thick liquid spilled into the straw. Mo Xi didn't let up for a moment, fucking him through his climax with short, sharp thrusts. Gu Mang came so hard he nearly lost his wits, his harsh breaths turning into sobs that transformed into shouts. "I...I can't anymore...You're going to fuck me to death... Mo Xi...Mo Xi... *Ah*... Stop... Stop... *Ahhh*..." His cries subsided into disjointed mumbling. "Please, please... Please... *Ah! Ah!*"

With one last spurt, Gu Mang went slack in Mo Xi's arms. But Mo Xi wasn't done with him, and the aphrodisiac wasn't either. Beneath the flood of pleasure that came with his release, a frisson of desire surged through him anew—this body would drive him insane. He realized that the bat demons hadn't exaggerated their urgency. Demonic instinct was much stronger than any human lust. He lay boneless beneath Mo Xi, dripping with sweat, come, and slick as he let himself be fucked. The man who was once called the Beast of the Altar was mating exactly like a beast, begging to be filled, owned, and viciously stuffed full. He was flushed and feverish, unable to catch his breath. He jolted with every thrust, helpless tears filling his eyes and slipping down his cheeks.

He couldn't beg Mo Xi to love him anymore. But at least in this moment, under pretense of submitting to carnal desire, he could earnestly beg Mo Xi to take him, to fuck him. "Mo Xi..."

The man behind him was just as unflagging as he was eight years ago. Only after Gu Mang came a second and then a third time did Mo Xi's breathing finally begin to hitch. By the time Mo Xi was ready to come, Gu Mang was on the brink of madness. After a few more wild thrusts, Mo Xi slowed his pace. Some rational piece of his mind yet survived; he gasped for breath and said hoarsely, "I'll pull out..."

But Gu Mang was delirious. He clutched Mo Xi's hand and turned his head to look back at him. Beneath sweat-soaked locks, blue eyes gazed tearfully, helplessly, at Mo Xi as his glossy lips parted. "C-come inside... Don't pull out."

Mo Xi's eyes darkened.

"I can't take it anymore..." Gu Mang whimpered, "My body...isn't the same as before..." He lay in the straw, his voice soft with tears. "Mo Xi, come inside... I want you..."

What he wished to say was, *I want to love you, I want to take everything you have to give, I want to return to the past with you*—but these were the only words that escaped his mouth. He bit down on his lip, burying his face in the crook of his arm. Only his soft, inky hair and a sliver of reddened ear remained visible.

Their final entanglement was no less frenzied than that of wild beasts. Gu Mang couldn't even stay up on his knees, while Mo Xi's thrusts were quick and feverish, the smack of skin against skin filling their ears as their breathing turned to harsh gasps.

"Ah...ah..."

"Did you mean it?"

"Come for me..." Gu Mang sobbed, lifting his hips in invitation. "Come inside, come for me..."

Mo Xi wrapped an arm around his waist and pressed them flush together, sinking deep into the straw. This angle pushed Mo Xi farther inside him, driving Gu Mang to cry out, but Mo Xi covered his mouth and snapped his hips a dozen more times before burying himself as deep as he could go.

Gu Mang sobbed into Mo Xi's palm, once again brought to orgasm, his spend nearly clear after so many climaxes. His body clenched rhythmically around Mo Xi's cock; he could vividly feel each and every spurt of liquid heat as Mo Xi released everything, hitting him where he was most sensitive. Gu Mang's toes curled; he shivered. Mo Xi had come inside him...

Even after, Mo Xi remained sheathed inside his sloppy hole, slowly moving inside him, plugging him so none of that fluid dripped out.

Gu Mang was barely conscious. The two collapsed panting into the straw. Only then did the realization steal over them: they'd gone to bed together again. Despite everything, they had really done it. Neither spoke, but Mo Xi slowly and hesitantly took hold of Gu Mang's limp hand, claiming the afterglow as excuse to interlace their shaking fingers.

His mouth was so close to Gu Mang's temple. He could kiss his cheek if he just dipped his head. Everything seemed so much like how it had been eight years ago, before this debt of hatred festered between them. The only thing missing was a kiss—but that kiss could never fall.

Gu Mang's breathing gradually slowed, and his lashes fluttered weakly. "Don't pull out..."

Mo Xi blinked and stilled.

"In a while, the demon blood will absorb it... Once it's absorbed... then..." He paused and hoarsely said, "Then I'll be fine."

But Gu Mang knew—this entanglement had merely satisfied his bodily desires. That hollow ache in his heart would forever eat at his bones, at his marrow...a lifetime without a cure.

At daybreak, they prepared to leave the hut.

Gu Mang didn't say a word after it was over. When he rose to get dressed, his hands were still shaking. Mo Xi glanced at him and saw, by the weak morning light, that a faint flush lingered on his earlobe beneath his loose black hair. Gu Mang kept his head down as he straightened his lapels, his inky lashes lowered but unable to hide the redness of his eyes.

The two of them took great care with their clothes, perhaps out of embarrassment, or perhaps because they worried the others would notice something amiss. Fortunately they had not kissed, so there were no love bites to hide.

Mo Xi paused. "Your body..."

"It's the faewolf." Gu Mang spoke without inflection, unwilling to elaborate. "The bat demon incense was just as effective on me." He paused for a moment, then stood up.

In the past, Gu Mang was always a bit feeble after they slept together, sometimes even stumbling. Mo Xi instinctively reached to help him up, but Gu Mang flung his hand off. He sniffed, his nose still red. "There's no need. I'm fine," he said hoarsely.

His body had truly changed; these days, he could recover quickly. Holding the ribbon in his mouth, he gathered and tied up his long hair. His lips parted as he sighed. "I hope you'll excuse my behavior, Xihe-jun."

Mo Xi's chest felt tight, but he closed his eyes and replied, "I said it was only for the poison." His voice was low. "Don't think any more on it."

"Mn." Gu Mang smiled. "It's just that, considering our current relationship, it must have been a sacrifice to help me; I can't help but apologize. Also, I behaved...rather embarrassingly." Eyes the blue of deep lakes were cast down as Gu Mang fastened the hidden weapon compartment in his sleeve. "If it's at all possible, Xihe-jun should try to forget about it."

As he spoke, he pulled aside the bamboo curtain. Seeing that the bat demons were all still in their huts, he strode off toward the cave where Murong Chuyi and the others waited.

Pale sunlight filtered through the black smoke over Bat Island, filling the woods with a clear coldness. Mo Xi turned to glance back at the thatched hut they had spent the night in. What had passed here mere hours ago was like a mirage; the excuse that allowed them to entwine so desperately was gone. In the daylight, he was Chonghua's Xihe-jun, and Gu Mang was a prisoner and slave of Xihe Manor, the great traitor to the nation. Neither of them would speak again of what happened last night, and neither would assign it any more meaning than an ephemeral dream.

In the end, Mo Xi swept a final look around the room. He let the bamboo curtain fall and caught up to Gu Mang. The two of them still smelled like each other yet acted like strangers as they trekked back in perfect silence.

The life crystal in Mo Xi's possession had shown Yue Chenqing's condition to be much improved. Just as it predicted, when they returned to the cave, they found Yue Chenqing sitting against the wall, awake.

But they were surprised to find Yue Chenqing's head lowered, tears rolling down his cheeks. His usually bright and shining eyes were swollen from crying, and he wiped his tears away over and over with the back of his hand. "Fourth Uncle... I... I really wasn't messing around..." Still sobbing, he pathetically tried to explain himself to Murong Chuyi, who was standing beside him with an icy mien. "I just wanted to find a cure for you. Every year, before my birthday, you say you don't feel well, that you don't want to come... I...I..."

"You what? I think you've lost your wits!" Murong Chuyi swept his sleeves back and berated him through clenched teeth. "Do you not know your own worth?! You're so unbelievably foolish as to come alone to these damned Dream Butterfly Islands?!"

Jiang Yexue was sitting off to the side. He was weak from giving blood to Yue Chenqing, but he still coughed and said, "Now now; Chenqing meant well. Xiaojiu, he's barely woken up. You don't have to scold him so..."

Murong Chuyi shook off the hand Jiang Yexue had laid on his sleeve. "I'll scold my own nephew if I please," he snapped. "Is it your place to act like a saint?!" He turned back to rail at Yue Chenqing. "Forget about bringing me medicine before your birthday! If you were a bit less lucky, this time next year I'd be bringing flowers to your grave! What will it be—peonies or roses?! Yue Chenqing, are you trying to kill me from stress?! Don't you know this life of yours came at the price of your mother's? Yet you hold it so cheaply!"

Yue Chenqing looked up, his piteous sobs dying in his throat. He stared at Murong Chuyi, eyes wide with a smarting pain. No one present—neither Mo Xi, Gu Mang, nor even Yue Chenqing himself—had ever seen Murong Chuyi so furious that the rims of his eyes were scarlet.

So Murong Chuyi had been holding back all this time, maintaining his outward impassivity out of concern for Yue Chenqing's health. If he was turning such rage on Yue Chenqing now, the gu worms must be entirely dealt with. But Murong Chuyi was already sick, and he had used forbidden techniques to keep Yue Chenqing alive, injuring his heart vein in the process. As fury filled him, he began to cough.

At the sight of Yue Chenqing's expression, Jiang Yexue knew Murong Chuyi had said too much. He reached out to pull on Murong Chuyi's sleeve again. Murong Chuyi's face drew taut with anger as he shoved Jiang Yexue away. "I've told you not to touch me!"

He hadn't held back at all, and Jiang Yexue had lost too much blood. He'd just been helping Yue Chenqing and wasn't sitting in his wheelchair; this shove sent him crumpling to the ground.

Everyone around the cave was stunned into silence.

Yue Chenqing stared blankly at Jiang Yexue, who'd collapsed with his wrists still bleeding. Yet Jiang Yexue seemed not to want to argue with Murong Chuyi; he'd always been humble and courteous, considerate and accepting of others' feelings. He tried to push himself up, lowering his lashes as he murmured, "If you're angry, don't take it out on Chenqing. If you're unhappy, vent it on me instead. You're the senior and we are your juniors, so it's fine if you push me or scold me..."

For some reason, Murong Chuyi grew only more incensed at this; his hands were shaking. He pointed at Jiang Yexue, his face alarmingly pale. "You—!"

Jiang Yexue dropped his gaze to the ground. "Whatever Xiaojiu likes."

Murong Chuyi was incandescent with rage. "H-how dare you..." He'd just raised his hand when a trembling voice cried out.

"Why are you always so *mean*!"

A deathly silence followed.

No one expected this shout to be targeted at Murong Chuyi. Even the man himself was momentarily stunned, his sharp phoenix eyes flitting about before it dawned on him. He slowly turned around.

Tears streamed down Yue Chenqing's face as he stared at his uncle with eyes full of heartbreak and grief. He lowered his voice, but it was saturated with disappointment and despair. "Do you only care for my mother? No matter how devoted we are to you—whether me, or...or him—you still only rage at us and blame us."

All color had drained from Murong Chuyi's face; it was white as paper.

Yue Chenqing's features crumpled in his sad little face. Speaking to his uncle like this hurt him more surely than a knife to the gut, but his uncle's harsh words had wounded him deeply too. Even his sobs had changed in tone. For the first time, he stood in front of Jiang Yexue. "If anyone's at fault here...it's me, isn't it? He got hurt so badly and lost so much blood, a-all to save me... How could you still strike him and yell at him..."

Jiang Yexue shook his head. "Chenqing..."

Murong Chuyi's lips were bloodless. His gaze flashed, his mouth moving as if he was struggling immensely with some unspoken grievance. In the end, his fingers curled into fists, and only a few bitten-off syllables passed his lips: "Yue Chenqing. What do you know?!" His piercing gaze fixed upon Jiang Yexue's face. Murong Chuyi's resentment was so deep the rims of his eyes were red, and he spoke through gritted teeth. "He's no more than a...*bastard*!"

Now it was not only Yue Chenqing's expression that changed, but Mo Xi and Gu Mang's as well. They'd known Murong Chuyi for some time, and though it was true that he was aloof, they hadn't found him a monster who didn't know right from wrong. Neither had understood why he would be named one of Chonghua's three poisons. But when this blade of a word fell from his mouth and sank to the hilt in Jiang Yexue's heart, they suddenly realized that Murong Chuyi's resentment was far too harsh and cutting.

Jiang Yexue's lashes trembled. He closed his eyes, then lowered his head and fell silent.

Yue Chenqing turned tearful eyes upon Murong Chuyi. "Fourth Uncle..." His voice shook, the syllables strained like a bowstring drawn until the arrow flew. He dissolved into sobs. "Is your heart made of stone?"

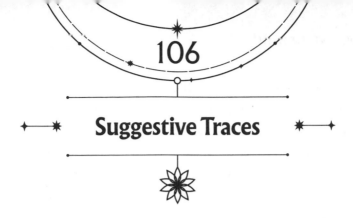
Suggestive Traces

N O ONE ON EARTH was less likely to criticize Murong Chuyi than Yue Chenqing. Since he was little, he had worshipped and loved Murong Chuyi, this uncle with whom he shared not a drop of blood. This was the reason a pampered young master like him would follow Xihe-jun to the northern frontier; this was the reason he would pore over all manner of books and records for any hint of a magical panacea.

He knew coming to Bat Island alone was a mistake. He'd started regretting it almost as soon as he set out, and had long since realized he was a failure who'd troubled his fourth uncle and the others to come to his rescue.

But no matter how he apologized, Murong Chuyi didn't soften in the slightest. He lashed out at Yue Chenqing, scolding him for not valuing the life his mother died to give him. He said such heartrending words to Jiang Yexue, who had opened his own veins to save his nephew. Yue Chenqing was devastated.

"Fourth Uncle...I know I'm no good, I'm too stupid and impulsive... I just wanted you to get better, but you won't tell me anything. What could I do but try to help you on my own... I'm sorry, I couldn't find a cure and caused you so much trouble...but...but..." He closed his eyes, tears flowing down his face. "Won't you even listen to my explanations...?"

He continued, "You say my life came at the price of my mother's, and Jiang... You say he's a bastard... But he didn't ask to be born to a concubine...and I didn't ask to kill my mother by being born! Why do you blame us? Fourth Uncle, I revere you and love you. For so many years, I've agreed with all you say and adored all you do. But have you ever turned to look at me?" Yue Chenqing sobbed. "Have you... Have you ever seen me as your nephew, even once?"

"Chenqing, forget it, Chuyi's—" Jiang Yexue murmured.

Murong Chuyi's face was ashen. He cut Jiang Yexue off, his bright brown eyes fixed on Yue Chenqing's face as he spat each word: "Let him speak!"

Jiang Yexue fell silent.

Yue Chenqing wiped at his tears, hanging his head and sniffing. "I don't know... I won't say anymore... I-I shouldn't be rude to Fourth Uncle... I shouldn't talk back to Fourth Uncle..." He muttered again and again, "I shouldn't disagree with Fourth Uncle" as though to calm himself. But as he mumbled on and on, he buried his face in his hands and sobbed like a whimpering cub. "Is it because you wish I was never born...?"

Murong Chuyi froze.

"But my mother is dead. I'm not Murong Huang, I'm Yue Chenqing!"

The atmosphere in the cave turned glacial. Everyone could see Murong Chuyi trembling with the clashing emotions in his heart; his jade-like face flushed faintly as his bone-pale fingers curled into fists. He looked at Yue Chenqing, then at Jiang Yexue, and closed his eyes. "Very well... Very well," he gritted out. He took a step back, and his sharp brows drew together as he coughed up bloody spittle. He covered his mouth with a sleeve, hiding it from sight.

Murong Chuyi opened his phoenix eyes, red-rimmed and glimmering. His gaze raked over his two nephews, its freezing glint hiding heartbreak. "I've heard your explanation. I won't reprimand you anymore, Yue Chenqing." His nails were digging into his palms so hard they nearly drew blood, but still he lifted his chin and assumed a cold calm. "Fend for yourself."

With a sweep of his sleeves, he turned to leave.

"Xiaojiu!" Jiang Yexue cried after him.

The sight of Murong Chuyi's expression seemed to wake Yue Chenqing from a nightmare. He stared at his uncle's retreating silhouette in blank confusion, tear tracks shining on his face. "Fourth Uncle..."

But Murong Chuyi was gone. He pretended not to see Gu Mang and Mo Xi as he swept from the cave mouth, his face as pale as the first snow of winter. He took not a single look back.

After more than a moment, Mo Xi broke the silence. "H-how did it end up like this?"

Jiang Yexue sighed. "As soon as Chenqing woke up, Xiaojiu started in on him. He asked why he would come to Bat Island alone, so Chenqing explained he wanted to find medicine for him. Xiaojiu...he felt it wasn't worth Chenqing risking his life, so he grew even angrier and berated Chenqing for being without sense... Xiaojiu's always had a temper, he doesn't mean it that way. I'm sorry, these Yue Clan matters...are rather embarrassing."

Finding himself in the middle of this mess, Mo Xi wasn't sure what to say either. It wasn't his nature to meddle in the business of others, so he paused and said only, "It's too dangerous out there. I'll go after Murong."

"Hey," Gu Mang grabbed his arm.

"What is it?"

"That hissy beauty is too smart to go far. He just wants to calm down—didn't you see his face when he left?" Gu Mang glanced at Yue Chenqing and Jiang Yexue, then lowered his voice so only Mo Xi could hear. "He was so angry he was on the verge of tears."

Mo Xi was stunned for a moment. Whose tears? Murong Chuyi's? Didn't he leave in a furious huff?

"Wouldn't it humiliate him if you went to look for him now? Give him some space," Gu Mang advised.

Mo Xi hadn't noticed any such vulnerability in Murong Chuyi's expression, but Gu Mang had always been the more observant one. Since Gu Mang had spoken, he wouldn't insist even if he did disagree.

Jiang Yexue was worried. "I'm afraid my xiaojiu..."

"Don't worry." Gu Mang stepped deeper into the cave, waving a hand. "You guys rest up a bit. I'll go find him in a little while, then we can set out for Chonghua."

"You figured out where to break through the barrier?"

"Duh. Did you forget who I am? I was already this great back when we hung around together."

They tidied the inside of the cave. Gu Mang was the most idle among them, leaning against the cave wall to rest. He summoned his demonic dagger, spinning it in slender fingers. After playing with it for a time, he felt a pair of hesitant eyes quietly watching him. Gu Mang looked down and met the feathered girl Rongrong's wide eyes.

Rongrong didn't expect Gu Mang to suddenly notice her. She averted her gaze, but it was too late.

Gu Mang smiled. "Hi, gorgeous. Why are you looking at me like that?"

"You, you..." Rongrong's pretty face was red. Stumbling and hesitant, she murmured, "You...you smell so strongly...of him."

His fingers spinning the dagger froze. "Who?" he asked in surprise.

Rongrong didn't make a sound, but her eyes flicked toward Mo Xi, who was standing next to Yue Chenqing, examining his wounds.

Gu Mang's lips quirked up into a smile. "Oh, him. It's normal; we were sitting close to each other."

"No, not that, you two seem like—"

With a smile, Gu Mang laid a finger on her lips, then patted her head and leaned over to whisper in her ear. "Don't worry, I know how astute you feathered people are. Demon blood runs in my body, and you're sensitive to demon scents, right? But, little beauty, demons and humans are not the same. While you're with us, you need to learn human rules—with some things, it's best to pretend you don't know. Behave, sweetheart."

Hearing the soft rustle of their movements, Mo Xi turned. "What are you two doing?"

Gu Mang drew back from Rongrong and grinned. "Nothing. I'm just teasing her." He reached out and flicked the flame marking on Rongrong's forehead. "Remember what I said. Why don't you get ready to leave the island with us?"

Thanks to the vulnerability Gu Mang found in the barrier, evading Bat Island's defenses was the work of moments. The two nut boats broke past the clouds, and by the time the patrolling bat demons spied them, they were much too far away to pursue.

Gu Mang had invited the feathered girl Rongrong onto the ship as well. Once they were deep in the sea of clouds, he brought her out from the cabin. "Mount Jiuhua is right below us here. Miss Rong, you can go home."

Rongrong leaned over the ship's rail and looked down. Beneath the vast layer of clouds, a greenish-blue mountain was visible, faintly glowing with the light of the feathered tribe's barrier. She couldn't help the pink flush that spread over her cheeks as she stared for a long while, lost for words, before turning to speak. "Thank you, thank you, Da-gege..."

"Da-gege?" Gu Mang smiled. "It's fine if you call us da-gege. Even if you're older than all of us, you look younger. You can call us whatever you'd like."

"You cured Chenqing of the gu," said Jiang Yexue. "It is us who owe you a debt of gratitude, so it would be too bold of me to accept your thanks." Jiang Yexue performed an obeisance. "Miss, take care."

Rongrong was eager to go home. After bidding farewell to all of them one last time, dazzling gold-red wings sprouted from her back, and she gracefully leapt into the sea of clouds and disappeared into that golden light far below.

Gu Mang sighed. "All right, we've performed the rescue and cured the poison. Time to go home and rest. But you guys can't sell me out," he warned. "I plan to keep pretending to be stupid when I return to Chonghua, just as we agreed."

Yue Chenqing was standing beside the mast with a thick coat draped over his shoulders, staring blankly at Murong Chuyi's pleasure boat in the distance. He'd not yet been apprised of Gu Mang's situation, and at these words, turned to Gu Mang in shocked silence. "What did we agree?"

Before Gu Mang could answer, Jiang Yexue cut in. "Don't worry, I'll explain it to him later. You two must've had a long night. Go back to the cabin and rest. Once we reach the capital, you'll need to report to His Imperial Majesty."

"Sure, I'll rest, but can you change rooms with Xihe-jun?" Gu Mang asked. "You can sleep with me, and Xihe-jun can sleep in a different cabin."

Jiang Yexue hesitated. "Did you two...fight again?"

"Haven't we been fighting the whole time? More like we never stopped." Gu Mang smiled. "Look, he hates me so much he's gnashing his teeth. Plus, he looks so deliciously pretty—don't forget I'm an insane Liao Kingdom demon. If I get too excited I might end up defiling and killing him. What would we do then?"

Mo Xi and Jiang Yexue stared.

"I'd really appreciate it. If it's too much of a bother, I'll go over to Murong-xiansheng's boat and make do for a night."

"It's no bother at all," Jiang Yexue replied. "And Xiaojiu is in a temper right now; we shouldn't disturb him." He gave Gu Mang a small smile. "If it makes Gu-xiong more comfortable."

"Jiang-xiong is as accommodating as ever; how nice." Gu Mang batted his eyelashes at him, lips curving into a smile. Then he lifted the bamboo curtain and ducked into the cabin.

Mo Xi stood silent for a moment, then announced, "I'll go rest too." He disappeared into the other cabin.

Yue Chenqing was stupefied. "Wh-what happened between those two?" he stammered.

"It's a long story. If you don't mind hearing it from me, I'll tell it to you from the beginning." With a twitch of his fingertips, Jiang Yexue wheeled his chair over to Yue Chenqing. "Chenqing, are you willing to hear me out?"

"I..." Yue Chenqing looked at Murong Chuyi's ship in the sea of clouds, then glanced down at Jiang Yexue's wounded wrist. He hung his head. "I'm sorry. I made things difficult for you all."

"You've said sorry many times. It's water under the bridge," replied Jiang Yexue. "Just don't be so reckless next time. You see how we all worry about you, whether it's your father, your bofu, your uncle... or me. You meant well; you didn't act out of mischief. I know this, and I'm sure Xiaojiu knows as well. His temper's always been like this when he's anxious. Don't think he doesn't care for you."

Yue Chenqing stood in dejected silence and didn't raise his head.

Jiang Yexue instructed two little clay people to bring cushions and desserts. "Sit down," he said to Yue Chenqing. "You've just recovered, so have a snack. You'll feel better if you eat something sweet like a flower cake. Give it a try."

The dawn breeze ruffled Yue Chenqing's hair. He sat down as told, watching the crooked little clay person that came to deliver snacks, then voiced his thanks and started nibbling on the cake. When half of it had disappeared, he reluctantly lifted his head. "Um..."

"Hm?"

"Did giving blood...hurt? The wound on your wrist looks really deep, I-I have medicine..."

"I have medicine too." Jiang Yexue smiled, his eyes like two clear pools scattered with jasmine blossoms, their subtle fragrance rippling outward. "Don't worry. It doesn't hurt, and I don't blame you. You don't need to be so nervous with me."

Yue Chenqing's eyes were a little red. His head hung so low his chin nearly touched his chest. "I-I'm sorry..."

Jiang Yexue sighed deeply. "Silly child, why are you apologizing again?"

"I-I treated you so badly before, but—but you still helped me like this. I... I feel very sorry." The light flush reddening his ears spread to his cheeks as his voice grew thick with shame and embarrassment. "I'm apologizing on Fourth Uncle's behalf too. We...we shouldn't have said that about you." He set down the flower cake, hesitated for a moment, then raised bright, limpid eyes. "Jiang...er, Qingxu Elder, thank you."

He still wouldn't call Jiang Yexue *dage*, but at least he didn't just say "hey," or call him by his full name with no mark of respect. Jiang Yexue smiled, his cheerful expression like pearls beneath water, like flowers in the wind or feathery snow falling over a river in the dead of night.

"I don't blame you, and of course I won't blame him," Jiang Yexue said softly. "I've lost many people—my mother, my wife...my family. I understand some things a little better than you. Nothing is so important compared to life and death. And I won't bother quarreling over unimportant things. Also, he...he's a good person. Back when we were at Yue Manor, he never bullied me."

"Do you still want to come back to Yue Manor?" Yue Chenqing asked.

"I'm teaching at the academy now, and all the disciples are very cute." Jiang Yexue turned and smiled. "Whether I come back or not—this isn't important either."

Yue Chenqing sighed softly. "You're so even-tempered. If only Fourth Uncle could be the same—"

"Then he wouldn't be Murong Chuyi," chuckled Jiang Yexue. "All right, let's speak no more of these things. Once he's cooled down, I'll talk to him properly. Weren't you curious about Gu Mang a moment ago? I'll tell you what happened."

Yue Chenqing nodded, pulling over a cushion and sitting closer to Jiang Yexue. Jiang Yexue's voice was soft as flowing water. "Have you ever heard of the Time Mirror...?"

By the time he finished telling the whole story, the sun was high in the sky. He produced a well-crafted yet very old little clock from his robes. This clock was unique—it held neither water nor sand, but scarlet beads. After looking down at it, Jiang Yexue said, "It's getting late. Use this time to rest before we return to the capital. Remember to keep Gu-xiong's secret. We made him a promise."

Yue Chenqing went off to sleep, and Jiang Yexue directed the little clay people to put away his cushion and the leftover tea and snacks. The walnut ship's sails fluttered in the wind as it soared under the vault of the sky. Jiang Yexue sat beside the ship's railing, looking into the distance at Murong Chuyi's vessel.

As he watched, the bamboo curtain on Murong Chuyi's pleasure boat rolled up, revealing a man's sickly face. Murong Chuyi seemed to have many things weighing on his mind and had opened the curtain for some fresh air. But he took not a single breath before he noticed Jiang Yexue watching him through the banks of clouds.

Murong Chuyi stopped cold.

Jiang Yexue gave him a tiny smile, his gentle face bathed in dazzling golden sunshine. With a twirl of his fingers, he conjured a paper crane and sent it gliding toward Murong Chuyi's bamboo window.

Murong Chuyi slammed the curtain down with a discourteous *crash*. The paper crane stuttered in midair. It turned with a rustle and gazed clumsily at Jiang Yexue. "Honk?"

"No matter if he's angry—send the message," Jiang Yexue instructed.

"Honk!" Having received its orders, the paper crane flapped its wings and transformed into a beam of golden light that darted unheedingly behind Murong Chuyi's tightly closed window curtain.

Propping his elbows on the armrests of his wheelchair, Jiang Yexue put a hand to his chin. Moments later, he watched the paper crane he'd folded tossed furiously out the window, crumpled into a tight ball.

Jiang Yexue arched a brow, unbothered. Then he shook his head, chuckling softly, and stepped into the cabin he now shared with Gu Mang.

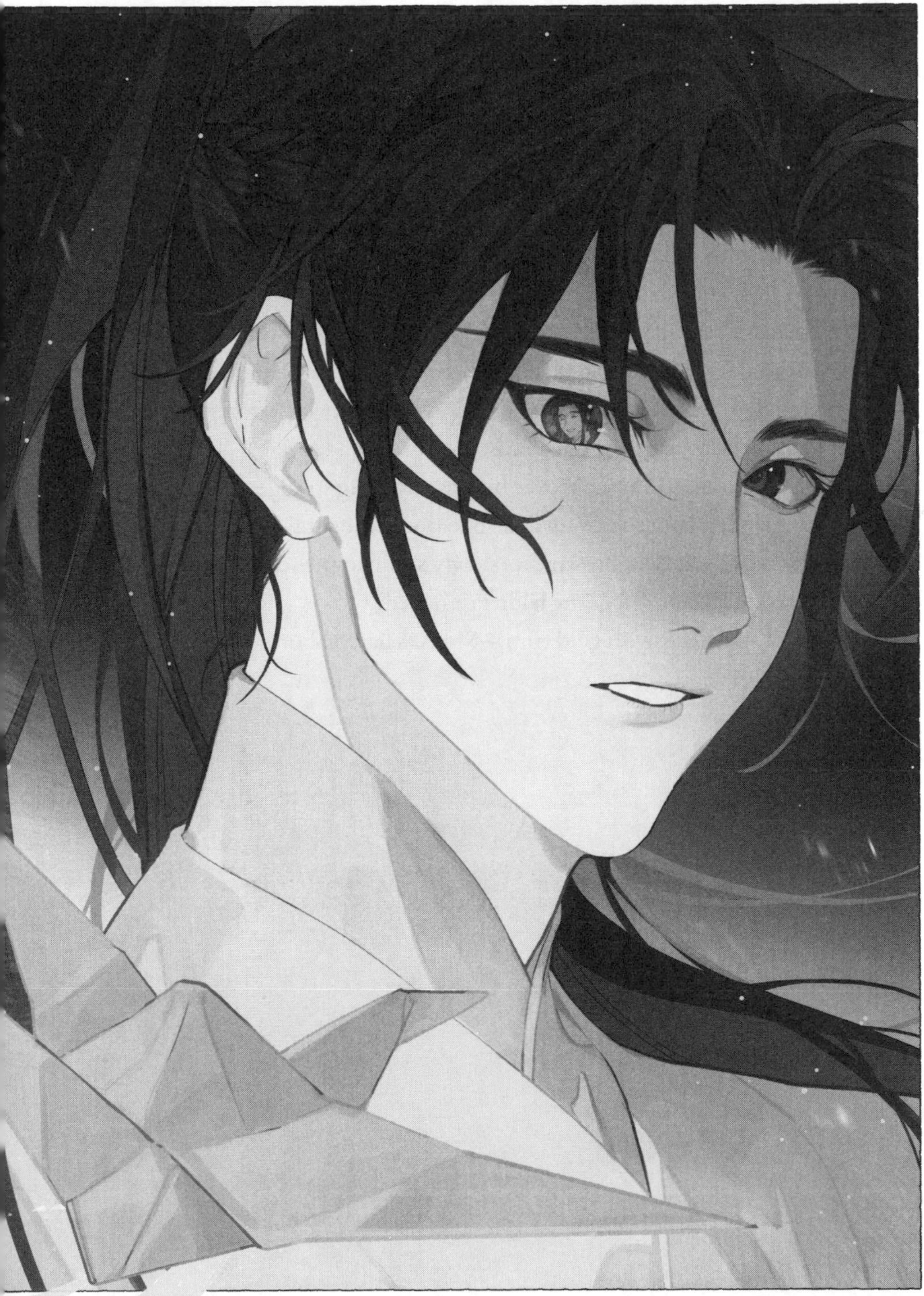

Gu Mang was exhausted; he'd already fallen asleep under the blankets. The faint scent of soap hung in the air; he must have just bathed. Yet this piqued Jiang Yexue's curiosity—Gu Mang was famously lazy and didn't like to bathe before sleeping. He'd always preferred to bathe in the morning.

Jiang Yexue had been his comrade for many years; he still remembered this quirk of Gu Mang's. Why would he suddenly change his habits? When Gu Mang had come in earlier, Jiang Yexue had noticed the heavy weariness in his eyes despite his efforts to feign alertness. What was going on...

He looked Gu Mang over but saw nothing strange. Just as Jiang Yexue was about to tidy up and go to bed, a thought occurred to him. He froze. His dark brown eyes slowly scanned the scene, landing on the hair ribbon Gu Mang hadn't removed.

It was black with gold trim—Mo Xi's hair ribbon.

His Only Stain

WHY WOULD GU MANG use Mo Xi's ribbon to tie up his hair?

Jiang Yexue's mind was spinning with thoughts. Mo Xi was a clean freak—he never used other people's things, and others had better not think of touching his. But even disregarding Mo Xi's peculiarities, this situation was bizarre. Under what circumstances would someone take another person's hair ribbon by accident? The two of them had to have undone their hair and then put it back up...

The more he thought about it, the graver his expression became. With a soft tap of Jiang Yexue's fingers, he sent the wheelchair gliding soundlessly over to Gu Mang and peered down. This hair ribbon trimmed in gold was embroidered with a soaring snake pattern. It definitely belonged to Mo Xi.

Could it be that...

Jiang Yexue's heartbeat sped up. With bated breath, his eyes traced down from the hair ribbon to Gu Mang's collar, where his lapels lay slightly open. But other than a mole on the side of his neck, there were no other marks.

And at this moment—perhaps because he'd stared too long—Gu Mang's senses prickled. His eyes flew open and he turned his head. As his gaze met Jiang Yexue's, all sleepiness vanished.

"Jiang-xiong." Gu Mang sat up, rubbing his hair. "Are we almost there? Is it time to get up?"

Jiang Yexue cleared his throat and tore his eyes away from Gu Mang's neck. "No, I just came inside to get ready to rest. I saw you were sleeping and didn't wish to wake you. I didn't think I'd disturb you." Although he spoke evenly, his face was a little red as he turned aside and ducked his head in embarrassment.

Gu Mang took note of Jiang Yexue's reaction. After a beat of silence, he summoned a lazy smile and said, "Don't worry, I wake easily. It's not your fault."

Jiang Yexue kept his eyes on the floor. "You should go back to sleep. I'll go wash up."

"All right."

The instant Jiang Yexue's figure disappeared behind the bamboo screen in the cabin, the smile on Gu Mang's face vanished. He quickly rose and stepped up to the copper mirror to scrutinize his face.

As far as he could remember, he and Mo Xi hadn't kissed—but his mind hadn't been clear, so he wasn't entirely confident of that. Jiang Yexue's reaction was strange enough that Gu Mang wanted to check himself over once more. After a long look, he found no marks whatsoever. Only then did he sigh in relief and lie back down in bed. He was probably overthinking...

When he and Mo Xi were together, he often worried that others would find out about their relationship. After each dalliance, he would pull Mo Xi over and check every inch of his exposed skin for kiss marks, then make Mo Xi do the same to him.

The intensity of their passion in those days had been too absurd. Gu Mang genuinely feared that others might discover them. Mo Xi was a noble of the highest, most unattainable class—he hailed from four generations of heroes, descended from a line of generals.

The daughters of the finest aristocratic families didn't dare dream of marrying him. If their secret were revealed—if it got out that the son of such heavenly lineage shared his bed with a filthy slave, what consequences would Mo Xi face? Gu Mang had nothing, so he didn't care if others criticized him. But Mo Xi was different. His status was high, his reputation clear, his nature kind and righteous. He was so young and so pure; his involvement with Gu Mang was the only stain on this noble youth.

Gu Mang feared such a stain would ruin Mo Xi's life. So he didn't see it as Mo Xi did. Mo Xi treated the most beautiful vision of their future together as his goal, heedlessly forging ahead in that direction, while Gu Mang hung up their most terrifying possible end as a warning bell, constantly reminding himself not to indulge in impossible dreams.

The contrast between them now was all the more stark. Mo Xi was Chonghua's most celebrated general, while Gu Mang had become the nation's most reviled traitor. In the time since his memories returned, Gu Mang had thought back on all the things Mo Xi had done since their paths crossed again—visiting him at Luomei Pavilion, protecting him at Wangshu Manor, asking for him in the throne room, even trying to stop the fight at the New Year's Eve feast.

He felt himself drenched in cold sweat. It was outrageous, all of it. Was Mo Xi crazy? Why did he still protect him? Everything he had done in the past—was it not enough to make Mo Xi hate him to the core? Had Gu Mang been lucid, he would've absolutely never allowed Mo Xi to behave so foolishly.

On the surface, nothing was obviously odd; Mo Xi's actions could be chalked up to the strength of their brotherhood, or to the depth of Mo Xi's grudge, so bitter he longed to torment this felon with his own two hands.

But from another angle? A decorated general of the empire, one known to keep his distance from men and women alike, went to a brothel again and again for a traitor. Not only did he pay to bed said traitor, he even asked the emperor for him before the assembled imperial court.

Upon taking custody of this condemned criminal, he had neither imprisoned nor brutalized him—rather, he'd given him all he could ask for in food and drink, personally taught the traitor to read, and taken him to the healer for medicine. This traitor slept in General Mo's bed, wore General Mo's clothes, shared food at General Mo's table, and listened to General Mo reading poetry on a snowy night... What the actual fuck was he doing?

Mo Xi was insane!

When Gu Mang turned his back on Chonghua, the last thing he wanted was any further connection to Mo Xi. But none of his careful planning had included his own amnesia or Mo Xi's mule-like stubbornness. He began to worry—if someone came to stir up shit and asked what kind of punishment that damnable traitor was enduring in Xihe Manor, how would Mo Xi answer? Despite racking his brains, Gu Mang was unable to think of a single acceptable response Mo Xi could give. What was he going to say, *This general swore at him once in a moment of boredom?*

Forget the absurdity of what had transpired last night. Neutralizing poison? Controlled by the drug? What a joke. The one who had been dosed with aphrodisiac was Gu Mang, not Mo Xi. Had any other traitor been inflamed by lust to the point of wishing for death, would a cold beauty like General Mo have lowered himself to personally relieve their torment? Hacking them to death would be considered merciful.

Gu Mang wasn't stupid. He knew Mo Xi still held him in his heart.

The enormity of it stunned him, but it also sunk him into utter despair. He could scheme over every black and white chess piece on the board—all of them save for his general, his lover, his princess. The piece he wanted to protect the most.

Mo Xi was not under his control.

And this man he couldn't control had made a mistake and slept with him again. But it couldn't go any further. Just like the secret affair and ceaseless lust of their youth, their love and desire stopped here. It could never stand in the light of day; it could never walk the honorable path. If what happened last night was made known, Mo Xi would fall into an endless hell alongside him, forever unable to cleanse his name.

With all this in mind, Gu Mang found himself glancing back toward where Jiang Yexue had disappeared. Lowering his head guiltily, he sniffed himself once, then twice to be sure. All he smelled was the faint scent of soap. Jiang Yexue wasn't of the feathered tribe; he couldn't have noticed any less-perceptible scents. He was probably overthinking...

Gu Mang sighed, burying his face in the bedding and digging his hands into the blankets.

Mo Xi, my princess, my little dummy... Oh, what should I do with you...

He slept until the sun sank below the horizon.

At twilight, their walnut ship finally reached the outskirts of Chonghua's capital. The tea stalls had long packed up, and the streets were mostly empty. Murong Chuyi touched down soon after. He disembarked from his pleasure boat and briskly turned to leave.

Yue Chenqing haltingly spoke up. "F-Fourth Uncle..."

Murong Chuyi acted as if he hadn't heard. Clad head-to-foot in clothes whiter than snow, he left without a backward glance.

Yue Chenqing's head drooped. Jiang Yexue comforted him. "Don't worry, he'll cool off."

"Mn..."

Mo Xi sighed inwardly at this pair of nephews, then gazed after Murong Chuyi's retreating back. Between the three of them, Jiang Yexue still seemed the steadier senior by every measure, despite Murong Chuyi being older by a few years. But these were the difficulties of a family he didn't belong to, and it wasn't his place to speak.

Just as he prepared to turn away, he glimpsed one of Chonghua Bridge's stone pillars. Mo Xi's gaze darkened for a moment. The old beggar from the Time Mirror was gone; he'd passed in the second year after Gu Mang defected. That familiar beggar's song would never ring out here again.

Gu Mang strolled over to Mo Xi, nudging him with an elbow and crossing his arms. "Hey, what's Xihe-jun looking at with those wistful eyes? Murong-xiansheng?"

Mo Xi immediately turned. "Don't speak nonsense."

"I got you, didn't I? You're just mad because you got caught, ha ha ha—"

After laughing a moment, he realized even Jiang Yexue and Yue Chenqing were looking at him sternly. Gu Mang tactfully pursed his lips and chuckled dryly. "Um, well, sorry everyone. Just trying to lighten the mood."

Mo Xi didn't bicker with him. "I'm leaving too," he said. "I'll go to the palace and report back to His Imperial Majesty."

"Don't I need to enter the palace too?" Gu Mang asked.

"No, go back to Xihe Manor without me."

Gu Mang smiled. "Can I stroll around instead? I'll change my features; no one will notice a thing."

"Where do you want to go?"

"Anywhere. The pastry stall at the eastern market, the shadow plays at the western market, Apricot Mansion in the south, the Perfumed Alley in the north..."

"Absolutely not," Mo Xi said coldly.

"I just want to look around. I won't bed anyone."

Mo Xi ground his molars. He didn't explode, but it looked as if he was using a lifetime's worth of forbearance to keep his cool. He lowered his head to look at Gu Mang and pushed out a sentence from between his teeth. "Go back to the manor and wait."

Seeing them fight again, Jiang Yexue sighed. "Gu-xiong, the matter of you recovering your memories will be revealed the instant you step into a brothel. Beauties are nice, but isn't your life more important?"

"Fair enough, Jiang-xiong's quite reasonable." Gu Mang heaved a sigh as well. "But frankly, Xihe Manor is far too cold and lonely. I didn't mind it when I was witless, but it's going to be a bore now. Why don't I come visit Jiang-xiong's manor instead?"

"I need to take Chenqing to Jiang Manor. Chenqing and Xiaojiu were both injured, so we'll need to ask Medicine Master Jiang to treat them and get some medicine for Xiaojiu."

"All right, all right, go on then," Gu Mang replied wearily. "I'll obediently go back and lie down. Mo Xi, can you at least bring me a pack of cards when you come back? Your manor is way too dull, I'd rather go to Luomei Pavilion..."

He was still speaking when Mo Xi turned to leave.

Mo Xi was a key minister in the Bureau of Military Affairs and the descendant of a prestigious family. In recognition of his status, the late emperor had bestowed a token upon him that allowed him to enter the core of the imperial city unannounced. Nonetheless, Mo Xi had always understood the rules: heavenly grace was one thing, but the emperor's heart was another. Though he had this sort of privilege, he never used it.

Just as he had in the Time Mirror, Mo Xi walked past the ranks of imperial guards. The soldiers turned toward him, lowering their heads to make their obeisance. Their armor shone in the last glow of twilight, scarlet feathers on their helmets rustling. Though Mo Xi had never taken note of it before now, he realized that the imperial guards from eight years ago seemed to have all been replaced. He didn't see a single familiar face among these inner guards of the imperial city.

"Aiyo, Xihe-jun, you're back!" The attendant Eunuch Li paid his respects to Mo Xi as soon as he saw him, sinking into a deep bow. "This old slave greets Xihe-jun."

Mo Xi stopped. "Could you please report that Mo Xi seeks an audience with His Imperial Majesty?"

"His Imperial Majesty is indisposed and has already retired for the evening," Eunuch Li replied.

In silence, Mo Xi glanced at the illuminated doors of the Great Hall.

"Xihe-jun, please don't misunderstand—the one inside the Great Hall isn't His Majesty," Eunuch Li hastily explained, following the direction of Mo Xi's gaze.

Mo Xi furrowed his brow. "Then who is it?"

As he was about to answer, a thought seemed to occur to Eunuch Li. Casting a sidelong glance at Mo Xi, he plastered on the sort of warm and suggestive smile the ladies of the harem knew well. Unfortunately, Mo Xi was not of the harem and had no idea what this smile implied. "What is it? Why are you smiling?" he asked, bemused.

Eunuch Li bowed and led him into the golden hall's library, smile never faltering. "Nothing, nothing, perhaps it's perfect timing. This old slave thinks the one inside the Great Hall would most certainly like to see Xihe-jun."

"Who?"

"Xihe-jun, if you please."

Eunuch Li wouldn't answer, and Mo Xi didn't like beating around the bush. He glanced suspiciously at Eunuch Li's stupid smile, paused a moment, and pushed open the doors to the hall.

The sandalwood doors creaked, and the night wind rushed in, setting the lights in the phoenix candelabras aflicker. The handmaiden Yue-niang started; she hastily fell to her knees and kowtowed. "This servant greets Xihe-jun!"

At this, the figure sitting in the middle of those piled official documents lifted her head and met his gaze. Mo Xi found himself at a loss for words.

Princess Mengze's pretty eyes widened in surprise, a smile blooming across her face like a lotus in clear water. "Ah, it's Mo-dage?"

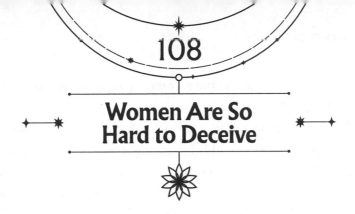

Women Are So Hard to Deceive

NO MATTER HOW OBLIVIOUS Mo Xi might be, it was impossible to misunderstand Eunuch Li's suggestive tone at this point. Seething, he turned around, only to find that the sly old fox had already made himself scarce. Mo Xi was rendered speechless. He sighed as he entered the hall and crossed to Mengze's desk. "What are you doing here?"

The night was cold and crisp, and Mengze's health was frail, so she wore a pale blue coat even indoors. She coughed, then said warmly, "Imperial Brother is ill. In the past few days he hasn't had time to go through the memorials, so I came to assist."

Murong Mengze, a mere woman, had not risen to the position of one of Chonghua's three gentlemen without reason. She treated the common people with lenience and virtue, was well-versed in matters both political and military, and was no man's inferior when it came to the management of a nation. Though she was physically frail, it was only because she had healed Mo Xi years ago and succumbed to a chronic ailment afterward. Before that, both her magical abilities and the strength of her spiritual energy reflected an extraordinary innate talent that left her contemporaries, male or female, in the dust. She could no longer fight on the front lines these days, but she could still sit in the command tent. If only the Nine Provinces had a precedent of women rulers, the emperor likely would've bestowed on her an official title and the accompanying authority to exercise her true capabilities.

Regrettably, women were still women in the eyes of too many; in their opinion, ladies should be arranging their hair in a window or making themselves up in a mirror. Even if they excelled in scholarship or strategy, it would be better to devote themselves to their husbands, fathers, or brothers—the real court officials. What need was there for any girl to show her face in public?

Thus, though Murong Mengze was of royal blood, the first princess of a nation, people would usually only mention her to say, *Oh, that's Xihe-jun's future wife—they just haven't tied the knot yet.* Though the healing techniques and military stratagems she'd devised in her youth were impressive, the public's most positive impression of her boiled down to "infatuated princess who sacrificed herself for her one true love."

And so the emperor had very little choice: in spite of Mengze's pure and noble character, her talent and her righteous nature, he could give her no important responsibilities.

Still, he was loath to hand these memorials, so central to imperial power, off to other nobles. His spirit was willing, but his body was weak. At a glance it was clear that, out of all his close siblings and cousins, he only had Murong Lian to rely on besides Mengze and Yanping.

There was no question of Yanping's capabilities. She had an ample bosom but no brain. Out of ten young masters she would sleep with nine; Young Master Mo was the only one who'd decline. She might do well if tasked with drawing erotic pictures, but the idea of having her look at military reports was laughable.

As for Murong Lian... Even ignoring the fact that his paternal grandfather had his own designs on the throne, the previous emperor had genuinely considered adopting Murong Lian as a son and naming him crown prince in the current emperor's stead. The emperor was destined to hold a grudge toward him.

Which left only Mengze.

Murong Mengze was clever, wise, clear-headed, and competent. She was unfortunately female, but who was to say this misfortune wasn't the emperor's greatest comfort? In the world as it stood, women could make no sweeping changes. They couldn't accumulate influence or win support; they had no mechanism whereby they could gather power into their own hands. As long as this woman remained unwed, the closest man to her on earth was her eldest brother, the emperor himself. Thus, with Mengze, he felt utterly at ease.

Mengze coaxed the candles in the library to burn brighter and turned to speak gently to her handmaiden. "Yue-niang, a pot of spring tea for Xihe-jun."

"Yes."

Yue-niang darted off and swiftly returned with a tray laden with tea and desserts. She arranged each item with care and smiled. "Xihe-jun, please enjoy. This servant will remain outside, awaiting orders." The handmaiden's gauzy red skirts fluttered as she left the room, and the sandalwood library doors creaked shut behind her.

Mo Xi lowered himself into a seat. "How is His Imperial Majesty? How did he fall ill so suddenly?" he asked.

"He won't say, and he doesn't allow the healers from Shennong Terrace to say much either." Mengze sighed. "I only know he was bedridden for the past few days... But it's nothing serious. I was permitted to visit him this morning. The most dangerous phase has passed, but he's still weak. I'm afraid it'll be another three or four days of recovery." She paused, then looked inquiringly at Mo Xi. "Mo-dage, did you come to report on the results of the mission?"

"Yes."

Mengze looked concerned. "Did everything go smoothly?"

Mo Xi gave her a heavily edited account: "Yue Chenqing and the others were wounded, but they've already gone to Medicine Master Jiang for treatment. There were no other issues."

"That's good." Mengze let out a breath. "But I'm afraid Imperial Brother won't be well enough to see you for a few days. Mo-dage should write a report when you return home; I'll pass it to him on your behalf."

Mo Xi thanked her. Seeing how tired she looked, swamped with documents, he wanted to help her with the memorials. But if the emperor had handed these to Mengze instead of assigning them to his officials, they were scrolls he didn't wish others to see. "It's getting late, so I'll be heading back. You should get some rest as soon as you finish."

Mengze's pretty eyes shone as she smiled. "Leaving so soon? You won't keep me company a while longer?"

Mo Xi didn't reply.

"I'm just teasing, Mo-dage. Look at you, so travel-worn—how could I have the heart to make you stay with me?" Mengze coughed lightly a few more times, covering her mouth, then added warmly, "You should return."

Rising, Mo Xi looked down at her. "The night's cold and wet. Have Yue-niang bring you another robe."

Mengze smiled. "I will."

Mo Xi took his leave. He'd no sooner walked through the library doors than Yue-niang stepped back in. She had served Mengze for many years; in front of others she was a deferential servant, but the minute she was alone with Mengze she let her tongue loose, unable to hide her thoughts. As she looked back at the doors through which

Mo Xi had departed, she stamped her foot, plainly dissatisfied. "My lady—"

"What is it?"

"Why did you let Xihe-jun go? Look, you've been back in the city for so long, but this is the first time the two of you have been alone together, and you didn't even try to keep him." Yue-niang pursed her lips in a moue of disappointment. "You should at least ask him to stay for dinner or something," she mumbled.

Mengze dipped her brush into the ink stone, speaking as she wrote. "Why would I keep him? He doesn't wish to be with me."

"How could that be? His spiritual core came at the cost of your health! My lady, if you ask Xihe-jun to go west, he definitely wouldn't turn east instead. The kindness you did him—he owes you an enormous debt!"

Mengze smiled. "It was only kindness. I don't plan on demanding repayment."

"What is my lady saying? Of course he must repay it!" Faced with Mengze's indifference, Yue-niang grew anxious. "Xihe-jun is handsome and courageous, and his reputation is excellent too. I heard that in the three years he was stationed on the northern frontier, he didn't touch a single woman, unlike those other young masters who have concubines lined up in rows. You'd be fortunate to marry a husband like that. Leave him be, and a mob of witches will be clawing at each other to become his wife or concubine... How can we let that happen?" The longer she spoke, the more fretful she became. "I won't stand for it, I won't! He can marry our princess and no one else! He can't be allowed to flirt with any other maiden!"

Mengze listened to the girl shouting insolently but continued writing without a word. Only after a long while did she casually ask, "Yue-er thinks Xihe-jun is very handsome too?"

"Of course he's—" Yue-niang realized she had been too bold and hastily backpedaled. "No no no, Xihe-jun is like a holy deity. It's not this servant's place to speak of him."

Mengze smiled as she pressed a seal to a silk memorial scroll on behalf of her brother and blew the cinnabar ink dry. "Don't worry," she said. "You don't have to say it; I know you girls all like men like him. Tall, righteous, and reliable—all good things."

Yue-niang spoke nervously. "My lady, even if this servant had a thousand, ten thousand times more courage, I wouldn't dare... wouldn't dare..."

"What are you frightened of?" Mengze asked kindly. "It's only chat, and I'm only picking a few of his good traits as an example. But Yue-er, have you never thought why such a remarkable person has yet to wed at his age?"

"It's because m-my lady remains indisposed," Yue-niang mumbled.

"Why is it my fault?" Mengze looked up, still smiling. "If he truly wanted to marry, he would have requested permission from His Imperial Majesty long ago." Her smile faded. "He doesn't want to. That's why he's been dragging it out."

"And that's why this servant wants my lady and Xihe-jun to spend more time together! Look—the two of you rarely have any chance to meet." Yue-niang paused and bit her lip as if steeling herself for what she was about to say. "And, my lady, you don't know, but I've heard people talk. While you were away, Princess Yanping tried to s-se—"

Yanping was still a princess; no matter how close Yue-niang was to Mengze, she didn't dare say the word *seduce*. In the end, she mumbled over it. "She tried to do *that* to Xihe-jun. Look at the initiative she's taking, my lady! Why are you still pushing Xihe-jun away? Don't you know you're the only reason he's alive right now? If it were me, I'd feel it wasn't worth it!"

Mengze shook her head. "A melon torn from the vine isn't sweet. I won't force him into it."

"My lady!" Yue-niang sounded indignant. "Ah, but given...given your health... If Xihe-jun doesn't ask for your hand now, how long does he plan to make you wait?"

"Don't talk nonsense." Mengze's voice was stern as she set down the brush. "Xihe-jun and I are not betrothed; who is making anyone wait?"

"But—"

"I don't want to hear you speak of this again."

Yue-niang bit her soft lip. In the end, she hung her head, dejected. "...Yes, my lady."

Taking up her brush, Mengze unrolled a new memorial. For a while, it was quiet inside the library. Yet soon Yue-niang started muttering sulkily once more. "Xihe-jun's so callous and ungrateful. He's already got another girl behind my lady's back—the shame he's brought to my lady!"

The tip of Mengze's brush stilled over the scroll. She looked up. "What do you mean by this?"

Yue-niang looked as if she was bursting to speak, but also as if it were unbearable to say. She held her tongue under Mengze's clear gaze for a long moment before finally blurting out, "His hair ribbon!"

"Hm?"

Yue-niang took a deep breath. "I wouldn't expect my lady to notice, but this servant is used to waiting on people; I always take note of the masters' clothes and ornaments. The hair ribbon Xihe-jun wore today was obviously not his own—it was raw silk, something only commoners use. But the embroidery was very fine, so it's a little tart who likes pretty things and dresses above her station..."

The words had already left her mouth, so Yue-niang barreled ahead with her eyes red and her cheeks puffed in a pout. "I could tell right away it belongs to some poor hussy who seduced Xihe-jun with her common wiles! You're the only one who could be calm about this! This girl's ribbon has already made it into Xihe-jun's hair-knot—how close must they be?! Yet you don't see it! I-I-I, I'm so mad I could die! How could he betray you like this!"

Mengze didn't say anything. Her brush had soaked up too much ink; a black splotch landed on the scroll and left a dark stain. She lowered her pretty face to dip her brush again. "It's only a hair rib- bon," she said in a low voice. "Maybe he just wanted to try something new. Don't think too much on it."

"You know how much of a rule-follower he is; he's not that kind of person!"

"Enough."

Yue-niang fell silent.

Mengze looked up at her. "No more of this," she said blandly. "Yue-er, come here and grind some ink for me."

"...Yes, my lady."

109

Coffin Library

I N THE RUSTLING NIGHT wind, Mo Xi left the palace, but he didn't return to Xihe Manor. The clues he'd discovered in the Time Mirror were still on his mind. As his long strides took him away from the Great Hall, he resolved on three questions to which he must have answers.

Firstly, the black-garbed man. Before defecting, Gu Mang had met with a man in a mask. That man had spoken of Chonghua's inequities and urged Gu Mang to turn traitor, and Gu Mang hadn't said a word to oppose him. So who was that black-garbed man?

Secondly, Warrior Soul Mountain. The black-garbed man had brought Gu Mang to Warrior Soul Mountain just before his defection. When Gu Mang visited the graves there with Mo Xi, he'd told Mo Xi the restricted area felt familiar. There was a good chance Gu Mang had done *something* on the other side of the barrier there. But what? What exactly was inside Warrior Soul Mountain's restricted area?

Lastly, the prison. After speaking to Lu Zhanxing inside the Time Mirror, Mo Xi was certain Gu Mang had secretly visited this man in prison before defecting. What had Gu Mang spoken to Lu Zhanxing about?

If he could get to the bottom of these three mysteries, he was sure the truth from eight years ago would surface.

But all of these events had occurred under a veil of extreme secrecy. Of those who had witnessed them, aside from Gu Mang himself, one person's identity was unknown, and the other was a dead soul beneath the Yellow Springs. Mo Xi didn't expect to loosen Gu Mang's tongue, so two paths of investigation remained.

The first was to turn back time. The second was to find the history scrolls from that year.

Turning back time required the Time Mirror, but the power of the ancient godly mirror was tremendous. Mortal bodies could only enter it once per decade; enter again, and the mirror would devour them and crush them to dust. The Time Mirror was no longer an option.

Mo Xi's footsteps slowed, and he glanced northward in the direction of the Imperial Censorate, where his hopes of answering these three questions lay.

A piece of history stone was embedded in each of Chonghua's palace halls and imperial pavilions. From the day an emperor ascended the throne, he wore a string of pendants made of history stone, not to be removed until the day he died. These stones faithfully recorded all that happened in the empire, and court historians gathered them each month into a volume that was stored in the Imperial Censorate.

There were sure to be secret records within the Imperial Censorate related to Gu Mang's defection. The issue with them was the possibility of falsehood. The royal family had always proclaimed the truth and reliability of the history stones to outsiders, but everyone knew that even if the stones couldn't lie, their keepers could destroy sections of the records. If the nation's ruler ordered historians to expunge some segments of history, who would gainsay him?

It was dark now; night had swallowed the final glimmer of sunset. The stars in the sky shone as bright as the lamps on earth. Mo Xi gazed at the faraway Imperial Censorate. In the distance, some palace maidens on night patrol wandered with lanterns like a winding snake, passing by the carved white jade railing one after another.

Yes, the scrolls inside the Imperial Censorate could be tampered with, but at least there was a chance. The emperor was ill tonight, so the imperial guards were mostly concentrated around his private quarters. It was the perfect opportunity to infiltrate...

Mo Xi watched the string of lanterns disappear into the darkness. After a moment of thought, he turned his steps toward the Imperial Censorate.

The compound had two points of entry and exit, each set with barriers, as well as layer after layer of guards. This was hardly a hindrance for the top general of the empire. Mo Xi made it into the main hall without much effort.

In contrast to the sumptuous extravagance of most palace buildings, the structure of the Imperial Censorate was unusual. It was more accurately described as a tomb rather than a hall. A lofty monument stood at the entrance, carried on the tortoiseshell back of a statue of Bixi, as was traditional for mausoleums. Four words were engraved upon its stone surface: THE PAST IS DEAD.

These words were the work of Chonghua's second emperor. Soon after Chonghua was established, its founding ruler suddenly perished of complications from a wound he incurred in battle. He died without penning any posthumous edict. There was no named successor, nor had it been decided whether the successor would be the eldest son, the one of most merit, or whether this new nation would use the system of fraternal seniority or patrilineal inheritance.

Everyone had greedily eyed the empty throne, from brothers of the royal family to powerful officials and noble relatives.

The bloody power struggle that followed devastated Chonghua for a full fourteen months, during which countless citizens were unjustly imprisoned and loyal souls perished with unresolved grievances. The storm only died down after the seventh son of the founding emperor finally ascended the throne.

But even sitting on the throne couldn't guarantee a ruler peace under these conditions. Chonghua's second ruler lived day and night tangled in schemes and conspiracies; plots targeted his empress, his sons, and even the emperor himself. He could never rest easy.

In the end, his paranoia escalated to compulsion—he visited the Imperial Censorate at frequent intervals to look through the records over and over again. Where did a certain imperial brother go today? Whom did a certain important subject visit yesterday? If he caught wind of the slightest aberration, he traced it like a man possessed, unearthing every detail and demanding the lives of all who thought to plot against him.

This second emperor was exhausted by such a life. It was only after he grew old and passed the throne to his son that he understood the past died with the passage of time, and that bygones should be left as bygones. He'd come to this palace hall that was so familiar to him and so significant to Chonghua, and set down a monument at the doorway, leaving behind these four words: *The past is dead.*

What was dead was dust; why obsess over it? Why look back? The third ruler was greatly moved upon seeing this monument. As a gesture of mourning for his imperial father and in honor of the late emperor's final wishes, he had the Imperial Censorate rebuilt in the style of a tomb. In this singular palace hall, the building was a cemetery and the past was the deceased, warning all those who visited to forgive and let go. If it wasn't important, they shouldn't pursue it. Even if it was, they shouldn't allow it to possess them.

In the time since, few came to the Imperial Censorate in search of the past. There were many guards, but they were relaxed and idle. Mo Xi entered without alerting them.

His steel-toed military boots clicked on the stone, echoing in the silence. The Imperial Censorate was cavernous, structured like a real mausoleum with twelve tomb beasts lining the path. The deepest passages delved at least a hundred and fifty feet into the ground. "Tomb rooms" lined either side of the main path. Within them, scrolls recording the history of the empire were filed by year and stored with a seal stone outside, carved with the dynasty and the generation.

Mo Xi swiftly reached the room with records from eight years ago. As he gazed at the glimmering gold inscription upon it, he hesitantly raised a hand and sensed a powerful barrier. The tomb beast carved atop the stone door rumbled to life and spoke. "Who..." *Who...* The sonorous voice echoed endlessly down the passage. "...goes...there?"

This was a talisman seal set down by the second emperor. The Imperial Censorate held the official records of the empire and should reasonably be open to the public. But if anyone could go in and investigate the pasts of others as they pleased, palace affairs would become even more of a bloodbath.

Thus the second emperor put down this barrier with a strict condition: anyone who entered the chamber must truthfully report their name to the tomb beast. If any incident occurred as a result of the information divulged here, they could be investigated. The emperor himself was not excepted from this rule.

This was a grave mistake, Mo Xi knew. But it was a measly price to pay to learn the truth. He put his hand over the spirit stone inlaid in the tomb beast's forehead and spoke clearly: "Xihe Manor, Mo Xi."

The beast's red spirit stone eyes shone as if to lay bare the truth of Mo Xi's words. After a moment the glow faded, and the giant seal stone made a thunderous noise. A voice that seemed to ring across the ages sang out. "The—past—is—dead—"

With this final warning from the second emperor to his descendants, the door swung open, revealing to Mo Xi's eyes a stone room with three hundred and sixty-five coffins emanating a bone-chilling cold.

Each coffin represented one of the three hundred and sixty-five days in the year. All that occurred in Chonghua each day was collected within a jade scroll, cataloged, and placed within its coffin. Mo Xi knew which days he needed to investigate as well as he knew his own hands; he walked without hesitation toward a row of coffins in the depths of the room.

The truth was so close. His heart raced. Mo Xi stopped in front of a coffin, his dark eyes flashing. Yet as he stretched his hand toward the wood of the lid, he suddenly tensed—

Mo Xi's eyes darted to the side of the coffin, where the dust had been disturbed. Someone had opened this coffin before him. When he pushed the lid aside, his galloping heart dropped like a stone into a ravine, tumbling endlessly downward...

It was complete disorder inside the coffin. The jade scrolls that held the records of the past were destroyed, some of the narrow slips more or less shattered to powder.

Even before he arrived, he hadn't expected this escapade to go smoothly. But Mo Xi felt he had taken a great blow upon seeing the state of things with his own eyes. He braced both hands on the side of the coffin, closing his eyes and forcing himself to calm.

The scrolls in the coffin were made of Kunlun spirit jade; they should be near impossible to destroy. If they had been shattered, it was with intention—someone who knew the secrets from that year didn't want them exposed. And this person was certainly someone who wielded great power in Chonghua.

Under his strong brows, Mo Xi's eyes flickered beneath his eyelids. Shadows flashed through his mind—

Murong Lian. Censorate officials. Or the emperor. Perhaps even Gu Mang himself, before he defected. All kinds of guesses flooded his thoughts.

In this moment of torment in which he felt his insides were splitting apart, a clamor sounded from outside, hauling Mo Xi back to the present. Footsteps and shouts rang out in the distance.

"Someone's trespassed into the Imperial Censorate!"

"Quick, find them!"

Mo Xi glanced toward the open stone doors, then down at the coffin filled with shattered jade scrolls. He might never get the chance to come back after today. Acting on impulse, Mo Xi waved a hand and summoned all the jade scroll fragments into his qiankun pouch, uncaring of whether they could be repaired.

The cultivators guarding the Imperial Censorate had assembled in the hall, weapons drawn. Mo Xi had planned to hide here, then quickly leave this chaotic scene before the cultivators spread out. But on second thought, he remembered he had already given up his identity to open this tomb; the guards only needed to question each tomb beast. It would take at most a shichen before news of him sneaking into the Censorate made its way to the emperor. What could he possibly accomplish in that time?

Mo Xi took a deep breath. He adjusted the fall of his robes before slowly stepping out from the depths of the room. Although the guards were still far off, the instant the captain noticed Mo Xi, he raised his sword and cried, "Thief! How dare you bypass the imperial guards and trespass—"

In the next moment, the words died in his mouth as a figure strode slowly out from the shadows. Moonlight fell upon his fine-featured face, and the clamorous imperial cultivators froze in shock. Some even fell to their knees out of habit.

"X-Xihe-jun!"

"This subordinate deserves death! This subordinate didn't realize the honorable Xihe-jun was here—this subordinate misspoke!"

Mo Xi's prestige in Chonghua was unmatched, and his image as a righteous and honorable man was deeply impressed in people's hearts. Had anyone else appeared unannounced in the Censorate, the imperial guards would assume they were here for some nefarious purpose. But because it was Mo Xi, the guards automatically assumed Xihe-jun had accepted some mission too sensitive for their ears. No one imagined Xihe-jun would defy heavenly will for anything or anyone.

He was depending on this; he gambled on his thirty years of spotless reputation as he walked in front of these dumbstruck guards, his sharp gaze sweeping over their youthful faces.

"There is no thief," he said. "A secret order from the Bureau of Military Affairs requires me to investigate records from these years."

The captain was stunned. "Does Xihe-jun have His Imperial Majesty's command token...?"

"I've already said it's a secret order." Mo Xi's pale lips parted, his frosty expression accompanied by an equally cold statement. "What command token?"

"But—"

"This is a military matter; it's highly classified. I'd hoped to keep it quiet, but I see the diligence of you gentlemen is to be commended." Mo Xi gazed at their leader. "If the captain suspects me, you may come with me to His Imperial Majesty's quarters to confirm the facts."

Who didn't know that the emperor had been severely ill the past few days? Asking for confirmation would not only offend Xihe-jun, it would earn the captain a tongue-lashing from the emperor and swift expulsion from the palace. Moreover, the man standing before them now was *Mo Xi.* The most upright and honest general of Chonghua, the empire's most decorated commander, fourth in a line of pure-blooded generals. What was there to suspect?

The captain of the imperial guard lowered his head and cupped his hands. "Xihe-jun, forgive me. This subordinate was only following procedure. I beg Xihe-jun to pardon any offense!"

"No harm done," Mo Xi said lightly. "You must only remember to tell no one what you saw here tonight."

"Understood!"

Calm and aloof as ever, Mo Xi left the Imperial Censorate. Only after stepping outside and feeling the night wind upon him did he realize sweat had soaked through his robes. This matter was dealt with for the moment, but there was no wall on earth that blocked every draft; the news of his visit to the Imperial Censorate would leak sooner or later.

Mo Xi lifted his face to the moon hanging above the capital, casting its frosty glow on city roofs. His fingers inside his sleeve curled around the qiankun pouch that held the fragments of jade scrolls. Such badly damaged scrolls could only be repaired by the finest master artificer. Mo Xi had not a minute to lose; he needed to somehow find an extremely powerful, extremely trustworthy artificer...

Almost as soon as the thought occurred to him, a suitable person came to mind.

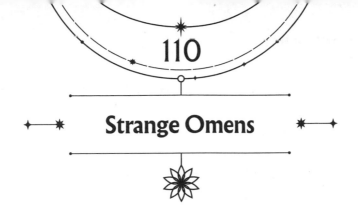

110

Strange Omens

OUT OF ALL THOSE who had the ability, the only one he could trust was Jiang Yexue. Mo Xi wasted no time rushing toward Cixin Forge.

The hour was very late. Cixin Forge was tucked away from the noisy heart of the city, so he encountered few people on the journey. Halfway there, a carriage burst from the cold fog; he could see as it neared that it was painted with vermilion bat sigils, the four corners of its elaborate canopy draped with golden bells that tinkled as the wheels spun. The coachman wore a short gauze hat, and his sleeves were narrow. With a crack, his crop landed on the flank of the golden-winged pegasus in the carriage traces.

"Make way! Make way for Wangshu-jun—"

Mo Xi frowned. Murong Lian? Where was he off to at this time of night?

He had no time for further thought before the carriage was hurtling toward him. It was too dark for the coachman to see Mo Xi's face. He shouted, "Make way, make way! Don't block Wangshu-jun's path!"

Mo Xi dove out of the way. A man behind him pulled his wife to the side and respectfully lowered his head to wait for Murong Lian's carriage to pass. The moment it rattled off, he spat in disgust, "It's the dead of night, but he's still yelling *make way, make way.*

Tch, is he shouting at the ghosts to clear the roads? There's barely anyone out; what's the point?"

Inwardly, Mo Xi sighed. Truly Murong Lian was an unpopular rich wastrel.

But as he turned back to glance at the dust kicked up by the carriage's passage, he felt vaguely that there was something strange afoot. Murong Lian was a lazy man; he wouldn't get out of bed early, and he definitely wouldn't leave his manor in the middle of the night if it wasn't urgent. So what was happening tonight...?

The Wangshu Manor carriage swiftly disappeared around a corner.

Mo Xi was overcome by an ominous premonition, his heart thudding violently. But at the moment, he had his own urgent task. He wasn't the type to put much stock in intuition, so he paid it no heed. Mo Xi turned away and strode toward his destination.

The rheumy-eyed Uncle Song opened the door to Cixin Forge. When he glimpsed Mo Xi's face in the clear moonlight, he stood stunned for a moment. "Ah... It's Mo-gongzi..."

"Is Qingxu Elder here?"

"Oh, Yexue." Song-laoban[7] coughed, voice thick. "Yexue isn't at the shop tonight. He said he had something to do and slipped out earlier." This man had the tendency of the very old to ramble, so he happily continued, "He said he'd get me some desserts from Lianhua Stall tomorrow morning. What a filial child; he knows that store has the best osmanthus cakes, I—"

If Mo Xi let the old man natter on, he'd be standing here all night. He gently cut him off. "Uncle, I have urgent matters to discuss with him. Do you know where he went?"

The old man beamed. "Of course, of course I do. He went to the academy; he probably won't be back until morning."

---

7   A term of address for a shopkeeper or the proprietor of a business that means "boss."

"I see... Uncle, many thanks."

Mo Xi coaxed Uncle Song back into the shop to rest. As he left, he closed Cixin Forge's doors on Jiang Yexue's behalf, then put up the "Closed" plaque before setting out for the academy.

But soon enough, Mo Xi crossed paths with another traveler. This time it was a black and blue carriage hung with silver skeleton bells, with an owl totem painted on the cabin.

This carriage belonged to the Sishu Terrace elder, Zhou He.

Zhou He was a noble quite close to the imperial family. His status wasn't as high as Murong Lian's, nor did he throw his weight around like Wangshu-jun. But all of Chonghua knew he was cruel, volatile, and eccentric, for he loved Sishu Terrace and its magical knowledge more than he loved his own Zhou Clan. He was an absolute madman when it came to spellcraft.

As Zhou He's carriage flew over the limestone path, Mo Xi found himself frowning. What was going on tonight? Despite the late hour, instead of remaining asleep in their beds, Murong Lian and Zhou He were rushing through the city streets. Could the emperor have taken a turn for the worse?

But if the emperor were that ill, Mengze wouldn't be going over scrolls so calmly, and he himself would've at least heard *something*...

He watched Elder Zhou He's carriage lights dwindle into two orange specks that flickered like stars, swallowed up by the endless night. The anxious thud of his heart grew stronger. He felt as if a shapeless outline hovered before him, the specter of a crisis yet to occur.

"Xihe-jun."

When he arrived outside the academy, those spiritual jade doors as tall as ten men were shut for the night. The guard was pleasant, but still conscientiously stopped Mo Xi. "It's very late; the academy doors are already locked. Is there something I can help you with?"

The academy was a unique place. Here, all of Chonghua's brightest young talents cultivated in seclusion before emerging into the world; hence its moniker, Dawn Academy. Since the academy was filled with inexperienced children, its protections rivaled those of the imperial palace. The same Xihe-jun who could go unannounced into the palace would be interrogated at the doors of the cultivation academy. Mo Xi knew the rules and remained calm. "I'm looking for someone. Is Qingxu Elder staying within the academy tonight?"

"So Xihe-jun is here for Qingxu Elder." The guard smiled. "Qingxu Elder is receiving a guest today, and the guest has not yet left. Would you like to wait?"

Jiang Yexue was a gentleman through and through, and many came to him with requests because they knew he was kind and easy to talk to. But Mo Xi was still surprised to hear a guest had come to call immediately after they returned from Bat Island and stayed so late. Mo Xi didn't wish to intrude, but the repair of the jade scroll could not be delayed. "No matter. I'll go see him myself."

In accordance with academy rules, he took a visitor's jade token and left his seal on the booklet. The great doors opened to him, and he stepped into the cultivation academy's grounds.

It was a quiet, clear night. The little cultivators had to abide by the rules set by the elders and were asleep by the hour of hai, shortly after full dark; this late, there was no one about. The eaves of the sprawling academy rooftops swooped up like wings, their golden tiles glowing in the silver light like a butterfly perched quietly on the curtain of the sky. Under the bright moonlight, it was like walking in a dream.

After graduating and enlisting, Mo Xi had rarely returned to the academy. Fortunately it had not changed much; neither the drill grounds and courtyards nor the halls and dormitories were much different from when he was cultivating and learning magic. Mo Xi didn't waste time reminiscing. He clutched the qiankun pouch holding secrets and hopes and strode purposefully toward the residences where the elders lived.

When he reached the white jade bridge that linked the elders' residences with the sword practice platform, he spied a figure walking toward him from afar. Mo Xi stared for a moment in some amazement.

...Murong Chuyi?

The man's head was lowered, so he didn't see Mo Xi standing at the other end of the jade bridge. He walked alone in silence. Absent was his usual immortal aura and floating grace. His steps were slightly unsteady, his hair-knot slightly askew, wisps falling loose around his jade-like face.

Mo Xi frowned. "Murong-xiansheng."

Murong Chuyi's head shot up. His usually aloof and proud face wore a layer of panic and distress he hadn't time to conceal. Yet what astonished Mo Xi most were the ends of Murong Chuyi's eyes, which were reddened as if he had endured some extraordinary disgrace. All his humiliation seemed to have transformed into scarlet fish tails, like rouge spreading in water toward the sharp corners of his phoenix eyes.

"You..."

Murong Chuyi bit his pale, dry lips. They were bleeding; scarlet appeared where his lips touched. He whipped his head aside—but as if afraid evasiveness would be more conspicuous, he forced himself to turn back before long, gazing at Mo Xi through eyes cold as frost and sharp as a knife.

Those eyes were misty. Perhaps Murong Chuyi thought he was hiding his emotions well and managed to look imposing. Mo Xi only felt that he was concealing his turmoil poorly. Vulnerability, resentment, shame... All of it was plain to see.

After a long silence, Mo Xi asked, "Xiansheng, are you well?"

A pause. "Yes."

They looked at each other, hearts heavy with their own concerns. Neither had a gentle temperament, nor were they especially close; expressing any more care was futile. Mo Xi didn't like meddling and Murong Chuyi liked it even less. "Good night," Murong Chuyi said.

They both performed a shallow obeisance and strode past each other.

The night wind set Murong Chuyi's snowy white robes aflutter, the faint scent of orange blossoms rising from his sleeves. Mo Xi tilted his head as he caught the hint of a second scent beneath that refined fragrance, one he had smelled on someone else before. But when he tried to pin it down, it was like grabbing smoky mist with his bare hands. It slipped his grasp.

Mo Xi frowned as he watched Murong Chuyi's silhouette melt into the darkness. "What did he come to the academy for...?" he murmured.

Of course he received no answer. Mo Xi stood for a moment, then turned back toward his destination. Although the elder's residences were all in the same area, they were well spaced out, and each was constructed according to the occupant's tastes. For example, the residence of Caiwei Elder, who taught wood elemental magic, was hidden within a jungle of plants and vines, the walls covered with rose climbers. Each flower was the size of one's spread hand, and bloomed thick and lush year-round. Changhong Elder, who taught swordsmanship, lived in a residence surrounded by a barrier the white-yellow of lightning. A large garden surrounded his house as well, but it contained neither plants nor stones. Instead, what sprouted from the ground were a few thousand swords of different shapes and ages.

Jiang Yexue lived in a simple wooden house with a row of elegant bamboo swaying outside. Among this crowd of crazies, his home seemed uncommonly restrained.

Mo Xi followed a narrow path of white gravel to Jiang Yexue's door. He crooked his slender fingers and rapped sharply on the wood. "Qingxu Elder."

There was no movement from within the house. After a few more knocks, the door opened with a creak.

A little clay servant falteringly peered out through the crack in the door. Someone had smashed its clay skull—only half its head remained, and it was sobbing pathetically. Jiang Yexue had always cherished these clay servants; he would never break them himself. Mo Xi's heart skipped a beat as he asked, "Where is your lord?"

"My lord... Lord..." The servant stuttered incoherently. It had been damaged too badly, and stalled on the same words over and over again as it tried to complete its sentence. "My lord... Don't... Lord..."

Seeing as the door was now ajar and the clay servant was broken, Mo Xi was afraid something had happened to Jiang Yexue. He pushed the door open and stepped into the room.

What he encountered inside was only more chilling. The bamboo flooring was splattered with blood. Next to the screen door, the exquisite Ru ware vase, with its round base and elegantly tapered top, lay in forlorn shards on the ground.

"Jiang-xiong!" Mo Xi strode into the inner hall and found it empty. He continued to the bedroom, opening the door to total darkness—

no lamps were lit, and the window screen was tightly shut. But the air was suffused with that familiar scent, the one he couldn't place. Mo Xi raised a hand and summoned a fireball, throwing light over the room. There was no one inside, but the bedding was in disarray. A few wrinkled, snow-white garments were tossed in the corner, but nothing else was out of place...

"Xihe-jun?"

A surprised voice sounded from behind him. Mo Xi whirled to see Jiang Yexue sitting in his wheelchair, clad in a loose bathrobe the color of flax. He was wiping at dripping hair like inky jade as he looked at Mo Xi in shock. "What are you doing here?"

111

Elder of the Black Magic Trials

UPON FINDING Jiang Yexue unharmed, Mo Xi first sighed in relief, then he frowned again. "You're asking me? What happened to you?"

Jiang Yexue smiled. "Did something happen to me?"

Mo Xi blinked. The doors were still open, showing the mess that covered the ground. No matter how one looked at it, it was out of the ordinary.

Sensing the question in Mo Xi's silence, Jiang Yexue explained, still smiling, "Oh, this. I made a new puppet that malfunctioned. It made quite a mess of the house." He shot a glance at that little clay puppet spinning around with its half-shattered head. "Look, it broke this one too."

"I see." Mo Xi cleared his throat. "Apologies, I thought Murong-xiansheng..."

Jiang Yexue's feathery lashes lifted. "You saw Chuyi?"

"Mn," said Mo Xi. "On my way here, I saw him leaving. I thought he was here to see you, that some...disagreement occurred."

Jiang Yexue paused to cover his mouth with a sleeve, cleared his throat, and smiled faintly. "Is that so? Well, he didn't come here." As if suddenly chilled, he pulled his bathrobe closer and smoothed the white fabric. Then he reached up and tied his long hair, binding it into a relaxed ponytail and fastening it with a green jade clip.

His face had a distinctive air of refinement. The lines of his features were as soft as spring-grown willow catkins floating on the water's surface, his skin pale as new snow fallen by the riverside on a winter's night. At the moment, he was fresh out of the bath, and so seemed even more like a beautiful piece of Hetian jade immersed in a natural spring's waters, soothing away all frustrations or doubts.

"The academy has many books on artificing. Xiaojiu probably came to borrow one, not to see me." He paused, smile unfaltering. "Anyway, it's so late. I wasn't expecting any guests, so I went to take a bath before cleaning this mess. I'm afraid I've embarrassed myself before Xihe-jun."

"The fault is mine. I'm the one who's bothered you at this hour."

"We're brothers who have shared life or death—nothing is too much bother." Jiang Yexue looked him over and asked without preamble, "Did Xihe-jun come tonight because of Gu-xiong?"

Mo Xi paused. "How did you know?"

Jiang Yexue's gaze slid away from Mo Xi's hair ribbon, his slender fingers interlocking over his knees. He said nothing about the mismatched ribbons as he lowered his lashes with a warm smile. "Other than military matters, the only thing that makes you so anxious is that dear brother of yours."

Mo Xi was silent a moment. Lifting a hand, he conjured a sound-vanishing barrier to ensure their conversation wasn't overheard. Then he looked squarely at Jiang Yexue, his face solemn. "I've brought something with me." After a pause, he asked, "Do you remember what I told you on Bat Island, that I learned of some strange events in the Time Mirror?"

"I remember."

"I found some clues regarding Gu Mang's defection eight years ago."

"Is that so? What are they?"

Mo Xi stepped forward and placed his gold-on-black qiankun pouch on the desk before Jiang Yexue. "Jade scrolls."

Jiang Yexue had been calm until now, but when he heard this, his eyes widened and his face paled. Incredulous, he murmured, "Did you...steal the history-recording jade scrolls?"

Mo Xi didn't speak. He pressed his lips into a tight line, then lowered his head and pulled open the ribbons of the qiankun pouch to pour the fragments onto the table. The pieces of the history-recording jade scrolls scattered in front of Jiang Yexue, glowing faintly.

"Someone destroyed the scrolls," Mo Xi said succinctly. "This proves someone wants to erase what happened in Chonghua back then."

Jiang Yexue was frozen in astonishment for a long while. Leaning back in his wheelchair, he murmured, "Mo Xi, you're out of your mind..."

At the same time, back at Xihe Manor, Li Wei's shrewd face was gleaming beneath the lights of the plum-blossom copper lamps. Lips curved in a flattering smile, he was attempting to have an amicable discussion with the crowd of guests standing stock-still in Xihe Manor's great hall.

These people wore purple robes trimmed in gold and embroidered with the insignia of a hundred birds. The man at their head looked to be in his early thirties. His countenance was stern, and the faint wrinkles between his brows were evidence of his love of frowning. His lips were thin and his eyes were cold, with an air of unbending arrogance; his entire aura was one that warded off strangers.

This was the leading elder of Sishu Terrace, Zhou He.

Everyone in Chonghua knew Zhou He was quite insane. He was enamored of foreign magic techniques; regardless of whether they were good or evil, black magic or holy arts, there were none he wouldn't touch. His methods were indiscriminate, ranging from standard theoretical research to dark and bloody dissection of intestines and brains. The only reason he hadn't been named Chonghua's Greed, Wrath, or Ignorance was because Murong Chuyi's absolute indifference, both toward people and propriety, was second to none.

In effect, though Zhou He was vicious, he at least followed the rules. He refrained from opening skulls the emperor didn't permit him to open—albeit just barely. Now that this Zhou bastard had come to Xihe Manor, he wasn't so easily dismissed.

Li Wei accepted a heavy tea tray from a serving girl. Bowing and scraping, he delivered it with a broad smile to Elder Zhou's table. "Elder, please have some tea and try some fruit and desserts."

Zhou He made no sound. His fingers instinctively caressed the pitch-black dagger at his belt.

Head lowered, Li Wei shot a glance at the blade. His heart pounded in his chest. The design was ugly, resembling nothing so much as a pair of fire tongs—yet everyone was aware that this dagger was the most cherished treasure of Elder Zhou of Sishu Terrace. The holy weapon Lieying had picked its way through countless brains and dissected innumerable hearts, befitting the falcon that was its namesake. How many of the techniques currently in use within Chonghua had been discovered by Zhou He wielding Lieying?

Many called the Zhou Clan vultures, searching for the secrets of magical techniques in piles of corpses. Zhou He, when he heard such things, sneeringly retorted that he didn't require a corpse—

many secrets could only be discovered while the subject lived. Any who didn't believe him were welcome to take a turn under his knife.

Purple with golden trim, totem of a hundred birds—the Zhou Clan were not solely carrion-eating vultures, they were also Chonghua's falcons. With eyes that saw every detail, they picked the secrets of enemy nations from within crimson blood and presented them all to the emperor.

Li Wei attempted to make conversation. "Elder Zhou, this tea was steeped with dew from Mount Cuiling..."

Zhou He cut him off impatiently. "When will Xihe-jun return?"

"Please wait a while longer. This subordinate has sent people to summon the lord. Very soon, they will—"

Zhou He produced an intricate water clock from within his robes and slammed it on the table. He looked up. "A quarter-hour ago, you said the same. I value efficiency. Let's have an exact time— tell me if Xihe-jun will return within a shichen."

"Um..."

"Don't hem and haw. Sishu Terrace's black magic gu worms have been ready since yesterday; all we lack is the test subject. Now the specimen has returned, but I can't take him away. Instead, I must wait for your Xihe-jun to come back." Zhou He narrowed his eyes. "All right then, I'll wait. I'll do Xihe-jun this favor on account of his status and authority. But this can drag on for another shichen at most. Housekeeper Li, listen up. Gu Mang is the test subject His Imperial Majesty personally granted me. When Xihe-jun brought him back to this manor, your master was ceded temporary custody. Gu Mang is a traitor, and has been named the most suitable subject for black magic experiments by imperial decree... I've spent so long gathering black magic gu worms, and now they're finally ready."

Zhou He grabbed Li Wei by the lapels with surprising force, tone laced with threat. "I haven't much more patience."

He shoved Li Wei away. Crossing one leg over the other, he said coldly, "Understand now?"

"Y-yes." Li Wei swallowed, shooting a glance at the water clock. "I do..." he murmured.

No I don't! Everyone knew Gu Mang would be used for Chonghua's black magic experiments, but damn it, you didn't tell anyone it would begin today, did you? You snuck around preparing everything without giving any notice, then rushed in to claim the prisoner. I don't have the means to stop your lordship, but shouldn't you at least stop by to chat when Xihe-jun's at home?

Who would dare give Gu Mang up when Xihe-jun isn't here!

The only person completely unbothered by the hostility filling the room was Gu Mang, who sat in a corner of the great hall. Despite suddenly finding himself Zhou He's quarry and a test specimen for Chonghua's demonic magic trials, Gu Mang was quite calm. When Zhou He arrived, Gu Mang had just finished bathing and was getting ready to sleep; now, he certainly couldn't go to bed. He sat on a chair with a loose bathrobe over his shoulders, inky hair framing his face.

Chin in hand, he gazed at this flock of vultures. He was quiet, as obedient as a tempered prisoner ought to be. It was just that his earlier obedience was real, while his current obedience was faked.

Although he'd recovered a majority of his memories since coming out of the Time Mirror, Gu Mang still couldn't recall some extremely crucial points. The absence of these memories was like a smoothly flowing poem missing its most important rhyme, rendering him unable to fully understand his current circumstances. Gu Mang could remember that the emperor had indeed decreed him a test subject for black magic experiments. Yet when he searched what memories he had, he couldn't figure out how he'd ended up like this. Nevertheless, he was ready; he knew what he was determined to do, so he could endure it.

"Quick, send another message to the lord," Li Wei urged the manor's messenger servant.

The servant was even more anxious than Li Wei; beads of sweat stood out on his forehead. "I've sent it seventeen or eighteen times, but I can find no trace of the lord!"

Li Wei was pacing in frustration, first sneaking a glance at the malicious-looking Zhou He, then peeking at the calm and composed Gu Mang. No matter which side he chose to offend, the consequences would be more than he could bear. He turned like a top again and again until inspiration struck. He came to a stop and waved the messenger servant over. "Come here, come here! Hurry up, I have a plan."

The messenger, thinking Li Wei had some new plan, waited with wide eyes. But the words Housekeeper Li mysteriously imparted were: "Send another message."

Speechless, the messenger replied awkwardly, "Housekeeper Li, didn't I tell you? I've already sent word seventeen or eighteen times, but..."

"Have you got a pig's brains?" Li Wei prodded frantically at the servant's forehead. "I didn't say send it to Xihe-jun!"

"Then to whom?"

"Princess Mengze!"

Li Wei's quick thinking impressed even himself. No one but Princess Mengze could afford the responsibility of letting Gu Mang be taken away. Li Wei prodded the messenger. "Emergency help, emergency help! Hurry and send a voice message to Princess Mengze!"

As soon as the servant heard this, his eyes gleamed. Had they not been watched, he would've given Li Wei an enthusiastic thumbs up. Excellent, Head Housekeeper Li was truly excellent! Gu Mang was kept in the manor like a concubine; even if their lord purported to hate this concubine so much his skin crawled, anyone with eyes in Xihe Manor could see Mo Xi cared for Gu Mang. Now that Zhou He wanted to take Concubine Gu away, was there anyone in the manor who could take the blame?

There was only one: the lord's first wife.

Though Mengze had yet to officially cross the threshold of Xihe Manor, she was solidly considered to be Mistress Xihe-jun in everyone's eyes. She had selflessly saved Xihe-jun's life once already, so the only one who could take responsibility for dealing with said "concubine" was her.

These two miscreants of Xihe Manor had found a piece of floating driftwood to cling to. They sent off a message to Princess Mengze in utter delight, but before the messenger butterfly so much as crossed over the wall, it was shot down by a bolt of black light.

Displeased, Zhou He raised his eyes to stare at Li Wei. "Who are you contacting?"

"P-Princess M-Mengze..."

Zhou He pointed Lieying at him. "Li Wei, listen well. I came here today to take the prisoner. I'm here to tell you I'm doing so, not to ask your permission. Don't think I'll give you the chance to find someone else to plead on his behalf."

Staring at the point of that holy weapon that had carved through endless gore, Li Wei broke out in a cold sweat. "Yes yes yes yes! The elder is c-c-correct—"

Zhou He turned away. A silence fell over the room, the water clock counting the minutes, drop by drop, next to Zhou He's hand.

Amid this crushing tension, a snort rang out, followed by a soft sigh. It wasn't a particularly loud sound, but in the silence of the hall, it was ear-piercing. Everyone looked toward the source, only to realize it had come from the black dog Fandou lying at Gu Mang's feet.

Fandou seemed as witless as his master. Since his master was sitting calmly, Fandou was also markedly relaxed, drooling as he whined and snored in his sleep. Amused, Gu Mang placed his pale, bare feet on his fluffy fur. Subjected to a stepping-on even in his sleep, Fandou whimpered and blinked open his beady eyes to see Gu Mang was just playing. He closed his eyes and went back to dreaming, letting Gu Mang's jade-pale feet sink deep into his fur as they rubbed his belly and soft ears.

But moments later, Fandou sensed something. He flattened his ears and stared in the direction of the receiving hall as he yipped out an inquisitive bark.

A servant ran inside. Thinking Mo Xi had returned, Li Wei was overcome with delight. But the servant's stunned expression wrung his relief instantly back into anxiety. "What's going on?"

"Head Housekeeper Li." The servant was visibly distressed. "Th-there's another group of people outside."

"Who?!"

Before the servant could answer, the newcomers pushed their way into Xihe Manor, heedless of decorum. The bootlicking servant at the fore shouted with unimaginable pomposity, "Wangshu-jun has arrived!"

112

A-Lian Wants Him Too

E VERYONE EXCHANGED stunned glances as Murong Lian
sauntered into Xihe Manor with his pipe held high. A group
of Wangshu Manor attendants followed in his wake.

The people he brought were all wearing the blue and gold of
nobility, the bat insignia embroidered on their robes flashing. This
crowd of glittering cultivators entered the manor like a knife, cutting through the attendants Zhou He had brought.

No one expected Murong Lian to come calling in the dead of
night, nor did they know what brought him here. The hall gazed at
him in confused silence.

Only Fandou showed no signs of ill will, perhaps because he remembered gorging himself on Murong Lian's stores back at Luomei
Pavilion. The instant he saw Murong Lian, he jumped up in excitement, rushing over to run joyous circles around him.

"Arf arf! Woof woof woof!"

Gu Mang felt like he'd been betrayed by a comrade.

The big black dog leapt up and down, barking as he nuzzled at
Murong Lian's left hand with enthusiasm. Murong Lian didn't care
for animals at the best of times; he waved his wide sleeves. "Where
did the damn dog come from? It's slobbering on this lord's clothes!
Get it out of here!"

"Yes, yes!" Li Wei hastily answered. "Aiya, Wangshu-jun honors us with his presence; please excuse this subordinate for not coming out to greet him. A thousand pardons, a thousand pardons."

As he spoke, he gestured for the other servants to collar Fandou and take him to the back courtyard. Fandou whimpered plaintively, his long tongue lolling as he looked back at Murong Lian with every step until the servants finally managed to drag him away.

Murong Lian sighed and rolled his eyes, then lowered his head to straighten his brocade robes. "Crazy dogs taking after their crazy owners," he muttered.

Only after the fuss was over did everyone return to their senses, each making their obeisance and greeting Murong Lian. None of those present held high positions; the only noble was Zhou He, and his station was a sight lower than Murong Lian's. Even he had to satisfy etiquette; he rose and performed his bow. Zhou He was a lunatic obsessed with magic techniques, but he respected people with actual ability. Trash like Murong Lian were, in his opinion, no more than scum whose veins ran with noble blood. His bow was indifferent. "Wangshu-jun."

The servants behind Zhou He lowered their heads and bowed as well. "Greetings to Wangshu-jun."

In this roomful of people, only Gu Mang hadn't moved. To others he looked like an idiot, but in fact he was surreptitiously observing this lord whom he had served for almost twenty years. Gu Mang knew Murong Lian's habits all too well, so it was only he who noticed something amiss—specifically, something about Murong Lian's style of dress.

Murong Lian was a man who adored extravagance. He constantly flaunted his noble birth and fabulous wealth like a peacock fanning its feathers. He wasn't like Mo Xi, who didn't dwell on his wealth or care for ostentatious food and sumptuous clothing. Neither was he like Mengze; though each garment she wore was eye-wateringly expensive, its subtlety was a mark of its quality. Murong Lian, on the contrary, belonged to a class of people whose every action screamed, *This lord is rich*; each puff of ephemera carried the scent of golden cowries. He preferred his clothing and accessories to impress his enormous wealth upon others from at least a mile away.

It was his habit, whenever he went out, to fasten the most costly gold or jade ornaments in his hair. Yes, they were heavy; no, it didn't matter as long as they were flashy. Best if they could dazzle the rabble's eyes until they couldn't see a thing.

But Murong Lian wasn't flashy at all right now. Though he was attired in a set of lavish sapphire robes with golden trim, the light blue layer that should've been worn beneath was absent; only the snowy-white of a silk inner robe showed beneath his collar. His hair-knot was unusual as well, secured by a simple sandalwood hairpin. It was obviously something he chose for comfort, a careless accessory he wore while holed up at home with no plans to see anyone. It seemed Murong Lian had rushed out the door so quickly he only had time to grab the robe. He hadn't even redone his hair.

Gu Mang found himself frowning, baffled. Zhou He had prepared the black magic gu worms yesterday. He wanted Gu Mang for experiments, so he hastened over to fetch him. What had Murong Lian come for?

As Gu Mang thought, Murong Lian lifted those sultry peach-blossom eyes and swept a glance around the room. His gaze paused momentarily on Zhou He, then landed on Gu Mang. In the instant Gu Mang met Murong Lian's eyes, he felt an earth-shattering pain spike through his skull, as if something in his head had let out a heartrending scream, trying to escape in terror and fury...

He clapped a hand to his forehead, screwing his eyes shut. Scarlet filled his vision as a twisted voice bellowed in his ears—

Let go of me... Let go of me! I'll make you live a life worse than death—a life worse than death!

Fresh blood rushed out like waves breaking on the shore, and scraps of vision flashed chaotically before his eyes. He saw corpses piled into mountains, gore seeping through the city walls, the earth bathed in sunset's bloody glow, broken weapons in the sand. A sadistic satisfaction rose in his heart as he clamored for more death. He seemed to be flying through this mortal hell, endless scarlet as far as the eye could see. The pungent scent of copper seeped into his bones. He couldn't tell what he was feeling; it was euphoric delight crossed with black despair. As if his soul was being cut into two...

"General Gu."

He tensed. This quiet address yanked Gu Mang from the surging pool of blood. He jerked his head up, panting through parted lips, clear blue eyes searching for the speaker. He met Murong Lian's fox-like gaze once more.

Murong Lian took a puff of ephemera, slowly exhaling smoke. "Let's see, did you have fun on your shameless little trip to Bat Island with Xihe-jun?"

Gu Mang said nothing. After a few heartbeats, that head-splitting agony receded; only the warm wetness in his blue eyes remained as his temples pulsed painfully. Gu Mang deliberately closed his eyes, straightening his back in his chair. His lips moved. Mimicking his manner from before, he quietly replied. "Mn. Had fun."

All these important guests had driven Li Wei to the point of tears. He looked at Murong Lian, then at Gu Mang, and finally at Zhou He. In the end, he lowered his head, fetched another tray of tea and snacks, and offered it to Murong Lian.

"Wangshu-jun, please take a seat and have some tea. Xihe-jun will soon—"

"No need, I'm not here for Fireball." The soft tips of Murong Lian's fingers tapped the tea tray as he pushed it away. He pointed at Gu Mang with his pipe, sneering. "I'm here for *him*."

Housekeeper Li was at a complete loss.

Murong Lian smoothed the front of his blue and gold robes. "You've had your fun idling around long enough. Get up."

Everyone looked between Murong Lian and Gu Mang in confusion.

"Come with me," Murong Lian commanded.

Other than Zhou He, no one in the hall had the faintest idea what was going on. Gu Mang didn't move, watching Murong Lian quietly.

The wrinkle between Zhou He's brows deepened when he was angry, making him look increasingly demonic. He said with mounting irritation, "Wangshu-jun, what do you mean by this?"

"What else? Does Elder Zhou not understand?" Murong Lian turned his head languidly, sultry eyes flicking toward Zhou He. "I've come to take the prisoner."

"You've come to take the prisoner?"

"That's right." Murong Lian took another lazy drag on his pipe, holding the smoke in his mouth before slowly blowing it in Zhou He's face. His indolent smile blossomed like a slumbering flower, but the tongue beneath was as venomous as any snake. He smirked. "Sishu Elder, this lord has come to claim him for black magic experiments."

If the entire hall had been confounded before, now the mood turned to one of alarm.

Zhou He's expression was ugly; he looked as if he wanted nothing more than to hack open Murong Lian's skull and turn his brains to mince. An entire lifetime's worth of self-restraint was all that kept him from exploding at Murong Lian. Even so, the sparks flashing in his eyes were terrifying, his gaze vulture-like in its ferocity.

"Wangshu-jun." Each word was forced through the gaps in Zhou He's teeth. "If I remember correctly, I am the top elder of Sishu Terrace, not you."

"Aiyo." Murong Lian bared his teeth in a mirthless smile, voice syrupy. "Elder Zhou, if this lord remembers correctly, I am His Imperial Majesty's cousin, not you."

Zhou He slammed the table in rage. "Why are you bringing that up?! What does it have to do with me?!"

"What *doesn't* it have to do with you? Both of us wish to do black magic experiments right now. Everything has been prepared; all we're missing is the test subject." Murong Lian pointed at Gu Mang. "What do you think? Will His Imperial Majesty give him to you, or to me?"

This was Murong Lian's most shameless trick. He liked to bring up the emperor whenever possible, name-dropping his cousin every second word, and no one could say a thing against it.

Zhou He's deep purple lapels rose and fell with his heaving breaths. He glared at Murong Lian. "Wangshu-jun, do you intend to pick a fight with me?"

"Who's picking a fight? It's simply an unfortunate coincidence." Murong Lian lifted his pipe to his lips and continued unhurriedly. "You happened to have prepared your black magic gu worms last night. It's the same for me—I received a set of the Liao Kingdom's black magic spells just today and I require someone to try them on. Look, we both need a dog. But—" Murong Lian paused, lifting his chin in Gu Mang's direction. "This dog happens to be one this lord has raised since childhood. By all logic and all rights, this lord should be the one to slaughter it."

Zhou He ground his teeth. "You're certain you wish to oppose me in this?"

Murong Lian's gaze drifted back to Zhou He, more enigmatic than ephemera smoke, his voice satin-soft. "Hm? So what if I do? Does Elder Zhou want to sulk about it?"

Zhou He was silent a moment. The veins at his temples stood out so far the servants across the hall could see them.

Li Wei thought: *The two of you can go ahead and start fighting; daggers or pipes, it's none of my business if you start stabbing each other with them. But could you have your squabble outside Xihe Manor? If this lunatic Zhou really blows up and stabs Murong Lian to death in our great hall, the blame will fall on my lord.*

As Li Wei was worriedly staging countless unspeakable and bloody outcomes in his head, Zhou He got his fury under control. When he spoke again, his tone was menacing. "What if I refuse?"

Murong Lian narrowed his eyes. "Then I'd suggest you use your little Lieying to poke around in your own brain," he said with a sigh. "Perhaps the contents have gone bad or rotted away."

The last shred of a cold smile vanished from Zhou He's face. "Very well. You're really insisting on making this difficult?" Gaze unwavering, Zhou He lifted a hand and spoke to the attendant standing behind him: "Bring it here."

"What do you think you can use against me?" Murong Lian asked carelessly. "I'm quite clear on your family's circumstances. You have a token of immunity from the late emperor that exempts you from imperial execution, but that'll be for saving your life, not getting your way."

Zhou He didn't bother to reply. The attendant returned carefully carrying a brocade box wrapped in pale yellow satin.

As soon as he saw the color of the box, the smile on Murong Lian's face froze.

"You must know what this is." Zhou He took the gleaming brocade box and opened it with a decisive *snap* to reveal a scroll of top-grade East Sea snowy mermaid silk. In all of Chonghua, this priceless sea-silk was used for one thing only.

Murong Lian's head shot up, eyes flashing. "When did His Imperial Majesty give you the edict?! Why wasn't I told?"

Zhou He coolly unrolled the imperial decree so Murong Lian could see the emperor's seal and inscription. "His Imperial Majesty gave me this edict the first year Gu Mang returned. Take a good look, Wangshu-jun. By decree of His Imperial Majesty, my Sishu Terrace shall be the first institution to experiment on Gu Mang." He paused, then icily spat two words in a tone that brooked no argument. "Step aside."

113

I'll Trust You Once More

WITHIN THE CULTIVATION academy, Jiang Yexue sat at a small poplar table inlaid with spirit jade. The legs of the table curved outward, and its frame was set with precious Guiyuan stone, flowing with abundant spiritual energy.

Most artificing workshops had a little table like this one, used to repair broken items. Nevertheless, each artificer had a different level of skill. Some could at most repair a broken bowl, while some, like Jiang Yexue and Murong Chuyi, could do much, much more.

These techniques appeared simple, but in reality, they made high requirements of the artificers who used them; the slightest imbalance in the flow of spiritual energy could trigger irreversible consequences. Any young cultivator who wanted to become an artificer would expect repair to feature heavily in their graduation exam at the cultivation academy. It was said that, for his final examination, the eldest son of the most renowned artificer family of his generation—Yue Chenqing's father, Yue Juntian—restored one hundred and seventy-eight broken treasures in an astonishingly short period of time to break the academy's century-old record. Yue Juntian loved to boast of this, and had even once tried to use it to intimidate his young brother-in-law Murong Chuyi. The story ended with Murong Chuyi losing his temper and destroying more than a thousand exquisite items in the Yue Clan's Pavilion of Treasures—and then, within a single incense time, restoring every single one before Yue Juntian's ashen face and putting a vicious dent his brother-in-law's pride. Yue Juntian never mentioned the old glory of his graduation exam again.

However, both Murong Chuyi and Yue Juntian had shattered things solely to show off their skills; those items were carelessly broken, not intentionally destroyed. Jiang Yexue's situation was different. Right now he was facing a pile of history-recording jade scrolls that had been ground almost to powder. Even disregarding the state they were in, the pieces were completely out of order.

"...What do you think?"

"No wonder the person who smashed these jade scrolls left them behind." Jiang Yexue sighed. "History-recording jade scrolls are imbued with spiritual energy. Even reduced to dust, they would still be easy to trace. But after destroying them like this, I'm afraid there are no more than three people in all of Chonghua who could restore them."

Mo Xi was silent for a beat. "My trespass into the Imperial Censorate won't remain hidden for long. I'm asking for your help—every scroll counts. Learning anything would be preferable to ignorance."

"If there was some secret motive behind Gu-xiong's old case, I'd want to uncover it too," Jiang Yexue said. "But..."

Mo Xi's gaze darkened. "Is it impossible?"

"It's not that." Jiang Yexue ran his fingers over a scroll that had been partially pieced together on the table. "But, as I'm sure you can see, I can only perform a rudimentary repair right now. I can't restore their original appearance. If you want perfect and unharmed jade scrolls, it would take at least a month."

Mo Xi shook his head. "I can't wait that long. His Imperial Majesty would definitely notice something amiss."

To this, Jiang Yexue had no answer.

"I want to at least learn something before he finds out what I did." Mo Xi raised his eyes, deep and black as an endless night. "Do you have any other ideas?" he murmured.

Jiang Yexue hesitated for a long moment. His gaze roved over Mo Xi's handsome and defined features, fixing on his hair ribbon before he lowered his eyes. He kept his head down and stroked those jade scrolls in silence.

But from this, Mo Xi seized a wisp of hope. "You do, don't you?"

Jiang Yexue closed his eyes, lifting slender fingers and carefully aligning a fragment at the edge of one of the scrolls. "Yes." Before Mo Xi could respond, Jiang Yexue quickly continued. "But Xihe-jun, this is too dangerous."

"Why? Because an incomplete restoration might show me a false version of the past, or because it would damage the scrolls and make a full repair impossible?"

Jiang Yexue studied Mo Xi. Rarely had he seen such uncontrolled anxiety on this man's face. But at the moment, Mo Xi was haggard from days of torment; his face held so many emotions he looked like a stranger.

"Because your body can't withstand it," said Jiang Yexue. "You know that even now, no one has fully restored the Space-Time Gate of Life and Death, first of the three forbidden techniques. But within the Nine Provinces, there are countless techniques and treasures derived from the Gate. Most have only mimicked the smallest fraction of it, or perhaps they're just a prototype reconstruction—like the Time Mirror you just experienced."

The haze of confusion in Mo Xi's eyes gradually dissipated. He gazed at the scrolls on Jiang Yexue's little table. "And these history-recording jade scrolls are the same?"

"Yes. The Space-Time Gate of Life and Death is the original, the Time Mirror is a copy, and these..." He tapped the edge of the table with porcelain-pale fingers. "These history-recording jade scrolls operate on the same principle. Their power is limited, but these too originate from the Space-Time Gate of Life and Death that Fuxi left behind. When it comes to this forbidden technique, the legends tell of a prophecy—whoever opens the Space-Time Gate of Life and Death is doomed to a grisly death. The Time Mirror and the history-recording jade scrolls don't have the power to change the past like the Gate, and they won't lay a curse on the transgressor's life, but..." He paused, looking into Mo Xi's weary face. "Every time you cross this boundary, it'll cost you your health... You already felt the effects on Bat Island."

Mo Xi neither confirmed nor denied this.

"Xihe-jun, we've known each other half our lives. Your bloodline is pure, and your spiritual energy is unmatched. In the past, you've never shown any weakness no matter how exhausted by battle. But ever since you emerged from the Time Mirror, both your spiritual energy and your physical condition have been pushed to the brink." Jiang Yexue heaved a sigh. "What will happen to you if you recklessly enter these unrepaired jade scrolls?"

Jiang Yexue's soft, white fingers slid over those icy-cold scroll slips, which glowed a soft ivory. "Your body might be torn apart, or your spiritual core could go berserk."

"I have to go. Gu Mang had some secret back when he defected, I'm certain of it."

The two of them had spoken at almost the same time. The room fell into silence. Bamboo swayed outside the window, a soft rustle in the breeze.

Mo Xi had heard Jiang Yexue's cautionary words. He lowered

his lashes. "Jiang-xiong. After all these twists and turns, I still choose to trust him."

Jiang Yexue looked back at Mo Xi, calm and silent. Those gentle black eyes seemed a little wet. "Mo Xi."

Mo Xi said nothing.

"You already trusted him once, back then."

Eight years ago in the throne room, a young general stood amid a full court of civil and military officials. He was extremely furious yet profoundly heartbroken, facing a horde of wolves and tigers alone.

Mo Xi's shaking voice seemed to filter through the sands of time to echo in their ears once more. "Who defected? How could Gu Mang ever defect?! Have you lost your minds? He didn't defect while leading our nation's great army, he didn't defect when his life hung by a thread and he was beset on all sides; he's given every last drop of his zeal and passion, he offered up the best of his youth to this land beneath your feet, and you call him a traitor? Have you lost your *minds?*"

Every official paled. "Xihe-jun..."

"Mo Xi!" the emperor thundered in rage. "Who gave you the guts!"

But Mo Xi was like a lonely beast that had lost its companion. No, he was hurt far worse than that. He was like an eagle shorn of its wings, a proud man with his legs torn away, an artist with his eyes blinded. Like a patriot gutted of their loyalty.

That naive, righteous, sorrowful youth faced them all, surrounded by whispers and criticism. He was the odd one out, opposing the nobles, yet those slave cultivators Gu Mang commanded could never take him into their midst. He stood alone in the middle of the hall, guarding the wreckage left by his brother, his beloved, his god.

The rims of Mo Xi's eyes were red and wet. Near tears, he still spoke with absolute faith. "He wouldn't defect."

No one answered him.

"I'm willing to swear an oath on my life, to testify on his behalf. He will definitely come back..."

In truth, he didn't know if he was speaking these vows for the emperor's ears, or as a final consolation to himself.

Jiang Yexue sighed. "You trusted him once, and you almost lost your life that time. Are you really willing to trust him again, to seek a truth that may not even exist?"

Mo Xi was silent for a moment. "That year, on the Dongting warship, I said something to him."

A string of waxen tears fell from a candle, flowing into the depths of the lotus flower lamp and quietly pooling at the bottom.

"I said I could accept anything as long as he turned back." Mo Xi closed his eyes, folding his fingers against his brow. He lowered his head, his voice a whisper. "As long as he turned back, it didn't matter if he killed me. Life, glory...none of it mattered to me anymore. But he didn't. He cut ties with me with that knife, then told me with the heads of thousands of soldiers that he had chosen a path of vengeance."

Mo Xi went on, "These past few years, he's killed countless cultivators of Chonghua. All lives lost at his hands. When those noble sons died, their parents and kin cursed me and hated me— they said back then, I had vouched for a devil. They said it was my brother who razed Chonghua's villages, who slaughtered the families of common folk... They said I was blind, that I had no conscience... Debts of blood piled up before my eyes, but still I didn't dare face him. I didn't want to fight a battle with him as an opponent."

As he spoke, he drew on all the pride and nobility in his bones to steady himself, but his voice was shaking. Jiang Yexue could hear the sobs caught in his throat, like a jug of wine kept sealed for eight years, soaked with such bitterness his words were barely discernible.

Mo Xi gradually opened his eyes. "They weren't wrong," he said hoarsely, self-mockingly. "Through the years, I've come to know of the thousands of lives he owes Chonghua. I've walked through villages devastated by war, I've seen cultivators fallen in pools of blood, their intestines pulled out and eaten by beasts, I've seen wives who lost their husbands, old men who lost their sons, children sobbing beside the corpses of their parents."

He kneaded at his forehead in pain. In all these years, was there anyone he could say these things to? He had stayed cold, controlled, and steadfast. Others at least had their wives, their sons, their parents—but whom did he have? The only light and warmth in his life had become his darkness.

What did he have left...?

It was only today—only when he stood to risk everything for a fragile hope—that Mo Xi finally said some of this out loud to Jiang Yexue. His shoulders shivered as he continued, his voice so hoarse it was unrecognizable. "I've seen the bones of a deputy general dismembered alive, I've seen enough corpses to fill a river—all the work of a man I spoke for." Mo Xi closed his eyes in grief. "The work of the Liao Kingdom cultivators under his command... Can you imagine how that feels?"

As if all those souls of the wrongfully dead were gathered round him, condemning him, cursing him, howling at him, begging him for help, demanding his life, screaming and thrashing in anguish— *your Gu Mang, your lighthouse, the one you admired and cherished most in your life—he killed us!*

Xihe-jun...Xihe-jun...

The fourth in a line of loyal subjects, the son of heroes... Chonghua's guardian deity... Save us... Protect us... Please, give us justice, take that incurable demon with his hands laved in blood to the gallows, please— kill him!

We're begging you to wash away the blood of innocents from your country.

Please... Please, give us justice...

Why aren't you doing it? Why aren't you meeting him in battle and fighting him to the death, why aren't you resolutely donning your armor, entering the fray, and taking his life? Do you still trust him? Do you still love him...?

Are you still so stubbornly hoping this devil will turn back, hoping he'll come to his senses, hoping for him to return to the past?

You too are a traitor... Coward... Traitor! Coward! Traitor!

Mo Xi buried his face in his palms, then covered his ears. These voices had followed him for eight years, tearing at him, tormenting him, whipping him—

Yes! He had once wished for Gu Mang to die! When he remembered an orphaned child wailing in his arms, mewling like a kitten, dying, unable to be saved from the Liao Kingdom's black magic poison as the demonic qi spread... When he remembered a hoary, wizened old grandpa, leaning on his cane in a broken and deserted village beneath the bloody dusk, weeping endlessly, losing his mind, repeating the names of his children who would never come home... How could he not wish for Gu Mang to be executed; how could he not want the general who committed these atrocities killed?!

Yet even when Gu Mang was captured, Mo Xi had chosen to say nothing. He'd left it to Chonghua, to the emperor, to deal with Gu Mang according to the law. But...

Tears dampened his long lashes.

But when he really saw him again...he discovered that his heart, which should have been tempered into steel long ago, was still made of flesh.

He was selfish.

He was ashamed of his selfishness; day and night he felt an unease that kept him from sleep; he would see the child in his arms open blood-red eyes to scream and curse at him, he would see that old man's face transform into a hideous mask of fury to snarl and shout at him.

Traitor! Traitor...

Jiang Yexue could hardly bear to see him like this. "Mo-xiong..." he murmured.

Mo Xi didn't answer. He paused for a while, a despairing smile spreading across his lips. "If the history-recording scrolls show me the truth from back then, if I find out he really had some secret reason—" He looked up, eyes glimmering as he gazed at Jiang Yexue. "Even if I died, I would be happy. At least, in this life, I didn't protect the wrong person or make the wrong judgment. I would... We would..."

His composure threatened to shatter once more. Mo Xi closed his eyes, swallowing thickly, and fell silent.

We would finally stop being a traitor and a coward. These eight years spent drowning in a sea of blood would finally come to an end.

114

Trials Begin

ABROKEN JADE SCROLL was spread out on the table, emitting a weak glow. It gave the impression of someone on the verge of death toppled over in the snow, waiting to see if anyone would hear the last wisp of truth issue from their dying lips.

"Xihe-jun, I'll warn you one last time," said Jiang Yexue. "I need you to fully understand this before you make a decision. The history-recording jade scrolls are not like the ancient godly mirror. In the end, they're only a common item. If you insist on prying into their contents, they will require your flesh, blood, and spiritual energy to fill in the cracks. You can still choose to wait. His Imperial Majesty might not discover you were the one who took the scrolls within the month. If you wait, you needn't put yourself at risk; the whole endeavor will be safer."

Mo Xi didn't make a sound, lowering lashes dense as smoke to hide the light that glistened in his eyes.

Eight years ago, as he watched Gu Mang fall into dissolution, he had chosen to wait. He had waited for Gu Mang to pull himself together, waited for time to slowly heal his wounds... But what had that gotten him? Time could not make a collapsed pillar stand tall once more. Its passage would only make broken ruins of what had been a majestic building.

"I've already made him wait too long," Mo Xi said.

Jiang Yexue looked at him, silent.

"Qingxu, please begin."

In the hall of Xihe Manor, Zhou He had one hand on the dagger Lieying at his waist and the other tucked behind his back. Beside him, Gu Mang was restrained by a handful of Sishu Terrace attendants. Zhou He's gaze swept over the anxious crowd from Xihe Manor, past Housekeeper Li with his forehead sheened in sweat and Murong Lian's glowering brows.

A small and icy smile played over Zhou He's lips. "No need to send us off. I'll see myself out." He readied himself to take Gu Mang away. A shichen had passed. There was no news from Mo Xi, and Zhou He had an imperial edict that named Sishu Terrace as the organization with priority access to Gu Mang for any experimentation. It was ironclad; even Murong Lian couldn't snatch Gu Mang from him.

"E-E-Elder Zhou!" Housekeeper Li was seized by an eleventh-hour desperation. "Won't you stay a little longer and have a cup of tea? Xihe Manor has Yaochi Flying Leaves from a thirty-year-old mother plant on the immortal Penglai Island! It was gifted to my lord by the late emperor on the appointment of his title!"

Housekeeper Li's words weren't without thought. Zhou He was a tea aficionado. In a necessary contrast with Sishu Terrace's gory day-to-day affairs, it was said that Zhou He's second-favorite hobby, after digging through people's brains, was tasting tea. Every year the auction house had first-class tea leaves, Zhou He would send someone to bid for them without fail. This was known to all of Chonghua.

As expected, Zhou He's pupils contracted slightly at the words *Yaochi Flying Leaves*. Housekeeper Li wasted no time turning up the charm. "This tea has been put away for more than ten years. We don't bring it out for ordinary guests—only connoisseurs like Elder Zhou are worthy of drinking it!"

Zhou He's hand caressed Lieying's hilt, as if torn between the joy of gouging out brains and the pleasures of tasting tea. But such commonplace pursuits were, after all, no match for deranged fixation. Zhou He pursed his lips, jerking his chin toward his subordinates. "There's no need. Take him away."

"Yes!"

Housekeeper Li looked like a dog who had failed to protect the house, terrified of his owner's punishment for letting a thief in. He gripped the doorframe as though on the verge of fainting.

The attendants had just about shoved Gu Mang into Sishu Terrace's waiting carriage when Murong Lian spoke up. "Wait a minute."

Zhou He glared at him. "Wangshu-jun, you've seen the imperial edict. What more do you have to say?"

With an impatient puff on his pipe, Murong Lian said, "Take him, then. But let's be clear: you can't have too much fun with him. I'm waiting to put this specimen to use too—if you spoil or kill him, and I can't carry out my experiments..." He looked at him, carelessly rapping his pipe against Zhou He's cheek. "Then your Lian-ge will be very angry," he crooned. "And if your Lian-ge gets angry, you won't find life in Chonghua so easy anymore."

Zhou He scoffed. "Murong Lian, how shameless can you be? You're only three months older than I. Where do you get the nerve to call yourself *Ge*?"

Murong Lian took another drag of ephemera and blew it over Zhou He's face with a smile. "Gege likes it that way. If you're not happy about it, your mom can shove you back in and birth you again. If you were three months older than me, I'd call you Ge too."

"You—!"

"Hold it, now." Murong Lian waggled a finger at him. "Don't *you* this or *me* that—your Lian-ge just had a good idea."

Zhou He glared at him.

"Why don't we do this?" Teeth on his pipe, Murong Lian swaggered over to his carriage. "Since His Imperial Majesty gave you the edict, I naturally can't stop you. You may take him tonight, and I'll come pick him up tomorrow. My black magic spells are also itching to be tested. One night with the subject will be more than enough for you, won't it?"

"No."

Murong Lian narrowed his eyes. This should have made his peach-blossom eyes look flirtatious and demure, but his irises showed the whites beneath, giving him a vicious air. "Sweetheart, don't assume you can do as you please just because you've got an imperial edict. After today, you'll still need to keep living in Chonghua."

Zhou He's light-brown eyes flicked toward him. "Which experiment has Wangshu-jun heard of that can be carried out in one night?"

Murong Lian stared at him. That water pipe in his hand seemed to have taken on his mood; smoke sputtered from it indignantly. "Fine. No time limit then. But I need some assurance this person will stay alive for my turn at the very least."

"What assurance?"

In answer, Murong Lian stepped forward and grabbed at the lapels of Gu Mang's robe to yank him over. He cast a lazy, sidelong look at Zhou He. "I'll leave a tracker." As everyone watched, he took a ring off of his left hand; the precious stone inlaid on its band glistened sapphire-blue. He cast a spell on it, then slid it onto Gu Mang's thumb.

The instant it touched him, Gu Mang was gripped by an inexplicable feeling of panic. His heart pounded with alarm.

"It's essentially no different from the tracking incantation Fireball laid on you before." Murong Lian grabbed Gu Mang's hand and examined it before nodding. "I've cast a spell so it can't be removed. Now I'll at least have some idea if you're dead or alive."

These words were not so much spoken for Gu Mang as for Zhou He. Murong Lian waved his hands as if bored. "All right, you little twerps can get lost now."

Gu Mang stared down at the ring on his thumb, the fear and shock ringing through his mind growing ever more vivid. Unthinking, he looked up to catch Murong Lian's gaze—but Murong Lian had already turned around, taking a long drag on his pipe and exhaling fragrant smoke.

He watched Murong Lian's figure from behind. There was something about this ring that was missing from his memories, and whatever it was, Murong Lian seemed to know it quite well. But even without his memories, Gu Mang knew Murong Lian; he didn't expect this man to tell him anything. And yet—as he stroked the blue stone of the ring, an uncontrollable feeling of familiarity assailed him. Gu Mang felt a bizarre conviction: this ring should have belonged to him from the start, it should always be wherever he was.

Why would he have such a thought? What memories were linked to this ring?

Zhou He left. Murong Lian stayed where he was, gazing out at the starry night as he slowly finished a pipe full of ephemera. After using such a strong hallucinogenic, it was as if his face had been immersed in spring water. A dreamy pleasure showed on his features, yet there seemed to be some warped emotion suppressed beneath. Only after a final exhale did that emotion disperse with the smoke, gradually disappearing...

"Li Wei."

"Ah, does Wangshu-jun have any orders?"

Back to the lights of the manor, Murong Lian stood a while longer, face upturned to the endless night sky. The wooden hairpin keeping his hair-knot in place was utterly at odds with his ostentatious gilt robes. After several moments, Murong Lian at last turned, his gaze shadowed. "Is Mo Xi dead?"

"...Huh?"

"It's been a full shichen, and you still haven't found him—is he dead or are you Xihe Manor people a bunch of useless insects?"

Li Wei hastily came to the defense of his lord and Xihe Manor, sounding chagrined. "Um... Wangshu-jun, you can't say it like that— you saw how it was. We've sent near a hundred messenger butterflies, but not a single one found the lord. Our lord is an important member of the Bureau of Military Affairs; if he's in his office, the messenger butterflies can't pass the barrier. And we can't possibly go look for him in the palace..."

He wasn't wrong, but Murong Lian's mood didn't improve in the slightest. Biting down on his pipe, he turned and began to pace. "Other than the palace, where in the capital are messenger butterflies unable to enter?"

Li Wei was shocked. "Wangshu-jun doesn't know?"

"What use does this lord have of this kind of worthless knowledge! Does this lord send his own messages?" Murong Lian snapped. "Tell me!"

"Ah, y-y-yes," Li Wei replied hastily. "Other than the palace, messenger butterflies can't reach the prison, the Jiang residence, Murong Chuyi's artificer workshop..." He named more than twenty places. Toward the end, Li Wei's voice sank to a murmur, and he snuck a glance at Murong Lian.

"What are you looking at me for?"

Li Wei braced himself. "And the entertainment hall and brothel Wangshu-jun runs."

Murong Lian glared at him, waiting for him to finish.

"And the cultivation academy."

"Send people to all those places to look for Fireball," Murong Lian ordered. "Right now—go."

"At this rate we'll be searching till tomorrow morning—" But when he met Murong Lian's eyes, Li Wei shrank back. "W-w-we'll go right away."

After handing out instructions, Murong Lian cocked his head in thought, running through those twenty-odd locations again. At last, he turned to his own attendants. "We're leaving."

"Does my lord plan to return to Wangshu Manor?"

"No." Murong Lian stepped onto a cushioned stool to enter the carriage, voice cold. "First to the prison, then to the cultivation academy. It might not be convenient for them to go to these places. I'll go."

An hour later, Jiang Yexue sat in a rosewood official's chair, his slender fingers folded over his knees. He stared fixedly at Mo Xi, slumped unconscious beside the history-recording jade scrolls.

The lights in the room were dim. Red spiritual energy flowed ceaselessly from Mo Xi's heart, enveloping the broken jade scrolls. They appeared more whole than before; his spiritual energy had bonded broken edges and filled in the jagged gaps.

Jiang Yexue lifted a hand to look at the water clock in his palm. Mo Xi had been under for a quarter-hour. It had taken a considerable amount of his spiritual energy to repair the scrolls to this extent. By now, Mo Xi could likely begin to read the information recorded within the history scrolls within the spell.

But at this moment, someone started pounding violently on the door. Jiang Yexue frowned and called out, "Who is it?"

Murong Lian's voice answered him. "Damn cripple, get out here and open the door!"

Jiang Yexue looked at the stolen jade scrolls on the table, as well as the unconscious Mo Xi. "It's very late. I'm afraid I'm not in a suitable state to meet with Wangshu-jun. I ask—"

With a loud *bang*, Murong Lian kicked open the door.

The two of them looked at each other through a floating haze of dust lit by the moon behind them. Murong Lian's gaze moved quickly away from Jiang Yexue, flitting across the interior of the room. He stormed toward the bedroom without another word. But after searching the premises to his satisfaction, he found no one. Murong Lian returned to the main room. "Mo Xi isn't here?"

Jiang Yexue's expression was unchanged, calm and at ease, but his pale, slender fingers were pressed to the most covert mechanism on the wheelchair's armrest. "Why would he be here?" He smiled faintly. "If Wangshu-jun was looking for Xihe-jun, you could've just asked. Did you have to burst in?"

But Murong Lian, with his temper, was accustomed to making trouble. He wouldn't knock on a door if he could push it open, and he wouldn't push it open if he could kick it in. Goody Two-shoes like Jiang Yexue pissed him off, so he was rude as a matter of course. He stared at Jiang Yexue, furious. "The dog this lord raised was left in the care of his manor, and now that dog's been taken by Zhou He for black magic experiments—shouldn't I make him pay?!"

Jiang Yexue stared at him. "Gu Mang was taken by Sishu Terrace?"

Murong Lian didn't bother to repeat himself. He gnashed his teeth. "Why can't I find Mo Xi anywhere... Could he really be in the secret meeting room at the Bureau of Military Affairs?"

Of course Mo Xi was not in the secret meeting room at the Bureau of Military Affairs. He was still collapsed beside the history-recording jade scrolls, inches from Jiang Yexue and Murong Lian. But Jiang Yexue had filled his bamboo house with a master artificer's mechanisms; by the time Murong Lian broke through the door, Jiang Yexue had activated the living room's illusion spell. Mo Xi hadn't moved from his original spot—but he was invisible to Murong Lian.

"All right then. If you see him, tell him what I said." Murong Lian took a gulp of smoke and exhaled as he spoke, his tone peevish. "I'm leaving."

"I won't see you off, then."

The moment Murong Lian disappeared through the open door, Jiang Yexue wheeled over and closed it before returning to Mo Xi's side. It was quiet in the room; he stared at Mo Xi for a while, then reached out a hand to take his pulse at his neck. He frowned slightly. Mo Xi was already in the midst of reading; if he were to pull him out of it now, this undertaking would become even more dangerous. He could only wait; he couldn't intervene.

He lowered his hands, eyes dark.

As for Gu Mang...what would he endure before Mo Xi woke from chasing those secrets of the past?

115

Back to Eight
Years Ago

IN THE JADE SCROLL'S illusory realm, Mo Xi slowly opened
his eyes.

He found himself lying in an endless, shapeless darkness beneath the boundless expanse of night. A ribbon of jade-blue light
unfurled in the sky, its tightly packed seal-script characters flashing
first bright then dim. A deep and solemn voice boomed down from
above, hoarse and cracked as the damaged scrolls. "What...dost thou
wish to read?"

The history-recording jade scrolls had been successfully pieced
back together; this was the invitation to revisit the past. Mo Xi
pushed himself upright and spoke to that jade-colored light twisting across the night like the Azure Dragon with fangs and claws
bared. "I want to know whether Gu Mang had some secret reason
for defecting in this year."

That ribbon of light hung in the air, shimmering and coiling.
Just as Mo Xi's hope slowly began to cool, just as he started to
wonder if the jade scroll hadn't recorded the relevant events at
all, the beam of light exploded into dazzling sparks. Innumerable
flashing seal-script characters gathered in the shape of a massive
illusory dragon. It had slender eyes and a long mouth, its whiskers
and mane flying.

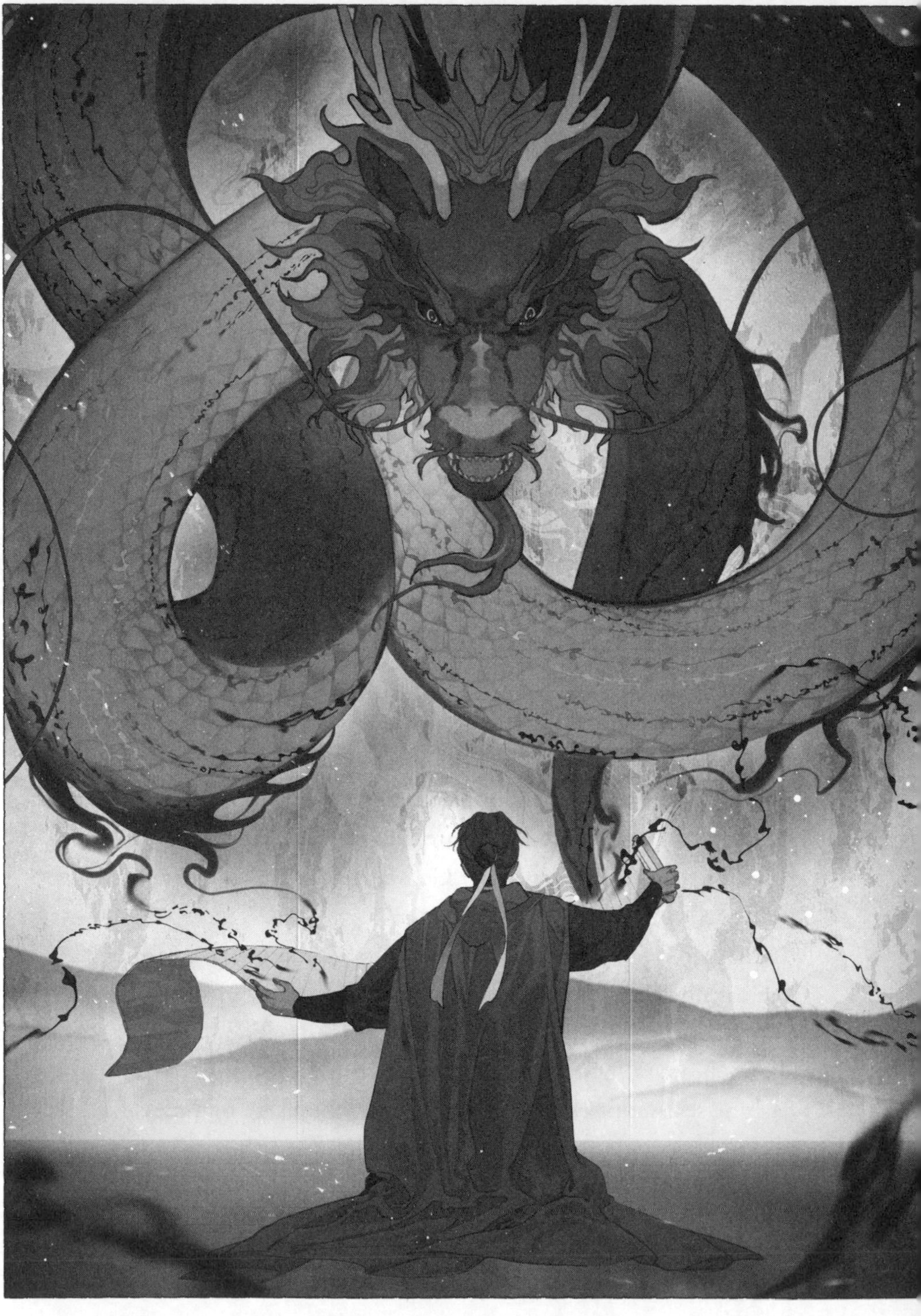

The sky within the jade scroll roiled with a thunderous storm, gales stirring the clouds like waves. Claws and scales flashed as the dragon soared up toward the nine heavens before suddenly diving down toward the minuscule figure that was Mo Xi. A sandstorm whirled to life, the burst of jade-green light blinding as thunder crashed overhead. The last thing Mo Xi knew was the massive dragon falling like a deluge from the dome of heaven, its light piercing his soul like a thousand arrows.

"The...past...is...dead..." A faint sigh, like a final warning to those who came to read the scroll. "Leave...it...to...lie..."

The interplay of light and color swept into his eyes like snow-flakes, sinking into his pupils as if trying to inscribe all those accounts carved within the jade scrolls into his flesh and blood.

The light went out.

Mo Xi panted, his vision flashing with interweaving afterimages. He stood rooted to the spot and blinked laboriously, shaking his head back and forth and trying to recover his sight as quickly as possible. He couldn't tell which day from eight years ago the history-recording jade scroll had brought him to. All he knew was that he had arrived somewhere very dim; he could hear rain pattering on the roof, drumming down and streaming over the tiles.

In time, footsteps approached, stopping a short distance away—

The rain tapped on the roof. There was no other sound. Just as Mo Xi was about to conclude he had hallucinated those footfalls, a familiar voice broke the silence.

"The commoner Gu Mang greets Your Imperial Majesty."

This voice, soft as drifting snow, was like a crack of thunder that sent shockwaves through all the blood flowing in Mo Xi's veins. A disjointed, colorful blur of images still danced before Mo Xi's eyes.

His eardrums were buzzing, but he endured his dizziness and turned around.

The night wind blew in, bringing the scent of rain and the sweet fragrance of midnight magnolia flowers. Smell, some said, was the sense engraved most deeply in one's memories, hardest to extinguish. Though he couldn't clearly see where he was, as soon as Mo Xi caught a whiff of this fragrance, he was immediately enlightened—

The Golden Terrace.

The history-recording jade scroll had brought him to the most secretive and difficult-to-reach palace hall in all of Chonghua.

The Golden Terrace was built at the edge of the palace's back mountains, with eaves like wings and interlocking brackets, towering above nine-hundred and ninety-nine steps. The entire edifice was built of yellow rosewood, and the hall had been constructed with mortise-and-tenon joints without the use of nail or glue. A field of dragon's-tongue magnolia from the immortal island on the East Sea flourished around it, the flowers a dark plum striped with white, in the shape of carp tails. They never wilted, and their fragrance was strong and unmistakable.

Dying with jeweled sword in hand to repay the trust of the king's command.[8] In every generation, only those subjects the emperor trusted and relied on most were permitted to ascend to its peak. From their youth, countless cultivators shouldered their parents' ardent hopes that in the future, they would receive an imperial edict and climb these nine hundred and ninety-nine steps secure in a glory few could hope to attain. From then on, they'd carry their greatswords into battle and leave an undying legacy of meritorious deeds. Even Mo Xi himself was only invited to the Golden Terrace

---

8   A line from Li He's poem "Song of the Yanmen Governor" about how the emperor exchanged his favor for the devotion of his hand-picked soldiers atop the golden terrace.

after he swore the Vow of Calamity and became one of these "most trusted subjects."

Never could he have expected that the first place the jade scroll brought him would be the Golden Terrace. Yet what was more astonishing was that the emperor had once summoned Gu Mang here. He had no time for further thought before he heard the emperor say, "General Gu, you've come at last."

The bright spots dancing across Mo Xi's vision were no longer as blinding as before. He closed his eyes and clenched his jaw. By the time he opened them again, he could finally see what lay in front of him.

It was a stormy night, the exact hour impossible to discern. The gauzy hanging screens on all four sides of the terrace fluttered like smoke in the rain and wind. The emperor knelt, straight-backed, on a spread mat. Beside him were lacquer railings carved with motifs of dragons and clouds, and a half-drawn bamboo screen. Outside, the rain flooded down in torrents; jade droplets splashed into the room, but the emperor paid them no mind. He turned from the distant, storm-shrouded mountains and looked through the hazy candle-light toward the entrance of the hall. Mo Xi's gaze followed his.

Once again, he saw the Gu Mang of eight years ago whom he'd glimpsed in the Time Mirror. But the Gu Mang in this history-recording jade scroll seemed somehow colder. As a clap of thunder broke the skies, a flash of lightning illuminated Gu Mang's face, stark and sinister.

"General Gu, come in."

Gu Mang pressed his lips into a tight line. He held a folded oil-paper umbrella, dripping with rainwater. There were no servants on the Golden Terrace, so Gu Mang leaned it against a pillar and strode slowly onto the terrace, bringing the cold night with him.

"Sit." The emperor gestured at the low table. "We've been waiting up for you, and now you're finally here."

Gu Mang took a seat on the opposite side. Besides coolness and apathy, there was a faint confusion in the set of Gu Mang's brows. He didn't seem to understand why the emperor had summoned him here; he'd certainly never imagined the emperor would let him set foot in such a place. As expected, after a short silence, Gu Mang said, "I'm unsure for which urgent matter Your Imperial Majesty has called me."

In lieu of an answer, the emperor toyed with the red clay pot on the table, waving a little black bamboo fan to help the tea fire burn more merrily. As the scalding steam rose into the damp, chilly wind, it was swallowed by the curtain of rain. Over the crash of the storm, the emperor spoke. "General Gu, do you despise us?"

The only sound was the rain outside.

"We heard when Xihe-jun took you out drinking, you told him you were very tired, that you couldn't bear it anymore..."

"Does Your Imperial Majesty have people tailing me?" Gu Mang's voice rang cold.

The emperor continued fanning the flame under the pot and didn't deny it.

"Why does Your Imperial Majesty make such an effort? You've stripped me of my rank, revoked my authority, detained my remaining soldiers." After a pause, Gu Mang continued. "And sentenced my dearest brother to death. These days, I'm a mere commoner. Broken wings cannot fly. Your Imperial Majesty needn't waste this sort of effort on a member of the rabble."

"We're just asking. General Gu, do you despise us?"

Gu Mang said nothing.

"In truth, you don't need to say it for us to know. You've fought wholeheartedly for the nation for so long, in so many battles, but now you have nothing left aside from yourself. We took it all from you—even when you begged us for gravestones for your brothers in front of the full court of civil and military officials, you received only mockery and derision." The emperor laughed softly. "If you could, General Gu likely would've cracked our bones for soup long ago."

"Did Your Imperial Majesty invite me here today just to chat?" asked Gu Mang.

The tea came to a boil in the crackle-glazed ceramic pot, which pinged sharply from the steam. The emperor lifted it by the hoop of its bamboo-wrapped handle and poured two cups of strong tea, one for himself and one for Gu Mang. He pushed the teacup toward Gu Mang with long fingers. "No. We asked to see you...so that we may exonerate a certain person."

Like a frozen lake splitting, the icy mask Gu Mang wore cracked to reveal human emotion. He looked up. Gu Mang's lips trembled as he stared into the emperor's eyes. After a long moment, one word stumbled from his mouth. "Who?"

Outside the curtain screen, lightning flashed. Pale light washed the sky and the mountains, reflecting in the eyes of the two staring at each other over candlelight. The emperor said, "Just who you're thinking of. Lu Zhanxing."

Thunder cleaved the skies with a *boom*. That earthshaking crash seemed to pierce the heavens like a sharp sword, the lingering rumbles puncturing the pavilion's roof to stab right into Mo Xi's heart. Cold entered his bones like waves overflowing, rushing up his spine...

Lu Zhanxing...had been falsely accused?

And more importantly, the emperor knew of it?

Rain slanted in the fierce winds, extinguishing several candle lamps. The light on the Golden Terrace dimmed. But even like this, Mo Xi could see Gu Mang's face, terrifyingly pale. It was obvious

Mo Xi wasn't the only one shocked by this news—Gu Mang was nailed to his seat, his eyes wide and blank. Only after a long while did he speak like a puppet receiving the breath of life. He paused with every syllable, his words halting. "What did you say?"

"Lu Zhanxing was falsely accused. Your brother was the victim of another's plot."

Gu Mang looked as pale as a corpse. Wind buffeted the burning candelabras on the high terrace, and the flickering light of the candles danced across his colorless face. Rain drummed down around them. A moth had hidden beneath the eaves to escape the monstrous claws of the downpour, never knowing its grave awaited it on the terrace. It fluttered around the hungry flame, as if about to dart into its fatal light at any moment.

Only after a long interval did Gu Mang speak. "Is Your Imperial Majesty joking?"

"We knew you would react like this." The emperor pushed the teacup toward Gu Mang's hand again. "Drink it. It'll get cold if you don't. This is Peach Blossom Springs immortal tea left behind by Imperial Grandfather. There are only five small bricks of it in total. Imperial Grandfather opened one to present to the Grand Chancellor at his appointment ceremony, as a show of respect. This second, we offer you today."

By now, Gu Mang's shock had yielded to fury and terror. He was like an animal spun cruelly round and round, dizzied by the carrot and the stick. What this man before him planned to do, what schemes he had in store for him, whether what came next would be honey candy or a whipping—Gu Mang knew none of it. He surged to his feet, chest heaving, and stared down at Chonghua's most respected, most powerful figure. "What does Your Imperial Majesty mean by this?!"

Mo Xi could see Gu Mang had to use a lifetime's worth of restraint to keep his voice below a shout. But Gu Mang's hands were shaking, and his nails sank deep into his palms.

The emperor picked up the teacup, looking indifferently at Gu Mang. The mournful wind caught his wide sleeves and sent them fluttering. Only then did Mo Xi realize the emperor wore neither imperial robes nor crown. He was attired in a set of unremarkable clothes with a white jade hairpin securing his simply dressed black hair.

"We mean to say that we're sorry, General Gu. We owe you an apology." He ignored Gu Mang's shocked and confused expression as he drank the strong tea in a single gulp, then showed Gu Mang the empty cup.

Gu Mang took a step back, stammering, his lips opening and closing around indistinct words. Even if he couldn't hear them, Mo Xi knew what he was saying.

Lu Zhanxing was falsely accused... Lu Zhanxing was falsely accused...

"What was he falsely accused of... What was he falsely accused of?" Gu Mang mumbled. His voice was hoarse, its pitch rising, yet his words still came slow as his mutters turned to hysterical shouts. "Was it that he didn't kill the envoy at Phoenix Cry Mountain?! Is that it?! Why didn't he tell me, why didn't he speak out? Why are you telling me this now, why are *you* the one to tell me this?!"

His pupils shrank to pinpricks as he stared, wild-eyed, into the emperor's expressionless face. He had lost his mind to the point that he, a common-born criminal, dared speak like this to the son of the imperial family. To the point that Gu Mang, who had always been cautious and prudent before the nobles, would dare use the common *you* to address his emperor.

As for the emperor, he slowly looked up. He had always been ruthless and paranoid, but he didn't berate Gu Mang for his discourtesy. "No. At the battle of Phoenix Cry Mountain, Lu Zhanxing was indeed the one who executed the envoy. No one framed him, no one coerced him. However." Looking at Gu Mang's shaking figure, the emperor paused. He produced a white chess piece streaked with scarlet blood and placed it gently on the table.

"Someone possessed him, and he became their unwitting pawn." The emperor drew back from the table as he murmured, "General Gu has dabbled in forbidden techniques. Take a look... Do you recognize this white chess piece?"

116

Lu Zhanxing's Injustice

T HE BLOODSTAINED WHITE chess piece sat on the pitch-black sandalwood of the tea table like the white of an eye spiderwebbed with blood vessels, staring vacantly, eerily in all directions.

Gu Mang squashed the emotions that threatened to overwhelm him and picked up the chess piece. At first, he noticed nothing strange about it. But after a moment's examination, his pupils contracted, and he looked up in astonishment. "Zhenlong Chess Formation?"

"General Gu has learned much from his dealings with the Liao Kingdom. It took Sishu Terrace three full days to recognize this technique, but General Gu can tell at a glance. You are correct. This is one of the three great forbidden techniques...the Zhenlong Chess Formation."

The Zhenlong Chess Formation was a bloody magic passed down since ancient times. Its caster could refine black and white chess pieces from their own spiritual energy and use them to control any living thing in the world, be it a beast of the field or a bird of the air, a human, monster, immortal, or demon. As long as they were implanted with a chess piece, they would become puppets that carried out the wielder's bidding. But this sort of forbidden technique had a significant restriction: the spellcaster's cultivation level had to be extremely high. It cost terrific amounts of spiritual energy to refine a single chess piece; those who weren't at the level of a grandmaster couldn't begin to attempt it.

Even so, among the three forbidden techniques, the Zhenlong Chess Formation left the clearest trail. Compared to the Rebirth technique with its hundreds of differing tales and the near-mythical Space-Time Gate of Life and Death, the bloody storms stirred up by the Zhenlong Chess Formation had repeatedly stained the history of the cultivation world. Countless ambitious tyrants had scrabbled madly through the land to collect scraps of scrolls about this magic. Although no one could yet use it as described in the forbidden texts—single-handedly refining tens of thousands of black and white chess pieces and creating an immense army with a scattering of stones—it was not impossible. No one had succeeded in mastering the Zhenlong Chess Formation to reshape the world and dye the land red, but cultivators who could make a few dozen or hundred chess pieces did exist. And sometimes, to spark a mutiny or topple a ruling class, it was enough to control the most crucial person for a single moment.

Gu Mang's eyes glimmered. "A white Zhenlong chess piece..." He mumbled, repeating the words with trembling lips. "So...so Lu Zhanxing was under control of the white chess piece?!"

"Yes."

The word was faint, barely discernible, but it seemed to re-ignite the glow that had gone out in Gu Mang. "Does Your Imperial Majesty tell me these things so I can redress Zhanxing's injustice?" he cried. "I'll do anything—"

"General Gu." The emperor cut him off, pouring another cup of tea. "Calm yourself. Sit."

"But—"

"Trust us. We brought you here to tell you the truth in person. We will certainly not let Subject Lu endure injustice for nothing."

His words were ingeniously crafted. What did it mean to *not let Subject Lu endure injustice for nothing*? At first it sounded like he meant to exonerate Lu Zhanxing. But with a moment's thought, there was another possibility. He would ensure the injustice done to Lu Zhanxing was for a worthy cause, so that this deputy general's sacrifice would not be in vain.

A worthy sacrifice...was also not for nothing.

But how could Gu Mang in his current state detect any cunning meaning in the emperor's words? He blinked teary eyes, gazing into the emperor's sincere face. In the end, he lowered his head and sat back down.

How easy it was to set alight this bundle of firewood named Gu Mang. A moment ago he was icy and cold, as if he would never trust or serve anyone again. All it took was the tiniest spark for him to once more offer all he had to the emperor.

Mo Xi closed his eyes, lashes fluttering. The heat of Gu Mang's reignited hope seared the pain deeper into Mo Xi's heart. He already knew—in the end, nothing would go as Gu Mang wished. This bright flare was no more than the final wisp of light Gu Mang left in Chonghua.

"Does General Gu know how we discovered this chess piece?"

Gu Mang shook his head.

"After Lu Zhanxing was taken into custody, the jailer interrogated him. They found his condition extremely strange. He could give no details, and all his reactions were unnaturally delayed. We were suspicious, so we asked Zhou He to perform a magical vivisection." He tapped the white chess piece on the table. "They found this inside him."

The emperor continued, "Zhenlong Chess Formation isn't a technique easily managed; since antiquity, no one has truly mastered it. This white chess piece doesn't have the power of those recorded in the texts. In that regard, it's a failure—but it can still control people for a short period of time and make them do the spellcaster's bidding."

Pausing, the emperor looked up. "General Gu, you've always been clever. Surely we needn't tell you who would benefit most from Lu Zhanxing executing an envoy in those circumstances."

After a beat, Gu Mang murmured, "Liao."

"Correct. The Liao Kingdom."

The emperor plucked the white chess piece from the table and set it on its edge. With a flick of his fingers, the white chess piece was set spinning. He continued, staring at the chess piece. "The spell-caster's cultivation was not high enough to maintain steady control with the Zhenlong Chess Formation in the long term. Nor could he control cultivators with powerful spiritual energy like you or Xihe-jun. But your deputy general Lu Zhanxing was keeping watch over the army alone. He became their best target."

It was as if layers of gauze had been unwrapped to expose the bloody truth beneath. Gu Mang's fingertips shook as he watched that unassuming white chess piece.

"Imagine, General Gu. Consider Lu Zhanxing's temper, his birth, and his status... That he executed the envoy in a rage was only to be expected. If not for Zhou He's meticulous examination, this case would be closed, and no one would find it suspicious."

The white chess piece spun on the table like a top. Over this madly whirling Zhenlong piece, over this narrow wooden table, an emperor and his subject regarded each other.

"A single chess piece brought Chonghua's bravest army to ruin, destroyed Chonghua's growing hopes of reform, and reduced us to a puppet of those old, conservative nobles. As for you—you, and others like you, will never again have the means to free yourselves. Can you imagine what that looks like?"

"Imagine?" There was a long pause. Dazed, Gu Mang's voice, hoarse and weary, came out as a whisper. "Your Imperial Majesty, I've been living it." He pressed his fingers to his brow, burying his face in his hands. "Since the day I knelt in front of the court, begging you to raise those seventy thousand gravestones for my brothers... I already...already..."

He was like a traveler who had trudged so long in the desert he had reached the brink of death. This sudden hope had choked him. From his vantage point, Mo Xi could see Gu Mang in profile, bright tear tracks at the corners of those slender eyes like swallowtail butterflies.

The emperor was silent for a spell. "Subject Gu, we apologize."

Faced with an emperor who had once ridiculed and impugned them in court, how many subjects, aside from fawning sycophants, could forgive without resentment? If it were Murong Lian or Mo Xi who stood here, neither would so easily accept this apology.

But Gu Mang was a general born to poverty. Others could be aloof and heroic and bold, but him? He had too often smilingly pestered noble masters for his soldiers' pay. He had shamelessly attempted to cozy up to the other commanders as he could. It wasn't as though he was really so pathetic as to happily turn the other cheek when others slapped him.

It was because he had no choice.

He only had so much. He was responsible for the lives and dignity of his hundred thousand comrades. His pockets were empty, and he had no powerful backer; all he could pitifully offer up were his smiles. He could nod his head and bend his neck. What other option did he have?

Gu Mang swiped his thumbs across his lashes and looked up. The remaining candles flickered in the wind. Mo Xi could see his tears hadn't dried, yet he still strove to smile. It was a smile utterly shattered, yet also surpassingly strong.

"It's nothing," Gu Mang said. "Elder Zhou hadn't discovered the Zhenlong chess piece at the time, and Your Imperial Majesty didn't know the truth. Your Imperial Majesty's reprimand was justified." As he spoke again, he carefully watched the emperor's face, eyes bright with tears. "Dare I ask... How does Your Imperial Majesty plan to reverse Lu Zhanxing's sentence?"

But the emperor said nothing. In the silence, the white chess piece slowed and wobbled, weary and dispirited...

Outside, lightning flashed again; in its harsh light, the distant mountains looked like demons burst from the bowels of the earth. Thunder shook the skies, and the rain was like a waterfall tumbling down into the mortal world.

The emperor said, "General Gu, we're afraid that won't be possible."

Gu Mang's eyes were wide in the thunder and lightning. The white chess piece on the table finally exhausted itself. Struggling with the last of its momentum, it wheeled a few more pathetic circles before falling down and lying still.

Everything returned to silence. It was as if the river god Feng Yi was churning in the depths, towering waves about to break the water's surface, the gleam of scale-clad justice so close to rising from the abyss. But the wind stilled, and the water calmed. The river god sank back into the deep, cold waters, leaving those on the shore empty-handed and hopeless.

"What?" Gu Mang tasted bitterness in his throat.

The emperor didn't answer directly. "Does General Gu know how Subject Lu fares inside the prison? Even now, he thinks executing the envoy at Phoenix Cry Mountain was a deed he did in a moment of impulse. He regrets it terribly. Zhou He said throughout the interrogation he kept asking to see you. He wanted to personally apologize for his recklessness."

Gu Mang closed his eyes. The hands fallen by his side twisted into fists, and the tendons by his temples protruded, his expression tortured.

The emperor stroked that pale white chess piece, caressing it with a fingertip. "Subject Lu doesn't know that those controlled by the white chess piece will do anything—they might commit any atrocity, whether it was murder, betrayal, or rape. They will believe they *wanted* to do it. He's no more than an innocent victim, the knife in the killer's hand. But he thinks he is the murderer."

Gu Mang stood up. He couldn't hold back, his voice shaking: "Then why didn't Your Imperial Majesty tell him?!"

"Why didn't we tell him?" The emperor seemed to ask this question to no one, or perhaps he was asking himself. He laughed softly, a little sorrowful. "Because we have a guilty conscience."

He turned to look out at the vast curtain of rain. It was a desolate sight, but his voice was bleaker still. "We don't know how to face him," the emperor murmured. "He isn't a rebellious subject; he is only a general who faced torment for Chonghua. Our heart is also made of flesh... We don't have the nerve to see him." He paused. "Do you think we don't wish to exonerate him, that we aren't willing to clear your reputations and give you justice? You're wrong. What ruler under the heavens would wish to disappoint his important subjects like this?"

The emperor rose and walked to the edge of the Golden Terrace, which seemed to waver in the wind and rain. Hands behind his back, he gazed into the endless night. He sighed. "General Gu, there's something you wouldn't believe, even if we told you on our knees."

The emperor seemed to hesitate before speaking again. "In our eyes, *your army* is the most precious treasure we inherited from our imperial father. Regardless of what was offered in exchange—no matter how rich the land, how beautiful the woman—we would not have given you up. We never wanted to lose you all."

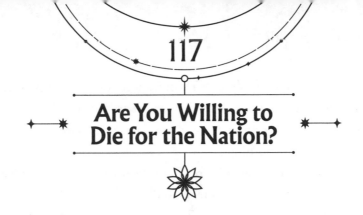

117

Are You Willing to Die for the Nation?

GU MANG MADE no sound; he felt this all extremely absurd. He wasn't alone. Mo Xi, too, found the emperor's words beyond ridiculous. Precious? Something he never wanted to lose? More like discarded like an old shoe, dissolved with delight... It would be more accurate to say Gu Mang's army was a thorn in the emperor's side. *A treasure?* Who would believe it?

At Gu Mang's silence, the emperor turned. "General Gu, what kind of person do you think we are?"

Gu Mang's lips parted, but almost immediately, he pressed them tightly together again.

"You don't have to say it, we know. All of you people think Imperial Father was a virtuous ruler, willing to give cultivators of slave birth a chance to distinguish themselves. In your eyes, the former emperor made great strides and enacted lasting change. And we?" The emperor smiled. "We're a stickler for tradition, stubborn and inflexible."

He looked at the deluge of water streaming from the eaves. "But have any of you stood in our position and considered our circumstances?"

The emperor murmured: "We have no other choice. General Gu, as a slave on the path to where you stand today, you met with every kind of criticism and countless hardships. We've witnessed them all.

What we felt most deeply wasn't admiration or pity, but a powerful sympathy. Your path and mine are equally hard to walk. We are both destined to bear the burden of endless curses and condemnation."

Gu Mang said nothing.

"No—in truth, we are less fortunate than you. At least you have a Xihe-jun you can trust wholeheartedly, and an army of brave and loyal warriors devoted to you. What do we have? Mengze? Yanping... or Murong Lian." The emperor chuckled, mocking himself. "In this vast imperial city, we have so many relatives, from side branches to direct descendants, but every one of them bears us ill will. Do you know why?"

Gu Mang shook his head.

"Because the path we took to the throne ran red with the blood of our brothers." As he spoke, he turned his face to the inky sky. "Let us share a rumor. No...better to say a forbidden tale. But tongues will wag. We think General Gu may have heard this story before."

When Gu Mang said nothing, the emperor took a breath and began, "This happened long ago, when we were born... Everyone knows we're the eldest di son of the imperial family and should have been heir apparent. But there has been a precedent of deposing the di son in Chonghua. Before one formally ascends the throne, anything can happen. When we were a month old, our mother secretly went to an oracle, who divined a star chart. The array showed great peril, and the oracle predicted we would suffer calamity in our life. It was written in the palaces of our Ziwei Star birth chart that we were destined for strife among siblings, unlikely to live harmoniously with our brothers. This star chart deeply troubled my mother, and she fell ill for many months. After she regained her health..." The emperor paused and closed his eyes. "From then on, none of the male infants born in the imperial harem lived to see their first year."

Mo Xi knew the emperor spoke true; as a child, Mo Xi went often to the palace with his father, but in all those years, he had seen but one imperial scion, now the current emperor. He had clear memories of an imperial concubine auntie, sweet and kind. She liked making pastries and desserts, and every time he visited, she would give him a few boxes of them to take home.

That concubine had a frail constitution, and when she later fell pregnant, it took everything she had to give birth to a child.

It was a young master.

Mo Xi remembered his parents discussing a suitable congratulatory gift. But before the gift had been settled, the mourning bells of the palace tolled throughout the capital—the little boy had passed.

Back then, Mo Xi had been too young, and too many years had gone by since; he didn't remember how the infant had died. Dimly, he thought it was some severe childhood illness. What remained seared in his memory was that, a few days later, while the handmaidens and guards weren't watching, that imperial concubine hung herself in heartbreak and grief.

This strange and suspicious incident became the talk of all of Chonghua. After the death of this concubine, the other ladies became afraid. It was whispered that, for these women whose rank depended on their children, a boy wasn't cause for celebration but a curse. How many mothers' tears had fallen, how many souls had met unjust ends among those countless deaths?

In the end, however, it was no more than hearsay.

The emperor gazed into the dark, eyes vacant, as if he saw in the rain his brothers of flesh and blood who didn't survive to adulthood.

"Whether such a series of misfortunes was truly coincidence or our mother's doing...it is not our place to guess. Regardless of the truth, everyone presumes we walked a bloodstained path to the throne.

Who among all the concubines of the late emperor would hope to see us succeed? Of all their families and all their relatives—which would truly take our side? They've never accepted us or treated us with sincerity in the first place. On top of all this, just before the late emperor passed, he considered abolishing our title to adopt Murong Lian instead. How solid do you think our position is?"

Gu Mang watched him and said nothing.

The emperor bit his lip, his eyes flashing. "It's not that we're unwilling to continue along the path the late emperor started on, nor is it that we think you're as insignificant as floating duckweed. It's because..." He closed his eyes. "We have no other choice. We are new to the throne, beset by internal troubles and external strife; our rule is precarious. To you all, it might seem that a single stamp of the cinnabar seal resolves matters big and small. In reality, we can't even touch Wangshu-jun's Luomei Pavilion. These are the circumstances Chonghua's new emperor faces—how ridiculous."

"Luomei Pavilion is no more than a brothel. What stops Your Imperial Majesty from closing it?" Gu Mang asked.

"A brothel..." The emperor scoffed, looking up at Gu Mang. "General Gu, have you any idea how deeply entrenched this brothel is within the capital? If you look from afar, you might only know it as a venue belonging to Wangshu-jun. But if you attempt to pull it out, you'll discover its root system runs beneath most of the imperial city. Touch it, and the relationships and stakes buried deep in the mud move as one to intimidate you, harangue you, and work against you.

"Luomei Pavilion has sheltered officials and facilitated cover-ups. It's at the heart of such scandals as fencing stolen goods and bribery... and this is just one brothel. In Chonghua today, ten thousand eyes watch whatever we do, one thousand mouths say no, one hundred arms shove us down onto the throne. If the day comes when we wish to reform the Ministry of Rites, the Bureau of Military Affairs, or even make sweeping changes to Chonghua's political system? How do you imagine that would play out?"

The wind buffeted the rain, blowing it into the Golden Terrace. For a moment, everyone sank into silence—Mo Xi as he spectated; the emperor; his subject. Eventually, the emperor spoke again. "It was not our wish to retreat, to uphold conservative ideals. We had no choice but to enact these policies, and we have no choice but to shoulder the blame."

No choice but to enact these policies...no choice but to shoulder the blame... These two phrases seemed to stab at Gu Mang's flesh and heart like nails; his chest heaved with it.

"General Gu."

Gu Mang raised his eyes.

The emperor laid slender fingers on the crimson lacquer of the railing. "Do you know what it is we've most wanted to do, all our life? We've wanted to shut up those shameless, toadying old nobles; we've wanted to make those useless sacks of shit spit out the meat in their mouths. Chen Tang was wrong to trust Hua Po'an. Thus the Liao Kingdom came to be, and slave-born cultivators became anathema to the people of Chonghua. But Imperial Father was right to trust in Subject Gu, and thus Chonghua gained an invincible general to oppose the Liao Kingdom. First there was Hua Po'an, but now there is you, Gu Mang, and him, Lu Zhanxing. The path the late emperor chose was correct—but we want to walk farther than he did."

As he paused, his distant gaze gained focus, his fingers slowly and subconsciously clenching into a fist as if he were about to face a thing he found abhorrent. "Those talentless officials who cling to the fringes of our court, those stick-in-the-mud old nobles...they've never cared for the nation of Chonghua. They think of nothing but what rewards they'll receive today and what titles they'll receive tomorrow. If they were to step onto the battlefield, they'd be useless—a crowd of armchair strategists! All these years, they've brandished the excuse of Hua Po'an's treason to relentlessly oppose letting capable officials or knowledgeable soldiers take initiative; the moment a slave-born cultivator stands out, they rush to surround them and fling a pile of baseless charges at them, dooming them to death in Fengbo Pavilion—"[9]

At these words, it was not just Gu Mang, but even Mo Xi who was shocked. When had the emperor ever said so much in one breath, so fervently and openly, his eyes flashing with intense light? It seemed to pierce the thick shell he wore in front of outsiders; at this moment, he looked like any zealous and passionate youth.

"They're afraid of Chonghua changing, they're afraid of understanding black magic techniques, they're afraid of all the possible upheaval the future brings. They want to grow old and live easy, striving for momentary gratification. They care nothing about how, in a hundred years, the country may fall, their families may perish— these are the nobles of Chonghua. My brothers," said the emperor.

"But you're different," he continued. "My brothers, my noble peers, those whose veins flow with the same blood as mine—they merely think how to suck another mouthful of blood from Chonghua, how to guard their glorious place at the top. But General Gu, you're different. *Your* brothers, your army—they're a sharp sword the likes of which Chonghua hasn't forged in hundreds of years. Even if you don't believe it, we meant what we said: this is our treasure."

---

9   Fengbo Pavilion is the name of the highest court during the Southern Song dynasty, where the loyal general Yue Fei was put to death on baseless charges of treason.

The moth, trapped by the rain and unable to escape, danced madly before the candle, finally throwing itself into the fire. With a sound like a sigh, flame licked up, emitting the acrid scent of char... The moth died for the light at last, falling into the pool of wax.

"We wish to do more in this life than follow in Father's footsteps—we want to curtail the power of the nobles, demote the fringe officials, and blaze a new trail, go where no one's dared before. Chonghua blindly rejects forbidden black magic techniques—but we must know them, we must master them! We needn't use them, but what's wrong with understanding them? We ask you: if Chonghua had studied more of the three great forbidden techniques, would Lu Zhanxing have met such an end?"

Gu Mang flinched.

"General Gu, one Subject Lu is enough...we don't want to see a second or third harmed by black magic while we languish in ignorance."

He looked to the heavens. Another bolt of lightning forked across the sky, and a boom of thunder rumbled in its wake. The emperor's eyes blazed. "It's high time Chonghua had a storm like this..."

The leaden clouds roiled overhead. On this dark night, most of the candles in the depths of the palace had already gone out. Only the Golden Terrace perched at the highest peak of the imperial city still glowed faintly amid the howling winds. It was like an icy sword pointed straight up into the nine heavens, piercing the thick clouds.

"General Gu, we need someone loyal enough, brave enough, and clever enough. We need this person to infiltrate the Liao Kingdom and send information back to us—to become the poison in the bellies of both Liao and those old nobles."

Gu Mang wasn't stupid. By now he'd guessed why the emperor invited him to the Golden Terrace today. As he anticipated, what the emperor said next was: "Subject Gu. Are you willing to endure a difficult mission as Chonghua's right hand?"

For a moment, Gu Mang was quiet. "Your Imperial Majesty wants me to pretend to defect?"

In the silence that followed, the sound of rain pouring over the roof tiles seemed to drill into their ears. Gu Mang was waiting for this answer, and so was Mo Xi. The atmosphere was taut as the string of a jade bow pulled to full draw, waiting for that last ounce of force.

The emperor closed his eyes. "Yes."

The bowstring snapped with a terrible sound, and the bow left behind couldn't stop shaking, couldn't stop trembling... Even as a passive spectator within the jade scroll, Mo Xi felt the tragic misery of this night slashing deep into his flesh. Blood surged to his head, where it congealed into dark ice; this single word from the emperor seemed to have frozen him solid. He couldn't feel his limbs.

It was cold, so cold.

Or perhaps it was because he had always been waiting for this line of exoneration, this explanation of the truth behind the treason. He had waited for eight years, grieved for eight years, suffered for eight years, and despaired for eight years. When he finally heard this—that Gu Mang really did have a secret, that he was in fact a chess piece Chonghua had pushed into the Liao Kingdom, every emotion he had felt for the past eight years transformed instantly into grievance and heartache...

Dying with jeweled sword in hand to repay the trust of the king's command...

How ironic.

Only those who truly ascended to this platform that thousands of people held in envy would understand what a "trusted subject" was. You would be thrust into an eternal darkness; every plot or scheme,

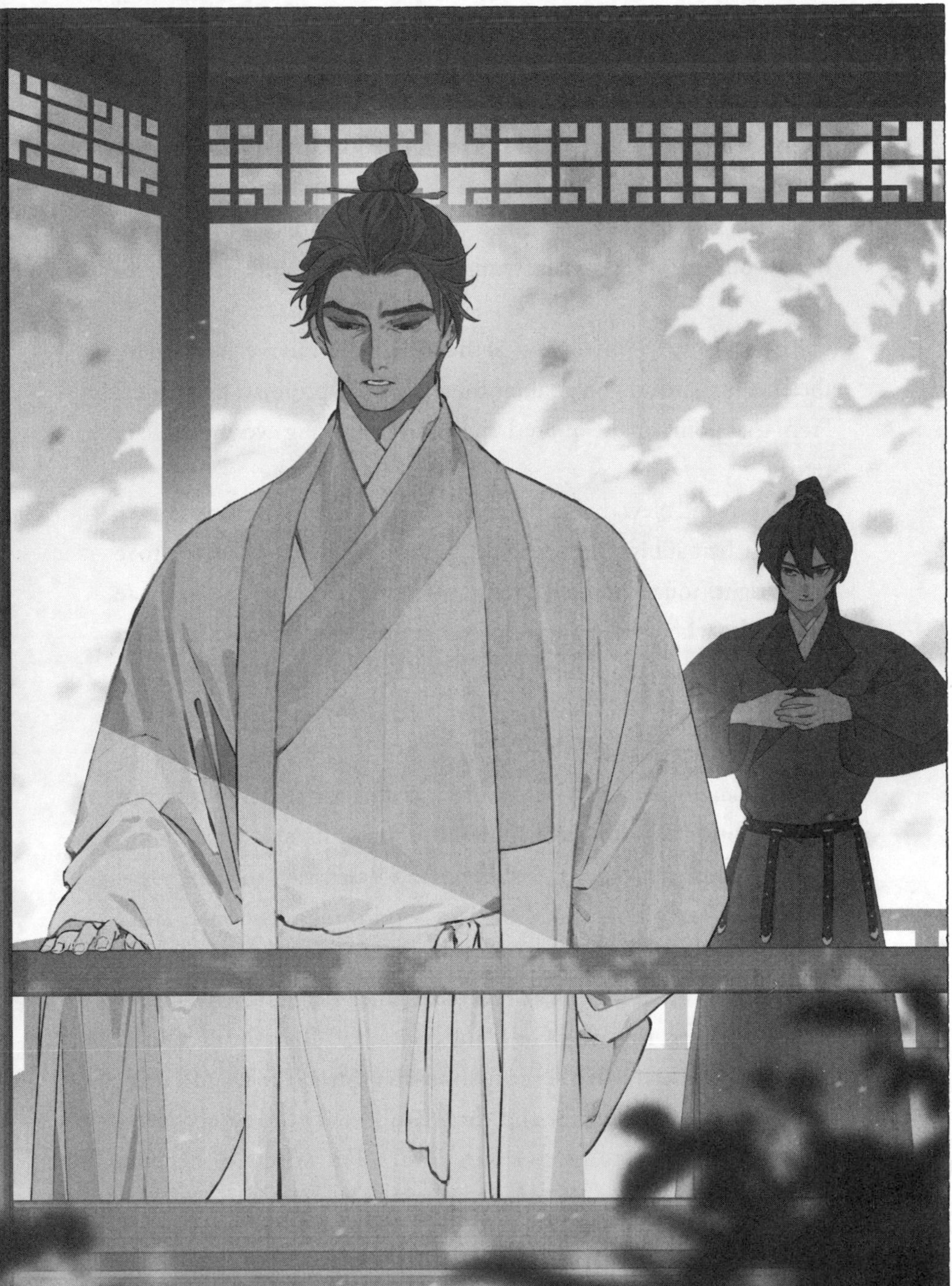

sacrifice or machination flew from the ruler's mouth to your ear. From then on, a brilliant and sincere smile was bloodily torn from your face, while a mask you had no choice over was locked in place. Once the bloodstains dried, the scars faded, and you raised your head, you'd never recognize your own face in the bronze mirror again.

This so-called hero nodded as the storm raged above, perhaps for the sake of a dream or a goal, or for a person, a promise, or an ideal. From that point on, he offered up his life, forsaking every avenue of retreat.

As the wind blew through his wide sleeves, Gu Mang tucked back the loose hair at his temples. "Your Imperial Majesty wants to prove you're right. You want to take on an earthshaking cause, to give those old nobles who don't believe in you reason to reconsider whether you're trash that stepped over the bloody flesh of your brothers to ascend the throne, or a monarch who can hold up the vault of the heavens. Is that not so?"

Gu Mang's tone was too measured, as if he was striving to repress some emotion. The emperor waited for him to finish.

"Your Imperial Majesty wishes to be a wise ruler, to reform the foundations of Chonghua. This is a good thing to be sure, and I admire it very much."

The emperor let out a soft breath of relief. Yet just as he parted his lips to speak, he heard Gu Mang continue: "But, Your Imperial Majesty, I've already died seventy thousand times. The wounds over my heart have yet to scab, and there are seventy thousand heroic souls who have yet to receive burials. Yes, I'm willing to become your sharp blade, the poison fed to the Liao Kingdom, the spy that gathers their secrets of black magic, the sacrifice you offer to placate the old nobles.

"I can agree to all these things, I'm willing to do all these things. As long as you, on behalf of my seventy thousand dead, let my brother live. I'm not some god of war. I'm merely one among those hundred thousand slave cultivators. I will become your traitor and endure a lifetime of infamy, but I ask that you give them the justice they deserve."

The emperor slowly closed his eyes, as if Gu Mang's words pushed him into pained unease. "We won't let you suffer for nothing," he said. "There will come a day... Subject Gu, there will come a day when we clear your name. On that day, we will personally bestow the blue and gold ribbon of heroes upon you. We will announce to the great breadth of Chonghua, announce to each and every safe and happy citizen, that they are only blessed with such a world because of your sacrifice..."

Gu Mang's eyes flashed, but he remained unmoved by the future the emperor painted. He was clearheaded yet, unwaveringly sinking his teeth into the boon he had asked, unwilling to let go. He faced the emperor squarely, tone solemn. "Then, what about Lu Zhanxing?"

The emperor looked at him, their gazes locked in some intangible battle. In the end, in this dead and unnerving silence, the emperor was first to concede. He closed his eyes. "Subject Gu, there is no way Subject Lu can live."

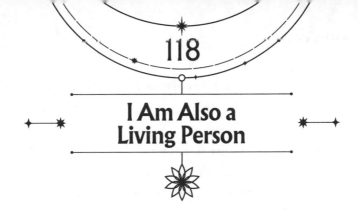

118

I Am Also a Living Person

GU MANG HAD predicted the emperor's response, but when these words crashed down like thunder, his voice still shook. "Why?!"

"Because this chess piece was tempered with demonic qi. Lu Zhanxing's spiritual flow is no longer pure. How many in all of Chonghua would let a man who bears traces of black magic on his body live in peace? Since antiquity, those stained with demonic qi are either drawn and quartered, or tormented to death upon the experimentation table. Do you prefer to clear his name only for him to die under torture, or is it better for his death to at least pave the way for Chonghua, for all of you?"

Gu Mang couldn't summon a reply.

"We want Chonghua to accept slaves and to understand black magic." After a pause, the emperor continued. "But the price is that the injustice Lu Zhanxing has suffered will only ever be known to the two of us. He must be sentenced."

In the squalling wind, another handful of lanterns went dark. The light on the Golden Terrace dimmed further.

Gu Mang raised his head slightly, blinking away the wetness in his eyes. It seemed he didn't want to keep arguing with the emperor. After a beat he asked, his voice low and hoarse, "Then...what next? What next, after the sentencing?"

"Next, we will lay down a logical path for your treason. After the autumn hunt this year, Lu Zhanxing will be executed, and the remnants of your army will be detained. We will betray not the slightest hint of gentleness or compassion toward slave cultivators. We will be meticulous; the entire court will believe we have chosen to cleave to the mores of the old nobles. Everyone will watch as we abrogate your authority, demote you, and replace you. We will set your feet on the road of despair. After the execution following the autumn hunt is complete, we will give you the last push and provide you sufficient reason to defect."

"To the Liao Kingdom?" Gu Mang asked.

"To the Liao Kingdom."

Gu Mang guffawed as if he had heard some absurd joke. "How far does Your Imperial Majesty plan to go for others to believe that I, Gu Mang, would choose the darkest, most depraved nation in all the Nine Provinces and Twenty-Eight Nations? Defecting to the Liao Kingdom..." The last traces of his smile twisted on his face, his hatred seeming to imbue his expression with a beastly malevolence. "How far would I have to be pushed to defect to the nation that has slaughtered countless of my comrades and stirred the flames of war across the Nine Provinces?!"

"You see why Lu Zhanxing must die," replied the emperor. "If Lu Zhanxing lives, no one would believe the once earth-shatteringly powerful General Gu, so devoted to his nation and its ruler, would pass willingly through the gates of the Liao Kingdom. Only if Lu Zhanxing dies does that seed of hatred sprout in your heart; only then do these events have a turning point, rational and believable."

He paused, then repeated, "Subject Gu, think about it. If Lu Zhanxing is saved, what would be lost? Everyone would see he's been wronged; his name would be exonerated. But he's infected with the black magic demonic qi—he's doomed to execution regardless. Perhaps you believe that if he dies this way, at least those seventy thousand graves, those thirty thousand heroes of your army, will be treated fairly. But we tell you now they will not."

The emperor's black eyes swirled with thick clouds and heavy mist. That darkness was a wall no one could break through anymore.

"If Lu Zhanxing doesn't die, we could try to redress the injustice done to your army and give your soldiers rewards or gravestones, but the old nobles would most certainly jump out with all sorts of bizarre excuses to stop us. Most terrifying of all...they might say, Deputy General Lu was infected with demonic qi. No one can say for sure whether other soldiers in the camp were infected, so it'd be safer to show no mercy—they might demand we execute every single one of those thirty thousand comrades you have left. Subject Gu, right now, your army is like an old manor that has caught fire. We will do our best to retrieve whatever can be rescued, but the first spark fell on Lu Zhanxing. He has been reduced to ash; we cannot save him. We are so very sorry."

Gu Mang was quiet for a long interval. Almost indifferently, he said, "Okay. I understand. We are treasures, but a single spark can reduce Your Imperial Majesty's treasures to ash." He looked up. "Your Imperial Majesty, do you know what my army is to me?"

This was an insubordinate question, but the emperor didn't rebuke him. His lashes trembled, and his expression was evasive, even sorrowful.

Gu Mang continued, "They are my blood, my eyes, my arms and my legs, my family, and my life. However precious a treasure may be, it's useless once destroyed, merely dust after the flames blaze through. But family and kin are different. Even if they die, even if they're burned, even if they're nothing but ash... They will have a tombstone in my heart. I will remember every one of their names, every one of their faces, until the day I join them in death."

"We didn't mean..." the emperor started.

"Then what *did* you mean?" Gu Mang showed him a gentle, hollow smile. "Your Imperial Majesty, you say we are your treasures, but treasures are not alive; we are living people! For you, we've shed blood; for Chonghua, we've shed tears. We've worked, we've given, we've tried—even died... I'm not sure if you've noticed?"

His questions came one after another, as if those seventy thousand dead had become vengeful ghosts, overtaking his body, the mass of them possessing his solitary figure. They demanded restitution from their emperor.

"General Gu..." The emperor's eyes dulled, but he raised them to gaze back into Gu Mang's. "We *have* noticed. But to sacrifice the lives of thirty thousand men and the glory of another seventy thousand, to give up the future of all slave cultivators in Chonghua to cleanse the reputation of one man—is it worth it?"

Gu Mang's shoulders shook; his lips trembled. He wanted to refute the emperor's words, but he couldn't speak. He was a preternaturally talented commander; of course he understood what the emperor said was true. His ruler's words were heartless, but they were also correct. This was the path involving the least sacrifice, yet how could he simply nod, how could he accept it...?

"That day in the throne room, when you knelt at our feet begging for gravestones for your dead men, to show mercy to your remaining soldiers, we said you were delusional. But now as we stand before you, we swear you this oath: we will not let Deputy General Lu's sacrifice be in vain. We will give you everything you asked that day, but for Lu Zhanxing's life. The rest is yours—those seventy thousand gravestones, and the safety of your thirty thousand remaining soldiers.

We promise that one day, we will show you a future where heroes can become heroes no matter the circumstances of their birth, and every life will be treated equally."

Gu Mang took a step back, shaking his head. The emperor's promise was too heavy, weighing him down until he almost seemed stooped. Only after a long while did he hoarsely mutter, "Lies..."

"We never lie."

Gu Mang was on the edge of insanity; he looked up, his gaze like a sharp sword unsheathing, eyes scarlet as he hurled a reckless shout at the emperor. "Liar!"

His voice was thunderous with rage. In the roiling storm and whipping wind, the blinded and declawed Beast of the Altar had been spun round and round by the carrot and the stick until he didn't know what he should believe. He railed at the master who tamed him, slamming over and over against the bars of his cage.

Mo Xi closed his eyes. The pain of a body that had endured the jade scroll repair could not be more than a cowering, bleeding, loyal heart.

Beast of the Altar... Beast of the Altar...

In the past, people had spoken this epithet as they spread stories of General Gu's glory. But now, Mo Xi could only see a bloody beast in truth, flayed of its skin, trapped and howling in a cage. The emperor's beast, Chonghua's beast—it hurt so keenly for its comrades that it longed for death, yet those who had raised it now tore off its hide, wrapping a new layer of skin over that mutilated body. They wanted to send it to another country, instructing it to endure the pain and burn up the last wisps of warmth and light it possessed.

The rain poured down around them. The emperor stood ramrod straight, supported by some power inherent to monarchs that allowed him neither to cower nor to shrink back in the face of

Gu Mang's intense emotion. His expression was unsightly, but still he persisted.

After a long silence, the emperor finally answered with a quiet question of his own. "Do you think we made this decision lightly? Do you think framing loyal subjects is something that brings us ease? Do you think tormenting our greatest general and chasing him off to another nation is something that brings us ease? Do you think that, as we stand here today, surrounded by thunder beneath the nine heavens upon the Golden Terrace, telling you these things, we can be at ease?!"

The emperor's voice became louder and louder. His fingertips were trembling, his eyes flashing with an unsteady light. "Subject Gu...you once said seventy thousand people died at the battle of Phoenix Cry Mountain, so you see seventy thousand wronged ghosts demanding justice from you day and night, reproaching you, cursing you, spurning you, asking you why..." His voice shook mightily, each word ground out from between his teeth, each phrase stained with blood. "Do you think...it is different for us?"

Gu Mang looked up with ridicule in his eyes. "What does Your Imperial Majesty see? Seventy thousand broken treasures? Or is it a mountain of destroyed clay servants, all identical?"

He'd gone mad; he must have gone mad. After having his arms torn off and his heart cut out, Gu Mang was no longer afraid of saying anything to the emperor's face. Irreverent words burst from his lips: "Your Imperial Majesty says over and over again that you think of us as people. Over and over again, you say you can see my dead brothers, your dead subjects... But you grieve that your invincible army lost seventy thousand soldiers. You grieve a number, a ledger full of heroes—you don't grieve for each and every human life!"

Outside the Golden Terrace was the endless storm; inside the Golden Terrace was boundless silence.

At length, the emperor squeezed his eyes shut, then opened them once more. His lips moved as if to speak, then he pursed them again... Finally, in a choked voice, he softly, sorrowfully, spoke a name—

"Xu Xiaomao."

Just one name. Gu Mang froze.

His fingers, originally shaking from rage, seemed to be locked in by black ice. He stood motionless, staring at the emperor in disbelief, as though he thought it might be a figment of his imagination. He was certainly mistaken to have heard this sort of pathetic, ridiculous name—the name of his brother, his comrade—from the mouth of the Son of Heaven.

But such names issued one after another from the lips of the emperor, clearly, sorrowfully, solemnly. "Lan Yufei, Jin Cheng, Sun He, Luo Chuan..." He recited them one by one.

With each name, a brother's voice and features rose before Gu Mang's eyes.

A man who liked to drink fiery, cheap shaodaozi wine.

A cousin who had a mole on the bridge of his nose.

A little scamp who always lost his money gambling but never learned any better.

And that little devil who recklessly squeezed himself into the squadron at the age of sixteen, his face so terribly young.

The invocation of these names seemed to summon their souls; Gu Mang bowed his head, his back bending. He buried his face in his palms, fingers digging into his hair, and cried brokenly, "Stop talking..."

"Qin Fei, Zhao Sheng, Wei Ping..."

Qin Fei's bright laughter seemed to echo back into the world of the living and ring in his ears.

Zhao Sheng had once run over to his commander's tent in one of the garrisons to bring him a pot of sweet wine from the village nearby. When he had clasped it to his chest, it was still warm.

Wei Ping was thirty years old already, but he looked so young. When he smiled, his canines would show sweetly, and he had grinned and laughed arrogantly when he requested to stay behind at Phoenix Cry Mountain. That had become Gu Mang's last farewell with the rascal.

Who would remember these men's names... Who would remember?!

General Gu...

General Gu...

In life, a hero among men; in death, a hero among ghosts.

No, no, all of this is meaningless. I only wanted every one of you to return safely after each battle. No one would want their brothers to receive posthumous glory after a horsehide burial.

"Stop reciting them..." Gu Mang clutched his head in pain, crumpling to his knees. He howled, on the verge of collapse, crying out like a trapped beast, "Don't say any more! Don't say any more!"

"I remember them too." The emperor walked over to Gu Mang, gazing down at the man who had buried himself in the dust in front of him, curled in on himself in the muddy sand, and murmured, "Gu Mang, I remember them all too."

He spoke frankly, setting aside the royal *we*. "I'm sorry. Unlike you, I never spent my days with them from dawn until dusk. I can't remember their ages, appearances, interests...any of those details. But since I received the list of soldiers who perished at Phoenix Cry Mountain, I've been committing their names to memory."

Gu Mang's icy forehead pressed pathetically against the floor. His tears fell in fat drops down his cheeks as he sobbed, howling in grief...

He had finally fallen apart.

He had silently endured the wounds that covered his body, had painstakingly subdued his own agony and licked away the blood, just barely enough to put on a brave face before others. But the emperor tore open the wounds that had begun to scab over, and scarlet blood and flesh spilled outward in a great rush. It hurt so much, it hurt so much...it hurt so much he was going to die.

"I thought," the emperor said, "that even if I can't openly give them the gravestones of heroes, I can still honor them in my heart... General Gu, every day and every night, I am engraving them into memory. We're sorry, we are powerless to change many things..." He gripped Gu Mang's arms, helping him to stand, letting Gu Mang slowly lift his head. The rims of the emperor's eyes were wet. "But we ask you to believe us. We have never, will never, see you as cheap pawns, as lowly slave-born bodies."

It was an unremarkable sentence, containing neither praise nor commendation, yet Gu Mang sobbed uncontrollably. He knelt and staggered forward; struggling free of the emperor's hands, he pulled himself to the edge of the Golden Terrace.

He looked up at those towering mountains and the vast sky. The sounds of his weeping seemed to be carved out of his throat, dripping with crimson blood. The torrential storm swallowed his sobs; the nation was an expanse of grieving rain. Gu Mang was completely drained; he pressed his head to the railing as his shoulders shook. The ends of his eyes and the tip of his nose were flushed red. He had nothing left to say.

Eventually, the emperor slowly crossed the terrace to stand next to him. "Subject Gu, do you believe us now? We meant every word;

we would not lie to you. We swear you this oath." He pressed two fingers to his temple, taking Chonghua's customary position for vows.

Under the lightning that arced across the nine heavens, there upon the Golden Terrace, Chonghua's new ruler made Chonghua's subject a most solemn promise: "If General Gu accepts our request, we swear to three things. First, General Gu's thirty thousand soldiers will receive proper protections. Second, the law allowing slaves to cultivate in Chonghua will never be repealed. Third, we will inter those seventy thousand souls lost at Phoenix Cry Mountain with all the customary national rites upon Warrior Soul Mountain, complete with inscribed gravestones. Should we renege on any of these promises, may we live without the love of our descendants and die without a place of burial. Chonghua's fortunes will turn to ash in our hands, and we shall be condemned for all eternity."

After a pause, those final words fell from his mouth. "In life and after death, we shall never know peace."

119

His True Intent Was This

G U MANG SHOOK violently. How could he not tremble? What he had was so little. Even as a famous general, he'd always had to shamelessly beg the nobles for favor and acknowledgment. Now the emperor was offering him everything he had so painstakingly asked for, promising him all of it, crushing him beneath its weight—how could his spine stay straight? Unbreakable pride was a privilege of the likes of Mo Xi or Murong Lian. It had never been his.

Perhaps the emperor was well aware of this; he was in no rush. He stood, hands behind his back, waiting for Gu Mang to calm down, to submit, to take the first slow step onto the path of no return. Waiting for the Beast of the Altar to see he had no other choice, to take up the bridle himself.

It was only to be expected when, after a long while, Gu Mang lifted his head, those tear-filled eyes, black as pitch, fixing on the ruler in front of him. His face was serene; it was only that the light in his eyes had become embers, his heart like ashes. "Then, I ask Your Imperial Majesty," Gu Mang murmured, "to please grant one more request."

"Tell me."

"Zhanxing... He shouldn't be kept in the dark. Allow me to go personally to the prison and tell him the truth."

The emperor closed his eyes and sighed. "Subject Gu, why bother—"

"Because I have a guilty conscience."

"It is better for him to never know the truth—for you, for us, and for Chonghua."

"No. He must know. He has sacrificed enough. I implore you, just this once...have some consideration for him." Gu Mang closed his eyes in torment, tears trickling between thick lashes and slipping down his face. "He's been wronged. And I can't...can't save him. But at least I can tell him..." Those final words were like a red-hot iron branding his heart. "At least I can tell him he did nothing wrong. At least I can prevent him...from dying in ignorance..."

As he finished speaking, his voice weakened, and his silhouette gradually became transparent. The scene before Mo Xi's eyes dimmed, and darkness swallowed the Golden Terrace; the last thing Mo Xi saw was Gu Mang slowly kowtowing, lowering his head at the emperor's feet. It looked nothing like a pledge of loyalty, but rather an exhausted prostration.

Night descended before his eyes. At the same time, a sharp agony exploded in Mo Xi's limbs. The history-recording jade scroll fed on his strength, but Mo Xi felt that what flowed from him wasn't spiritual energy—his very soul seemed to be drawn out, pulled from his body and ground to fine powder.

But it didn't seem to hurt.

The words spoken on the Golden Terrace eight years ago echoed in his head. Gu Mang's harrowed expression lingered before his eyes.

One rainy night, one scheme, one sacrifice, deceived the world for eight years.

"General Gu, we need someone loyal enough, brave enough, and clever enough. We need this person to infiltrate the Liao Kingdom

and send information back to us—to become the poison in the bellies of both Liao and those old nobles."

"Are you willing to endure a difficult mission as Chonghua's right hand?"

Are you willing...? From now on, in all the world, only one other will know the truth. The countrymen you protect will spurn you, your former subordinates will misunderstand you, all the friends you've ever had will become your enemies.

You will gouge out a blazing heart, offer up your lifetime's worth of passion, yet the world will only remember your treason and infamy.

Subject Gu, General Gu, Gu Mang. Are you willing?

Each question seemed to thunder from the depths of the storm clouds, like heavenly sound piercing the sternum, like a sharp awl boring through the heart. The scene swam before his eyes, the colors seeming to scatter like snowflakes only to coalesce once more. Mo Xi fell helplessly among these fluttering fragments as if tumbling into a bottomless chasm. He opened his eyes; only when scalding tears burned at the corners did he realize he was crying.

His body didn't feel like his anymore; his soul felt like it had been cut into separate halves locked in heated combat within the dispersing vision. His past conversations with Gu Mang resurfaced one by one in his mind, crushing him into dust—

Gu Mang said, "They are my blood, my eyes, my arms and my legs, my family, and my life."

Yet Mo Xi had once rebuked him furiously, "As you bathed your hands in blood and killed your own comrades—Gu Mang, when did you ever feel the slightest bit of regret?!"

Gu Mang said, "How far would I have to be pushed to defect to the nation that has slaughtered countless of my comrades and stirred the flames of war across the Nine Provinces?!"

Yet Mo Xi had once said, "There was more than one path before you, and more than one country you could have fled to. Yet you went to the Liao Kingdom. You wanted revenge. For your dashed prospects, for your dead comrades-in-arms, for your own advancement. You didn't care whose blood you spilled."

Gu Mang said, "They will have a tombstone in my heart. I will remember every one of their names, every one of their faces, until the day I join them in death. They will never become rubble."

And Mo Xi had once slapped him, had stabbed a single word through Gu Mang's heart. He'd called him... As that word rose to mind, Mo Xi began to shake uncontrollably, horrified by the malice in what he'd said.

He had actually called him *dirty*.

Gu Mang had lost his memories, but he instinctively longed to wear the forehead ribbon bestowed upon Chonghua's heroes. He instinctively yearned for the day he would be exonerated, once more able to openly and honestly don his uniform and ride into battle, stand before the soldiers of three armies and watch the sun glinting off their armor. In all the years he had spent undercover, this thought was perhaps Gu Mang's only comfort. All he had was this empty illusion, this sentimental imagining.

Yet Mo Xi had scorned him as dirty.

"I should have it... I should have it, too..." The blue-eyed Gu Mang who had lost his mind had fought him for the ribbon. That voice filled with stubbornness and sorrow seemed to grate again in Mo Xi's ears through the flow of time. The vicious slap his past self had landed on Gu Mang's cheek seemed to whip across his own face, stinging sharp and hot.

How dare you. How could you be worthy...?!

Mo Xi was surprised he'd kept from sobbing, that he could

somehow bear this. He was unsure whether his pain had subsided into numbness, or if his heart had been forged into stone by the weight of despair.

Naught but one among the heavens and earth knew the events that had played out upon the Golden Terrace.

He felt his limbs were about to be torn from his body. The jade scroll gnawed at his soul, but in the depths of his skull, a voice spoke faintly, circling him, interrogating him without cease.

Do you wish to keep reading? Mo Xi, Xihe-jun. What are you made of? Can you face this bloody past, this bloody truth?

Each word, each phrase was like a sharp knife cutting open his heart, but his body no longer seemed to belong to him. Fresh blood filled his chest, but he couldn't feel it.

He opened blank eyes like a walking corpse. *Pain? Death? Shattered core? None of that matters anymore.* He murmured— *Blame me for being stone or ice. Let me keep reading. I want to know everything, these truths that have been hidden away, swallowed up, painted over.*

Why did you hide it from me... Why... Before you stepped onto this path... You pushed me away... You kept me in the dark... Why! Why...

"Since thou hast decided," the jade scroll intoned, "offer up thy flesh and blood unto me—to soothe your heart's regret—"

His chest throbbed with pain, as if an invisible claw covered in barbs had torn through his chest and seized his heart. The spiritual flow from his core fluctuated as if it would explode. Jiang Yexue had warned him: reading these half-repaired jade scrolls required one's vital spirit and spiritual energy; he would suffer excruciating agony. But at that moment Mo Xi only marveled that the pain was no more than this... It couldn't outweigh even a fraction of the pain brought on by these buried truths.

Innumerable years swirled and remerged like clouds as he watched. The Golden Terrace vanished. What appeared in its place was the Chamber of Ice in the imperial prison.

This was the cell he had seen in the Time Mirror, where Lu Zhanxing had been kept. The jade scroll had returned him to that ghastly hell bereft of light. As the scene in front of him came into focus, the taste of copper surged in Mo Xi's throat. He endured waves of dizziness, lifting his eyes to watch the truth surfacing once more.

In that prison cell eight years ago, one lamp cast a weak glow. It spat out listless flames, as if its light would shrivel and burn out at any moment.

Lu Zhanxing sat on the narrow and icy stone bed. This Lu Zhanxing, who hadn't yet seen Gu Mang, seemed a completely different man from the calm and guilt-free Deputy General Lu in the Time Mirror. He leaned against the wall, despondent, his face buried deep in the shadows. Strands of matted hair fell in front of his eyes, and his entire body emanated a sense of misery. Right now, he was truly a wretched prisoner.

The prison doors creaked open.

"Bastard Lu, the interrogation official sent by His Imperial Majesty is here!" the warden called out. "If you have any grievances, speak them; if you have any requests, make them; but remember to behave! You'd better not go crazy!" He put on a flattering smile and said to the man standing outside, "Your Excellency, if you please."

"You may withdraw."

The masked interrogation official stepped into the cell. Magic came to his fingers, and he closed the door with a wave of his hand. Within the cramped room, no one could hear their conversation—save for Mo Xi, who was invisible as he watched.

Lu Zhanxing showed no stir of emotion at the arrival of this interrogation official—many such people had come in the past few days, but not a single one had brought him hope. He kept his head down, resting his sturdy arms on his knees. He dully repeated the request he had perhaps already made thousands of times. "I want to see Gu Mang," he said flatly.

No one answered him.

"There's nothing else I want. I have no grievances to report, I have nothing else to appeal," Lu Zhanxing muttered without the slightest spark of life, as though he had been stripped of all vitality and left with a singular obsession. "I want to apologize to him in person. Afterward, you can kill me...drawn and quartered or death by a thousand cuts or boiled alive, whatever. I won't cry foul."

The interrogation official didn't speak. He knelt before Lu Zhanxing's dirty bed and kowtowed three careful times.

Lu Zhanxing finally reacted, somewhat stunned. "What...does this mean?"

"Before the battle at Phoenix Cry Mountain, we were playing dice. We hadn't finished ten rounds before I had to leave. We promised to keep playing after we returned victorious." The visitor produced a pair of wooden dice from his qiankun pouch. "We can no longer have victory. But I brought the dice."

Two wooden dice, with a red lotus mark in place of the sixth dot.

Lu Zhanxing seemed to have been struck by lightning. He leapt off the bed, grabbing this interrogation official by the lapels before the man finished speaking, before the mask even came off. These two brothers who had grown up together had the familiarity of siblings. Lu Zhanxing stared into the black eyes behind the mask. In his entire life, he had never seen anyone with eyes brighter or livelier than his dear brother, his Mang-er. Lu Zhanxing was a strong and sturdy man, but he immediately choked up. He looked into Gu Mang's eyes and cried, "Mang-er! It's you?!"

The interrogation official reached up and slid off the mask that hid his features. Gu Mang's face, soaked with tears, was revealed to the dim light.

The last time these brothers saw each other, they were a mighty and invincible general and a heroic and courageous commander. In the blink of an eye, one had been demoted to a commoner, and the other was condemned to die.

"It's me." Gu Mang's voice was terribly hoarse, the rims of his eyes red. "I'm sorry, it's been so long...and I've only just come to see you now..."

Reunited at last, they wept piteously in each other's arms. Eventually, Lu Zhanxing wiped away the tears on his face, tightly gripping Gu Mang's hand. He had so many questions to ask—*how did you get here, why have you come, how are you now*—but as Lu Zhanxing gazed into his brother's face, the first tear-thickened question that rose to his lips was: "Mang-er, the battle at Phoenix Cry Mountain... Do, do you blame me?"

"Zhanxing..." Gu Mang squeezed out between sobs.

But Lu Zhanxing was mired in his guilt; he had stifled these words in his heart for so long, they had long since flooded their confines. He couldn't stop himself from muttering, "I was impulsive, I don't know what happened... It was like some demon took hold of my mind. I suddenly thought shedding blood and offering up my head for this nation wasn't worth it at all; I suddenly thought nothing we've done was worth it... But... But...that's not how I really felt... Perhaps I wondered about these things here and there in the past, but that's really not how I felt! I let down my seventy thousand brothers at Phoenix Cry Mountain... I don't know what happened to me, Mang-er. I betrayed your trust; I betrayed our brothers' trust..."

Each word and sentence was heartrending. Lu Zhanxing was the picture of woe and regret. Those red-rimmed eyes, wet with tears, were like hooks viciously driving into Mo Xi's flesh. How could the Lu Zhanxing in front of him, so remorseful for the great wrong he had done, be the same person as that sloppy and careless man in the Time Mirror? Everything Lu Zhanxing said in the Time Mirror had been insane—

"Having me ruin his life is still better than seeing him ruin his own and the lives of others. His Imperial Majesty was right...to strip him of his power!"

No...

No, no, no, that wasn't true! None of it was true. The truth was nothing like that.

Mo Xi watched Lu Zhanxing kneel before Gu Mang, choking on his unbearable regret and agony. His ears were ringing... *It was wrong...all wrong!* He heard Lu Zhanxing apologizing to Gu Mang over and over, he heard Lu Zhanxing say to Gu Mang: "Mang-er, I'm sorry."

Bitter cold coursed through Mo Xi. In hindsight, the Lu Zhanxing in the Time Mirror had already known his death would save thirty thousand lives, which was why he'd embraced his guilt. He wasn't a lunatic who destroyed his brother's dream and thought himself infallible. Rather, he was keeping this secret from Mo Xi all the way to his death, never letting on that he was a hero cast in the mold of a villain,[10] a loyal subject falsely accused.

---

10   From a couplet about the general Yue Fei. "The green hill is fortunate to be the burial ground of a loyal general, the white iron was innocent to be cast into the statues of traitors." Statues of the people who brought about Yue Fei's death were cast, kneeling, at Yue Fei's grave.

To protect Gu Mang, to protect his remaining comrades, the emperor handed him the mask of a guilty subject, the mask of a reckless brute, and he wore it until death. But in truth, Lu Zhanxing had never betrayed Gu Mang. He was Gu Mang's true friend; he was Gu Mang's worthy second-in-command. They were much the same, these brothers, both willing to die for their ideals.

With great difficulty, Gu Mang calmed Lu Zhanxing and helped him sit on the edge of the stone bed. Voice breaking on sobs, he said to this man racked with guilt, "Zhanxing... You never betrayed us. From beginning to end, you've always been our brother."

Though Lu Zhanxing had recovered himself somewhat, at this, he broke down again. He buried his head in his hands, kneading his face. "No... I was the one who killed that Rouli envoy. I was the one who lost control, who was blinded by my selfishness."

The rims of Gu Mang's eyes were a vivid red as he interlocked their hands tightly. "It wasn't like that."

Lu Zhanxing said nothing.

Gu Mang's next words were like lightning breaking through the heavens, piercing through heavy clouds—

"Listen to me. What blinded you wasn't your selfishness, but the Zhenlong chess piece the Liao Kingdom planted in your body."

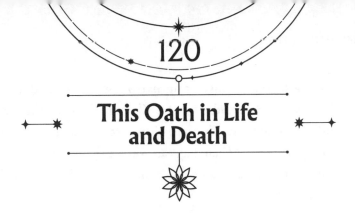

120

This Oath in Life and Death

L U ZHANXING WAS like a caged beast; his emotions were running high, and it took Gu Mang a long time to explain everything clearly.

As a spectator, it was difficult for Mo Xi to describe Lu Zhanxing's expression after he heard the truth. When Gu Mang began to explain the matter of the Zhenlong white chess piece, Lu Zhanxing's countenance fluctuated constantly. From astonishment to blankness, from blankness to wild joy, from wild joy to rage, from rage to sorrow, stuttering with shock countless times between.

After Gu Mang finished, Lu Zhanxing fell upon that icy stone bed as if freed. His wide eyes stared vacantly at the low ceiling of the prison. Only after several long minutes did he murmur, as if dreaming, "I...didn't betray you all..."

Gu Mang's gaze was gentle, his voice hoarse and low: "You never have."

"I didn't betray you all... I didn't betray you all... Ha ha...ha ha ha ha!" Veins bulged at Lu Zhanxing's temples as the overwhelming emotion flushed his cheeks red. But as he laughed, he began to weep. Perhaps embarrassed, he flung his arms over his eyes, but crystalline tears still seeped from beneath them, rolling down to soak into his temples.

Gu Mang sat on the edge of his narrow stone bed and looked at Lu Zhanxing. He couldn't see Lu Zhanxing's eyes—they were still hidden behind his sturdy arms. He was still for a moment, then asked in a quiet voice, "Zhanxing, can you see them too?"

It was such an inexplicable question, but Lu Zhanxing understood. So did Mo Xi.

Can you see them too? See those seventy thousand soldiers crossing the river of the underworld to come to your side? Those who fought shoulder to shoulder with you, those who drank their fill of strong wine before countless battles with you, those brothers who swore their oaths with you—do you see them flocking to your side? You're surrounded by seventy thousand dead, whispering day and night without rest. Gradually, you stop being able to see the world in front of you. Bit by bit, so slowly you hardly notice, you begin living with the dead. You become a living tombstone, the names of those dead souls carved into your heart.

Can you see them too...?

Lu Zhanxing mumbled from dry lips. The first time, nothing intelligible came out. Only on the second attempt did he manage to say, "Always. I've seen them all along."

They were still for a long time before Gu Mang replied, "Me too."

The candle flame in the prison shed a string of waxen tears.

"Zhanxing, after Phoenix Cry Mountain, we are both the living dead. Do you blame me?"

Lu Zhanxing slowly lowered his arms, half a teary eye showing. "What?"

"I tricked you...tricked you all into following me onto this path. I promised you a grand future, but with me, none of you lived well for long. Instead, you became guilty subjects and reckless brutes."

Gu Mang hung his head and stared into his hands. "Recently, I've been thinking about what kind of person I am."

His dense lashes trembled, casting a soft shadow on the bridge of his nose. "I know Chonghua has expressed many judgments of me. I've been praised, mocked, slandered, flattered... I never cared; I always felt I was doing the right thing. That I, Gu Mang, had never betrayed my conscience."

He went on, "But after the battle of Phoenix Cry Mountain, I can't justify it to myself anymore. All along, I've said again and again that I want to change Chonghua's, and even the Nine Provinces', views on slaves. I always told the people who followed me that I would take them home, that I would give them a future much brighter than the present. But it turns out one defeat is all it takes for me to be beaten back to my original state like a pathetic clown. I'm the general of an army, but I can't even wrangle the slightest fairness for my brothers."

Those whispers he had never heeded seemed to ring in his ears.

Power threatens kings! The higher the lowly slave climbs, the lower he'll fall! That man is the next Hua Po'an!

No, how could he compare to Hua Po'an? At least Hua Po'an established a country, at least his brothers received rewards and gained advantages. He, Gu Mang, was a dog rolling in the mud. Even if he'd had Hua Po'an's nefarious intentions, he didn't have the ability to deliver on them. He was a charlatan. Tricking that crowd of fools into following him to their deaths. What would they gain by following him? Dreams?

Some Beast of the Altar he is, ha ha ha ha...

Mocking laughter circled him like a vulture. Gu Mang slowly closed his eyes. When he opened them again, it was to look down at his calloused palms. "Now I finally understand. I'm no more than a gravedigger, expending so much time and effort just to bury all my brothers in a pit."

Lu Zhanxing didn't make a sound as he turned his head. He looked at Gu Mang contemplatively. "His Imperial Majesty won't be reversing my sentence, will he?" Before Gu Mang could answer, he continued. "I know the answer. The old nobles, the black magic curse... Our new emperor is too green. Even if it were someone else in my place, he wouldn't be able to save them."

Gu Mang lowered his head. "Zhanxing, I'm sorry. Other than telling you the truth, I can't do anything."

Lu Zhanxing turned his blank gaze back to the ceiling. The tear-stains at the ends of his eyes were already dry. "It's fine. I don't blame him, nor do I blame you."

Freed of the shackles of a guilty subject, Lu Zhanxing had relaxed entirely. Anyone would have complicated emotions when facing a death sentence, but Lu Zhanxing seemed content. "It was my bad luck to be planted with the Zhenlong chess piece." Lu Zhanxing picked up the two wooden dice Gu Mang had brought, running his fingers over them. "Do you remember? When we played dice as kids, I'd lose every time and have to give you my sweets. My luck has always been bad; it's no one else's fault." As he spoke, he tossed the dice carelessly onto the bed. The two wooden cubes tumbled, eventually rolling to a stop: snake eyes. "See, was I wrong?"

Gu Mang looked down again, his shoulders shaking. "Some time ago, I heard there was a gambling demon in Chonghua who showed up wherever he went in a green copper mask. If you chanced upon him, he would always win—he never tallied a single loss at the gambling tables... That person was you, wasn't it?"

Lu Zhanxing stiffened.

"You always get whatever number you roll for. What bad luck?" Gu Mang rasped. "It's only that you've always indulged me. You wanted to share your sweets with me."

Looking at Gu Mang, Lu Zhanxing heaved a soft sigh. Of course he wanted to protect this little rascal. This had been destined upon their first meeting, more or less.

Back when Lu Zhanxing had just been sold into Wangshu Manor, he came across Murong Lian bullying Gu Mang, then only four years old. The young master had smeared oil paints all over Gu Mang's face and forced him to stand frozen with a bowl of water balanced on his head.

Murong-gongzi laughed wildly. "Stand there for a full shichen. If a drop of water spills from the bowl, every slave in the entire manor will go hungry along with you!"

Lu Zhanxing had inwardly despaired. He must have met with eight lifetimes' worth of misfortune. This little brat was so young—how could he endure such a thing for so long? It looked like Lu Zhanxing would go hungry his first day in the manor.

But against all expectations, the cook handed him two big and fluffy steamed buns when dinnertime came around. That was how Lu Zhanxing learned the little child had actually gathered all his willpower and stood motionless for a full shichen. This greatly upset Murong Lian, so even though the other slaves escaped hunger that night, Gu Mang was still given nothing.

Lu Zhanxing ate one steamed bun, then pocketed the other and went looking for that little kid. He searched the whole of the sprawling Wangshu Manor before he finally found Gu Mang crouching in some grass in the flower garden.

"Hey." He patted Gu Mang's shoulder.

A brightly colored little face scribbled with oil paints turned to him. The child chewed silently, his lips covered in dirt. Lu Zhanxing couldn't make out his features clearly; what struck him were those pitch-black eyes, as brilliant as the stars in the night sky. "Wh-why are you eating dirt…?" Lu Zhanxing asked, startled.

Gu Mang was so pitiable. He was only four years old, his childish voice nasal with tears. "Gege, I'm hungry."

As Lu Zhanxing gazed into those helpless eyes like a little cub's, his heart melted. He hastily dug out the second steamed bun and said gently, "This is for you, don't cry. Aiyo… Gege will protect you. Look at you, you poor little thing."

In the cold prison, Lu Zhanxing studied Gu Mang in front of him. Stripped of his battle armor and his glory, the present Gu Mang was not so different from that little rascal who had eaten mud with his head down. Just as helpless, and with just as little to his name.

They had struggled for almost half their lives, but they never truly gained anything.

Lu Zhanxing's grimy face gradually showed a flicker of exasperated warmth. He reached out a dirty hand to stroke Gu Mang's cheek and wipe the wet corners of Gu Mang's eyes. "Mang-er, don't cry."

Gu Mang said nothing.

The corners of Lu Zhanxing's mouth curled in the wisp of a smile. "Gege will protect you. Look at you, you poor little thing."

Gu Mang squeezed his eyes shut, his features filled with pain as he swallowed thickly.

"This is the last time Gege can protect you. In the future, whether you advance or retreat, whether you forge ahead or set down your sword and retire—it's all up to you. Mang-er, I'm happy you could tell me the truth. Even if nothing can be changed, at least I know— I never betrayed my seventy thousand comrades, I never betrayed you.

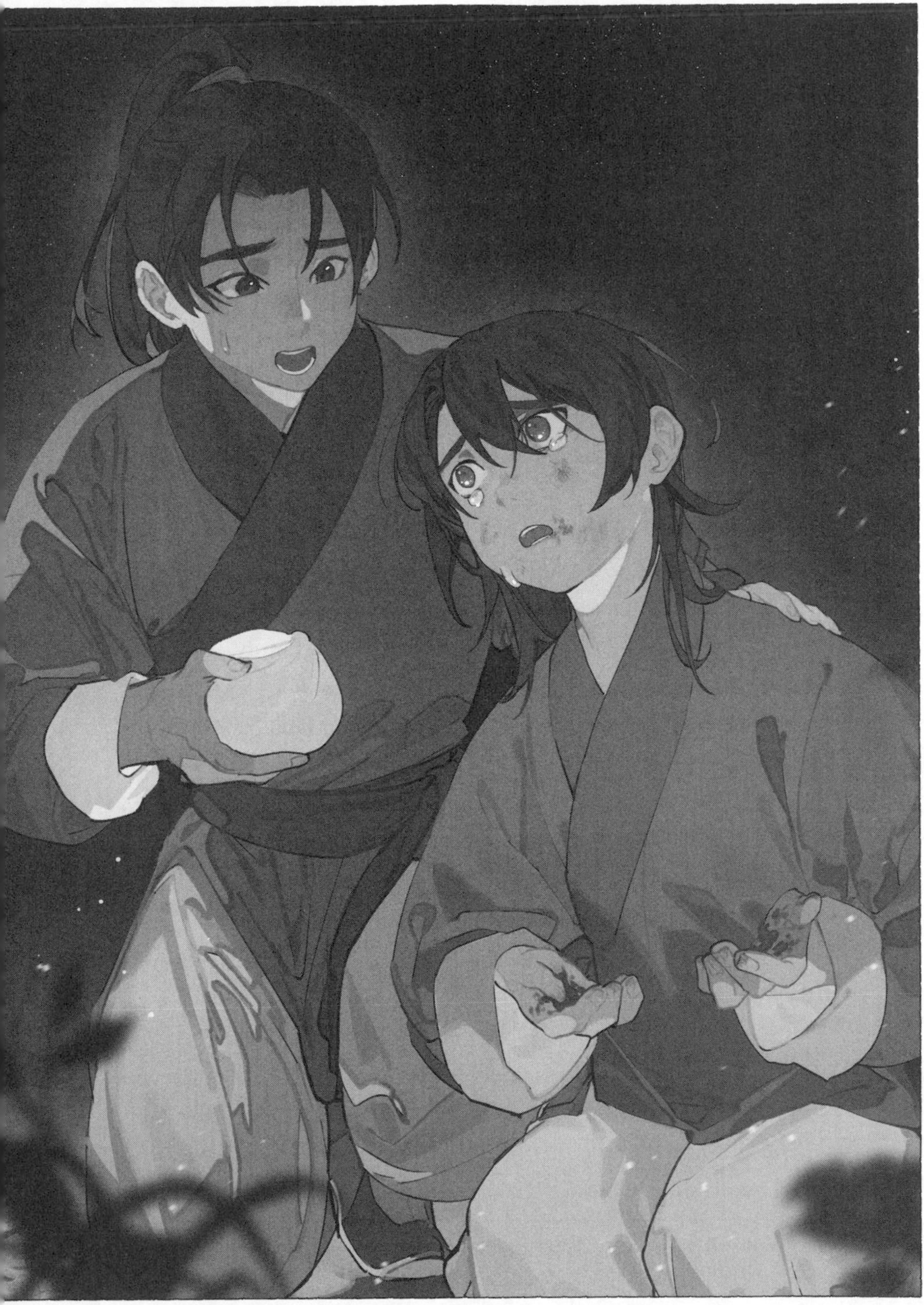

I can finally be at ease. Keep going. Whatever you choose, your Lu-ge will be happy for you."

As he spoke, he bit his lower lip, trying to hold back his emotions with all his might. At last, he grabbed Gu Mang, who had long been weeping silently, and pressed their foreheads together. He clapped Gu Mang on the shoulder. "After all, you're my brother. Even if we've never sworn."

Gu Mang swiped tears from his face, then looked up through bright black eyes. "Let's swear it."

Before Lu Zhanxing could respond, Gu Mang replaced his mask and left the room. Very soon, he returned to the cell with a jar of pear-blossom white wine.

Holding back tears, Gu Mang schooled his tone to solemnity. "Lu Zhanxing, after today's farewell, the two of us will meet again at the autumn execution. I was born without a family, without a father, without anyone to rely on. I've never dared be reckless, never dared be unbridled, never dared overstep my bounds. Before others, I've always endured in silence and rarely showed my true feelings. Except...except with Lu-xiong, who showed me what it feels like to have a family. To have a big brother."

As Gu Mang spoke, the rims of Lu Zhanxing's eyes also reddened. Memories of the care they had shown each other since their youth, all the times they leaned on each other, sprang vividly to their minds, flashing past one by one.

"Xiongzhang,[11] thank you for these twenty years of care."

Lu Zhanxing raised his head. He'd thought that, since he was to be executed in a few months, he had no more need for deep connections with other people. But upon hearing Gu Mang speak, each word sincere and agonizingly heartfelt, he was overwhelmed;

---

11 A respectful term of address meaning "older brother."

passion welled up in his chest. He blinked back hot tears and took the pear-blossom white from Gu Mang's hand. "I was born to a life as insignificant as drifting duckweed, and never expected I would have a rightful and proper brother. Even less had I expected that right now, with my infamy spread far and wide and as the end of my life draws near, the heavens would still give me the chance to become your sworn brother. I once disliked, distrusted, and disdained these rites, but today... Today, I, Lu Zhanxing, could not be happier. All right, let's swear!"

He continued, "Even if we were born slaves, even if the end is nigh, even if the future is vast and unknown—today, we'll swear for the hell of it! The two of us didn't ask to be born together and can't ask to die together, but we can carve this into our hearts, never to be forgotten even in the Yellow Springs."

Both tilted their heads back to drink. They bowed to each other, then broke into laughter, hand in hand. But that laughter held tears, and those tears filled their eyes.

"Dage," Gu Mang said.

Lu Zhanxing laughed out loud. "From now on, neither of us are alone anymore. Even when I walk in the underworld, I'll know I have a true brother."

That tragic yet bold, despairing yet glorious laughter surrounded Mo Xi as the scene in the prison began to blur. It gradually lost definition, the figures of those two brothers becoming hazy.

Lu Zhanxing... Gu Mang...

Brothers.

So Gu Mang had once gone to the prison to see Lu Zhanxing. The two of them had sworn to each other as brothers, and sworn to each other as family. All of Lu Zhanxing's reactions within the Time Mirror had been an act. He had never been a traitor who carelessly destroyed Gu Mang's dream and heartlessly deserted his seventy thousand comrades. His true intent... His true intent was—

"This is the last time Gege can protect you. In the future, whether you advance or retreat, whether you forge ahead or set down your sword and retire—it's all up to you."

"Keep going. Whatever you choose, your Lu-ge will be happy for you."

"After all, you're my brother."

When the blade whistled down at the autumn execution, leaving them on opposite sides of death, it didn't merely take Gu Mang's last comrade. When that executioner's blade fell, it took his only family. Newly sworn, so recently gained that the times he called him *dage* could be counted on one hand—in all the world, his only big brother.

121

The Long Winter Will Pass

AGONY BURST from Mo Xi's heart and spread through his body like cracks opening in the earth. Within the history-recording jade scroll, Mo Xi went down on one knee, striving to endure it, and spat out a mouthful of blood.

The image of the prison had shattered, leaving behind a blur of light and shadow. Or perhaps it wasn't the light that was blurry, but his vision. The jade scroll was stripping his spiritual energy and tearing at his flesh. The pain in his soul and the torture of his body broke across his insides like the tide.

The icy voice of the jade scroll spoke again, echoing in his ears. "This scroll is damaged, its pages ruined beyond repair. Shouldst thou persist, thou wilt suffer severe injury to the flesh..."

Severe injury to the flesh...

What did he care about *severe injury to the flesh*? What physical suffering could be more painful than these truths? Gu Mang...

He was clearly a loyal subject charged with a mission, but he had buried himself in filthy mud, unable to escape.

He clearly knew the truth, but had silently endured unimaginable torment.

He was clearly a flame that wanted to warm the world, but he was trampled again and again, stamped out, ground to ash.

He had clearly just sworn an elder brother of his own...

Mo Xi coughed blood, swallowing the shattered sobs in his throat, closing his eyes with a shiver. Tears escaped his eyes, flowing freely down his cheeks—he was on the verge of collapse.

Back then...what must Gu Mang have felt?

He had just gained a sworn brother, and he'd only gotten to call him *dage* a few times before sending him to the executioner. He knew his dage was innocent, but he couldn't exonerate him nor tell anyone the truth.

When Gu Mang smiled as he swore that oath and kowtowed to Lu Zhanxing, what had he felt?

What physical injury could hurt more than the sorrow of being a spy?

Knowledge that couldn't be shared, love that couldn't be spoken. A pair of hands...stained against his will with the blood of his brothers, his comrades. Watching as the demons and beasts around him devastated the nation he used to protect, but having to laugh and shout as if delighted. Hearing the wailing of civilians from his motherland, the crying of infants, the enraged shouts of soldiers— but having to put on an indestructible mask, unable to shed a single tear, unable to show the slightest mercy, unable to expose the tiniest hint of hesitation or sorrow.

How must that have felt...?

His Gu Mang, his Gu-shixiong, Chonghua's General Gu, was someone who would take the military records in both hands and carve the names of each and every faceless soldier into his memory. He was so gentle, so kind, so quick to smile, so deeply caring and reverential toward every life. He could hardly bear to trample a flower on the battlefield, yet he had wielded the knife that personally stabbed those living bodies—he may as well have carved out his own heart!

Mo Xi was choking on blood, slowly staggering forward. All around was formless darkness; the only spark of light was in the distance. He knew it was the next memory he needed, stored in the history-recording jade scroll.

He walked onward. With each step it felt like invisible hands ripped into his insides, frantically plundering his body for blood and vitality. The jade scroll had consumed his spiritual energy down to the dregs, but that light was still so far from him. So far it resembled Gu Mang from eight years ago, a shabby cloth sack on his back carrying his sworn brother's head, leaving Chonghua in the setting sun, setting his steps to the strains of that old beggar's sorrowful folk song.

> *Time as swift as the shuttle does fly*
> *Yet before it I think two paths lie:*
> *In bygone days was I envy of all,*
> *Careless years passed in careless thrall.*
> *Alas, today is my purse light;*
> *Each hour, minute a yearlong blight.*
> *I, too, once rode a splendid horse,*
> *My flag bid thousands on their course;*
> *One cry dispersed the demon crowd;*
> *Godlike, before my feet all bowed.*
> *Today none mark my glories past,*
> *Men once called friends all turn their backs;*
> *By day I starve, my nights lack sleep,*
> *Streetside I sing here for my keep.*
> *Too high a flight, too far a fall;*
> *I blame not heaven nor kin for't all.*
> *But knowing now my bitter end,*

I rue th'demons I once called friends.
And now that naught can change my state
I beg you all to avoid my fate.

And now he'd come to find out that was not the retreating silhouette of a traitor, but a hero's farewell.

Gu Mang stood upon Chonghua Bridge, looking back over the capital city, knowing that he would soon fight a battle with no one to support him, soon enter the fray splattered in blood and gore. Knowing he was walking into hell.

In a soft murmur, he had said, *Goodbye.*

Then he carefully pocketed the only travel ration his homeland would grant him—the pastry the old beggar gave him, already stone-cold. He lowered his head and walked toward his seventy thousand dead brothers.

Gu Mang... Gu Mang...

Stop walking, will you... Why can't I catch up to you...?

Mo Xi took step after step toward that light, tears ceaselessly flowing down his face. The darkness around him seemed to take the form of innumerable dancing shadows, mocking him and cursing him; all the vicious things he said in the past pierced his bones once more.

"Traitor!"

"Don't you know how dirty you are..."

"You wanted revenge! For your dashed prospects, for your dead comrades-in-arms, for your own advancement. You didn't care whose blood you spilled!"

It wasn't like that...

It wasn't like that.

Don't curse him, don't curse him, he's innocent...!

Mo Xi was being driven crazy by those wild shadows in the dark. He could no longer feel the torturous pain inflicted by the jade scroll; his only wish was to wade back into the river of time to tell his past self: It wasn't like that. The truth wasn't like that.

Gu Mang, he...had never thought of revenge, had never thought of ambition. He only wanted to guard those seventy thousand gravestones, the last dignity his brothers deserved. He only wanted to see Chonghua sprouting green after the snow melted, red peach blossoms blooming again on the shore. He only wanted... He only wanted to see realized those promises the emperor had made to him on the Golden Terrace: a peaceful world of equality that would blossom from bodies that had been trampled into mud. To see the old replaced by the new, verdant growth replacing spilled blood, right replacing wrong, happiness replacing sorrow.

He only wanted to see heroes becoming heroes regardless of their birth, to see the gravestones of martyrs receive a jug of clear wine and a burned slip of paper peace.

When did he ever bear the slightest hatred...?

He just wanted to bring his brothers home.

Mo Xi staggered along, step by step, walking toward that light— as if each step could bring him closer to that General Gu from eight years ago.

It hurt too much...

His spiritual energy was spent, but he didn't stop. The jade scroll began to pull power from his core, threatening to crack open his heart. But he didn't feel the sickening pain; he just had a thought—

The instant it occurred to him, his tears fell like rain. He thought: When Gu Mang's core had shattered, did it feel like this? Did his little shixiong who was so afraid of pain, who was so very gentle and cried so easily, feel ten or twenty times this agony?

Even while in that much pain, had he endured the scorn and the judgment of his comrades, with no one to care for him, no one to look after him, no one to recognize how much he had sacrificed?

When that smiling General Gu turned to leave Chonghua, no one knew what he felt exactly.

"Gu Mang..."

As he labored onward, Mo Xi had a vision. He saw, in that faltering light, a Gu Mang who wore the military uniform of Chonghua. He was smiling, and followed by Lu Zhanxing, followed by the figures of all those brothers who had died in battle—Zhao Sheng, Wei Ping, Luo Xiaochuan... They surrounded him. Gu Mang looked so happy: sharper, more polished, more high-spirited and heroic than Mo Xi had ever seen him.

Mo Xi walked toward them. Gu Mang seemed to notice him, his black eyes flashing with surprise. An impossibly brilliant smile crinkled the elegant ends of his eyes. He smiled so brightly, without the slightest pain or shadow in his eyes. He held out his arms to Mo Xi. "Shidi, stop crying, it's fine... Look, this is the dream I've had all my life. I hope one day the world will right itself, here in Chonghua or within the entire cultivation world. Don't laugh at me for being naive or idealistic. I know things will get better and better, just as flowers will bloom, rain will cease, and winter will pass... My princess, my royal highness, believe me. When has your Gu Mang-gege ever lied to you?"

Gu Mang had once said these words to the young Mo Xi as they lay on the riverbank in their academy days. Now, as they crossed time and space, tears streamed down Mo Xi's cheeks.

Flowers will bloom, rain will cease, winter will pass. Believe me... My princess, my royal highness. Because...if even you lose faith in me...

The light dimmed. Gu Mang's silhouette distorted, and the military uniform turned into snowy-white slave robes as a pitch-black collar locked itself around his neck. The figures of Lu Zhanxing and his brothers scattered and faded behind him like swirling snow.

In the darkness, in the unending night, Gu Mang fell to his knees with his hands soaked in blood, curling up like an abandoned beast.

If even you lose faith in me, then I truly will be fighting on my own. I will really be alone.

Believe in me, won't you...?

His figure became smaller and smaller, more and more stooped. Mo Xi rushed toward him as if crazed, heedless of anything else, shouting in grief—

"Gu Mang!"

Gu Mang. I believe you... I believe what you said, that flowers will bloom, rain will cease, winter will pass... Will you turn back? Will you turn from that dark road?

In his thirty-three years, his Gu-shixiong had been a slave for more than twenty, a traitor for five, a prisoner for three. If you made a reckoning of his life like this, he had never lived a single good day. It hit Mo Xi then that Gu Mang had never once thought of himself. He had never wondered where he would be, with his filthy body and bloody hands, on the day the flowers bloomed, the rain ceased, and the winter passed.

Yet Mo Xi had once said to that selfless and noble commander— *You didn't care whose blood you spilled!*

When had Gu Mang ever not cared whose blood he spilled? By the time he was forced to kill his first innocent citizen of Chonghua... he was probably already dead and buried in his own heart.

That beam of light at the end of the jade scroll flickered. Gu Mang grew more and more distant; Mo Xi couldn't catch up.

He heard Jiang Yexue's voice from far away, as if he were speaking across the sea. "Mo Xi! Mo Xi! Wake up! If you keep going, your core will shatter! Mo Xi!"

The illusory Gu Mang stopped walking and turned. "Mo Xi... don't chase after me anymore."

Flimsy snow-white robes fluttered in the wind, ink-dark hair framed his hollow cheeks. In the many years since he had gone from worshipped commander to despised traitor, he had thinned so much, weakened so much. He would never be as strong and healthy as he used to be; even the color of his eyes had changed. But those eyes, which had seen untold death and blood, hidden countless secrets and sorrows, were still so bright and so gentle. Even in the furthest depths of suffering, they held the strongest hope.

"Don't follow me any farther. Everyone has their own path. I chose this one long ago... It's not an easy road to take. But I know it was right."

"Gu Mang..."

"It was the right one, so I don't regret it."

The wind rose, fluttering through Gu Mang's robes. Slowly, he scattered in the breeze like crushed flower petals. Gu Mang smiled at him before he dissolved, a smile so radiant it was like the first golden bloom of winter jasmine, bravely poking its head from the snow. As if to say, *Look, I didn't lie to you. Spring will come. Spring has already come.*

A sudden force yanked him out of the darkness. The afterimage of Gu Mang lingered in his vision, but Mo Xi had at last returned to Jiang Yexue's residence.

He hadn't yet come to his senses. Blood streamed endlessly from his split skin and from his mouth, but he couldn't feel the pain. He heard Jiang Yexue calling for him, anxious, his fingers on Mo Xi's heart vein as he passed him spiritual energy.

He felt nothing.

His eyes were open. He didn't blink; he was afraid, if he did, what remained of Gu Mang's smile would disappear completely. Tears left tracks on his bloodstained face, rolling down his temples.

"Mo Xi..." Jiang Yexue saw that Mo Xi's spiritual energy was exhausted, that his core, once damaged by Gu Mang, was again on the precipice of failing. He found himself asking, voice rough, "Why... What was this all for...?"

Mo Xi didn't respond, as if his soul had died. After a long while, his lips moved. Gently, he withdrew his hand from Jiang Yexue's grasp.

"Mo Xi...?"

Even in this state, he struggled arduously to his feet. Mo Xi forced himself to stand, bolstered by some unknown strength, and walked unsteadily toward the door.

At the sight of him on the verge of collapse yet still obstinately moving forward, Jiang Yexue turned pale as a sheet. "Where do you think you're going?"

Mo Xi paused. "Home."

He had to go home and see Gu Mang... He had to tell Gu Mang, who'd recovered his memories, the truth he'd seen... He needed to get home as soon as possible...

He needed to rush back to belatedly say, "Wait for me," as he should have said eight years ago. He needed to add, "I believe you."

I'm sorry...

I'll never let you be alone again. In darkness or in infamy, I'll endure it with you... I will brave it...with you...

"He's not at Xihe Manor anymore!" A sudden shout, like a peal of thunder. Mo Xi turned.

Jiang Yexue's expression was unsightly, as if he couldn't decide whether to speak or not. But at last, he gritted his teeth. "When you were reading the scroll, Murong Lian came by. Sishu Terrace has taken Gu Mang away."

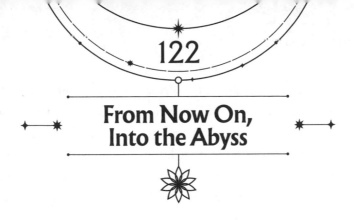

122

From Now On,
Into the Abyss

I N CHONGHUA'S SISHU TERRACE—

"Elder Zhou!"

"Greetings to Elder Zhou!"

Zhou He was a strict person, and he had a rigid habit of changing his clothes. Outside, he wore the formal robes of his own family, but the moment he returned to Sishu Terrace, he went first to the bathing room to change into Sishu Terrace robes, no matter how important the tasks awaiting him. Given his station, no one would give him grief for wearing formal robes, but Zhou He insisted on the uniform of Sishu Terrace cultivators.

Every agency in Chonghua had a uniform that represented their function. Most popular among young men were the tailored black combat uniforms of Mo Xi's Bureau of Military Affairs with their narrow waist, tapered sleeves, turned-down collar, golden buttons at the hems, and golden tassel at the lapels. Most popular among young women were the uniforms of Shennong Terrace, jade-green robes of peacock silk perfumed with eaglewood incense, and a gauzy white silk coat worn over top.

In comparison, the standard attire of Sishu Terrace was less appealing—a pale blue robe with a standing collar and narrow sleeves, nothing else.

Some interpreted Zhou He's obsession with his uniform robes as a compulsive disorder, while others attributed it to superstition, among various other theories. In reality, the reason Zhou He insisted on changing was a simple one: he loved his work. With every assignment he accepted, he felt an indescribable sense of ceremony. Changing into the uniform robes marked the beginning of a ritual.

He was about to enjoy an intoxicating ecstasy.

"Elder Zhou, the gu worms and magical implements have been prepared. The specimen is waiting in the Asura Room and is currently in stable condition."

Zhou He strode down the long corridor as he adjusted the steel claw gauntlet on his left hand. At this, he paused in shock. "Stable? How stable?"

The attendant nodded. "Extremely stable. There's no strong reaction as of yet."

Zhou He didn't immediately respond. After a long moment he murmured, "The legendary Beast of the Altar indeed."

Sishu Terrace's Asura Room was deep underground. As Zhou He neared it, the iron chains over the doors retracted with a *clang*, and the stone doors carved with the indomitable figure of the stalwart warrior Xingtian slowly swung outward.

A gust of freezing air swept from the gap.

The guards flanking the stone door performed obeisance toward Zhou He. One of them shook out a sable overcoat, preparing to drape it over the elder's shoulders. Zhou He raised a gauntleted hand: there was no need. He walked straight in.

The Asura Room was a cold cell roughly twenty yards wide. Because most experiments were best conducted at freezing temperatures, the inner walls of the Asura Room were built of bricks cut from ancient Kunlun ice. The walls, ceiling, and floors were all ice, and at first glance, it was like walking into a mythical palace of mirrors.

At present, Gu Mang was sitting in the middle of the Asura Room, his eyes closed in meditation.

Zhou He walked over and looked at this man with interest. He'd seen many test subjects during his tenure here. Most broke down in terror as soon as they crossed the threshold of Sishu Terrace, never mind the Asura Room. He had never seen anyone like Gu Mang, who acted as if this was nothing out of the ordinary.

Had this person lost his mind so completely that he didn't know what he would face here? Or had the Liao Kingdom's black-magic tempering given this mortal's body some special ability, making him unafraid of pain or death?

Either way, it was bound to be a fascinating examination. Zhou He grew more and more excited; he licked his lips, his long fingers gripping Lieying, the falcon at his waist.

Perhaps because of the exceptionality of Gu Mang's identity and reactions, Elder Zhou He, who had grown accustomed to seeing his specimens as beasts, felt a fresh curiosity toward this subject. He couldn't help wondering—what was Gu Mang thinking right now?

Gu Mang seemed to have read his mind. He slowly opened his eyes to reveal a lupine blue stare and spoke two words: "It's cold."

It's cold? That's it?

Zhou He stared intently into those clear blue eyes, as if trying to dredge up some more turbulent emotions. But there were none. How could there be any? How could Zhou He uncover the slightest hint of his true feelings if Gu Mang didn't want him to? Who did he think Gu Mang was?

The emperor's unsuspected spy.

The agent who had infiltrated the Liao Kingdom for more than five years.

The General Gu who had endured endless judgment, criticism, abuse, death, and guilt, yet had gritted his teeth and walked down the long road into the dark.

When he'd first defected to the Liao Kingdom, the Liao officials hadn't dared believe it. They'd tried hundreds of different tortures and all their malicious methods, but none had pried a solitary secret from his mouth. How could *Zhou He* possibly succeed?

"It doesn't matter," Zhou He said. "Very soon, the cold won't bother you." He raised a hand. At the beckoning of his fingers, the assisting attendants entered the Asura Room. "Begin," Zhou He intoned.

Through dense lashes, Gu Mang looked up at those Sishu Terrace cultivators standing in formation in their pale blue robes. Each held a wooden tray arranged with daggers, gu worms, magical implements, and medication. The daggers were for slicing open flesh, the gu worms and implements were for conducting black magic experiments, while the medicine was something quite precious— the finest Divine Tincture of Life, for preserving his life at critical moments.

The cultivator closest to him lifted a tray with a roll of snow-white bandages. Gu Mang knew this wasn't for binding wounds, but to fill his mouth and keep him from biting through his tongue to end his own life.

Gu Mang closed his eyes. He remembered now that this was the second time he was experiencing such a scene, the first being in the Liao Kingdom. Though the Time Mirror hadn't returned much of what passed in the years he defected, this scene was so painful it must've been an exception—

He had buried Lu Zhanxing's head on the shores of the Soul-Calling Abyss. Then, just as the emperor planned, he put on a show of having been pushed to the edge and defected to the Liao Kingdom in a fit of rage.

The great hall of the Liao Kingdom was paved with golden-red bricks, such that the entire hall seemed to be aflame. The full court of civil and military officials resembled a horde of monsters and demons, each with their own grotesque elements. Liao's youthful ruler wore the beaded crown and sat atop the lofty throne. He was a child of no more than sixteen, and exerted no control over the demons skulking beneath the throne. Their true master was the golden-masked man who stood at his ruler's side.

The guoshi of the Liao Kingdom.

Gu Mang remembered taking a knee, bowing as he offered up proof of his allegiance—a jade scroll containing detailed records of Chonghua's secret techniques from the past century.

Though the most important techniques had been excised, this scroll was still one of Chonghua's most important classified records. The Liao Kingdom court officials' eyes shone when they glimpsed it, and even the King of Liao craned his neck, anticipatory glee showing on his face.

Only the guoshi chuckled through that golden mask with its grinning eyes. "General Gu, let's not talk about the offering yet. Why don't we first discuss why you wish to turn your back on Chonghua?"

Gu Mang indignantly recounted his experiences after the defeat at Phoenix Cry Mountain to the gentlemen of Liao. When he mentioned his sworn brother's execution, tears flowed down his face, his voice breaking with sobs.

Even before his defection, many in the Liao Kingdom had heard rumors of Gu Mang's treatment after Phoenix Cry Mountain. Now, as they heard the tale from his own lips and gazed at that jade scroll filched from his own nation, their suspicion began to fall away.

"I've thoroughly experienced the disgrace Hua-guozhu[12] felt back then," Gu Mang said in the end. "Instead of remaining in Chonghua to be humiliated, I'd rather follow in the footsteps of Hua-guozhu and defect."

Hua Po'an was the founding ruler of the Liao Kingdom. Was there anyone at the scene who couldn't see the similarities between Hua Po'an and Gu Mang? The Liao ruler was immediately convinced, his voice shaking slightly with barely concealed excitement. "S-since this subject has had such a realization, then..."

Halfway through, he suddenly felt he had overstepped. He snapped his mouth shut and shot a glance at the man beside him, meeting the guoshi's smiling eyes. Cold sweat soaked through the Liao ruler's heavy robes. He swallowed and hastily added: "Th-th-then we'll await the guoshi's counsel!"

The guoshi narrowed his eyes in a smile, clasping both hands behind his back and turning toward Gu Mang, who was kneeling below. "General Gu, Beast of the Altar. This one is indeed familiar with your famous military prowess. The sworn fealty of a mighty beast is naturally a blessing from the heavens to our Liao, a cause for great celebration. But..."

The guoshi's voice grew soft. His eyes, which had been curved in a smile, suddenly snapped wide, glinting with cold light as he looked out at Gu Mang through the eyes of the golden mask. "But, General Gu," the guoshi said, "do you know what Hua-guozhu did first, when he forsook Chonghua?"

As those cold, slender eyes studied Gu Mang, he felt a pain like

---

12   Honorary term of address for the founding ruler of a nation.

the bite of a venomous snake. The guoshi smiled faintly, but those black eyes held not a hint of mirth.

"Hua-guozhu ordered his most loyal attendants to tie him up, and over the course of three days and three nights, tore Chonghua's techniques and all its magic from his body... Then he poured the breath of black magic into the vessels of his heart. With one determined act, he broke all ties—with Chonghua, and with his *honored teacher* Chen Tang."

The ominous glint of cruelty gleamed brighter with every word he spoke. By the end, that golden mask seemed to have melted through from hot malice; one could almost see that terrible and wicked face beneath.

The guoshi smiled a menacing smile. "General Gu, since you seek to follow in Hua-guozhu's footsteps, you know what proof of your allegiance we require. Do you not?"

And thus Gu Mang was escorted into the Liao Kingdom's Soul-Tempering Room.

It was a room remarkably similar to Chonghua's Sishu Terrace—a cold chamber built from dark ice, its attendants dressed in near identical pale blue robes. The trays that held magical implements, gu worms, daggers, and bandages—all were exactly the same.

The interrogation and the tempering were conducted simultaneously over three days and three nights. The flesh of his back was flayed open along his spine. Gu worms that ate spiritual energy were seeded deep in the wounds, and thousands of puppet strings crawled along his blood vessels, snapping and scrambling every meridian that ran with Chonghua's magic and making a gory mess of his viscera.

That guoshi sat in a rosewood chair, legs crossed, arms folded over his knees, studying Gu Mang. While he suffered, while he wailed, while he endured a life worse than death, saliva dripping from the corners of his mouth, his flesh mangled, his organs sliced to pieces, the guoshi would gently ask him, "General Gu. Do you regret it?"

He asked him: "Going from white to black is as difficult as going from black to white. You need to be sure—once your body is filled with black magic spiritual energy, only the Liao Kingdom, in all of the Nine Provinces and Twenty-Eight Nations, will take you in. Does your hatred of Chonghua run so deep?"

Gu Mang was already soaked in his own blood, but this was nothing; the greater agony came from the puppet strings burrowing deep into his back like the eight limbs of a crab. Those thousands of steel-silk threads had surely been refined with truth-compulsion magic. Whenever he lied, the strings threaded through his body bristled with sharp thorns, their barbs sinking deep into his flesh, ready to tear him apart.

His vision had long since gone blurry with blood, tears, sweat... everything. He heard the Liao Kingdom's guoshi crooning a question: *Do you really hate them? Hate them enough to meet them with blades drawn, hate them enough to become their enemy for life?*

Convulsing, Gu Mang felt himself about to vomit. He lowered his head, choking as he laughed. *Yes... Yes, I hate them, I hate them so deeply...*

Steel thorns pierced bone and his entire body twitched. But Chonghua's Beast of the Altar still clamped his mouth shut, not saying a word, not revealing a thing. He endured the agony of his body, lips tremoring as he spat out fragmentary words.

Yes. I hate. I don't regret.

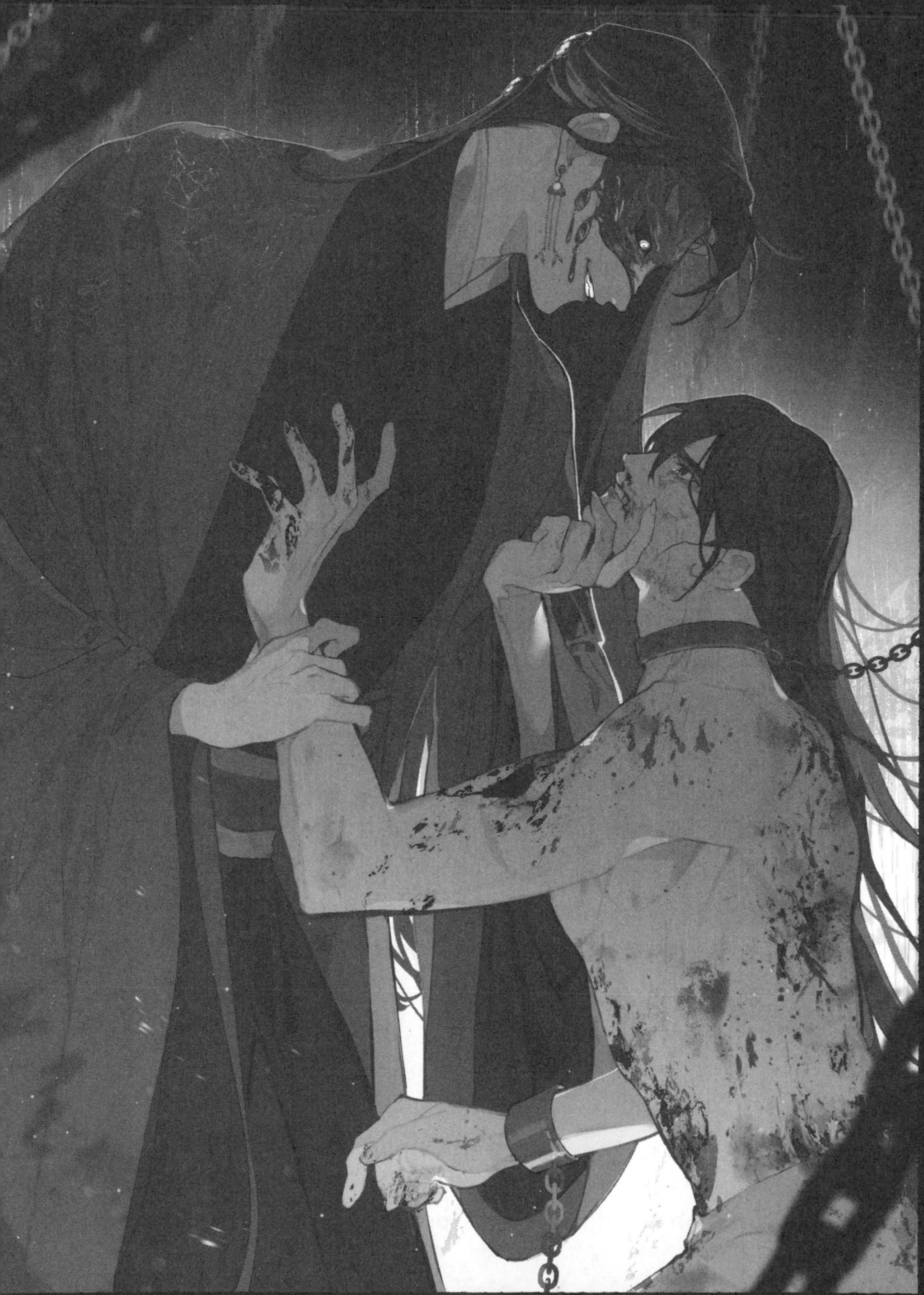

From now on, I, Gu Mang, cut all ties with Chonghua. I, Gu Mang, am defecting to the Liao Kingdom, swearing loyalty to the Liao Kingdom. For vengeance, I am willing to be tempered, to fall onto the demonic path; never will I feel regret.

Never...regret...

Bloody tears streamed down his face. He had been tortured to the point of madness, his hair disheveled and face covered in filth, like a vengeful ghost cackling in despair. He didn't know how he kept his mouth shut, but whenever he couldn't bear it, he would work to remember the past.

He thought of the emperor speaking on the Golden Terrace. *General Gu, we ask you to believe us. We have never, and will never, see you as cheap pawns, as lowly slave-born bodies.*

He thought of Lu Zhanxing telling him, *Mang-er, keep going. Whatever you choose, your Lu-ge will be happy for you.*

He thought of Mo Xi...

He felt a heart-wrenching pain the moment he thought that name.

He remembered the cool summer breeze the first time he saw Mo Xi, and the clarity of Mo Xi's eyes when he turned. He remembered the first smile Mo Xi had shown him and the sorrow on his face at their last farewell.

It had been more than ten years since. And it wasn't that he'd never been moved, that he'd never wanted to recklessly risk it all and accept what Mo Xi offered, to believe the two of them could truly cross that chasm and share a lifetime together.

But... When all was said and done, they couldn't overcome fate or defeat destiny.

How would his princess, his highness, his little shidi, feel after learning of his defection? He would probably hate him, wouldn't he?

Hopefully he would.

Don't be so impulsive anymore, don't be silly and oppose the court, don't try to vouch for me... You absolutely mustn't do anything like that...

Mo Xi.

I'm sorry. Your shixiong really, really loves you.

Every uttered "I love you," every word of warm affection I ever said was true. And from now on, every "I hate you," every mocking insult will be false.

You absolutely, absolutely...mustn't regret that when Shixiong defected, you weren't at my side, that you couldn't attempt to persuade me one last time, that you couldn't stubbornly attempt the impossible.

Because...

Gu Mang's tears fell endlessly down his cheeks, mixing with his sweat and blood, soaking that ruined, nearly inhuman face.

Because the one who transferred you to the frontier and delayed your return wasn't the emperor at all... The person who suggested that was me! It was me... I was the one who was too weak; I was too afraid to let you see me leave, too afraid to hear you try to convince me, too afraid to see the heartbreak in your eyes again. I was afraid that if you looked at me, I wouldn't be able to leave.

I'm sorry, I have to go, I must go. I'm sorry—in the end, I still chose Chonghua, chose my brothers, chose this path, and so I had to part with you.

I'm sorry...

More blood trickled from his forehead into his eyes. That handsome face he held so dear slid away with his tears, and Mo Xi disappeared. In his hazy scarlet vision, he saw the flames and defeat at Phoenix Cry Mountain. He saw brains smeared into the ground. He saw those with whom he had once sat round a fire, drunk wine in the snow, advanced and retreated, chatted about daily rations and the nation's ideals. They looked at him from across the shores of the flowing river of the underworld.

Gu Mang had a vivid hallucination. He saw himself floating on that vast netherworld river, just about to swim across, just about to take hold of their hands—

Wait for me.

Wait for me—I'm coming, I'll bring you home, I'll take you back.

An excruciating agony assailed him. The demon claw clinging to the white bones of his spine had drunk its fill of Chonghua's magic techniques and spiritual energy. It ripped itself from his flesh, yanking back against exposed bone.

He screamed.

Seventy thousand comrades, his unblemished soul, the future he dreamed of—all vanished with this vicious tearing. Black magic spiritual energy mixed with faewolf blood flooded into his body.

Those brilliant, smiling faces of his comrades and his brothers dwindled to nothing in that field of scarlet...

Gu Mang heaved. From now on, he could never go back. Never again...

He knew he could never again walk among them.

"Tsk, tsk..." The guoshi took the opportunity to grab his face, stroking a thumb over that cheek mottled with blood and tears as he cooed. "General Gu. Do you regret it? Do you grieve for that bright and honorable magic of your motherland that's been stripped away?"

Gu Mang convulsed and shivered. His body was not strong. He had a great dread of pain and suffering; he would balk at pulling a thorn stuck in his nail or drinking medicine even when sick. But this fragile body contained a soul that hadn't the same softness. Gu Mang looked up, his eyes blood red, and hoarsely said, "No."

Surprised, the guoshi stared into his eyes but couldn't find the slightest waver or hint of deceit in those black irises.

Gu Mang's soft lips quivered. He weakly, stubbornly, and softly said, "I don't regret it, I want revenge..." Weeping, he let his face crumple, a ferocious howl tearing its way from his throat. "I want revenge!"

The guoshi finally seemed moved. He released Gu Mang's jaw. Slowly, he lifted that hand to gesture to the attendants. "Come."

At his command, his subordinates nearby responded immediately. "Awaiting the guoshi's orders!"

"Carve all the black magic spells of Liao into his bones."

"Yes!"

The guoshi reached out and patted Gu Mang's head with a hand covered in his own blood, caressing it as if Gu Mang had somehow proven himself. "General Gu, do you know what this means?" An indecipherable light glinted in the guoshi's deep brown eyes. "For the rest of your life—no matter if you lose your memories, or if your bones shatter, or if your eyes are gouged out and your tongue is cut away—as long as but a single shard of bone remains, you will be under the control of our black magic. You will never escape. Everything you can use, the only thing you *will* use, will be our filthy techniques carved into your bones, scorned by all the world. You will never be able to forget them."

He grinned, exposing sharp, white fangs in an eerie smile. "Congratulations, General Gu. You belong to my Liao Kingdom now."

Gu Mang's vision flickered, dreams overlapping reality. That golden mask disappeared, replaced by Zhou He's scowling face. Zhou He lifted Gu Mang's chin with Lieying's sharp tip. "What are you thinking about?"

Gu Mang made no sound.

Whether he had been an acceptable general he didn't know, but at least he had always been an exemplary spy. Even if his memories were broken and shattered, even if he found himself confused and bewildered at many points, he had guarded this secret with his life. Regardless of whether it was the Liao Kingdom, or Lu Zhanxing, or Mo Xi, he'd always held safe those truths he must not say. In this respect, he had never failed at being a spy.

Gu Mang's silence appeared to anger Zhou He. "I'd very much like to see how long you think you can last," he growled darkly.

An array glowed to life. Chains rattled out from all sides, restraining Gu Mang's limbs and neck. Zhou He turned to his attendants. "You may begin."

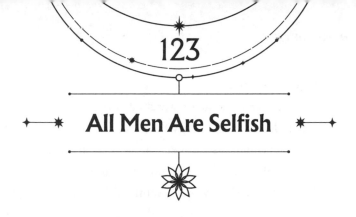

123

All Men Are Selfish

EVERY NATION had its dark side. And any country's ministry of secret techniques would forever be one of its dirtiest, bloodiest, most unspeakable places. This was true in the Liao Kingdom, and it was just as true in Chonghua.

Zhou He sat in the rosewood chair spread with silver fox fur, one leg crossed over the other as he observed the scene in front of him.

Black magic trials were terrifyingly cruel, but they were also fast. Scarcely an incense time had passed since he'd given the order and two rounds of experiments had already been conducted. Gu Mang hung, strung up by the chains. Zhou He had used no numbing or suppressing herbs on him due to the requirements of the spells, and Gu Mang could feel each slice of the knife and each bite of the gu worms.

The bandages that gagged his mouth and pressed against his tongue were already soaked with blood. A nearby cultivator cut another length of gauze and took hold of Gu Mang's unconscious face to replace the bloody cloth. Gu Mang didn't react at all, his slender neck lolling. His face was paler than ice; even his lips were completely bloodless.

"How is his spiritual flow?" asked Zhou He.

"Extremely weak."

"What about the heart vein?"

"In complete disorder."

The Sishu Terrace cultivators watched three important indicators in these trials: spiritual energy flow, the heart vein, and mental strength. If preserving the specimen's life was of any importance at all, then these vitals had to be constantly monitored.

Zhou He frowned slightly as he examined Gu Mang's white and lifeless face, and his grip tightened on the armrests of his roundback chair. Beyond reporting to the emperor, he still had...*that* person's orders to complete. But given his current state, Gu Mang might not withstand much more. No one could endure such torment when their spiritual flow and pulse were both approaching collapse. He would break.

Biting his lip and closing his eyes in apprehension, Zhou He scowled. His grip on the chair slowly relaxed. He sighed, somewhat vexed, and asked with an air of resignation, "How is his mental strength?"

The cultivator monitoring Gu Mang's condition put their fingertips to Gu Mang's forehead, soaked in cold sweat. Their eyes flew open at once. In disbelief, they checked again.

"How is it?" Zhou He asked impatiently.

"E-Elder, to answer your question," the disciple turned, stammering, "Gu...um, th-the test subject's mental strength remains strong. His mind shows no signs of deterioration."

Zhou He blanched. How could that be? Over the course of his long tenure at Sishu Terrace, subjects whose willpower hadn't collapsed in the first round of trials, much less the second, were rare as phoenix feathers. And those were by and large sturdy, durable, and healthy people. Gu Mang's physical condition was poor; the Liao Kingdom's tempering had left the marks of countless old wounds on his body, and three years at Luomei Pavilion had weakened him further. Now his heart vein and spiritual flow had reached their limit. How could he still...

Jumping to his feet, Zhou He strode over to Gu Mang and reached up with a spell at his fingertips to examine his icy forehead.

In that single touch, Zhou He's astonishment multiplied. Gu Mang's mental fortitude showed no sign of crumbling whatsoever. If you ignored his bloodstained body, Zhou He would've never believed this was the mental strength of a man who had been ravaged by black magic experiments until insensible. His steadiness seemed carved into his bones, so stubborn and formidable was the mind under Zhou He's fingers.

What exactly drove his persistence?

"Elder, what do we do next? The test subject's body can bear no more, but based on his mental strength, perhaps we could still..."

Zhou He gestured for silence. He stared into Gu Mang's face, an intense unease pricking at his heart.

In addition to completing the emperor's black magic experiments, he had also, due to a personal relationship, secretly accepted a request from a close friend—

He had to scramble Gu Mang's memories.

What in Gu Mang's memories was worth scrambling, he didn't know. After all, he already had amnesia and his mind was slow. But since they'd spoken, Zhou He wouldn't shrink from this favor. He had thought it more convenient to tend to this task after the trials were through, when Gu Mang's mind was nearly destroyed. But it seemed things hadn't gone as smoothly as expected.

Zhou He paused, deep in thought. "You may withdraw."

"Yes!"

When the attendants had left the room, Zhou He approached Gu Mang and lifted Lieying. Inch by inch, he polished it to a gleam.

He extended the blade, its icy surface pressed to Gu Mang's equally icy cheek. The holy weapon sensed at once that the body before it held a strong soul—this bloodthirsty falcon began shaking with excitement in Zhou He's hand.

Zhou He leaned down and brought his lips to Gu Mang's ear, murmuring to the unconscious man, "General Gu, I've conducted thousands of trials and wrung innumerable men of steel into puddles of muddy water. You alone are the exception. Honestly, I admire you."

Lieying flashed bright, its glare intensifying until it was a blinding white.

"Unfortunately, I've been entrusted with the task of breaking your mind."

No response came.

"My apologies."

With a flick of his wrist, Lieying transformed into many transparent chains coiling in his palm. They were as thin as willow branches, darting between his fingers like snakes as they hovered beside Gu Mang's head.

"Lieying," Zhou He commanded in a low voice, "Soul Chaos!"

As the order left his thin lips, Lieying emitted a shrill like a predator finally receiving its master's command. Those fine chains flew out, drilling into Gu Mang's skull.

"*Ah—!*"

Blood sprayed. Gu Mang was jolted awake by the devastating pain of that strike. He lifted his head, whimpering through a mouth gagged with gauze... His screams were weak with exhaustion, but tears flowed down his bloodstained cheeks. His blue eyes opened wide, pupils contracting violently. Strung up midair, he struggled with all his might as the restraints holding him clanked.

The fine chains of the holy weapon flailed madly within his skull like a violent intruder, screeching as they shattered his memories. Those scenes he had so painstakingly recalled, recovered, and come to possess—his priceless lucidity.

Gu Mang stared through wide blue eyes. In the throes of this agony, the delighted shouts of his brothers on the frontier were erased.

The emperor's promise upon the Golden Stage was erased.

Lu Zhanxing's sorrowful, bold laughter in the prison's Chamber of Ice was erased.

In the depths of his memories, Mo Xi's tender gaze when he looked at him, the love and devotion he had promised him over and over....were all erased.

Every memory Lieying tore apart Gu Mang strove to recollect, resisting and trembling in despair. He had been stripped of his mind once already, and now, he was about to suffer it once more at Zhou He's hands.

A feeling of outrage suddenly overwhelmed him. Why did they treat him like this... Why did they reduce him to this? *Why?!*

For the promise of a better world, he'd offered up his flesh, his elder brother, his conscience, his lover, and his reputation. He had nothing left. He had even forgotten *himself*—he had even thought he really betrayed his country and betrayed its people, that he really had been willing to sacrifice anything for his ambition and vengeance.

Because of this, he had once agonizingly knelt before Mo Xi and before Murong Lian; he had knelt before each martyr's tombstone on Warrior Soul Mountain, kowtowing to them one by one, imagining ways he could start anew.

Later, the heavens showed him mercy. The Time Mirror somehow allowed him to recover those memories from before he defected.

Even if they were painful, at least—at least he could know he was a spy, an undercover agent, the knife Chonghua had sent into the belly of the Liao Kingdom. He wasn't a traitor...

Tears spilled from Gu Mang's eyes. He was allowed so little; he only wanted to remember who he was. They had to take even this away?!

His mouth had been gagged; he couldn't speak, but the blue eyes he turned on Zhou He were almost beseeching. This was the first and only time Gu Mang had looked at him this way since the trials began. Like a cub that had been driven to a dead end regarding the hunter in front of it with despair.

Gu Mang's resistance was rewarded with Lieying's chains puncturing his mind even more frenetically. Gu Mang howled, a heart-stopping, lung-splitting sound. The tendons in his neck stood in stark relief, his nails gouged deep in his palms. He was gagged by the bandages, but still wailed a hopeless, unintelligible plea: "Don't..."

Please, no more... Don't take my mind. Don't take my memories. I've had them for so little time...

I haven't yet had the chance to take a look at the Northern Frontier Army, to see what those youths who marched beside me look like now. I haven't had the chance to walk through the streets and alleys of Chonghua, to see if my country is a little better than before.

I haven't yet gone to the shores of the Soul-Calling Abyss, to offer a jug of wine and light a stick of incense under that old pagoda tree where Dage's head is buried.

I haven't yet made proper arrangements for my silly princess's future... I don't want to forget.

I don't!

The holy weapon in Zhou He's hand emitted a buzzing cry. Lieying burst with a despairing and enraged light, unable to strike the killing blow. With a *boom*, the spiritual energy chains retracted from Gu Mang's skull, solidifying into a bloodstained dagger once more. Zhou He took a stunned step backward, staring at the holy weapon in his hand, then at Gu Mang, his face ashen.

How could this be...? Why was this person...

Before he could finish the thought, Gu Mang went limp, scarlet spurting from the wounds in the side of his head. All the vitality flowing through his organs seemed to have been spent in that split second. He curled in on himself, spasming uncontrollably, blood streaming from his mouth and nose. The gauze between his teeth was completely soaked through.

Zhou He heard a commotion outside the Asura Room—the Sishu Terrace disciples outside seemed to be arguing with someone. He stood frozen, unable to react, until someone flung open the stone doors with a *bang*—

A man in a state not unlike Gu Mang's stood outside the Asura Room. Disciples timidly clustered around him, trying to stop him without daring to make a move.

Zhou He couldn't believe his eyes. "Xihe-jun...?"

MO XI STOOD outside the door, looking as if he had just crawled out of a sea of corpses. His face was white as paper, his clothes mottled with bloodstains, and his gaze was terrifyingly wild.

Jiang Yexue had also come, but unlike Mo Xi, he looked uneasy in the extreme. His expression was gloomy as he sat in his wheelchair, looking in helpless sorrow at the two people on either side of the stone door. They were both filthy with blood and riddled with wounds, yet they showed the same stubbornness, the same unbreakable will.

The instant Mo Xi caught sight of Gu Mang, his composure crumpled. It was as though he hadn't felt any of the pain from his own body until then; yet now, the weight of their combined anguish crashed over him. His feet carried him toward Gu Mang, but only the first few steps could be described as walking. By the end, he was rushing forward in staggering steps and lurching stumbles. "Gu Mang…" That murmur fell from pallid lips. He called again, his emotions breaking loose as if some shackles had fallen away. "Gu Mang, *Gu Mang*!"

Even with his spiritual core on the brink of failure, he recklessly summoned Shuairan, breaking the chains that held Gu Mang with a single whip-strike. That body, soaked in fresh blood, fell limply down, and Mo Xi caught him in his embrace.

"It's okay, it's okay... I'll take you away, I'll take you away right now... It's okay, I'll..." The man in his arms was so cold the tips of his fingers were purple. Dark blood dripped from his temples.

With a trembling hand, Mo Xi pulled the gauze from Gu Mang's mouth, his vision blurred by tears that fell onto Gu Mang's small and filthy face.

The truth was, his shixiong had never been big or tall. His features were soft, naive, bursting with a sense of innate childishness. But those around him had grown used to his strength, his courage, his hard-charging spirit, his unfailing warmth. It was these qualities that made him their lighthouse, and why they saw him as invincible.

Only as Mo Xi held him now did he discover how frail and thin the man in his arms was. Time had sapped Gu-shixiong and General Gu's vitality; what was left for Gu Mang was merely a mortal body covered in scars. These scars, both new and old, wove together before Mo Xi's eyes. Sorrow and anguish racked him as he realized—

Gu Mang had been shattered too many times. The deaths of his comrades, his brother's execution, his secret mission as a spy, his tempering at the hands of the Liao Kingdom, those five years on enemy lines, being forced to slay his own brothers.

Fate had pushed him from great heights again and again. He had fallen and shattered into innumerable shards, but each time had pieced himself back into human shape, again and again. He had tried his best to glue himself back together. Anyone else in his place might have been smashed to powder, reduced to dust, never able to stand again. But Gu Mang had always gritted his teeth and endured, because behind him were those brothers who would never return, and before him was the dawn he yearned for.

"Gu Mang..."

Lieying had dealt Gu Mang too great a shock; though he had escaped its worst, the memories he had painstakingly recovered had been irrevocably damaged. He turned tearful blue eyes and gazed hazily at Mo Xi.

Mo Xi knew Gu Mang still wanted to feign strength; perhaps he even wanted to push Mo Xi away. Before he could, Mo Xi caught the hand he raised, holding that icy palm covered in purpling bruises from the chains.

Gu Mang's eyes were half-lidded, exhausted, his gaze unfocused. "Mo Xi..."

"It's me, I'm here, I'm here," Mo Xi said through hoarse sobs, taking Gu Mang's hand, wet lashes trembling as he pressed a kiss to his fingertips. "I'm right here."

Gu Mang stared blankly at the man in front of him. His awareness had gone murky. The shattered remains of his memories whirled in his head as if they might dissipate at any moment. Those snowy nights in the barracks, those sunny afternoons at the academy, their desperate entwining on the night of Mo Xi's coming-of-age, each and every time his princess, his royal highness, had promised him a future together. Everything seemed to be covered in one layer of snow, then another. A snowstorm swirled over his mind, threatening to cover the traces of the past, little by little.

Gu Mang knew he might not be able to hold on much longer. The agony of losing something he had just regained was filling his body. His most beloved person was right next to him, yet he was about to forget him too.

At that moment, in the throes of torment, Gu Mang suddenly felt an unhappiness and vulnerability he had never known before. His fingers tightened around Mo Xi's hand. Eyes widening, he panted urgently, gazing at Mo Xi's face, his voice roughened and weak: "I..."

But what should he say?

I'm not a traitor? I'm not a bad guy?

It wasn't that I didn't love you, it wasn't that I was unwilling to be with you, it wasn't that I wanted to push you away.

Will you trust me?

But he couldn't say a thing. Even now, he wasn't able to say anything; he *couldn't* say anything!

The years-bygone storm on the Golden Terrace poured over his burning mind, extinguishing that single spark of selfishness. He seemed to hear the emperor's voice once more, imploring but oh so awe-inspiring, presenting the dream he had chased after his entire penniless life.

"We can even promise you that one day, we will show you that future, where heroes can become heroes no matter the circumstances of their birth, and every life will be treated equally."

Heroes, regardless of their background. Everyone treated as equals.

Never again would there be someone like Lu Zhanxing, pulled unwittingly into a fight between old and new powers and dying an unjust death.

Never again would there be someone like him, who couldn't protect his own brothers or do what he most wanted...who was beaten down all his life because of his lowly birth.

Never again lovers who, because of blood and lineage, were forced to sneak around and hide, too afraid to give their hearts to one another...

"General Gu, we need someone loyal enough, brave enough, and clever enough. We need this person to infiltrate the Liao Kingdom and send information back to us—to become the poison in the bellies of both Liao and those old nobles."

"Subject Gu. Are you willing to endure a difficult mission as Chonghua's right hand?"

The rumbling thunder and flashing lightning above the Golden Terrace seemed to light up his mind once more. He opened his eyes, extinguishing all his human selfishness and swallowing all his words back into his stomach.

Yes, he was a spy. From the day he agreed to the emperor's request, he had relinquished any hope of turning back.

But...

As if the heavens took pity on him, as if even the heavens felt his lifetime of suffering should have some measure of sweetness in it—though he hadn't said it, he felt Mo Xi grip his hand, heard him murmur: "I trust you."

Vacant blue eyes turned sluggishly to stare at Mo Xi's grieving face.

"I'll always trust you... I'll never leave you again."

Gu Mang knew he should have been shocked. He should have asked why Mo Xi would say this now, what he had discovered and experienced—but perhaps because his mind was already a mess, his strongest feeling just then was that it was all so unfair.

I trust you.

After five years' defection and three years back home, he suddenly realized with impossible clarity—he had always been waiting to hear this sentence. Even in his sleep, in his dreams, he had longed for someone to say this. But no one ever had. No one had gifted him these three words.

Until today.

Living as a spy for so many years still hurt so much, far too much.

Tears spilled from Gu Mang's eyes at last. His throat worked, as if trying to say something, but his mouth was filled with blood.

He couldn't make a sound; only his lips were moving, trembling, shivering, his silent tears adding their marks to his bedraggled face.

Never had Mo Xi seen Gu Mang cry so despondently, so helplessly. He lifted a bloodstained hand to caress Gu Mang's face; he wanted to wipe away Gu Mang's tears, but his clumsy touch left streaks of filth in its wake.

Mo Xi's tears were also falling uncontrollably; his fingers shook as he stroked Gu Mang's soft, icy cheek. He gave up trying to wipe his tears and stared at Gu Mang. There were so many people around them, but he didn't care anymore. He lowered his lashes, heavy with tears, his vision filled with one person alone. Mo Xi said hoarsely, "Shixiong, I'm sorry, I've made you wait too long. I've come to take you home."

He scooped Gu Mang up, putting his arms over his shoulders. Only then did Zhou He seem to wake from a dream and shout, *"Xihe-jun!"*

Mo Xi didn't answer.

"Don't you know His Imperial Majesty has given orders that Gu Mang is a test subject? He—"

Mo Xi didn't let him finish; his phoenix eyes flicked up, their rims bright red. "His Imperial Majesty gave orders to do many things, some of them completely unknown to others. Right now, all I want to know is when His Imperial Majesty gave you this assignment, whether he did so with guilt."

"Have you gone mad?! Have you any idea what you're saying?!" Zhou He turned and cried, "Detain him!"

Mo Xi *had* gone mad. Without another word, he lifted his free hand. Blue light gathered in his palm. Jiang Yexue's face went deathly pale. "Mo Xi! Stop!"

But why would he stop? Eight years' worth of time separated him from his shixiong. If he stopped now, how could he catch up to

Gu Mang from eight years ago, who walked away alone with a bag on his back, surrounded by song? Mo Xi closed his eyes and called with a furious shout: "Tuntian! Come!"

A whipping gale spun up, and a blue scepter appeared in his hand. Mo Xi felt a pang of agony like a knife twisting in his heart. Fresh blood seeped from the corner of his mouth—fine cracks spread over his spiritual core, each wisp and shred of magic doing irrevocable damage to his body.

The light at the scepter's tip blazed in Mo Xi's eyes. Channeling his spiritual energy, Tuntian lengthened into a scepter ten feet tall, towering over any man. It had a white rod and a golden finial emblazoned with a sun totem, the sapphire inlaid within emitting a dazzling light.

A clarion whistle sounded.

Tuntian's full form possessed an earth-shattering spiritual energy. The instant it touched the ground, it rumbled with waves of energy; some weaker disciples found themselves forced to their knees.

"Xihe-jun..." Zhou He's face twisted in anger. "Are you unaware that by pursuing a personal grievance within the ministry and wielding a holy weapon, you have broken martial law?!"

"Indict me, then." The blue and gold light of the scepter illuminated Mo Xi's handsome, pale, and resolute face. "I'll wait."

Zhou He was speechless.

"Mo Xi..." Jiang Yexue whispered.

Tuntian was a fearsome holy weapon that could cover ten leagues in corpses with a single flourish. Even if no one believed Mo Xi would genuinely use it against his fellow countrymen, the full form of this sun-tipped scepter was terrifying in his hand. Never mind Sishu Terrace—even the Bureau of Military Affairs, with all its martial talents, wouldn't dare stand in his way.

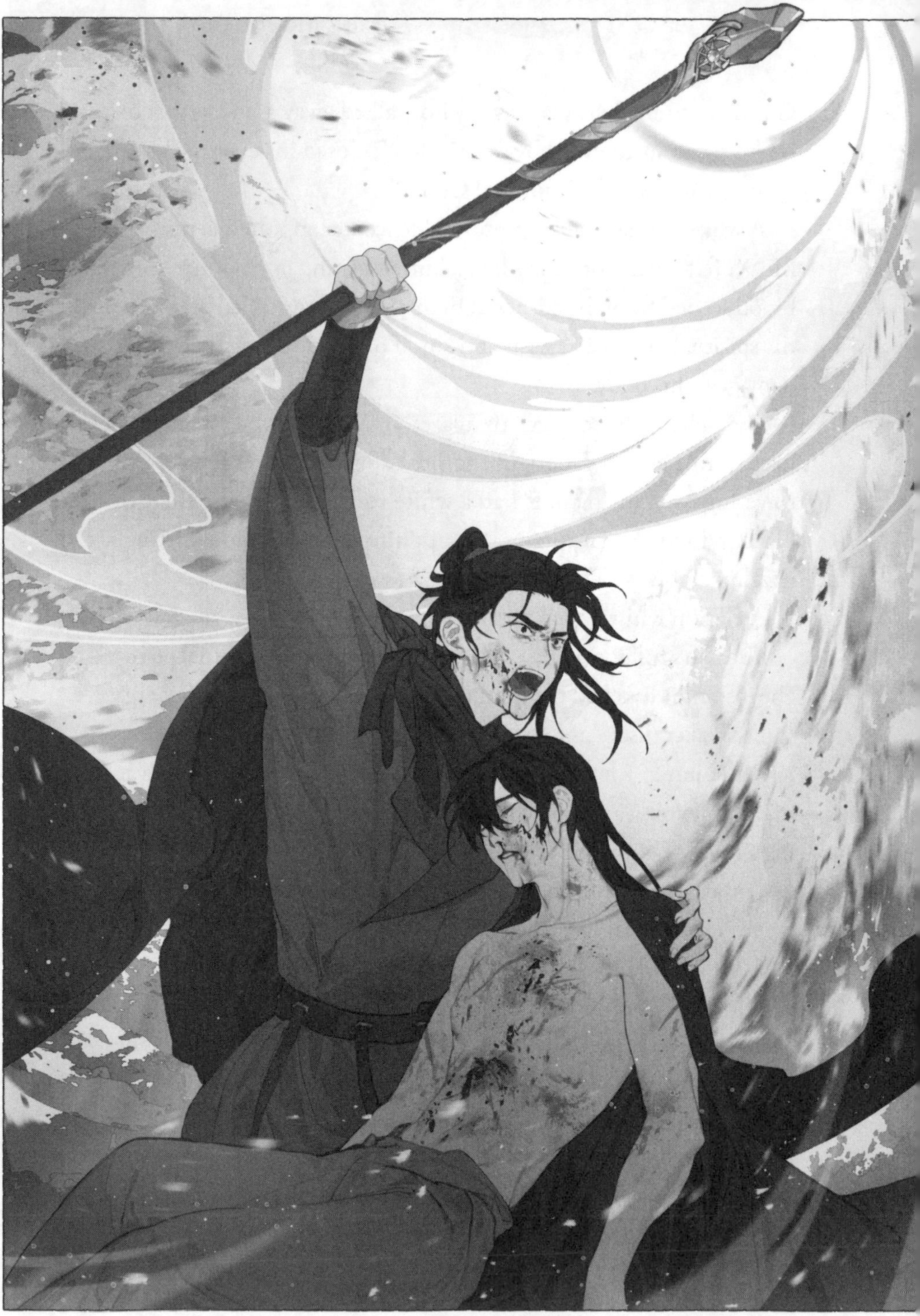

Mo Xi swept a glance over the crowd as they cowered from him and tightened his grip on the unconscious Gu Mang. The two of them, both covered in wounds, nestled close. Carrying Gu Mang in his arms, Mo Xi slowly walked out of that bloodstained hell.

125

Severe Injury

As Zhou He watched Mo Xi stride off, his expression was ugly.

"Elder, what...what should we do?"

"What else *can* we do? Report to His Imperial Majesty! Say that Mo Xi flouts the law of the land—he trespassed into secure locations, opposed the emperor's decree, and fought within imperial walls over private matters!"

Jiang Yexue frowned. "Elder Zhou, this situation is complex, and His Imperial Majesty is indisposed. I ask you to think carefully."

Zhou He instantly blew his top. "Bastard Jiang, do you too think to oppose me?!"

Jiang Yexue blinked at him.

"A member of the Bureau of Military Affairs dared trespass into my Sishu Terrace and seize a test subject in our custody. If I bore this in silence, how could I hold my head up in the future?! I know you're his brother, but you need to understand, your brother has broken the law! Are you trying to excuse his crime?!" With a wave of his sleeves, Zhou He barked at his attendants, "What are you staring at? Hurry up and report to His Imperial Majesty!"

"Yes!"

One hour later, in Xihe Manor.

The damage the black magic experiments had wrought on Gu Mang was severe. He had fallen unconscious upon leaving Sishu Terrace and not awakened since.

In this long slumber, Gu Mang dreamed a somber dream.

He and Mo Xi were in their early twenties. They were walking near a long dike on the outskirts of Chonghua. It was dusk, and the setting sun had shed half its painted face; crimson rouge and brilliant gold powder were smeared across the gloaming, floating over the horizon for endless leagues.

Gu Mang pulled a blade of foxtail grass, twirling it as he walked. "I really didn't expect His Imperial Majesty to give you command of the attack on Fan City." After a pause, he continued. "It'll be your first command, right? Are you nervous?"

Mo Xi lowered his lashes but didn't answer the question. "I will win."

Gu Mang smiled. "That's right. Remember, the most important thing for a commander is to never let them see you falter. No matter what happens, your men will draw strength from you as long as you don't crumble. Once the general loses his resolve, his army becomes a handful of loose sand, useless no matter how courageous its soldiers may be. You are the soul of the army. The moment you take up the position of general, the lives of each of your brothers are in your hands."

Mo Xi nodded and lifted a hand. Turning into the tawny gold of the setting sun, he looked into Gu Mang's face. "I will." After a pause, he added: "Wait for me to come back."

"Why are you suddenly so serious?" Gu Mang grinned. "Is there something I should know?"

The young man was very earnest and also very awkward, but still clung to his facade of composure. "His Imperial Majesty said if I come away victorious, he'll allow me to leave the Mo Clan and establish my own independent household."

"...So?"

Mo Xi bit his lip, too afraid for a moment to meet Gu Mang's eyes. He turned to the glimmering surface of the river, flecks of gold filling his eyes and gilding his lashes. Maybe it was the rosy sunset, or maybe it was something else entirely, but Mo Xi's face looked a little red, and the tips of his ears were faintly flushed. "I'll have my own residence."

Gu Mang blinked at him. He was also slow to react. For both of them, this was their first relationship, and truth be told, neither was much wiser than the other. Gu Mang looked at Mo Xi in confusion. He hesitated. "That's nice... Then...congrats?"

Almost simultaneously, Mo Xi asked softly: "Will you come live with me?"

They stared at each other in silence.

Mo Xi's elegant features flushed redder. He coughed quietly, and then, as if wanting to recover his pride, or not wanting to pressure Gu Mang overmuch, he lowered his lashes evasively. "I-if you don't want to, that's fine too. I can wait. No, that's not what I meant— what I mean is, I, I've already looked at the plans, I..."

The longer he spoke, the more embarrassed he became. The harder he tried to hide his softness and inexperience, the more obviously they were laid bare. Finally, the usually calm and composed Mo Xi pushed Gu Mang away. He walked over to the dike and buried his face in his hands, mumbling morosely, "I'm sorry, I was only asking..."

As Gu Mang had watched this young man clumsily, stubbornly, try to express his intent, he suddenly understood something. This little shidi of his hadn't yet left on his campaign or fought his battle, but he was so certain of victory that he'd secretly gone to look at plans...

He felt heartsore. He knew Mo Xi had always been sincere with him. He was just too scared to accept it.

Perhaps it was because Mo Xi was about to leave for the front lines, or because there had always been some selfishness hidden in the bottom of Gu Mang's heart; in any case, back then he hadn't rejected Mo Xi's suggestion. This had delighted the young man to no end. That night, neither returned to their own abodes. They spent the whole night making love in an inn outside the city. It passed like a dream.

By the end, Gu Mang had not a drop of energy left. He lay there with his face buried in the sheets, eyes still wet with tears, silent and dazed. His eyes were half-lidded, lashes quivering.

In this hazy state, he heard Mo Xi softly say, "There's something I want to give you."

Gu Mang hadn't the wherewithal to ask many more questions, and Mo Xi had already taken hold of the hand he had burrowed into the sheets, his broad palm covering Gu Mang's fingers. He felt a faint prickling sensation as two arrays glowed red where their hands were joined. The light glided over their interlocked fingers and floated up to the side of Gu Mang's neck.

Still foggy with exhaustion, Gu Mang asked quietly, "What is it?"

"A tiny sword array." Mo Xi released his hand and reached up to stroke Gu Mang's neck with lightly callused fingers. "I know people are always trying to bully you. They're afraid of stirring up trouble and too scared to use magic, so they only dare press their physical advantage."

He looked down, turning his head to gently kiss Gu Mang on the neck.

"I gave a drop of blood to form this array. I haven't fixed its form, so you can shape it into whatever you want—a character, a flower... anything. When I'm not here, it will protect you. Of course, if you don't want it...you can seal it off too."

Gu Mang felt that soft kiss brush over his skin as he listened silently, tangled in the bedding. A whole host of emotions welled up in his heart. He wanted to laugh with glee; he wanted to weep with sorrow.

He knew he wouldn't go live with Mo Xi in his residence. It would be a house, not a home. A home was somewhere two people could rightfully and openly make a life together. It wasn't somewhere one needed to hide, or love one another as if carrying on a clandestine affair, covering their tracks as if ashamed. Mo Xi could give him a place to stay, but he couldn't truly give him a home. They were not the same; their paths were always destined to diverge.

He knew he would refuse Mo Xi in the end. But as he looked at this youth's earnest and beseeching face, he couldn't say a thing. His body had become pliant under the hands of his little shidi, and his heart too had long since melted into a puddle.

Moving as if pricked by guilt, he turned to caress Mo Xi's face. "Will you only leave a sword sigil for me?"

"Hm?"

He smiled, his dark eyes gentle. "Then what if someone tries to bully *you*?"

Mo Xi blinked at him. Of course no one would dare pick a physical fight with Mo Xi. But it was as though something compelled these two people doomed to separate paths to leave some secret on each other's bodies, known only to the two of them.

Gu Mang bit his own finger and rolled over, tapping the side of Mo Xi's neck. He diligently transformed the mark into a red lotus.

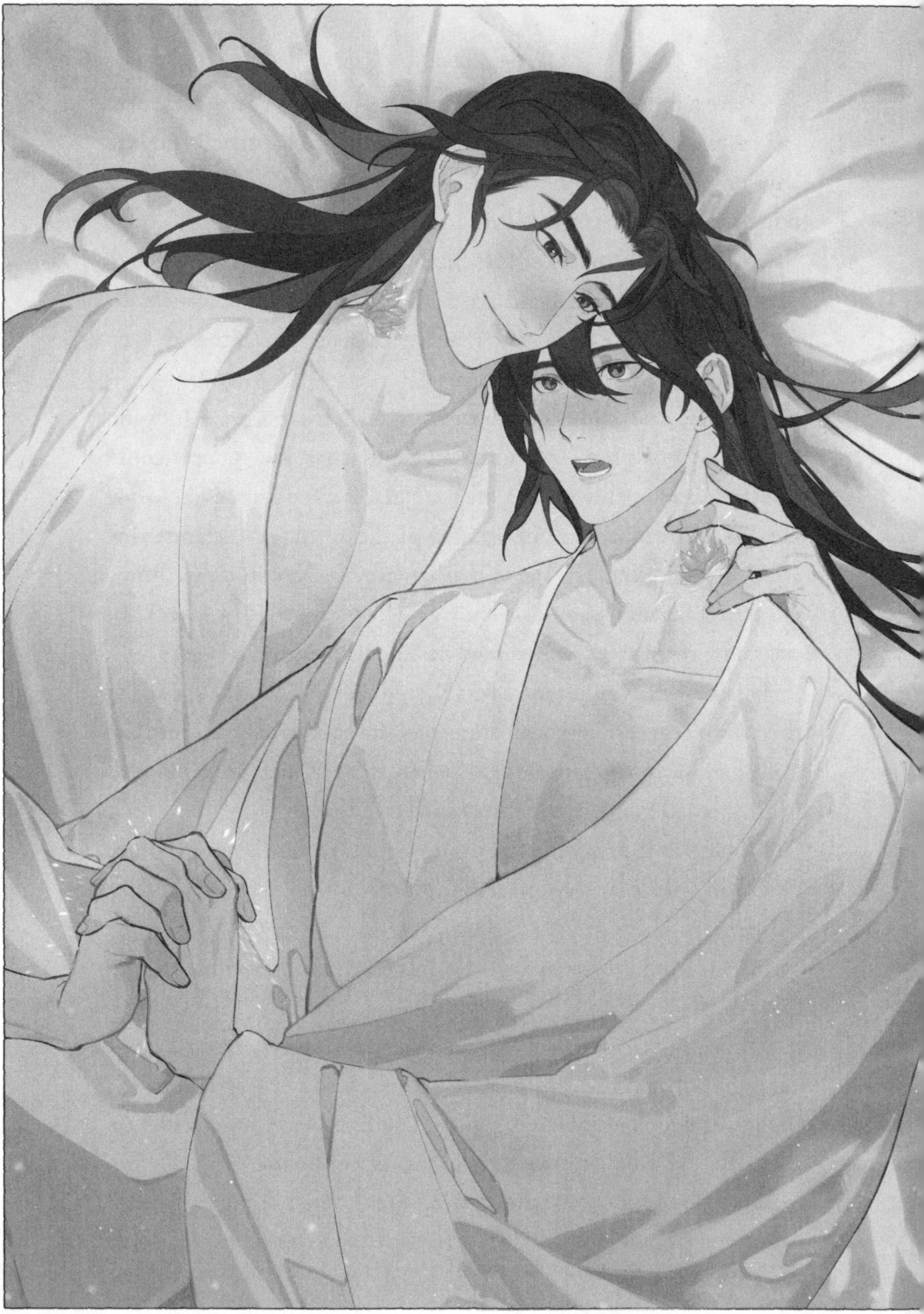

Then he took hold of Mo Xi's hand, covering it with his own, and smiled. "I left a drop of my blood too. Make it into a protective sword array on my behalf, so it'll count as me staying by your side. Okay?"

Mo Xi's eyes shone brilliantly in the dark. Gu Mang didn't have the heart to dim that light.

"Okay," Mo Xi said, and folded Gu Mang into his arms from behind. His warm chest pressed against Gu Mang's curled back as he stroked his hair and kissed his warm neck, his slightly cool ear.

"You have to wait for me to come back. When I come back, everything will be better. You have to trust me..."

Trust me.

Mo Xi's voice in that vision of the past drifted out of his reach, just like the memories Lieying had skewered, scattered and smashed, falling to pieces.

Wait for me. Everything will be better.

In the depths of his awareness, Gu Mang was struggling, falling to his knees, prostrating again and again to that wholeheartedly devoted Mo Xi—*I'm sorry, I wish I could have waited for you too. I wish everything would have gotten better. I always trusted you.*

But...Mo Xi, some things must be done, some sacrifices must be made. When fate comes knocking, you have to face it if you don't want to be a coward. We all have our paths to walk.

You painted a picture of that future and that home for me. I lived that beautiful and carefree lifetime through your eyes. That's more than enough. So when you return in fathomless glory and I'm not here, don't be sad...

I do love you. All my life, every "I love you" that left my lips was true.

Mo Xi...

Though he didn't wake, tears fell from the corners of Gu Mang's eyes, wetting his temples.

A crowd of cultivators buzzed around Gu Mang's bedside as the elder at their head issued a steady stream of commands. "Open another three blood-clotting arrays. Place soul-stabilizing needles at the Shenting, Fengchi, and Renying acupoints." When one disciple didn't immediately move, his white brows drew low in anger. "Why are you spacing out? Hurry up!"

The disciple answered hastily, "Oh...oh." He looked away from Gu Mang's face in a panic but couldn't keep himself from thinking— *Looks like the black magic experiments really were terrible. Otherwise, why would Gu Mang cry while he's not even conscious...?*

"Place needles at the three acupoints," his shifu barked. "Your hands have to be steady."

"Understood!"

The healers had gathered in front of the bed in Xihe Manor's bedroom. The dove-gray hui-patterned canopy hung low, and soothing incense wafted from golden beast figurines, but they did nothing to allay the anxiety filling the room. The doctors of Shennong Terrace came in and out, replacing basin after basin of bloody water from cleaning wounds, bringing in prepared tinctures and concocted ointments one after another.

No one dared to speak. Sweat beaded on the foreheads of every cultivator and slave. There were two patients in the room: one was Gu Mang, lying in the bed, and the other was Mo Xi, sitting by the desk.

What exactly Mo Xi had been through, no one knew—how he had sustained such injuries, or why he ignored them for the sake of that...that traitor lying unconscious on the bed. The healers urgently summoned from Shennong Terrace were utterly bewildered.

One cautiously stepped forward. "Xihe-jun, the top-grade flesh-regrowth ointment is here. Your wounds..."

"Give it to him."

The cultivator stared.

"Use all of these top-grade healing salves on him." The rims of Mo Xi's eyes were scarlet, his eyes never moving from the bed. "I'm fine."

The healer tending to Mo Xi's wounds turned a waxy yellow at this. He wanted to cry, *Dage! You're not fine! Your spiritual core is about to shatter, in what world is that 'fine'?* But when he saw Mo Xi's determined face, he didn't say a thing. Head down, he continued silently bustling about the room.

Suddenly one of the household servants ran in. "My, my lord!" they cried anxiously.

"What is it."

"H-his Imperial Majesty sent Eunuch Zhao with a decree. H-he says you must go outside to accept the edict."

Official messengers were required to read the imperial orders they delivered directly to the subjects involved. But Mo Xi didn't speak, nor did he move. His hand was still on the gleaming black sandalwood desk as the healer treated his wounds. After a tense silence, three words issued from his thin lips. "Let him wait."

The entire room gaped in shock. One cultivator nearly dropped the bowl of medicine in his hands, staring goggle-eyed at Mo Xi. All had the same thought: *Could Xihe-jun have gone insane?!*

The servant stammered, "H-h-how...could..."

Mo Xi repeated unblinkingly: "Wait."

The servant could do nothing but stumble from the room with this message. Mo Xi's gaze never left the figure enclosed in talisman arrays.

According to the grizzled medicine elder, the Liao Kingdom had reshaped Gu Mang's body in a very strange fashion. Dense yin energy ran in his veins, as if his was a body thousands of people had cursed.

Chonghua's healers had little experience treating someone with Gu Mang's constitution, and his injuries were severe. Drawing on all their skill and effort, the healers could just barely keep Gu Mang breathing. But they couldn't heal the mental damage he had once more sustained.

The medicine elder wiped sweat from his face. "How is his mind?"

The cultivator who had been casting spells to stabilize Gu Mang's skull shook his head. His face was pale and drawn from the effort. "Nearing collapse," he said. "He was missing two souls to begin with, and now..." He coughed up a mouthful of blood, completely drained.

Mo Xi's ears rang, his entire body cold as if he'd fallen into a frozen lake. "What do you mean?"

The healers exchanged glances. They kept their heads down, none daring to answer.

"What will happen to him?"

At this point, it was left to the elder to deliver the news. His countenance was dreadful, but he braced himself and said, "I'm afraid that he...might not remember anything... He might be unable to speak. If his mind has deteriorated completely, he might even lose the use of his eyes..."

Mo Xi leapt to his feet, shaking all over. His pale lips had gone more bloodless still. The healer who had been attempting to stabilize his pulse was thrown off by the burst of spiritual energy that exploded from him. "Xihe-jun, you can't keep moving recklessly! You—"

"Mo-dage." They were cut off by the soft sigh of a melodious female voice. "Is this how you risk yourself with the core I gave you?"

All eyes turned toward the door, then lowered in a deep obeisance.

"Princess Mengze!"

"Greetings to Princess Mengze!"

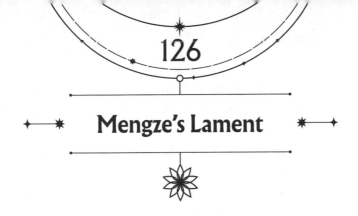

126

Mengze's Lament

PRINCESS MENGZE wore robes of pale gold with a cape thrown over top, her thick hair wound in a low bun. As she stepped out of the shadows of the flowers beside the doorway, her handmaiden Yue-niang followed at her heels, carrying a sandalwood box wrapped in golden brocade.

Mengze entered the room, eyes sweeping across the faces of everyone present. Her gaze took in Gu Mang, insensible beneath the gauze canopy, then finally came to rest on Mo Xi's bloodless face. "You were about to risk yourself again, weren't you?"

Mo Xi said nothing.

Broken light glimmered in Mengze's eyes. "The last time your heart shattered, it was also because you wanted to redeem this shixiong of yours. He nearly killed you that time. It was I who rescued you, and I asked nothing of you. My only wish was that from then on, no matter what people or situations you encountered, you would first consider whether it was worth your life."

The room was terrifyingly silent save for the sound of Mengze's low, heartbroken voice. "Mo-dage, so many years have passed. I ask you now, are you going to be just as stubborn as you were back then and make the same choice?"

Mengze was of course speaking of the battle at Dongting Lake. Mo Xi had tried to barter his life for Gu Mang's return and been rewarded with a stab through the heart. It was a blow so decisive and final that ever afterward, Mo Xi felt bitter devastation at the very thought of it.

But now that he knew the truth, recalling it once more merely made him feel Gu Mang had suffered too much.

Who do you think you are? You think that if you die, I'll feel guilty and turn back? Don't be a fool!

As a general, as a soldier, and as a person, you can't be too attached to past affections.

What had Gu Mang felt when he spoke those words and did those deeds?

Mo Xi closed his eyes. There was no way to explain all this to Mengze in a short time; the twists and turns were too difficult to follow. His heart was in chaos. He wanted to preserve Gu Mang's mind, wanted to protect this man covered in bloody wounds, wanted to demand the justice this spy who had immersed himself in evil for a full five years deserved. But the Shennong Terrace elder's words echoed unceasingly in his head—

Might not remember anything...might lose the ability to speak. If his mind has fallen apart completely, he might even lose the use of his eyes.

The brilliant and gentle black eyes in his memories curved in a smile, twinkling like the reflection of stars on water. They blinked. When they opened again, they had become an azure blue, as if a lake unpolluted by the dust of the mortal world flowed from them.

Before he was tempered, Gu Mang's eyes danced with laughter; afterward, they gazed at Mo Xi with quiet obedience. Those eyes called to him—*Mo-shidi, Mo Xi, my princess, my lord...*

Mo Xi's hands were trembling. He didn't respond to Mengze but walked straight to Gu Mang's bedside. Mo Xi bent to stare fixedly at that face; with the blood wiped away; it was white as bone. After a long silence, he turned to the elder from Shennong Terrace. "Continue."

Mengze's eyes finally flashed with anxiety. "Mo Xi—"

"I will explain everything to you afterward, if you only trust me."

Mengze fell quiet.

"I have to save him."

In the silence that followed, it was as if an invisible current churned beneath the surface. Almost everyone believed Mengze would lash out or explode or break down. But she only went still for a long time and then slowly said, "Very well. If this is your choice." Pausing, she stepped forward. "Then I will help you."

"Princess!" Yue-niang exclaimed.

Mengze seemed to be doing her utmost to restrain some emotion. She had always been proficient at enduring hardship in silence, but this time, there was no one who couldn't see the hurt and pain filling her eyes. Her lips parted slightly as if to say more, but it seemed she had overestimated her ability to remain stoic; the rims of her eyes reddened before any sound left her mouth. She turned away, eyes downcast.

Yue-niang's heart ached for her mistress. Disregarding the lines between master and servant, she wailed, "Princess, wh-why are you doing all this..."

Mengze closed her eyes, lashes trembling. As she strove to master herself once more, she finally swallowed down that overflowing grief. Her eyes opened. "Bring me my medicine chest."

Everyone was stunned. Did Murong Mengze plan to work the healing arts herself after all this time?!

Chonghua was home to two grandmaster healers. The first was Jiang Fuli of the three poisons Greed, Wrath, and Ignorance.

The second was Murong Mengze of the three sages Virtue, Mind, and Wisdom. In order to save Mo Xi many years ago, Mengze had overdrawn the power of her spiritual core; there were many spells she could no longer perform on her own. After painstakingly tending to her health for so many years, her body was only just starting to recover. If she used healing magic now, the results were sure to be unparalleled—but she might come out a complete invalid. How could Mo Xi allow her to make another sacrifice like this?

He caught her wrist, stopping her quietly. "Mengze, go home. I already owe you a life. I cannot let him owe you more."

Murong Mengze's slender eyes gradually filled with tears. Perhaps all her waiting and endurance had been too much; this imperial princess who never let her emotions slip fell so far as to show red-rimmed, wet eyes before a staring crowd.

"Mo-dage...you're so sad when something happens to him. But have you ever thought of me?"

The crowd had never heard Princess Mengze express herself so frankly, and for a moment, all of them were at a loss. This wasn't something they should see or hear—but they couldn't leave, so they could only stand as still as statues.

Mengze's voice shook. "If you come to any more harm, what do you think will happen to me? I can never cultivate the proper path again. Was my life worth so little in your eyes that it couldn't buy you more than a few short years of peace?!"

As she spoke, a tear finally trickled from her eyes, rolling down her luminous cheek and landing on the back of Mo Xi's hand. "This shixiong of yours...if he's that important to you, I'd rather use forbidden techniques to bring him back! Mo-dage...I've done everything I can do. I only ask you to have more consideration for me in the future... Then I could... I could at least..."

She closed her eyes, fat teardrops falling like beads off a broken string.

Mo Xi's mind was like a bowstring strained to its limit. Gu Mang's treatment could not be delayed—he urgently needed to ask the Shennong Terrace elder if there was anything else they could try—but here Mengze was in such a state. Mo Xi had never known how to deal with women. He was anxious and miserable, at a loss for how to stop her from intervening in this matter.

He knew how painful it was to owe a favor he could never repay. He couldn't look upon Mengze without feeling guilt and self-reproach. Yet this guilt and blame could never be absolved—what Mengze wanted was something he'd long since given to the man on that bed. He couldn't possibly give it to her.

Because of this, he had never known what to say in front of her, or what to do, as if he were bound by invisible strings. There were many things he would do if Mengze asked that he would never do otherwise. Mo Xi found this lack of agency unbearable. He couldn't let Gu Mang, too, bear a debt of grace he could never repay.

At this moment, the healer who had been maintaining the stability of Gu Mang's mind coughed up a great mouthful of filthy blood. The magical light array in his hands flickered and failed.

"What happened?!" the Shennong Terrace elder exclaimed.

"H-his condition is too strange. Vicious intent suddenly burst across his mind. This disciple is unskilled and could not withstand it..."

At that instant, on the bed, Gu Mang's eyes snapped open, but not because he'd woken up. His eyes were darting side to side, his pupils eerily unfocused, his lips moving as if to lay a curse. Bloody tears streamed from his eyes, flowing along those edges that were slender as phoenix tails.

An inexperienced young healer cried, "What's going on?!"

"This is...the backlash from the black magic curse within his body..." Mengze murmured. She looked up at Mo Xi. "His mind is breaking down. Already I'm unsure whether I can save him. If the damage isn't brought under control, Mo-dage—he will die."

Mo Xi's face instantly paled.

Mengze took note of his panic. "If you want to preserve his life, let me help," she offered sadly. "After all... After all, in your heart, I'm..."

But before she could finish, a voice from outside cut her off. "Princess, why so pessimistic?"

That voice was slow and unhurried, carrying a note of innate scorn and arrogance. "That man on the bed is tough as nails. He won't die, and his mind won't break." These words echoed into the room. A man wearing wide-sleeved green robes with a golden pin through his hair sauntered into the room. "I'm here, aren't I?"

If these medicine cultivators, who admired skill with healing magic above all, were apprehensive over Princess Mengze's presence, then this new arrival's entrance left them ready to fall to their knees.

"Greetings to Medicine Master Jiang!"

Mengze was also stunned. "Medicine Master Jiang..."

Jiang Fuli's expression was indifferent, his eyes narrowed. This was his distinctive habit—his vision had never been good, probably because he spent too much time counting his money. Without his liuli eyepiece, those almond eyes were hazy, as if cloaked in misty Jiangnan rain.

Jiang Fuli brandished a golden cowrie note pinned between pale, slender fingertips. He turned to Mo Xi. "Was it you who sent the spiritual messenger beast to bring this to me?"

"Your wife said you left for the southern frontier..." replied Mo Xi.

"Yes. But I hadn't gotten far. Besides, when have I ever been unwilling to take money? I rushed back as soon as I saw this." Jiang Fuli flicked that dazzling golden note, glancing at Gu Mang on the bed. "But his condition is dreadful. I'm tripling your fee."

Mo Xi anxiously started, "My shixiong's life—"

"Both his life and his eyes are salvageable." Jiang Fuli paused, then walked forward and tapped Gu Mang on the forehead. "Hard to say if the same applies to his mind, but he won't be left with nothing. I'll have to heal him first to know for sure. Regardless, I will do my best."

Jiang Fuli was a heartless man with no moral convictions. The single principle underlying his actions was money, and making more of it. As long as he was paid handsomely, he would spare no effort.

Sitting at the edge of the bed, he pulled open Gu Mang's robes and examined the wounds on his body. He sighed. "You've spent so much time and only gotten this far? Rank amateurs."

The cultivators from Shennong Terrace could only stare in silence.

Jiang Fuli extended slender fingers and tapped Gu Mang's critical acupoints in a few rapid motions, staunching the flow of blood. He lifted a hand and said, "Bring it over."

He didn't name what he needed, assuming bystanders would intuit the line of his thoughts. The healer closest to him hastily handed him a medicine chest.

"Why would I want your little box? Gauze!" Jiang Fuli snapped.

Pinned by that almond-eyed stare, the cultivator shivered and frantically offered him the gauze he wanted.

Jiang Fuli wiped the blood from Gu Mang's most severe wounds. When he reached Gu Mang's arm, Jiang Fuli suddenly paused.

"What is it?" Mo Xi asked at once.

The medicine master frowned as he examined a spot on Gu Mang's arm. "This petal-shaped mark..."

"It isn't new, he's had it since he was young."

"Of course I can see it's not from a recent injury." Jiang Fuli's gaze remained on that mark. "It just looks familiar. Why do I feel I've seen one just like this, but on a different patient?" He hesitated and shook his head. "Possibly there were just similarities, and I've misremembered."

With that, he tossed the bloodied gauze aside and sat up to begin healing Gu Mang's wounds with magic.

The water clock by the table in the bedroom dripped. A hush fell over the room as Jiang Fuli sat at Gu Mang's bedside. Two slender fingers hovered at Gu Mang's wrist, monitoring his pulse while passing spiritual energy into his body.

Jiang Fuli's healing spells were distinct from Chonghua's standard treatments; the medicine cultivators around them could barely follow what he was doing. They merely watched as the wounds marring Gu Mang's flesh reknit at an astonishing rate, and the bruises on his face faded.

"Jiang Fuli, the cunning reverser of fate, lives up to his name," Mengze murmured.

"The princess flatters me," Jiang Fuli calmly replied.

The Shennong Terrace elder edged closer. "Medicine Master Jiang, do you... Do you need anything? Can we lend a hand?"

"Oh yes, I do need something," said Jiang Fuli.

"Medicine Master Jiang, only say the word," the elder hastily replied. "We are at your command."

"I need your silence," Jiang Fuli answered.

He didn't get his wish. Moments later, a servant dashed in as if flames were licking at his heels, shouting at the top of his lungs: "Bad news, bad news!"

Mo Xi turned. "What is it this time?"

"Bad news!" the servant cried again. "My lord, Housekeeper Li can't stall them any longer. Eunuch Zhao is furious. He says if my lord refuses to respect the imperial edict and meet him, his people will charge in and escort you to the palace!"

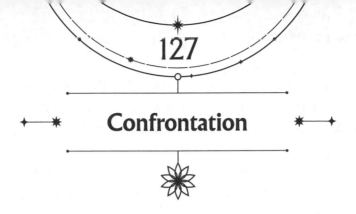

127

Confrontation

L I WEI STOOD BENEATH Xihe Manor's plaque in the middle of the main entrance, arms crossed and hands tucked into opposite sleeves. His eyes were fixed on the ground. Behind him were the manor's great doors, heavily secured, and before him was the stone residence pillar conferred by the previous emperor, engraved in lesser seal script with the glorious merits of four generations of Mo Clan heroes.

"Housekeeper Li, this is an act of rebellion! Does Xihe Manor choose to defy the imperial edict?!"

"What are you saying, Eunuch Zhao? Haven't I already explained? Xihe-jun is indisposed. He can't come out to receive the imperial edict. Once his condition improves, I'll report the imperial order. You mustn't get angry; you'll make yourself sick."

Eunuch Zhao was seething with rage. Jabbing a finger toward Housekeeper Li's nose, he snapped, "Li Wei! Do your lies know no bounds?! The news of Xihe-jun's trespass into Sishu Terrace has already spread through the heavens! He stole that Gu traitor from Elder Zhou himself and now you stand out here saying he's unwell—who are you trying to fool?!"

Li Wei rubbed his nose and sighed. "It's a long story. I'm afraid there have been several misunderstandings…"

"What misunderstandings could there be! This night, Shennong Terrace has gone in, Princess Mengze has gone in, Jiang Fuli has gone in—Xihe-jun can receive all of these people, but the mouthpiece of the emperor is kept outside? What nonsense is this?!"

Li Wei clapped his hands together. "Aiyo, you're right! Then you've noticed—everyone who went in is a healer, and all of them are here to treat the lord! The lord is very gravely ill."

"You—!"

A creak interrupted their argument as the manor doors opened.

Mo Xi stood framed within the great doors. In the moonlight, his eyes were sharp, undulled by his exhaustion.

Li Wei had deflected these messengers for as long as humanly possible. Upon seeing Mo Xi emerge, he heaved a great sigh of relief and hastily darted out of the way. He lowered his head. "My lord."

Mo Xi stepped over the threshold, his voice low, unhurried, and intense. "You've done well. You may withdraw."

"Understood."

After Li Wei left, Mo Xi strode out. His gaze swept down the manor steps and landed on Eunuch Zhao. Even as the emperor's closest, most trusted servant, Eunuch Zhao was not immune to the pressures of hierarchy and status. Plus, Mo Xi naturally possessed a glacial aura. When he wasn't speaking or smiling, the iciness he exuded intimidated all around him.

Eunuch Zhao's earlier boldness shrank to nothing. He lowered his head and performed his obeisance. "Xihe-jun."

Mo Xi didn't speak. He turned his face up to the starry night sky, eyes flashing with an indescribable light.

"His Imperial Majesty asks you—"

"How is His Imperial Majesty's health?"

Eunuch Zhao was stunned. He had imagined all sorts of reactions—acceptance, fury, defiance...but he was strangled into silence by this question out of the blue.

"Mengze said his illness flared up these past few days. How is he now?"

"...Xihe-jun's consideration is appreciated. His Imperial Majesty is naturally protected by the heavens and has mostly recovered."

"All right. That's good." Mo Xi's steel-toed military boots clicked over the stone. He descended the stairs and said lightly, "Lead the way."

They arrived at Zhuque Hall in the depths of the imperial palace, the warmest place in the entire compound. This imperial hall wasn't large, but it was built entirely of volcanic rock from the far south. Warming incense spiraled through the air, and the floor was covered in thick woolen rugs. The emperor always came here to rest and recuperate when his illness plagued him.

Mo Xi followed Eunuch Zhao to the hall's entrance. Eunuch Zhao went in to make his report, then returned with his horsetail whisk in the crook of one arm. He bowed to Mo Xi. "Xihe-jun, His Imperial Majesty invites you in."

He strode through the hall doors. Mo Xi had never liked this place; the rugs here were too thick. His feet sank deep into the soft pile whenever he came here, like a wild beast trapped in mud, or a moth stuck in a spider's web. That feeling of helplessness crept up his spine, lingering in spite of the luxurious scents suffusing the room.

Eunuch Zhao closed the doors behind him. The bejeweled Zhuque Hall was filled with a heavy fragrance, as if the air itself had grown dense and solid.

The weather had warmed in the last weeks, but a coal brazier blazed fiercely in the middle of the hall. The emperor reclined on a couch of ebony sandalwood. He was wrapped in thick fox fur, his lashes lowered as he fiddled with a bracelet of dzi beads carved of bodhi wood. His complexion was pale and wan—even the fire's light gilding his features put no warmth on his face.

At the sound of Mo Xi's muffled steps, the emperor let his fingers fall from the beads. He spoke with a sigh thinner than paper. "Xihe-jun, you're here."

Mo Xi said nothing.

To be honest, he'd felt an overflowing rage since the moment he learned the truth. He'd wanted to run off to the palace to question the emperor at once—but Gu Mang was still in jeopardy, so he couldn't very well leave. Only after Jiang Fuli rushed over and successfully stabilized Gu Mang could he finally come to the palace and face this man who had known the truth all along.

Now that he was actually standing before the emperor, his rage was not as sharp and volatile as it had been in the beginning, but it was deeper. He suppressed his own fury with great difficulty as he stared at that ruler wrapped in fox fur.

"We requested your presence tonight over a small matter," the emperor began. "Zhou He related quite a strange story to us, and we felt that it should be shared with Xihe-jun. Would Xihe-jun like to hear it?"

Mo Xi made no move to answer, so the emperor continued. "Zhou He said he was conducting the black magic experiments as we ordered tonight. In the middle of an important trial, someone burst in, disregarding all reason and defying imperial orders, and insisted on taking the test subject away. They even went so far as to flout the law and summon a holy weapon, coming just short of shedding the blood of our own Sishu Terrace's cultivators. Does Xihe-jun feel that this thief must be a wicked, evil villain?" The emperor spun one of the beads on his wrist and burst into laughter. "So did we. Until Zhou He said this hero who had come to the rescue..." He paused, slowly looking up. His face was lined with fatigue, but those eyes were cold and sharp. "...was you."

These two words seemed to have been pushed through bared teeth. The emperor sat up straight, his brows stark over the dark shadows of his eyes. Emperor and subject gazed at one another over the blazing coal brazier, over the rising heat and smoke. Their images reflected in each other's eyes were hazy and distorted.

The emperor's voice was dark. "Xihe-jun, you've disappointed us deeply. We ask you—when we handed Gu Mang to you, what did we say?"

Mo Xi remained silent.

"We warned you that, in light of the great crimes Gu Mang has committed, he ought to have gone to the executioner's block long ago. We kept him alive solely because the Liao Kingdom techniques written into his body were worthy of further study. That there would come a day when he would be taken for such study, and on that day, we hoped you would not forget who you are and take the wrong side on impulse."

These had indeed been the emperor's words. Back then, Mo Xi had only felt suffocated. Hearing them for the second time now, he found them absurdly mocking and terrifying.

Mo Xi studied the emperor's face, seeking the slightest hint of guilt, sadness, or hesitation. But there was none. The mask he wore was exquisite; every line and angle of emotion seemed to have been measured a hundred times before it was portrayed. There was not the merest waver in his eyes.

Hardest to read was the heart of the king... When had this saying been wrong?

Mo Xi closed his eyes. Coldness and rage, disappointment and sorrow filled the veins that flowed through his body, but the emperor's words stabbed into his eardrums like scorpion venom. "Xihe-jun, as we see it, you've gone blind; you've discounted all the warnings we gave you. You've forgotten you are the top general of Chonghua, and forgotten who stabbed you in the heart. You've forgotten who rescued you and gave you a second chance at life, forgotten who killed tens of thousands of our nation's people. You've entirely forgotten who the traitor is, haven't you."

A piece of prickly ash burst inside the brazier with a crackle, and a trail of bright sparks flew up, dancing in the air.

Mo Xi opened his eyes.

He held back his fury, so intense it threatened to overwhelm him; he endured the trembling of his hands, so enraged they were shaking, pushing down his fiery anger that surged like lava. He spoke, voice low. "Is Your Imperial Majesty done?"

The emperor stilled. He stared dark-eyed into Mo Xi's face. He'd finally realized the state Mo Xi was in; looking at him more closely, he found that even his spiritual flow was fluctuating wildly.

Could it be—!

The emperor was filled with an extreme unease, unconsciously tightening his grip on the dzi bead bracelet. The last bit of color in his face faded. In this fraught moment between ruler and subject, it seemed as if everything had been laid bare.

"If so, then I, too, have a strange tale. I'm not sure if Your Imperial Majesty dares listen to it."

After a long while, the emperor reclined deep into the couch. He had already guessed what Mo Xi was about to say—there was only one thing that could change his mind so suddenly and resolutely. That last layer of paper between them shuddered, waiting to be punctured.

Mo Xi's eyes never left the emperor's, pausing between each word as he tore through that paper screen. "Many years ago, there was someone I knew. That man performed outstanding military achievements for the nation, fighting for years on end and only ever recording a single loss. Later, for the price of seventy thousand gravestones, for the equal world his emperor promised him, he went deep into the enemy's ranks, suffering a mission in unceasing torment for a full five years. In those five years, not a single day passed when he didn't rue the blood he spilled, when he didn't hope for his emperor to show him that old promise fulfilled..."

The emperor's face paled with every word he spoke. Each one was like a sharp knife piercing that flawless mask, shredding his many falsehoods into tattered scraps. Each and every word Mo Xi set down before the emperor was soaked in glaring scarlet.

"In the end, this man returned to his nation but lost his memories. Other than the emperor he'd once entrusted with his life, no one knew he wasn't guilty. He was universally reviled, debased, and imprisoned. The nation hated him, blamed him, humiliated him, wished for his death. And his emperor, who had once promised him that he would one day be exonerated, that he would be bestowed that blue-gold ribbon of heroes—said he was only left alive as fodder for black magic experiments!"

Explosive fury ignited Mo Xi's eyes. No matter how he tried to suppress it, by now his voice was quaking. His black eyes seemed to spark with flame. "Your Imperial Majesty. I'm not sure you're familiar with this story?"

The emperor's face was whiter than paper. In this dangerous silence, he tried to put the bracelet back onto his wrist. His hand was trembling slightly, and he didn't succeed on the first try; only on the second attempt did he wrap the beads properly.

"Mo Xi." The emperor looked up. "What nerve you have... You dared trespass into the Imperial Censorate to steal the history-recording jade scrolls..."

"So..." Mo Xi closed his eyes, his voice shaking from rage. "*You* were the one who destroyed them." His eyes snapped open. The emperor had never seen such anguish and frigid cold in those pupils. It chilled him to the bone.

The emperor was of an age with Mo Xi; they had essentially grown up together. He knew too well the character of this youthful commander of the empire.

His father had once said: "The Mo bloodline is loyal, strong, brave, stubborn, and tenacious... They are ruled by absolute principle. They will never covet your throne, nor will they do anything to oppose you without real cause. But if a day comes when he believes something you've done violates the tenets he believes in, he will stand against you, with no fear of death nor thought for reputation. He will become the sharpest needle in your eye and the most painful thorn in your flesh."

He had never forgotten his father's words for a single moment. In all matters regarding Mo Xi, he had ever been cautious and prudent.

But Mo Xi had still ended up on the opposing side.

Mo Xi spoke, voice resounding through the hall. "Your Imperial Majesty, he's done so much for you, yet you insist on hiding the truth?!"

For a moment, Zhuque Hall was terrifyingly quiet. The twisting jiao dragons carved onto the roof beams seemed to come alive, staring with sharp claws outstretched at the confrontation below.

After a lengthy silence, the emperor spoke. He could no longer evade nor conceal the truth. He looked up and asked softly, "...And if I do?"

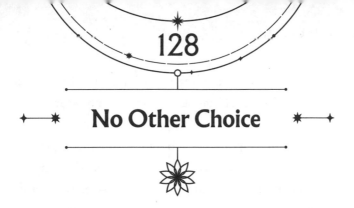

128

No Other Choice

T HE WARM ROOM was suddenly filled with a piercing cold. The emperor leaned back deep into the couch, looking down at Mo Xi. He wrapped the fox fur more tightly around himself and slowly said, "The past is the past. There is no reason whatsoever for us to keep those records. Xihe-jun, let me ask you. These jade scrolls you risked your life to repair—can they strengthen our nation, or bring security and happiness to the people? Can they bring down the Liao Kingdom or guarantee peace in the Nine Provinces?" The emperor paused. "They cannot."

He continued, "Preserving those scrolls...would only cause unnecessary confusion and discontent. It would only cause... See, it would only cause what has come to pass today, an emperor and his subject at odds. Do you recall the stone plaque erected at the door of the Imperial Censorate? It says, 'The Past Is Dead.' These four words are quite correct. Some events, some secrets, *ought* to be buried by the passage of time. If they are unearthed, they stand to harm the present in a hundred different ways, without conferring the slightest benefit."

After a few beats of silence, the emperor said blandly, "We didn't expect you would find it so hard to accept."

Mo Xi's eyes were shot through with scarlet. Lava seemed to roil in his chest; blood rushed into his head. His fingers curled into fists, and his voice was dreadfully hoarse. "It's not that I can't accept it. But rather, Your Imperial Majesty...it's that you have accepted it far too easily."

He pressed on. "Eight years ago on that stormy night upon the Golden Terrace, you promised Gu Mang everything he wanted. You used every pretty phrase at your disposal—you said you'd never thought of him and his men as insignificant beasts, you said you would shape for them a world where everyone is treated equally, that there would come a day when you would personally bestow the martyr's ribbon upon him. All these guarantees you gave to him, all the promises you made, were they no more than schemes and lies?!"

"Xihe-jun." The emperor's gaze was like solid ice. The bridge of his nose wrinkled slightly, his stare growing predatory. "You forget yourself!"

"What have I forgotten?!" Mo Xi retorted. "I merely want right to be right and wrong to be wrong. I merely want him to receive the respect he deserves instead of more false accusations. It's been eight years... This secret festered in his heart for eight years, yet even during the worst of his suffering, he never betrayed you or revealed the slightest hint of the truth. Now he's been hollowed out, he can't serve you anymore—is it really so hard for you to return him the innocence he deserves?! You led him down a dead-end road then washed your hands of him. Your Imperial Majesty, he was your chess piece before, so who is your pawn now? Me?!"

The emperor rose to his feet, upending the table with an explosive crash. Fruit and cakes rolled over the floor. The bean cakes were crushed, the grapes destroyed, their juices pooling on the ground. Redness rushed into his face. "Mo Xi! We're warning you—do not forget the oath you have sworn!"

He had blurted this out in shock and in desperation. Regret came instantaneously.

Light flashed in Mo Xi's eyes. He put a hand to his brow and tilted his face to the sky, shoulders shaking with self-mocking laughter as he murmured, "The Vow of Calamity... Ten years of my life I give to make this oath of blood. From now on, slave cultivators will never take up arms and rebel, nor will I take up arms and rebel. I pledge my loyalty to Your Imperial Majesty and to Chonghua with my life."

The memory of helplessly swearing the blood oath and lowering himself to the ground in a long kowtow was vivid in his mind. Mo Xi swallowed thickly and closed his wet eyes. "What a colossal joke," he murmured. He was still for a moment with an arm over his eyes, striving to harness his own emotions—but it was futile. At that moment, his teeth-gnashing hatred was plainly engraved on his thin face.

He lowered his arm. When those black eyes opened once more, they were bright with a knife-like chill.

The emperor tensed and instinctively flung up a hand in defense. But Mo Xi's wrathful outburst, even with his core damaged, was more powerful than he'd imagined. With a crackle, the snake-whip Shuairan appeared in his hand and viciously struck the barrier the emperor had created. The whip's scarlet light tore through the air, transforming into a razor-sharp sword that came to a stop a hairsbreadth from the emperor's throat.

The emperor blanched. "Xihe-jun, make a move against us and you will disperse as ashes on the wind and die without an intact corpse!"

Mo Xi's eyes were bloodred. He stepped forward, holding the sword level, teeth gritted and voice dark. "You don't need to remind me. Your Imperial Majesty, back then, you already knew. You had

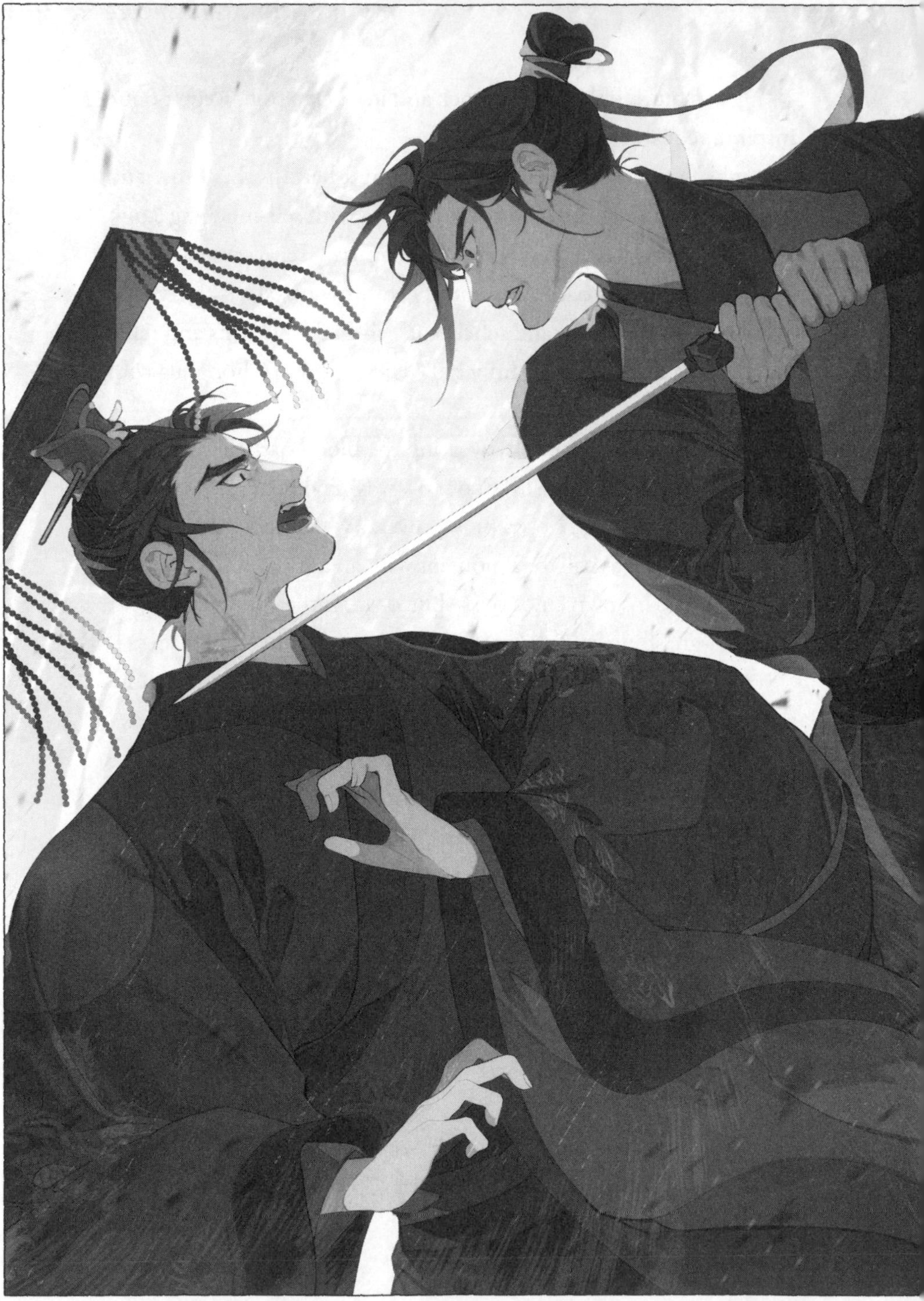

already made up your mind not to touch Gu Mang's surviving soldiers—but you still had to get another reassurance from me."

"Xihe-jun..."

"You used the same chip twice: first to secure his undying devotion, and second to ensure my eternal loyalty. Two birds with one stone—I would expect nothing less of Your Imperial Majesty. An excellent ploy!"

The emperor turned his face aside. "We couldn't explain it to you then... Recall that we'd been evading you the entire time. But you knelt before our hall for three days and three nights..."

He whipped around to face Mo Xi, the glare of the sword illuminating his face with a malevolent light. "Three days and three nights! What could we do? Send you away? Refuse to see you? Xihe-jun, take a moment to think about us! All the thousands of eyes of the court are fixed upon us! Think what you would have done if we told you the truth! Could you have merely looked on as that dear shixiong of yours went to suffer for so many years in the Liao Kingdom and endured so many years of disgrace?! You couldn't!"

At this point, the emperor's eyes, too, were bloodshot from rage and obstinance. He stared at Mo Xi, and his voice shook. "With everything you've done, when *haven't* you forced our hand? Do you think we wanted this?! Do you think, after all of it, we could really feel no guilt and sleep in peace?!"

"If Your Imperial Majesty felt so guilty, how could you do something as cruel as what you did today?" Mo Xi furiously shot back.

"What choice did we have?" The emperor stared at him through scarlet eyes. He pointed behind him at his own throne. "Why don't you sit there and see what it's like? There is much we cannot control. If you haven't sat there, you can't see any of the threats that lurk around us!"

He panted, "Do you think we don't want to clear his name? Do you think we don't want to see our god of war ride armored once more onto the battlefield? Do you think we don't want to take his hand and tell the entirety of Chonghua—his faith never wavered, their General Gu is still their General Gu, a loyal heart forever true? Do you really think we don't want that?!" As the emperor spat out those last words, he began to choke up. "I'll tell you the truth... Every day and every night, even in my dreams, I yearn for that day..."

The emperor turned, fighting an agitation unseemly for a nation's ruler as he turned his face away. Finally, he calmed himself enough to resume using the royal *we*.

"But we can't do it. The root system sustaining Chonghua's old nobles is as strong as it ever was, the situation with slave cultivators has improved but not enough, and the Liao Kingdom still threatens our nation's borders at every turn. In the matter of black magic curses, Chonghua is still in the dark; we can only react to them. How do you propose we clear General Gu's name? Do you want us to announce to the world that Gu Mang was actually a spy we sent into the Liao Kingdom? Or explain nothing and exempt him from punishment by fiat?"

The emperor laughed bitterly. "Xihe-jun, wake up. There is too much blood on Gu Mang's hands, the latter is impossible. And if you would just consider it calmly, you could guess the results of the former. Yes, the stain on his reputation would be washed clean, but what next? The Liao Kingdom would know Gu Mang had relayed the most closely guarded secrets of their magic to Chonghua and fortify their defenses accordingly. The old nobles would learn of the arrangement we made with General Gu back then and grow uneasy and restless. Internal troubles and external threats would combine to render General Gu's five years of spying, three years of humiliation... all his suffering, everything he sacrificed—it would be wasted!" The emperor paused, his eyes flashing as he turned to Mo Xi. "This is not what he wanted. Xihe-jun, you are the person he treasures most. You should understand his choice."

The longsword in Mo Xi's hand quivered with the trembling of his heart.

How could he not understand?

Gu Mang had spoken to him of his dream countless times. In the beginning, he was so timid, as if terrified his companions would mock the naivete of his ideals. Later, he'd spoken resolutely, decisively. At that time, Gu Mang had already chosen to follow this principle to its end and would never turn back from his aim.

How could Mo Xi not understand the choice he made? From the moment he saw Gu Mang kneel on the Golden Terrace, he knew what kind of path Gu Mang had laid out in his heart.

But—when he thought of that blood-soaked man in Sishu Terrace tonight, thought of the man who fell into his arms, tears streaming down his face as he begged not to have his memories stripped away, how could he accept it?

Torn in a thousand directions, Mo Xi felt like he was burning alive; he felt like his body had been cleaved into two. Half his heart ached for the suffering Gu Mang had endured and clamored for him to give up. What "righteousness and loyalty to the nation and the world"? How could there be "equal treatment for all, with peace throughout the land"? His shixiong was far too naive—the world would never give him anything, yet he still offered up his chest full of passion, his pristine reputation, and his body of flesh and blood. *Mo Xi, when his mind was collapsing, he begged you so pitifully. He's afraid of pain—how could you not save him?*

The other half of his heart murmured, *No...* Ever since he was young, Gu Mang had hungered for a world where all were equal. His shixiong had walked this path for so many years, covering his body with blood and filling his eyes with wounds, just for the realization of that day. *If he were awake, with how stubborn he is, he would definitely want to persevere... Mo Xi, how could you betray him?*

The two halves of his heart battled, locked in mutual torment.

His spiritual core was nearing collapse; though the elder of Shennong Terrace had done all in his power to stabilize it, it was still dangerously weak. Now, as his emotions surged, his jeopardized core throbbed with a pain so violent he coughed out a mouthful of blood.

Upon seeing his condition, the emperor relaxed slightly. "Xihe-jun..."

With a turn of his wrist, Mo Xi flipped the Shuairan longsword down to prop himself up. The blade's sharp point sank into the golden brick below. He panted, wiping blood from the corner of his mouth, and rasped through lips and teeth stained scarlet, "Even if...you can't clear his name right now, then let me ask you—" He blinked laboriously, tendons protruding in his neck and his hands tightly clenched, each word bitten out. "Why do these black magic experiments?!"

That sentence landed like a stone in the sea, sinking into silence.

Mo Xi looked up, staring at the emperor's pallid face through furious and grieving eyes. His bloodstained lips moved slowly, and the words he spat were equally raw. "Even if you were bound by circumstance and couldn't ensure his safety...as the ruler of the nation, could you not at least spare him some suffering after he returned?"

Mo Xi's voice cracked like a shattered xun. The rims of his eyes were alarmingly red. "Black magic experiments are excruciatingly painful! Your Imperial Majesty! What are you doing this for? Putting on a show? Performing blood-for-blood vengeance for those who don't know the truth? Or was it because *you* wanted to learn more secrets of black magic curses?!"

The emperor's face was ashen. He parted his lips to speak but stopped himself. In the end, he bit his lower lip and turned his face away. "Xihe-jun, there are many things you don't understand—"

"There are indeed many things I don't understand. I don't understand what you've been thinking all these years, I don't know which of the things you've said are true and which are false. It's precisely because I don't know anything that I was kept in the dark for a full eight years! But, Your Imperial Majesty, do you think you know all the truth?"

Light flickered in the emperor's eyes. "What do you mean?" he slowly asked.

Caught in the grip of his surging emotions, another burst of coppery bitterness filled Mo Xi's throat. He closed his eyes, tilting his head slightly without answering.

At that moment, those two little golden beasts on the brazier of Zhuque Hall awoke. They inhaled smoke into their bellies, then hiccupped, raising their voice to shout:

"His Imperial Majesty's fortune floods the heavens!"

"His Imperial Majesty's might covers the world!"

Mo Xi silently listened to these two magic-imbued beasts belching flattery and praise. He began to laugh, the sound filled with endless sorrow.

The emperor's expression strained tighter. "What about Subject Gu do we not know?"

Mo Xi didn't answer him directly. "Your Imperial Majesty, Murong Lian gifted you this brazier and incense burner to demonstrate his allegiance and give you peace of mind. Countless people bend their knee and praise you for the sake of their own titles and status, for their lives or the lives of their families... If you wanted to find someone in Chonghua whose heart is truly steady, immovable in its loyalty to Chonghua, there are actually very, very few. Gu Mang is one of them. Because of your many difficulties, you did not make good on your promise. But he is not the same. The things he promised you...were sworn with a gentleman's word. He achieved all of them."

As Mo Xi spoke, he smiled softly. That smile held a boundless, aching sadness. "Your Imperial Majesty, what you don't know is that Gu Mang recovered most of his memories while we were on Bat Island."

Distant light flickered in the emperor's eyes. After a moment of blankness, shock followed. "He did...?"

Mo Xi's eyes were almost cruel as he took in the emperor's rattled expression. He cut into his ruler's heart with every word he spoke. "Aside from those five years he spent in the Liao Kingdom, he more or less remembered everything. He remembered the promises you made him, the kind of person he is, Lu Zhanxing's death, the defeat at Phoenix Cry Mountain, everything you said on the Golden Terrace—he remembered it all."

The emperor's cheeks were bloodless. He shook his head, murmuring as he took a step backward. His face was blank as if he hadn't realized the implications of those words, but he was trembling all over as if he understood completely. "How could that be..." He took another step back, looking at Mo Xi in disbelief. But his eyes were empty, as though whatever convictions had supported his cruelty had collapsed to pieces. A crack had appeared across the emperor's usually indifferent expression, and increasingly vivid emotions began pouring from the split. The emperor shook his head again and again, his voice rising until it sounded almost wild. "How could he possibly have remembered? If he really remembered everything, then...then wouldn't it be..."

Mo Xi blinked back his tears. "He knew the truth, he knew you had forsaken him, yet he continued to keep your secret. Eight years have passed. He's seen his reputation destroyed and his body covered in wounds; he's received none of what you promised him—but he still kept this secret for you. He didn't come to question you, nor did he confess his grievances to any other. When Zhou He cut him open to carry out the black magic experiments you ordered...*his mind was clear*..." Mo Xi steadied his shaking voice, but his vision blurred. "Your Imperial Majesty, do you understand now...? When he went with Zhou He, he knew he was innocent!"

The emperor collapsed back down into his throne. His lips were nearly blue, as if his illness might flare up again at any moment. "He knew... He already knew... Then he... At that time..." The emperor stumbled over his words. He lifted slender fingers to bury his face into his hands, murmuring in hoarse fragments, "Subject Gu... Subject Gu..."

Despite knowing he had been discarded, he had walked silently into the Asura Room. What had he felt...?

The emperor closed his eyes in grief, his voice catching in his throat and turning into a sorrowful gulp. The shock of this truth was too much for him. For a long, long time, the emperor could not recover. He mumbled to himself, the rims of his eyes overflowing and his palms filling with tears. His head was down, his shoulders crumpled pathetically, his neck bent as if an invisible claw had broken it.

In all the years Mo Xi had known him, he had never seen the emperor like this. The man sat sunken into the soft middle of the throne as the minutes ticked past. He stared vacantly at that glowing brazier, watching the firewood crackle within. His eyes were empty when he spoke, defeated. "Mo Xi."

He was met with silence.

"Do you think we have a heart of stone? That after making use of Subject Gu, we carelessly abandoned him without any feeling, or the slightest intention of keeping our promises?"

The emperor looked up, the rims of his eyes and the tip of his nose still red. He closed his eyes. Amid this silence, he seemed to make some decision. He rose to his feet. "There is nothing we can say that you will believe. And so it is... To be honest, of those history-recording jade scrolls, one yet remains. We have always kept it at our side."

Mo Xi tensed.

When the emperor next spoke, it was with an air of heavy weariness. "Since it's come to this, we have nothing left to hide. We ask you to come with us."

129

The Truth of Warrior Soul Mountain

THE EMPEROR LED Mo Xi to a back courtyard terrace of Zhuque Hall. A pool of dream-gathering water lay there, which could gather the past into the present and bring it in front of the viewer's eyes.

The emperor stood motionless beside the pool, watching the reflections of himself and Mo Xi within. Then he slowly took that string of bodhi dzi beads off his wrist and passed it through his hands. The bodhi beads had been polished by time; he moved his fingers over each one and stopped at the seventh.

"Mo Xi...we might have chosen to destroy the jade scrolls in the Imperial Censorate, but..." He closed his eyes, wringing his hands. "But, believe us, we never thought of lying to Subject Gu. We've always kept this dzi bead that can clear his name with us. In the event we achieved what we promised during our lifetime, we of course intended to publicly announce his innocence. But, if we were defeated by fate, we would have ensured this dzi bead containing the truth remained on this earth. When the time came, there would be descendants who would reveal that oath on the Golden Terrace to the realm."

The night wind rose, rustling through the leaves of the parasol trees at the pool's edge.

"In this way, under the Nine Springs, we would at last be worthy of seeing our loyal subject again."

As he spoke, he tapped that dzi bead with a fingertip. The bead shone with dazzling light as a wisp of silver-white memory floated from it and fell into the Dream-Transfiguring Pool. The water rippled, shattering the frosty moonlit reflection as a cold mist rose from its surface.

The mist coalesced into a vision. Faint sounds emanated from the depths of the fog; gradually, they became crystal clear. A brothel echoing with the voices of women unfolded before their eyes.

"The fragrance of blackberry rose on the wind, cuckoo song and red flowers filling the trees. An empty happiness, only wishing the one I long for thinks the same."[13] The sound of the paired-stanza water fairy[14] music came hazily from the stage in the brothel, the songstress's tremulous voice drifting through the pleasure house like a floating skein of silk.

"The hazy shadow of flowers at dusk. The daylily flourishes without mercy, the pomegranate blossoms deepen yearning. Heavy is the ache of farewell."

The fog rising from the pool grew denser, enclosing the entirety of the terrace at the back of Zhuque Hall in a sensual illusion.

Apricot Mansion.

Mo Xi and the emperor stood amid that thick fog. Slowly, the scene came into focus. Mo Xi saw once more that night from eight years ago he had seen in the Time Mirror, the eve of Gu Mang's defection. In a side room of the brothel, Gu Mang was speaking with that mysterious black-garbed man.

He hadn't known who the black-garbed man was back then. In hindsight, it seemed it was none other than the emperor himself.

---

13   From "Spring Evening" by the Yuan dynasty poet Li Zhiyuan.
14   A type of poem with a rigid rhyming scheme, originating in the Tang dynasty.

The emperor walked to Mo Xi's side, eyes on that black-garbed man who had materialized from the mist. "This was the last meeting we had with Subject Gu before his defection. At the time, he knew he was soon to leave. He was distraught, so we agreed to come find him that day at midnight to take him to see something on Warrior Soul Mountain."

The conversation they watched was identical to the one in the Time Mirror. In the illusory realm, the black-robed emperor pushed a bundle toward Gu Mang and set it on the table. "I brought this for you. You should change into it."

Gu Mang's actions were exactly the same. He lifted a hand, turning down a corner of the cloth only to quickly wrap it back up. "What do you mean by this?"

"If you're going there, you'd best prepare, hadn't you?" The emperor said, "If I tell you what's there, I doubt you'll believe it. Tonight, I'll take you there in person, so you can see the truth with your own eyes."

The scene around them darkened. When it lit up once more, the thick fog around them had become the foot of Warrior Soul Mountain.

Both Gu Mang and the emperor wore black hooded capes, thoroughly covered from head to toe.

When Gu Mang reached the start of the curved footpath, he looked at the little cobblestone road snaking upward and lowered his hood, gazing at that lofty mountain path.

"Are you not going?" asked the emperor.

"Just thinking about how I'll be leaving soon, and my hands will be stained with the blood of Chonghua's soldiers. I..."

The emperor cut him off. "Chonghua's current state is as you've seen. You experienced it yourself after Phoenix Cry Mountain.

When you and your army fell from grace, all you found were those who would kick you when you were down, none who would offer help in your hour of need."

Seeing Gu Mang about to protest, he continued. "You don't need to tell me that if Xihe-jun were here, he would side with you. His support is useless. You're a clever person; you understand that Chonghua has always been ruled by the nobles. You cannot change anything with your power alone."

Gu Mang said nothing.

"It's come to this," the emperor said. "The pieces are already in place for your treason; this move cannot be taken back."

He lifted a hand in the cold mist, taking hold of Gu Mang's icy fingers. Gu Mang turned to look at him in surprise, twitching slightly as if he wanted to break free. But in the end, he did not.

Mo Xi watched it all unfold in front of him. The first time he'd seen this piece of the past in the Time Mirror, he thought this black-garbed man was a Liao Kingdom agent, and that Gu Mang's trembling upon having his hand caught was from hesitation and indecision. Knowing the truth, his emotions were incredibly complicated. The first coherent sentence that came to mind was: "Were they cold?"

The emperor, standing at his side, was taken aback. "What?"

"His hands," Mo Xi whispered. "Were they very cold?"

This was something that had happened eight years in the past. No one would remember such details for that long. But after a moment of blankness, the emperor understood. He lowered his lashes. "...Yes."

Mo Xi didn't reply.

"I'm sorry, we pushed him onto this road of despair."

Mo Xi made no sound as the emperor in the illusion repeated just what he'd said in the Time Mirror. "General Gu, none who seek to blaze a new path have hands unsullied by blood. Before you have a single innocent life on your hands, you should walk up Warrior Soul Mountain one more time. You won't have the chance to do so in the future."

Gu Mang closed his eyes. The night wind tousled the wisps of hair at his temples. It was a long time before he gently pulled his hand from between the emperor's palms. His fingertips still trembled; no one could warm those hands of his. "Let's go."

In the Time Mirror, this was as far as Mo Xi had seen. But this vision was different. This time, dense fog unfurled, and he finally beheld what Gu Mang and the emperor had gone to Warrior Soul Mountain to see—

The emperor and Gu Mang arrived before the barrier that guarded the forbidden area of Warrior Soul Mountain. Raising a hand, the emperor cut his own palm, smearing fresh blood onto the array. The blood was instantly absorbed by the magical barrier, and a voice seemed to rumble out from the depths of the earth. "Courageous achievements immortalized in stone."

The emperor answered, "Graves of commoner heroes carved with names."

Courageous achievements immortalized in stone, graves of commoner heroes carved with names.

This simple paired verse was the dream Gu Mang had held dear all his life. As soon as he heard this reply, the rims of Gu Mang's eyes reddened. The emperor, taking note, sighed and patted Gu Mang on the shoulder. "There's no one else here," he said softly. "You may take off your cloak."

Gu Mang unfastened the ties and let the cloak fall. Beneath was a set of white military mourning robes, trimmed in black.

"Let's go."

They passed through the barrier and entered the forbidden area of Warrior Soul Mountain. Mo Xi already had an inkling of what awaited them and thought himself ready. But when he laid eyes on the scene within, he felt his heart had been struck a heavy blow.

The entire forbidden area of Warrior Soul Mountain, fully half of the slope, was covered in neat rows of gravestones. Of those plaques, some were already carved with names, traced over with fine golden lacquer, while some were still blank. Seeing the vast expanse of them grouped together, it was as if those common-born heroes' souls had returned from the underworld, crowding around the peak in a noisy bustle.

Gu Mang stood stunned for a long interval. Then, as though afraid of shattering this beautiful dream, he took a few careful steps forward. Slowly, his cautious movements became staggering stumbles, and he lurched forward, ever closer. By the time he saw the engraved words on the first tombstone, tears had overspilled the rims of his eyes.

He reached out, caressing the gleaming gold inscription on the stone, tears flowing freely. "You've come home…" Choked sobs escaped his throat as he knelt. In grief, he huddled in front of that incomplete field of tombstones, kowtowing again and again to those seventy thousand comrades he left behind at Phoenix Cry Mountain. "You've come home…"

The emperor stood at his side. After a long while, he put a hand on Gu Mang's shoulder. "This forbidden area is the first promise we've fulfilled for you. Seventy thousand tombstones, each with names carved by our own hand, each gravestone personally erected. General Gu, it is our belief that, should we see through the plan you've made with us, there will come a day when the forbidden area of Warrior Soul Mountain will no longer be off-limits."

Gu Mang made no sound. Attired in formal military mourning dress and with white hemp binding his hair, he wept, kowtowing again and again. He saw no living people; his vision was filled only with those deceased and long-gone brothers.

The emperor didn't disturb him; he kept Gu Mang silent company as he watched from the side.

Eventually, Gu Mang staggered to his feet. He pressed his palms together, praying a few more times before the graves with his hands to his forehead, mumbling in a low voice.

"Is there anything else you want us to do?" the emperor asked.

Gu Mang closed his eyes. When he spoke, his eyes were damp. "If it's not too bold... I...have three things I'd like to ask Your Imperial Majesty to grant."

"Speak."

Gu Mang ran his fingers over the golden text on one of the gravestones, tracing the characters from top to bottom.

"For the first: if I'm really unable to return... I ask Your Imperial Majesty not to erect a tomb or gravestone for me on Warrior Soul Mountain. When I leave for the Liao Kingdom, I become a spy. I will inevitably stain my hands with the blood of my comrades. Even if I had no choice, even if I had a secret reason, those whose lives I take will still die by my hand. I have no right to be buried with them."

The emperor seemed uneasy. "But—"

"I ask you to hear me out. For the second request... Xihe-jun's character is pure and kind; he's a noble of great merit, yet he shares a deep friendship with me and has offended countless ancestral patriarchs on my behalf. When I defect, he is bound to disbelieve it; he may even take extremely disobedient and unfilial actions. I ask Your Imperial Majesty to keep the truth from him, no matter what.

I ask Your Imperial Majesty to understand his sorrow and refrain from punishing him."

Hearing this, Mo Xi couldn't hold back anymore. Tears poured down his face. He involuntarily stepped forward, eyes fixed on Gu Mang in the illusion, with his proper military uniform and solemn expression. "Gu Mang..." he murmured.

But the illusion of Gu Mang from eight years ago couldn't hear him. He stood in the chilly mountain air, his sleeves fluttering. He was not going to meet his death—rather, he was going beyond death, and right now, he was methodically briefing the emperor on his last wishes.

"The third thing," Gu Mang began, and then fell silent. He lowered his lashes and looked at his hands. After some time, he whispered, "The third thing. I want to play the soul-calling song for them, while my hands are still clean. But, Your Imperial Majesty, I only have a paltry little suona. May I borrow your holy weapon?"

He raised his head, the crisp wind stirring the hair by his temples. Under the moonlight, he looked imploringly at the emperor.

When Chonghua's soul-calling song was performed for martyred heroes, a ceremonial official customarily played it on their holy weapon. Gu Mang couldn't hope for a ceremonial official to come console his brothers. He could only ask for recognition from this man in front of him.

"With your devotion, what would we refuse you?" A jade-green bamboo xiao appeared in the emperor's hands. He handed the flute to Gu Mang.

Gu Mang thanked him, taking the xiao reverently with both hands. He raised his chin and gazed forward, as if to carve all of the seventy thousand gravestones on Warrior Soul Mountain into his heart. Under the light of the bright moon and the shadows of the pines, he pressed the bamboo xiao to his lips and closed his eyes.

"Our sons went forth with swords held brave, their blood and bones in distant grave. Last year this self was yet intact, last night this body spoke and laughed. Your loyalty I safely keep, your valiant deeds I freely speak. For when these heroes' souls come home, throughout the land shall peace be known..."

The song came to an end.

When Gu Mang lowered the xiao, his eyes brimmed with tears.

He turned to restore the instrument to the emperor, then knelt once more before the forest of graves. After a few moments of silence, he lowered his head, his voice small. "Your Imperial Majesty, I'm leaving soon. I don't know when I'll be back, if ever."

"Subject Gu..."

"When I'm gone, I ask you to visit them often on my behalf... No need to burn too much gilt paper money... Just...just bring some jugs of good wine, a few different dishes." By the end, his voice was a tearful whisper. "When they were with me, the military rations were never enough. They would look at the rations for the other armies, and often they would joke with me, and tell me..." He pressed his forehead to the icy stone plaque, tears falling like beads off a broken string. "Tell me they were hungry... That they wanted a proper meal."

The emperor said nothing.

"All these years, I heard all of it, even if I never said anything. There were always those who said we wanted to seize power...that we wanted to revolt... called us insatiably greedy and wildly ambitious..." Gu Mang slowly tilted his head back. "But Your Imperial Majesty, did you know? Their greatest, wildest ambition...was actually just to eat a filling meal..."

The emperor in the illusion wore a mask. No one knew what his expression was on hearing these words. But Mo Xi could see that, despite how many years had passed, when the present emperor beside him heard Gu Mang say this once more, his expression was dull with pain.

"Come visit them on my behalf, would you? Bring them some more army rations."

"Subject Gu...rest assured, we will do as you ask."

"Could there be wine, too?"

"We'll bring the finest wine in Chonghua for your men."

"Shaodaozi is good enough, they're used to being poor. They wouldn't have the heart to drink expensive wine."

"Shaodaozi then."

Gu Mang no longer had any requests. He knelt on the mountain, tilting his head to gaze at the plaques his brothers had become. He didn't move for a long time.

The emperor in the illusion sighed softly and raised a hand. Yet instead of dispersing the jade bamboo xiao, he pressed it to his own lips and played the soul-calling song again.

The notes of the flute echoed under the pale moonlight, carried on the crisp breeze. To the sound of this mournful tune, the surrounds of Warrior Soul Mountain disappeared. The illusory fog and the scene it showed dispersed, but the moving song of the xiao seemed to pass through illusion into reality and resonate from the foothills of Warrior Soul Mountain eight years ago. The mist scattered, yet the notes lingered in echoes.

A long moment passed back on Zhuque Terrace. Eventually, the emperor replaced that dzi bead and gazed up at the pristine moon peeking from the clouds. "Fireball," he murmured. "These eight years, we've worn this bracelet at all times, guarding this secret. Whenever we could bear it no longer, we transfigured this section of memory and watched it over again. Every time, we would remember once more that we did not walk this path alone, that we carried the hopes of more than just ourselves. It's been eight years. Every day and every night, we never forgot; we did not dare to forget."

The emperor caressed the dzi beads on his wrist, voice a murmur. "We don't have a heart of stone. It's only that...sitting on high is like being held in a cage..." By the end, his voice was tearful. "In all honesty, has there ever been a moment we did not feel shame for our treatment of Subject Gu...and of you...?"

Neither spoke. The birds and the cicadas in the ancient trees by the pavilion sang in the night. On the terrace of Zhuque Hall, Mo Xi and the emperor gazed at each other in silence, both grieving, eyes wet.

130

Going Home

MO XI RETURNED to his manor, where he stayed in seclusion for three days. The capital buzzed with curiosity about what had transpired. What had taken place when Mo Xi went to the palace such that the emperor did not punish his great offense? After everything, he was merely placed under house arrest for a handful of days, and that was the end of it.

No one could know the truth.

In those three days, Jiang Fuli never once left Xihe Manor. Gu Mang's injuries were too severe. He sent everyone away to treat him; no one was allowed near the patient's room.

On the third day, sunlight streamed through the window lattice. Time passed, and ink-dark shadows flowed across the floor. Mo Xi sat at his sandalwood desk, looking at the stack of letters in front of him.

He had already flipped through and reread these letters countless times in the past few days. They were the intelligence reports Gu Mang had sent the emperor from the Liao Kingdom during the years he had been gone from Chonghua. The emperor had kept them in the qiankun pouch he carried on his person all this time.

Five years' worth of reports, a thick stack. The earliest letters were smudged and faded, and even the latest had begun to yellow at the edges. The only thing that hadn't changed was the handwriting. Mo Xi couldn't be more familiar with those characters;

the penmanship was slightly slanted and messy, the ends of certain strokes distinctively curled.

> *Your Imperial Majesty, I've entered the Liao Kingdom. The guoshi of Liao was very wary and caused some slight difficulty. Everything has been settled, no need to worry. Wishing Your Imperial Majesty well.*

And another:

> *Your Imperial Majesty, Liao plans to attack Lan City at the northern frontier after the fall harvest. There are many civilians in Lan City; I ask Your Imperial Majesty to have sympathy for the people and prepare in advance.*

And another:

> *Your Imperial Majesty, I am stationed with the Liao Kingdom army at Mount Tiandang. As a general of Liao, I cannot avoid killing on the battlefield. In seven days, in the attack on Lan City, I will have no choice but to face my comrades, the soldiers of Chonghua. For this, I beg forgiveness on my knees.*

There was even the missive Gu Mang sent to the emperor after the battle of Dongting Lake. The handwriting on that note was messier than on any previous letter. The brushstrokes seemed to shake, as if Gu Mang was so distraught while writing he couldn't calm down to pen each stroke properly. The anxiety he felt was palpable in the form of the words themselves—

I had no choice but to stab him in the heart—General Mo is far too naive and stubborn. I sincerely hope Your Imperial Majesty will take attentive care of him. I have one more request: General Mo and I share a deep brotherhood, and I'm afraid I can never again face General Mo in battle...

Every time Mo Xi read to this point, he couldn't help but imagine how Gu Mang must have felt writing this letter. And every time, it hurt too, too much; once he thought it, he couldn't console himself.

Other than updates on the Liao Kingdom's military and reports of their black magic techniques, what Mo Xi saw most as he flipped through the letters were Gu Mang's accounts after each battle, of how many people he killed and how many cities he destroyed. These were not so much apologies to the emperor as Gu Mang's ledger of the lives he owed.

By the fifth year, Gu Mang had stopped counting. Probably because he, too, had realized: however he calculated or counted, those people were dead by his own hand. There was nothing to salvage. Instead, at the end of every letter, where one would usually sign their name, he would write a line in very small print: *The guilty subject Gu Mang kowtows once and once again.*

Mo Xi stroked the words curled up in the corner. *The guilty subject Gu Mang...* His tears fell just like that, dripping onto those shameful and guilt-ridden words.

He flipped to the last letter.

In this final missive, Gu Mang wrote a few simple lines of text explaining the reason the emperor must use him for black magic experiments.

When I first entered the Liao Kingdom five years ago, Liao tem-
pered my body, injected wolf blood into my veins, and carved black
magic spells into my bones. Throughout these five years, my mind
has gradually become chaotic, more and more difficult for me to
control. I can guess what the Liao Kingdom will do next: very soon,
they will break my mind and destroy my memories, then send me
back as a peace offering to Chonghua. My life is insignificant and
is already soaked in filthy blood. Your Imperial Majesty need not
trouble yourself to treat me. If Your Imperial Majesty truly pities
the suffering I have endured, I ask you to have me sent to the prison,
to be dissected and experimented on, so that methods to counter
the Liao Kingdom's black magic path can be found more quickly.
With this, my remaining wishes shall be fulfilled.

At the end of the letter, there was once again that line of small
and shameful characters. *The guilty subject Gu Mang kowtows once
and once again.*

The emperor's last words from Zhuque Hall still echoed in his
ears. "Fireball, do you know how we felt upon seeing this letter? In
the first missive he sent five years ago, he told us the Liao Kingdom
had some slight difficulty with him, but everything had been dealt
with, and there was no need to worry. It wasn't until five years later—
when he realized that the Liao Kingdom would likely dispose of him
next—that he revealed the truth. The 'slight difficulty' he spoke of
referred to the tempering of his body and the carving of his bones
with black magic runes.

"Do you understand now? The Liao Kingdom sent him back
because the demonic curse and monstrous blood in Gu Mang's
body could no longer be controlled. Even they didn't know what he
would become with his mind fully consumed by black magic. Nor

did they dare to carelessly kill this mutated, demonic body. So they sent him back to Chonghua."

The emperor paused then, and repeated himself. "Fireball, we had no choice. The black magic trials are cruel, yet this was the only method we could think of to save him. Otherwise, when the day comes that the demonic energy in Gu Mang's body explodes, both Chonghua and Gu Mang will be destroyed..."

A sharp knock sounded from the half-closed door. Mo Xi swiftly came to his senses, surfacing from those wretched memories. He wiped away the tear tracks that had not yet dried and tidied up the letters. "Enter."

Li Wei took a few steps inside. In the past few days, he was the only person who could enter this room without being kicked out. "My lord, good news! He's been saved!" he exclaimed.

Mo Xi started, jolting to his feet as if he might run out the door. "He's still sleeping," Li Wei hastily added. "Medicine Master Jiang instructed that he absolutely mustn't be woken up. The medicine master is waiting for you in the back courtyard; he says there is something he must speak to you about."

Jiang Fuli was leaning against a pillar beside the lotus pond in the back courtyard of Xihe Manor. He gazed at the pool full of flourishing, fragrant lotus blossoms, his eyes glimmering with an inscrutable light. Whatever he was pondering seemed to have left him perplexed; his brows were drawn together slightly, his thin lips tightly pursed in thought.

Mo Xi strode down the winding corridor and arrived at his side. "Medicine Master Jiang."

Perhaps he was depleted from three days of healing, or per- haps it was for some other reason that Jiang Fuli showed a rare unresponsiveness. He continued to stare blankly at the fish swimming in the pool.

"Medicine Master Jiang?"

Only upon Mo Xi's second greeting did Jiang Fuli react as if waking from a dream. "Oh, it's you. You're here."

Mo Xi was thinking of nothing but Gu Mang; he took no notice of Jiang Fuli's strange demeanor. "How is my shixiong?"

"There were some slight complications, but you don't need to worry," Jiang Fuli replied. "Sit down, I'll tell you."

Mo Xi was restless, but Jiang Fuli's attitude seemed to say, *I won't talk unless you sit*. He had no other choice; he took a seat across from Jiang Fuli.

"Let me first ask you: before Zhou He began the black magic experiments, had Gu Mang already recovered a majority of his memories?"

He was very straightforward, and so Mo Xi made no attempt to deny it.

"I don't concern myself with the machinations of the court. I won't ask anything more; you can be at ease. I'm only curious—he lost two souls, so it should be impossible for his memories to recover to such an extent. What did you experience on Bat Island? What was it that put him into this state?"

"The Time Mirror," Mo Xi answered.

Jiang Fuli was silent for a beat. "No wonder. Now I understand. I'll explain it this way, Xihe-jun. The Time Mirror can indeed return Gu Mang's mind and memories, but human souls cannot be replaced. What the Time Mirror did was only a flashback, and not a true recovery."

"A flashback..."

"Correct," Jiang Fuli said. "It's like a flash of dying lucidity, it doesn't last long. In another month or two, the memories returned by the Time Mirror will disappear." He paused before continuing. "My apologies. Even I have no way of reversing this."

In truth, Mo Xi had more or less expected this. When the shangao had called the Time Mirror, he had shouted something about "flashing back" Gu Mang's memories. Even back then Mo Xi had been alarmed by the shangao's choice of words, but when he heard this confirmation from Jiang Fuli, his heart still plummeted. He cast his gaze downward. "I understand… Many thanks," he said in a low voice.

"I'm paid to help with such problems, there's no need for thanks. Gu Mang's other injuries won't cause him further trouble. All he needs now is sufficient rest and care. However, there's something I must remind you of." Jiang Fuli's expression became solemn. "His mind absolutely cannot endure another major shock."

Mo Xi's heart seized. He asked, urgent, "He's still unwell?"

"How could he not be?" Jiang Fuli held up three fingers before Mo Xi. "First, he lacks two souls. Second, an ancient godly mirror forcibly returned some of his memories. Third, Zhou He cut into his brain…" He curled a finger with every item he mentioned. "Let me put it like this, Xihe-jun—this Gu-shixiong of yours is extraordinarily strong. If it were anyone else, they would have gone mad from any one of those three." By the time all three fingers were down, even someone as arrogant as Jiang Fuli couldn't help a sigh of admiration. "He went through all that, yet he still didn't lose his sense of self."

A breeze blew over the lotus pool, scudding across the shimmering water. Jiang Fuli turned to gaze at the ripples, speaking softly. "In truth, as a healer, I'm very curious. I can't imagine what kind of mental willpower he must possess to make him so indestructible."

Both men were still for a moment. Jiang Fuli's almond eyes watched the fish in the pond circle each other and disperse. Suddenly, he asked, "Xihe-jun, I have a question for you. Gu Mang was sent to the Liao Kingdom as a spy, wasn't he?"

Looking up, Mo Xi stared at him. Jiang Fuli had used up three days of sheer effort; he was deeply weary, leaning against the pillar for support. He turned his head and squinted at the rippling lotus pool. "Don't worry, I didn't peek at his thoughts while healing him," he said in a leisurely tone. "Considering his mental fortitude, he might not tell me the truth even if I fed him the Draught of Confession. It's just a personal hunch, no more than an offhand question. You don't have to confirm either way."

Mo Xi's throat hurt terribly. After a spell, he said, "Why...why would you think so?"

"It's very simple," Jiang Fuli replied. "A traitor who fell onto a path of vengeful murder merely because he couldn't bear disappointment would not have the kind of willpower he does. I have no evidence, nor do I wish to involve myself in the intrigues of the court, but as a healer, I am certain he isn't a cruel person."

Sunlight filled Jiang Fuli's eyes, smoothing those features that were usually so obstinate and unimpressed by the world. In this light, he looked somewhat melancholy, even gentle.

Mo Xi was struck by a faint sense of déjà vu.

"Take good care of him, Xihe-jun. The state of his mind is perilous, like a cracking sheet of ice. If he should endure a fourth trauma to the mind—" Jiang Fuli paused, tone grave. "He will go mad. At that point, unless you find his two souls, even an immortal from the highest of heavens couldn't save him."

In the evening, a crescent moon hung overhead. The canopy of heaven was lustrous with stars, and the Milky Way looked like a soaring dragon, or like a bright sword, glimmering with light as it flowed across the deep blue of the sky.

On this night, many in Chonghua found their minds heavy with the weight of their own difficulties.

In the imperial palace, the emperor lay curled within the soft bed canopies of Zhuque Hall, wrapped in fox fur. His eyes were closed as he caressed the bodhi dzi bead bracelet at his wrist.

In Yue Manor, Murong Chuyi's feet took him to the door of Yue Chenqing's bedroom. After hesitating a long time, he finally lifted a hand and rapped on the wood. He waited without response, then gently pushed the door open. Within, a singular lamp was lit, both the bed and the desk were neat, and Yue Chenqing was nowhere to be found. A servant walking past told him Yue Chenqing had gone to the academy to study with Jiang Yexue. Murong Chuyi did not respond. After a long while, he closed his eyes.

In Medicine Master Manor, Jiang Fuli had announced he must set out on a long journey and was urgently packing his bags. His wife stood by the door as if she wanted to say something, but in the end, she never spoke.

In Wangshu Manor, Murong Lian lay on the bamboo bed in his courtyard, taking long drags of ephemera. Clouds of smoke slowly drifted from his lips and were blown toward the blossoming foxglove trees. Biting his pipe, Murong Lian stretched his hand in front of him and stared vacantly at his own fingers, his gaze flickering.

As for Xihe Manor—

After so many twists and turns and bloody storms, the inhabitants of this manor finally returned to a temporary peace. Gu Mang lay on the spacious bed in the master bedroom, covered with a light blanket, slumbering still. Mo Xi had dismissed the servants, keeping a solitary vigil at his bedside.

He sat patiently, unbothered by Gu Mang's long sleep, or the fact that Gu Mang had taken his bed. After all, he'd once sworn to give Gu Mang those things.

"I promised to give you a home." Mo Xi took hold of his hand, bringing it to his lips and kissing it gently. "I'm sorry, Shixiong. I've made you wait too long."

The man on the bed lay obediently, his thick sweep of lashes fanning across his cheeks. He no longer had any need to pretend, endure, or exhaust himself. He looked so weary, so weak. As Mo Xi gazed at the man before him, he could scarcely recall how his Gu Mang-gege used to look—healthy, sturdy, resplendent with sunlight. Time had ravaged him terribly.

Mo Xi lowered his head, burying his face in his hands and pressing his forehead to Gu Mang's slightly cool palm. Quietly, he choked out, "Shixiong, you're home now."

Warm tears streamed down his cheeks, soaking Gu Mang's hand.

As if awakened by that murmur and the passion it entailed, after a few moments, Gu Mang's fingertips twitched. Slowly, he opened his eyes.

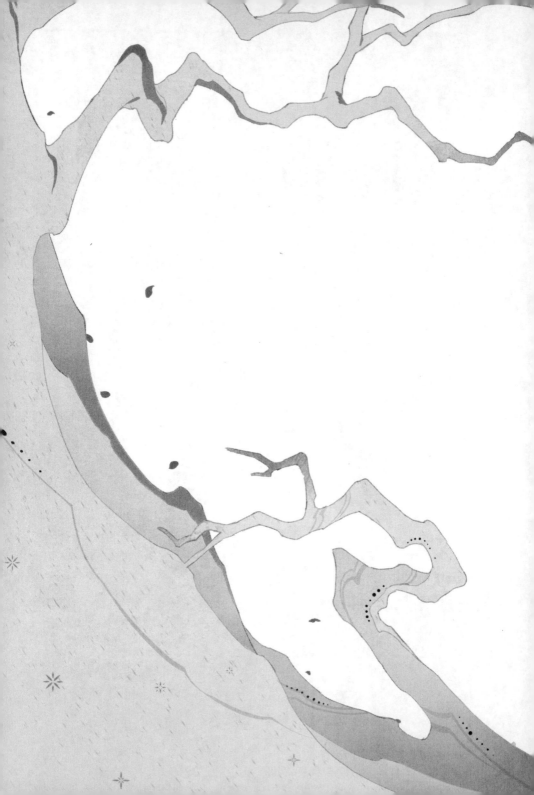

THE STORY CONTINUES IN
Remnants of Filth
VOLUME 5

Characters, Names, and Locations

Characters

Mo Xi

墨熄　SURNAME MO; GIVEN NAME XI, "EXTINGUISH"

TITLES: Xihe-jun (羲和君 / "sun," literary), General Mo

WEAPONS:

Shuairan (率然 / a mythical snake): A whip that can transform into a sword as needed. Named after a snake from Chinese mythology, said to respond so quickly an attack to any part of its body would be met immediately with its fangs or tail (or both). First mentioned in Sun Tzu's *The Art of War* as an ideal for commanders to follow when training their armies.

Tuntian (吞天 / "Skyswallower"): A scepter cast with the essence of a whale spirit.

The commander of the Northern Frontier Army, Mo Xi is the only living descendant of the illustrious Mo Clan. Granted the title Xihe-jun by the late emperor, he possesses extraordinary innate spiritual abilities and has a reputation for being coldly ruthless.

Gu Mang

顾茫　SURNAME GU, "TO LOOK"; GIVEN NAME MANG, "BEWILDERMENT"

TITLES: Beast of the Altar, General Gu

WEAPON:

Yongye (永夜 / "Evernight"): A demonic dagger from the Liao Kingdom.

Fengbo (风波 / "Wind and waves"): A suona used by General Gu.

Once the dazzling shixiong of the cultivation academy, Murong Lian's slave, and war general to the empire of Chonghua, Gu Mang fell from grace and turned traitor, defecting to the enemy Liao Kingdom. Years later, he was sent back to Chonghua as a prisoner of war. His name comes from the line "I unsheathe my sword and look around bewildered" in the first of three poems in the collection "Arduous Journey" by Li Bai, lamenting the sense of loss and obstruction the poet faced upon being sent away from the capital by Emperor Xuanzong.

Murong Lian
慕容怜 SURNAME MURONG; GIVEN NAME LIAN, "MERCY"

TITLE: Wangshu-jun (望舒君 / "moon," literary)
WEAPON:

Water Demon Talisman (水鬼符): A talisman that becomes a horde of water demons to attack its target.

Gu Mang's former master and cousin to the current emperor, Murong Lian is the current lord of Wangshu Manor and the owner of Luomei Pavilion. He is known as the "Greed" of Chonghua's three poisons.

Jiang Yexue
江夜雪 SURNAME JIANG; GIVEN NAME YEXUE, "EVENING SNOW"

TITLE: Qingxu Elder (清旭长老 / "clear dawn")
Disowned son of the Yue Clan, Yue Chenqing's older brother, and Mo Xi's old friend, Jiang Yexue is a gentleman to the core.

Yue Chenqing
岳辰晴 SURNAME YUE; GIVEN NAME CHENQING, "MORNING SUN"

TITLE: Deputy General Yue

Young master of the Yue Clan and Murong Chuyi's nephew, Yue Chenqing is a happy-go-lucky child with a penchant for getting into trouble.

Murong Chuyi
慕容楚衣 SURNAME MURONG; GIVEN NAME CHUYI, SURNAME CHU, "CLOTHES"

Yue Chenqing's Fourth Uncle, Chonghua's "Ignorance," and all-around enigma, Murong Chuyi is a master artificer whose true motivations remain unknown.

SUPPORTING CHARACTERS
(IN ALPHABETICAL ORDER)

Changfeng-jun
长丰君 "LONG, ABUNDANCE"

An older noble worrying himself sick over his daughter Lan-er.

Chen Tang
沉棠 SURNAME CHEN, GIVEN NAME TANG, "FLOWERING APPLE"

Chonghua's legendary Wise Gentleman, who was once the head-master of the cultivation academy as well as guoshi of the nation. He perished in battle with Hua Po'an, a slave cultivator-turned-traitor whom he had personally taught.

The Emperor
君上

TITLE: His Imperial Majesty, "junshang"

Eccentric ruler of the empire of Chonghua. Due to the cultural taboo against using the emperor's given name in any context, he is only ever addressed and referred to as "His Imperial Majesty."

Fandou
饭兜　"BIB"

A loyal black dog and Gu Mang's best friend.

Guoshi of the Liao Kingdom
国师　"IMPERIAL PRECEPTOR"

A mercurial and immensely powerful Liao Kingdom official who conceals his true identity behind a golden mask.

Hua Po'an
花破暗　"FLOWER BREAKING THE DARKNESS"

Chonghua's infamous first slave general. After learning cultivation under the beneficence of Chen Tang, Hua Po'an turned on Chonghua and became the founding monarch of the Liao Kingdom.

Jiang Fuli
姜拂黎　SURNAME JIANG; GIVEN NAME FULI, "TO BRUSH AWAY, MULTITUDES"

Also known by his title of Medicine Master, Jiang Fuli is the finest healer in Chonghua, dubbed the "Wrath" of Chonghua's three poisons.

Lan-er
兰儿　"ORCHID"

A sweet little girl with a dangerously volatile spiritual core.

Li Wei
李微　SURNAME LI; GIVEN NAME WEI, "SLIGHT"

The competent, if harried, head housekeeper of Xihe Manor.

Lu Zhanxing
陆展星 SURNAME LU; GIVEN NAME ZHANXING, "TO EXHIBIT STARS"

Gu Mang's oldest friend, who grew up with him as a slave in Wangshu Manor. Later his deputy general of the Wangba Army.

Murong Mengze
慕容梦泽 SURNAME MURONG; GIVEN NAME MENGZE, "YUNMENG LAKE"

A master healer and the "Virtue" of Chonghua's three gentlemen, Princess Mengze's frail constitution and graceful, refined manner are known to all.

Su Yurou
苏玉柔 SURNAME SU; GIVEN NAME YUROU, "JADE, SOFT"

Known as the most peerless beauty in Chonghua. Jiang Fuli's reclusive wife.

Zhou He
周鹤 SURNAME ZHOU, GIVEN NAME HE, "CRANE"

WEAPON:

Lieying (猎鹰): A pitch-black dagger.

The leader of Sishu Terrace. Obsessed with discovering new magical techniques using any means necessary.

Locations

Dongting Lake
洞庭湖

A real lake in northeastern Hunan, named "Grotto Court Lake" for the dragon court that was said to reside in its depths.

Luomei Pavilion
落梅别苑 "GARDENS OF FALLEN PLUM BLOSSOMS"

A house of pleasure where the nobility of Chonghua could have their pick of captives from enemy nations.

Shennong Terrace
神农台

The healers' ministry of Chonghua. Shennong is the deity and mythological ruler said to have taught agriculture and herbal medicine to the ancient Chinese people.

Warrior Soul Mountain
战魂山

Where the heroes of Chonghua are laid to rest.

Cixin Artificing Forge
慈心冶炼铺 "KIND HEART"

A shabby forge in Chonghua's capital where uncommonly humane spiritual weapons are refined.

Dream Butterfly Islands
梦碟岛

An archipelago of demonic islands not far from Chonghua. The archipelago is composed of around twenty islands, and different types of demons live on each one.

Bat Island
蝙蝠岛

One of the Dream Butterfly Islands, Bat Island is inhabited by fire bats, demons descended from the feathered tribe of Mount Jiuhua. The bats on their island are led by their queen, Wuyan.

Sishu Terrace
司术台   "OVERSEEING MAGIC"

An organization in Chonghua specializing in magical techniques and healing.

Golden Terrace
黄金台

The most secretive and secluded hall at the back of the imperial palace, reserved for the emperor's most trusted subjects.

Name Guide

Diminutives, nicknames, and name tags

A-: Friendly diminutive. Always a prefix. Usually for monosyllabic names, or one syllable out of a two-syllable name.

DOUBLING: Doubling a syllable of a person's name can be a nickname, e.g., "Mangmang"; it has childish or cutesy connotations.

XIAO-: A diminutive meaning "little." Always a prefix.

LAO-: A familiar prefix meaning "old." Usually used for older men.

-ER: An affectionate diminutive added to names, literally "son" or "child." Always a suffix.

Family

DI/DIDI: Younger brother or a younger male friend.

GE/GEGE/DAGE: Older brother or an older male friend.

JIE/JIEJIE/ZIZI: Older sister or an older female friend.

-JIU/JIUJIU: Maternal uncle.

Cultivation

SHIFU: Teacher or master.

SHIXIONG: Older martial brother, used for older disciples or classmates.

SHIDI: Younger martial brother, used for younger disciples or classmates.

DAOZHANG/XIANJUN/XIANZHANG/SHENJUN: Polite terms of address for cultivators. Can be used alone as a title or attached to someone's family name.

ZONGSHI: A title or suffix for a person of particularly outstanding skill; largely only applied to cultivators.

Other

GONGZI: Young man from an affluent household.

GUOZHU: The ruler of a nation.

-JUN: A term of respect, often used as a suffix after a title.

LAOBAN: A term of address for a shopkeeper or the proprietor of a business that means "boss."

-NIANG: Suffix for a young lady, similar to "Miss."

SHAOZHU: Young master and direct heir of a household.

-XIANSHENG: A polite suffix for a man, similar to "Mister."

XIONGZHANG: Respectful term of address meaning "older brother."

Pronunciation Guide

Mandarin Chinese is the official state language of mainland China, and pinyin is the official system of romanization in which it is written. As Mandarin is a tonal language, pinyin uses diacritical marks (e.g., ā, á, ǎ, à) to indicate these tonal inflections. Most words use one of four tones, though some (as in "de" in the title below) are a neutral tone. Furthermore, regional variance can change the way native Chinese speakers pronounce the same word. For those reasons and more, please consider the guide below a simplified introduction to pronunciation of select character names and sounds from the world of *Remnants of Filth*.

More resources are available at sevenseasdanmei.com

NAMES

Yú Wū

Yú: Y as in **y**ou, ú as in "u" in the French "tu"

Wū as in **woo**

Mò Xī

Mò as in **mo**urning

Xī as in **chi**c

Gù Máng

Gù as in **goo**p

Máng as in **mong**rel

Mùróng Lián

Mù as in **moo**n

Róng as in **wrong** / c**rone**

Lián as in batta**lion**

Yuè Chénqíng

Yuè: Y as in **y**ammer, uè as in **whe**lp

Chén as in ki**tchen**

Qíng as in ma**tching**

Jiāng Yèxuě

Jiāng as in mah**jong**

Yè as in **yes**

Xuě: X as in **sh**oot, uě as in **wet**

Mùróng Chǔyī

Mù as in **moo**n

Róng as in **wrong** / c**rone**

Chǔ as in **choo**se

Yī as in **ea**se

GENERAL CONSONANTS

Some Mandarin Chinese consonants sound very similar, such as z/c/s and zh/ch/sh. Audio samples will provide the best opportunity to learn the difference between them.

X: somewhere between the **sh** in **sh**eep and **s** in **s**ilk

Q: a very aspirated **ch** as in **ch**arm

C: **ts** as in pan**ts**

Z: **z** as in **z**oom

S: **s** as in **s**ilk

CH: **ch** as in **ch**arm

ZH: **dg** as in do**dg**e

SH: **sh** as in **sh**ave

G: hard **g** as in **g**raphic

GENERAL VOWELS

The pronunciation of a vowel may depend on its preceding consonant. For example, the "i" in "shi" is distinct from the "i" in "di." Vowel pronunciation may also change depending on where the vowel appears in a word, for example the "i" in "shi" versus the "i" in "ting." Finally, compound vowels are often—though not always— pronounced as conjoined but separate vowels. You'll find a few of the trickier compounds below.

IU: as in **ewe**

IE: **ye** as in **ye**s

UO: **war** as in **war**m

APPENDIX

Glossary

Glossary

While not required reading, this glossary is intended to offer further context for the many concepts and terms utilized throughout this novel as well as provide a starting point for learning more about the rich culture from which these stories were written.

GENRES

Danmei

Danmei (耽美 / "indulgence in beauty") is a Chinese fiction genre focused on romanticized tales of love and attraction between men. It is analogous to the BL (boys' love) genre in Japanese media and is better understood as a genre of plot than a genre of setting. For example, though many danmei novels feature wuxia or xianxia settings, others are better understood as tales of sci-fi, fantasy, or horror.

Wuxia

Wuxia (武侠 / "martial heroes") is one of the oldest Chinese literary genres. Most wuxia stories are set in ancient China and feature protagonists who practice martial arts and seek to redress wrongs. Although characters may possess seemingly superhuman abilities, they are typically mastered through practice instead of supernatural or magical means. Plots tend to focus on human relationships and power struggles between various sects and alliances. To Western moviegoers, a well-known example of the genre is *Crouching Tiger, Hidden Dragon*.

Xianxia

Xianxia (仙侠 / "immortal heroes") is a genre related to wuxia that places more emphasis on the supernatural. Some xianxia works focus on immortal beings such as gods or demons, whereas others (such as *Remnants of Filth*) are concerned with the conflicts of mortals who practice cultivation. In the latter case, characters strive to become stronger by harnessing their spiritual powers, with some aiming to extend their lifespan or achieve immortality.

TERMINOLOGY

COWRIE SHELLS: Cowrie shells were the earliest form of currency used in central China.

CULTIVATION/CULTIVATORS: Cultivation is the means by which mortals with spiritual aptitude develop and harness supernatural abilities. The practitioners of these methods are called cultivators. The path of one's cultivation is a concept that draws heavily from Daoist traditions. Generally, it comprises innate spiritual development (i.e., formation of a spiritual core) as well as spells, talismans, tools, and weapons with specific functions.

DI AND SHU HIERARCHY: Upper-class men in ancient China often took multiple wives, though only one would be the official or "di" wife, and her sons would take precedence over the sons of the "shu" wives. "Di" sons were prioritized in matters of inheritance.

DUAL CULTIVATION: A cultivation technique involving sex between participants that is meant to improve cultivation prowess. Can also be used as a simple euphemism for sex.

EPHEMERA: In the world of *Remnants of Filth*, a drug from the Liao Kingdom. Its name is likely a reference to the line, "Life is like a dream ephemeral, how short our joys can be," from "A Party Amidst Brothers in the Peach Blossom Garden" by Tang dynasty poet Li Bai.

EYES: Descriptions like "phoenix eyes" or "peach-blossom eyes" refer to eye shape. Phoenix eyes have an upturned sweep at their far corners, whereas peach-blossom eyes have a rounded upper lid and are often considered particularly alluring. Almond eyes have a balanced shape, like their namesake.

FACE: Mianzi (面子), generally translated as "face," is an important concept in Chinese society. It is a metaphor for a person's reputation and can be extended to further descriptive metaphors. "Thin face" refers to someone easily embarrassed or prone to offense at perceived slights. Conversely, "thick face" refers to someone who acts brazenly and without shame.

FOXGLOVE TREE: The foxglove tree, *Paulownia tomentosa* (泡桐花 / paotonghua), also known as empress tree or princess tree, is native to China. In flower language, the foxglove tree symbolizes "eternal waiting," specifically that of a secret admirer.

FOXTAIL GRASS: In flower language, green foxtail grass, Setaria viridis (狗尾巴草 / gouweibacao), symbolizes "secret, difficult yearning," often in reference to star-crossed love.

GENTLEMAN: The term junzi (君子) is used to refer to someone of noble character. Historically, it was typically reserved for men.

GU POISON: A legendary poison created by sealing many types of venomous creatures in one vessel until only one survivor remains, which would then possess the strongest and most complex poison. The term may be used as a stand-in for dark poisons of all types.

GUOSHI: A powerful imperial official who served as an advisor to the emperor. Sometimes translated as "state preceptor," this was a post with considerable authority in some historical regimes.

HORSETAIL WHISK: Consisting of a long wooden handle with horsehair bound to one end, the horsetail whisk (拂尘 / fuchen, "brushing off dust") symbolizes cleanliness and the sweeping away of mortal concerns in Buddhist and Daoist traditions. It is usually carried in the crook of one's arm.

IMMORTAL-BINDING ROPES OR CABLES: A staple of xianxia, immortal-binding cables are ropes, nets, and other restraints enchanted to withstand the power of an immortal or god. They can only be cut by high-powered spiritual items or weapons and often limit the abilities of those trapped by them.

INCENSE TIME: A measure of time in ancient China, referring to how long it takes for a single incense stick to burn. Inexact by nature, an incense time is commonly assumed to be about thirty minutes, though it can be anywhere from five minutes to an hour.

JADE: Jade is a semi-precious mineral with a long history of ornamental and functional usage in China. The word "jade" can refer to two distinct minerals, nephrite and jadeite, which both range in color from white to gray to a wide spectrum of greens.

JIANGHU: A staple of wuxia and xianxia, the jianghu (江湖 / "rivers and lakes") describes an underground society of martial artists, monks, rogues, artisans, and merchants who settle disputes between themselves per their own moral codes.

KOWTOW: The kowtow (叩头 / "knock head") is an act of prostration where one kneels and bows low enough that their forehead touches the ground. A show of deep respect and reverence that can also be used to beg, plead, or show sincerity; in severe circumstances, it's common for the supplicant's forehead to end up bloody and bruised.

LOTUS: This flower symbolizes purity of the heart and mind, as lotuses rise untainted from muddy waters. It also signifies the holy seat of the Buddha.

LIULI: Colorful glazed glass. When used as a descriptor for eye color, it refers to a bright brown.

MERIDIANS: The means by which qi travels through the body, like a magical bloodstream. Medical and combat techniques that focus on redirecting, manipulating, or halting qi circulation focus on targeting the meridians at specific points on the body, known as acupoints. Techniques that can manipulate or block qi prevent a cultivator from using magical techniques until the qi block is lifted.

MYTHICAL CREATURES: Several entities from Chinese mythology make an appearance in the world of *Remnants of Filth*, including:

AZURE DRAGON: The Azure Dragon (苍龙 / canglong, or 青龙 / qinglong) is one of four major creatures in Chinese astronomy, representing the cardinal direction East, the element of wood, and the season of spring.

BIXI: A legendary figure who was the sixth son of the Dragon King, usually depicted as a dragon with the shell of a tortoise and traditionally used as the base of commemorative tablets.

FLAME EMPEROR: A mythological figure said to have ruled over China in ancient times. His name is attributed to his invention of slash-and-burn agriculture. There is some debate over whether the Flame Emperor is the same being as Shennong, the inventor of agriculture, or a descendant.

GUHUO NIAO: A mythical bird created by the grief of women who died in childbirth; their song mimics the sound of babies crying as the bird seeks to steal chicks and human infants for itself.

SHANGAO: A small piglike animal said to live in the mountains, vivid scarlet in color, with a decidedly foul manner of speech.

TAOTIE: A mythical beast that represents greed, as it is composed of only a head and a mouth and eats everything in sight until its death. Taotie designs are symmetrical down their zoomorphic faces and most commonly seen on bronzeware from the Shang dynasty.

TENGSHE, OR SOARING SNAKE: A mythical serpent that can fly.

XINGTIAN: A mythical deity who was decapitated in his battle with the Yellow Emperor but nevertheless continued to fight; a symbol of perseverance.

XUANNÜ: Also known as the Dark Lady, the goddess of sex, longevity, and war.

ZHEN NIAO: Also known as the poison-feather bird, this mythical creature is said to be so poisonous its feathers were used in assassinations, as dipping one in wine would make it a lethal and undetectable poison.

NINE PROVINCES: A symbolic term for China as a whole.

PAPER MONEY: Imitation money made from decorated sheets of paper burned as a traditional offering to the dead.

QI: Qi (气) is the energy in all living things. Cultivators strive to manipulate qi through various techniques and tools, such as weapons, talismans, and magical objects. Different paths of cultivation provide control over specific types of qi. For example, in *Remnants of Filth*, the Liao Kingdom's techniques allow cultivators to harness demonic qi, in contrast to Chonghua's righteous methods, which cultivate the immortal path. In naturally occurring contexts, immortal qi may have nourishing or purifying properties, whereas malevolent qi (often refined via evil means such as murder) can poison an individual's mind or body.

QIANKUN POUCH: A common item in wuxia and xianxia settings, a qiankun pouch contains an extradimensional space within it, to which its name (乾坤 / "universe") alludes. It is capable of holding far more than its physical exterior dimensions would suggest.

QIN: Traditional plucked stringed instrument in the zither family, usually played with the body placed flat on a low table. This was the favored instrument of scholars and the aristocracy.

QINGGONG: Literally "lightness technique," qinggong (轻功) refers to the martial arts skill of moving swiftly and lightly through the air. In wuxia and xianxia settings, characters use qinggong to leap great distances and heights.

SEAL SCRIPT: Ancient style of Chinese writing developed during the Qin dynasty, named for its usage in seals, engravings, and other inscriptions.

SHICHEN: Days were split into twelve intervals of two hours apiece called shichen (时辰 / "time"). Each of these shichen has an associated term. Prior to the Han dynasty, semi-descriptive terms were used. Post-Han dynasty, the shichen were renamed to correspond to the twelve zodiac animals.

HOUR OF ZI, MIDNIGHT: 11 p.m.–1 a.m.

HOUR OF CHOU: 1–3 a.m.

HOUR OF YIN: 3–5 a.m.

HOUR OF MAO, SUNRISE: 5–7 a.m.

HOUR OF CHEN: 7–9 a.m.

HOUR OF SI: 9–11 a.m.

HOUR OF WU, NOON: 11 a.m.–1 p.m.

HOUR OF WEI: 1–3 p.m.

HOUR OF SHEN: 3–5 p.m.

HOUR OF YOU, SUNSET: 5–7 p.m.

HOUR OF XU, DUSK: 7–9 p.m.

HOUR OF HAI: 9–11 p.m.

SOULS: According to Chinese philosophy and religion, every human had three ethereal souls (hun / 魂) which would leave the body after death, and seven corporeal souls (po / 魄) that remained with the corpse. Each soul governed different aspects of a person's being, ranging from consciousness and memory, to physical function and sensation.

SPIRITUAL CORE: A spiritual core (灵核 / linghe) is the foundation of a cultivator's power. It is typically formed only after ten years of hard work and study. If broken or damaged, the cultivator's abilities are compromised or even destroyed.

SUONA: A traditional Chinese double-reeded wind instrument with a distinct and high-pitched sound, most often used for celebrations of the living and the dead (such as weddings and funerals). Said to herald either great joy or devastating grief.

SWORD GLARE: Jianguang (剑光 / "sword light"), an energy attack released from a sword's edge, often seen in xianxia stories.

A TALE OF NANKE: An opera by Tang Xianzu that details a dream had by disillusioned official Chunyu Fen, highlighting the ephemerality of the mortal world and the illusory nature of wealth and grandeur.

TALISMANS: Strips of paper with written incantations, often in cinnabar ink or blood. They can serve as seals or be used as one-time spells.

THREE DISCIPLINES AND THREE POISONS: Also known as the threefold training in Buddhist traditions, the three disciplines are virtue, mind, and wisdom. Conversely, the three poisons (also known as the three defilements) refer to the three Buddhist roots of suffering: greed, wrath, ignorance.

WANGSHU: In Chinese mythology, Wangshu (望舒) is a lunar goddess often used in literary reference to the moon.

XIHE: In Chinese mythology, Xihe (羲和) is a solar goddess often used in literary reference to the sun.

XUN: A traditional Chinese vessel flute similar to the ocarina, often made of clay.

YIN ENERGY AND YANG ENERGY: Yin and yang is a concept in Chinese philosophy which describes the complementary interdependence of opposite/contrary forces. It can be applied to all forms of change and differences. Yang represents the sun, masculinity, and the living, while yin represents the shadows, femininity, and the dead, including spirits and ghosts. In fiction, imbalances between yin and yang energy may do serious harm to the body or act as the driving force for malevolent spirits seeking to replenish themselves of whichever energy they lack.

ZIWEI STAR: A star known to Western astronomers as the North Star or Polaris. As the other stars seemed to revolve around it, the Ziwei Star is considered the celestial equivalent of the emperor. Its stationary position in the sky makes it key to Zi Wei Dou Shu, the form of astrology that the ancient Chinese used to divine mortal destinies.

ZI WEI DOU SHU DIVINATION: Zi Wei Dou Shu (紫微斗数/ "purple star astrology") is a common system of astrology in Chinese culture, which predicts one's fortune by plotting the position of certain stars at the time of one's birth. The presence of stars in certain "palaces," or sections of the sky, indicates either an auspicious or inauspicious destiny with regard to different aspects of one's life. Zi Wei, also known as Polaris, the North Star, is a primary star that represents the emperor or leadership.

ABOUT THE AUTHOR

Rou Bao Bu Chi Rou ("Meatbun Doesn't Eat Meat") was a low-level soldier who served in Gu Mang's army as a cook. Meatbun's cooking was so good that, after Gu Mang turned traitor, the spirit beast Cai Bao ("Veggiebun") swooped in to rescue Meatbun as it passed by. Thus, Meatbun escaped interrogation in Chonghua and became a lucky survivor. In order to repay the big orange cat Veggiebun, Meatbun not only cooked three square meals a day but also told the tale of Mo Xi and Gu Mang as a nightly bedtime story to coax the spirit beast Veggiebun to sleep. Once the saga came to an end, it was compiled into *Remnants of Filth*.

Seven Seas

耽美 *Danmei*
Seven Seas Entertainment
sevenseasdanmei.com

晋江文学城
WWW.JJWXC.NET

The Husky and His White Cat Shizun ©肉包不吃肉
(Rou Bao Bu Chi Rou) / JJWXC / Seven Seas Entertainment

Case File Compendium ©肉包不吃肉 (Rou Bao Bu Chi Rou)
/ JJWXC / Seven Seas Entertainment